A Toga of a Different Color

By Kass Evans

An Alexander the Alabarch

Mystery of Ancient Rome

A TOGA OF A
DIFFERENT COLOR

BY

KASS EVANS

Terra Expressions

Brandon, Florida
2018

Published 2018 by Terra Expressions Publishers, an imprint of Terra
Enterprises (Tampa, Florida)
http://TerraExpressions.com ;
copyright 2018 by Katherine G. Evans

ISBN: 978-1-941790-08-3 (pbk.)
ISBN: 978-1-941790-09-0 (ebook)

Libraries: MARC record is available for free download at publisher Web
site.

Evans, Kass.
A Toga of a different color / Kass Evans.

Brandon, Florida. : Terra Expressions, 2018
350 pages : Illustrations ; 23 cm.

Series: Alexander the Alabarch; 1

DESCRIPTION
Rome, 12 A.D. As darkness reigns over the Palatine Hill, a man in an augur's
striped toga removes the famous statue of Victory from its temple. He says it's
for a procession, but the Victory disappears not to be seen again. At first,
Alexander thinks little of it. He's a Jew, so a Roman goddess has nothing to do
with him. Then a Jewish art dealer is arrested for the theft. As the man's patron,
Alexander decides he must find the Victory if he is to free his client. At
Alexander's side are his boyhood friends: Claudius the emperor's ill-loved
nephew, Rutilus the poorest patrician in Rome, and Agrippa a Jewish prince and a
bit of a rogue. Standing in their way is an elite group of Praetorian guards who
don't want the art dealer freed. But why? Seeking the stolen statue soon
becomes a very dangerous pursuit.

ISBN: 978-1-941790-08-3 (pbk.)

1. Alexander, Alabarch, active 1st century--Fiction. 2. Claudius, Emperor of Rome,
10 B.C.-54 A.D.--Fiction. 3. Jews--Rome--History--Fiction. 4. Rome--History--
Augustus, 30 B.C.-14 A.D.--Fiction.

PS3605.V367 T645 2018
813.6 EV92

Dedication

FOR MY SISTER

NANCY KAY EVANS

THE INSPIRATION FOR NIKE

CONTENTS

MAJOR CHARACTERS
denotes an historical figure

Aemelia	Roman matron, mother to Rutilus and Rutila (Aemelia Scaura)
Agrippa*	Jewish prince and grandson of Herod the Great (Marcus Julius Agrippa)
Alexander*	Jew from Alexandria and Roman citizen; client to Augustus (Gaius Julius Alexander)
Amarantus*	Alexander's servant (nickname Ranti)
Antonia*	Claudius' mother, daughter of Marcus Antonius, niece to Augustus (Antonia Minor)
Apollonius, Saul	Jewish merchants from Alexandria, clients of Alexander
Augustus*	"First Citizen" and ruler of Rome; heir of Julius Caesar, formerly known as Gaius Julius Caesar Octavianus
Berenice*	Agrippa's mother and Jewish princess; friend of Antonia
Claudius*	Alexander's friend and future Emperor of Rome (Tiberius Claudius Nero)
Electra	a prostitute at the Venus House
Germanicus*	older brother of Claudius; adopted son of Tiberius (Julius Caesar Germanicus)
Gnaeus Pulcher	powerful Roman senator and art collector
Hermias, Ephigenia	Aemelia's servants

Lucius Servilius	an augur, a priest of Rome's State religion
Sejanus*	Member of the Praetorian Guard, Augustus's elite personal guard (Lucius Aelius Sejanus)
Sextus Fadius	Aemelia's husband, stepfather to Rutilus and Rutila
Rutila	Rutilus' sister
Rutilus	Alexander's patrician friend (Aulus Rutilus)
The Rat	your basic, low-life blackmailing scum
Theon	Jewish art dealer from Alexandria, client of Alexander
Tiberius*	adopted son of Augustus and heir apparent; uncle of Claudius; adopted father of Germanicus (Tiberius Julius Caesar Augustus)
Vatinius	priest at the temple for the goddess Victory

AUTHOR'S NOTE

Alexander the Alabarch was an historical person who lived in the first half of the first century A.D. in Alexandria, Egypt. He was a Jew and was, almost certainly, a Roman citizen as well.

Many tantalizing little details of Alexander's life are known. He was "old friends" with the Emperor Claudius, but was thrown into prison by the Emperor Gaius (Caligula). He was the 'guardian' in Egypt for Antonia Minor, daughter of Marc Antony and mother of Claudius.

Alexander was related through marriage to Agrippa I, King of Judea. At some point, Alexander had the nine gates of the great Jewish temple in Jerusalem plated with silver and gold. Alexander's son, Tiberius Julius Alexander, burned those same gates down when he attacked Jerusalem as a general with Titus (the future Roman emperor).

Philo of Alexandria, Alexander's brother, is still studied as an important philosopher and theologian from the first century.

The historical evidence seems clear that Alexander was a man whose influence spanned across Rome, Egypt, and Judea. He was a Roman and a Jew, but what did it mean to be a Roman Jew in the early first century and in each of those places?

For me, Alexander's life is a story that begs to be told.

. . . And here is how I imagined that it all began.

ROME IN 12 A.D.

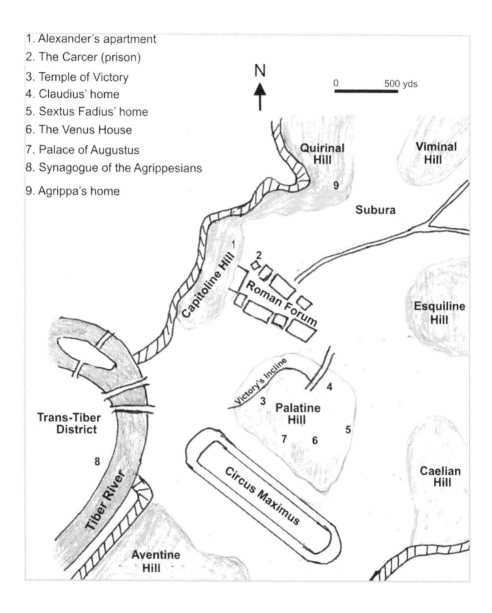

1. Alexander's apartment
2. The Carcer (prison)
3. Temple of Victory
4. Claudius' home
5. Sextus Fadius' home
6. The Venus House
7. Palace of Augustus
8. Synagogue of the Agrippesians
9. Agrippa's home

N

0   500 yds

Quirinal Hill

Viminal Hill

9

Subura

Capitoline Hill

1

2

Roman Forum

Esquiline Hill

Victory's Incline

3

4

Palatine Hill

Trans-Tiber District

7   6

5

8

Tiber River

Circus Maximus

Caelian Hill

Aventine Hill

ROME

SUMMER OF 12 A.D.

YEAR 39 OF THE
FIRST CITIZEN

GAIUS JULIUS CAESAR OCTAVIANUS
CALLED
AUGUSTUS

ADOPTED SON
OF THE DEIFIED
GAIUS JULIUS CAESAR

PROLOGUE

THEON jerked his head back on his shoulders.   That tends to happen when one notices four hairy fingers balled up in a fist and heading for your face.   Wait, no.   *Three* hairy fingers; the fourth was completely smooth.   No matter.   The outcome was about to be the same.

Not that it was totally unexpected.   Theon knew it had been a risk to come here.   He knew, too, that he was in the right.   The Lord knew he had to try.   ... but he had failed.

As the semi-hairy fist stopped just short of his chin, Theon quickly closed his mouth to any further protest.   His shoulders drooped as he acknowledged defeat and was shoved roughly out the door.

***

"What did you expect, Theon?   You thought that you could walk right into a rich Senator's house and demand payment?   And he would, *what*?   Just give it to you?   Apologize for the delay?   Perhaps, offer a cup of wine?"

The oldest of the three companions shook his head gravely. "You knew it was never going to happen, Theon.   You're not even a Roman citizen ... *none* of us are.   Romans see us merchants from Alexandria as nothing but barbarians.   To that Senator, we're even less than that."

Theon angrily kicked at a stone on the path.

"Do you think I don't *know* any of that, Saul?   I know better than to try to do business with the likes of Gnaeus Pulcher, but he didn't give me much of a choice. I deal in fine statues. He collects the same. That would be fine if the Senator didn't *insist* on choosing what *price* he will pay."

Theon paused to let out a long breath. "In the past he's paid me enough to at least break even. But *this* time … if I sell him the statue for so little, I'll be ruined."

The youngest of them, Apollonius, gave his friend a worried look. "*What* can you do, Theon?"

"I will have to find another buyer for the Neptune and fast."

Apollonius sucked in a loud breath and exchanged a wide-eyed look with Saul before turning back to Theon.

"I know you've heard what they say about *him*. We've all heard it, and, I don't think it's just idle talk. They say Gnaeus Pulcher is completely ruthless when he wants something. Theon, if you don't sell him the statue he wants, only the Lord knows what he might do."

Once again, Saul shook his graying head.

"I *knew* this could come to no good. Selling graven images of their gods is …. it's *blasphemy*. We're Jews. This is not what we do."

Apollonius smiled and rolled his eyes. "Saul, you are too traditional. Jews know these statues are nothing but chunks of marble or bronze. For us, it's just business."

The men started at the sound of the approaching footfalls of servants carrying a litter. The three friends, all merchants from Alexandria, had met about half-way up Victory's Incline, the path that led from the top of Rome's Palatine Hill to the marketplace below.

"Well, let's not discuss it here in the middle of the road. There are a lot of people on the Incline today, and they don't need to hear your business," Apollonius took his friends by the elbow and steered them to the side. Glancing up, he noticed they were near the path that led to the temple of Victory.

Apollonius tilted his head and pointed his chin toward the temple.

"*Ever seen it?*" he asked. "That statue of Victory is said to be sculpted by the Greek master Phidias himself."

Saul gasped, "Of course not! Surely, even *you* would not enter a pagan temple!"

"*I've* seen it," Theon replied distantly. "Replicas of that particular statue of Victory are quite popular, particularly with the Roman military. They think the statue will bring them success in battle."

Theon rubbed at the whiskers on his chin as he regarded the temple thoughtfully.

"In fact," he mused, "there is a certain Roman collector who has offered me a small fortune if I could ever obtain the original."

Saul turned ashen. "*Be silent!*" he hissed. "Not even in jest should anyone speak of the theft of a Roman goddess. Especially not a Jew. You could get us all expelled from Rome."

Apollonius was quick to respond. "Oh, Saul, you exaggerate. You know that there have been no purges of Easterners in years. To most Romans, one of us *barbarians* is the same as another. Jews are no different than the Gauls, Germans, Parthians, or any of the other foreigners living in the city."

Saul gave him an incredulous look.

"To *most* Romans, perhaps. But you know very well that recently there have been murmurs of trouble. We've all heard about it in the synagogue. There are some Romans who resent that of all the peoples, it is *only the Jews* who don't worship the Roman gods. Only the Jews have been granted the right to worship our Lord and no other. ... And you know what *those* Romans would do about it, if they could."

Apollonius bit into his lower lip and looked away. Saul may be old fashioned, but on this matter he *was* correct. Theon's careless words could prove very dangerous if they were overheard. Better that they all be quickly on their way.

Wrinkling his nose, he spoke up a bit too loudly. "*Merda.* We seem to have stopped near a sewer cover. The smells are quite noxious today. Come, friends, let us return to my house. It is time for lunch and today I shall be host."

As the three men hurried away, the nearby sewer cover scraped lightly. A pair of filthy fingers emerged through one vent and gripped the top. A second pair of equally filthy fingers emerged through another vent. Then the entire stone cover began to slowly rise.

A sewer cover on a cobblestone street in the Roman Forum.

***

Five days passed. Once again a small group of men paused on Victory's Incline to regard the temple of the goddess Victory. This time the group turned onto the path that led to its doors.

It was the ides of July, three hours after the sun had set, and the path was cloaked in darkness. The small party made its way to the temple with the silence broken only by the rumbling wheels of their large ox cart. At the foot of the temple steps, the man who was their leader stopped.

"You and you, come with me," he pointed at two men then ascended the steps.

The temple's doors were closed and locked for the night. At a nod from their leader, a slave banged on the door. They waited long moments, but there was no response. Impatiently, the leader glanced at the second man who was wearing a freedman's cap, then jerked his head to the door. This man joined the slave, and the two began banging on the door with their fists.

Finally, they heard the sound of the cross bar being drawn from within and the door edged open a crack. A faint light revealed the disheveled countenance of the old priest who slept at the rear of the temple.

"What is the meaning of this?" he cried. "There is no silver here to steal. Think you that this is the temple of Saturn?"

"What is your name, priest?" the freedman asked.

"This is naught to you, villain. You show no repect to disturb the goddess at night. Be gone, or I shall summon the *vigiles*."

The freedman and slave stepped aside and looked toward their leader. The old temple priest had brought a small oil lamp with him to the door. He held it up and peered out as the third man stepped forward from the shadows.

Unconsciously, the priest sucked in a loud breath as he recognized the *trabea,* the maroon and purple striped toga of an *augur*. They were the only priests of Rome who could interpret the omens sent by the gods. *This* was an important man – a lot more important than a small temple priest.

The *augur* paused to draw a fold of his toga over his head in a sign of piety, and then brushed past the priest into the temple. The priest and the other two men followed him in. Once inside, the *augur* stepped back haughtily and looked the priest up and down. The old priest stared back dumbfounded.

The *augur* spoke.

"Your name," he demanded.

"I... I am Vatinius. *Uh*, I... I have been the priest and caretaker for the goddess Victory since our esteemed First Citizen Augustus had the temple restored near thirty years ago."

The *augur* stared at the old priest a moment longer and then gave him a curt nod. He gestured for his freedman to continue.

"We've come for the statue of the goddess," the freedman said.

When the priest looked puzzled, he added "for the procession tomorrow."

The priest still looked puzzled. The freedman sighed and adopted the tone of one speaking to an imbecile.

"Tomorrow is the procession of Victory. We have come for the statue to prepare her to be carried in the procession."

That broke the old priest's silence.

"But no one has told *me* anything of this," he blurted out. "And there *is no* procession for Victory."

"There is *now*," the freedman replied. "Tomorrow morning there will be a procession from the Forum to the Circus Maximus. And then during Victory's games three days hence, there will be another procession around the stadium."

"But, but I have heard *nothing*!" the priest protested. "How can there be a procession that no one knows about? *Who* has decided this?"

"The old man did," the freedman answered. The *augur*

cleared his throat meaningfully.

"I mean our esteemed First Citizen, Augustus," the man corrected himself. "You know how he's felt about Victory ever since she helped him defeat Antonius and Cleopatra."

The priest nodded absently. Everyone knew that Augustus had brought a small golden statue of Victory back to Rome and set it up on an altar in the Senate house. *Still,* this didn't seem quite right, so he objected.

"I can't. I can't just release the goddess like this. I've never done that before. I think that I must see the Pontifex Maximus first," he stated invoking the highest of all of Rome's priests who also happened to be Augustus himself.

The priest gave a single sharp nod as if to assure himself. "Yes, yes. That is what I must do. If the Pontifex Maximus says to release the statue, then I will release her."

The *augur* strode forward, drew himself up and stared down his nose at the old priest.

"Do *you* question *my* authority?" he demanded.

The priest gaped back trying to gather his wits. *"Now which augur is this?"* Up to this point he had only thought of him in terms of his robes of office. The toga *trabea* was maroon in color, instead of the usual white. It also had a distinctive series of four purple stripes along the top, bottom, and two across the middle. That type of toga was only worn by *augurs.* Clearly, this late night visitor to the temple had to be an *augur* – and a very traditional one, too. He still wore the style of toga that was worn during the Republic. Under Augustus, togas had gotten longer and fuller.

The priest lifted his small oil lamp a little higher. The lamplight was dim and his eyes were old, but slowly he made out the features. Medium height, slight build, late 50s, wrinkled face and he could see that *the augur* was going bald under the folds of the toga draped over his head.

Of course! This must be the *augur* Lucius Servilius. He was one of the most senior of the *augurs*. The priest decided that his mind must have been addled not to have known him instantly.

"Do *you* question *my* authority?" the *augur* repeatedly slowly with more menace in his voice.

"N-n-no, L-L-Lucius Servilius," the priest sputtered. "I b-beg your pardon. It's just that I was asleep, and it all happened so suddenly."

"Very well," the *augur* replied and he stepped back and gestured for his men to begin work.

One man went to the door and whistled down to the others waiting by the cart. In seemingly no time at all, the workers had set up a small winch and lowered the larger than life marble statue of the goddess from her pedestal. Another man was waiting with rolls of linen and they reverently wrapped the goddess in layers. Then it was lowered into a wooden crate lined with straw. Four men lifted the poles attached to the crate and carried it down to the waiting ox cart. The whole thing had been accomplished with a swiftness that had made the old priest's head spin.

The *augur* moved to follow the statue disappearing down the temple steps. But then paused at the door and turned toward the priest.

"I commend your cooperation and I shall return her to the temple *personally* following the procession. … For your trouble," and he dropped a handful of coins into the priest's palm.

Slowly, exuding all the dignity of office, the *augur* gathered the folds of his maroon and purple striped toga to his side and descended the temple steps. Then the ox cart set out into the night.

The old priest stood at the door and waved into the darkness as the ox cart crunched down the temple path to Victory's Incline. When he could no longer hear the cart, the priest re-entered the temple, looked at the coins in his hand and gasped.

Silver *denarii,* all of them! A whole handful. For him, it was a small fortune.

After all these years of serving the goddess, she had finally smiled upon him with favor. And now that the goddess was getting her own procession more people would begin to visit the temple bringing gifts for the goddess … and her servant.

The priest retired to his screened enclosure at the back of the temple and carefully stowed away his new fortune. Then he lay back on his pallet wearing a smile of anticipation.

1
THE LETTER

"RUTILUS, your toga is dragging the ground again."

Aulus Rutilus turned a half circle as he twisted his head over his shoulder to look at the back of his toga.

"Oh, yeah," he grinned back at Alexander. "I always forget to keep my shoulder straight."

He grabbed a handful of fabric and deposited a rumpled wad back onto his shoulder where a series of neatly overlapping folds should have been.

"*Alexander!*" called another voice from somewhere beyond Rutilus. "It's good we found you. We brought you a letter."

Alexander turned his amused look from Rutilus's sagging toga to the second man behind him. This one, also a friend from boyhood, moved a little slower and with a noticeable limp. Tiberius Claudius Nero was the great nephew of Augustus – not that the imperials had much use for a young man who limped and often stuttered when nervous.

Claudius held out a small papyrus scroll.

"We stopped by your apartment and your slave, Amarantus, said a letter had just arrived from your father. I told him that we would bring it to you."

Alexander hesitated, then reached out and accepted the scroll. His father did not write to him that often and not usually this time of year. Turning the scroll in his hand, he studied the design on the clay seal that held the scroll shut. The image of a hand holding several shafts of wheat was indeed his father's mark. The next wheat shipment was not scheduled to arrive from Egypt for weeks. So what could this be about?

"Go ahead and read your letter, Alexander," Claudius said. I'll take Rutilus over here and try to straighten what's left of his toga."

Alexander popped the seal and unrolled the scroll as Claudius began to fuss over Rutilus.

"Really, Rutilus. Where is your sense of *dignitas*? You are a patrician. People see the purple stripe on your tunic and they look up to you. What will they think if ..."

Alexander's attention was immediately diverted to the letter as several troubling words stood out. He took a deep breath and read the short scroll in full.

Gaius Julius Alexander, Alabarch, to his son Gaius Julius Alexander many greetings and good health. Return to the City by the end of the month of Sextilus also called August. You are needed to manage the local affairs in Euhemeria. Travel to Ostia by the 7th and then take passage on the ship contracted by the firm Nikodemus and Sons.

I have betrothed you to the younger daughter of Ananus the High Priest of our Temple. Her father is of noble birth and she has the Roman citizenship so she is a suitable wife for you. Your brother Philo greets you and asks that you obtain the remaining scrolls of Ovid if you can find them. Everyone greets you by name. Farewell.

Alexander staggered a step back as his mind reeled in disbelief. *"Return to the City?"* That could only mean Alexandria, Egypt, his family's home. But it wasn't *his* home; not really. Twelve years had passed since Alexander's father had brought him to study in Rome. After schooling, his father had written him to stay in Rome and take charge of the family's shipping office. In all these years, Alexander had only returned to the family estate in Alexandria once. *And his own father?* He hadn't seen him in years.

Alexander re-read that other troubling line.

"I have betrothed you to the daughter of Ananus the High Priest of our Temple."

Of course, every Jew knew the name Ananus ben Seth. He was the High Priest of their great Temple in Jerusalem -- had been for what five or six years now?

But ... he was *betrothed* to the High Priest's daughter? His father had made a betrothal without even consulting him? He supposed that as the head of the family, his father did have the right. It's just that ... well, it had never occurred to Alexander that his father would actually do it.

Alexander read the letter again wishing that his father had learned to write his letters in Latin rather than in the cryptic Greek style so prevalent in Alexandria. If the letter had been written in the Roman style, Alexander would probably now know *why* he was being recalled and every detail of this betrothal as well. Not that he cared to know that much. After all, this priest's daughter ... well, she was not the one for him.

"Alexander. ... Alexander!" The voices finally broke into his thoughts and Alexander realized that his friends Claudius and Rutilus had been talking to him.

"Alexander, what has happened? You look worried." Claudius could always read him well, although Alexander doubted his face in any way hid his current sense of dismay.

Even Rutilus sensed the rawness of Alexander's emotions. "Alexander, what is it? I can see something bad has happened. Is it your trade? Has one of the wheat ships sunk?"

Alexander glanced down at the papyrus letter in his hand.

Then he crushed it as he formed a fist and shook it at his bewildered comrades.

"I've been recalled to Alexandria. *I'm leaving Rome.*" He glanced at Rutilus and decided to hold back the part about the betrothal.

His friends' responses were gratifyingly shocked and incensed. *"No!" "This cannot be!"*

"B-but, why?" Claudius finally demanded.

"My father has sent for me," Alexander replied. "He says he needs help with the family estates."

Rutilus was skeptical. "But, Alexander, what could you *possibly do* back in Egypt?"

Alexander sucked in a quick breath to control his sudden irritation at the ignorance in his younger friend's words. Even though Rutilus had known Alexander for years, he still seemed completely bewildered as to why Alexander spent hours in the family's shipping offices or meeting with other businessmen.

Things were different for Rutilus because he was a patrician. True, Rutilus' family fortunes had mostly disappeared with the death of his father. He had been reduced to living off of the meager income of a small farm in the country. But despite his near poverty, it would never occur to Rutilus to look for a job. Patricians in Rome simply did *not* work at a business or a trade. They lived off of the income of their estates – or in Rutilus' case, *estate* in the singular.

Alexander could not resent Rutilus for it. After all, everyone in Rome could only be exactly who they were born to be. Instead, he shook his head and answered with an exasperated smile.

"What could I do in Egypt? Work, Rutilus, I could work. Unlike you patricians, *I* work for a living. All this wheat my family exports to Rome doesn't just magically appear from nowhere. The estates take careful management."

Rutilus remained skeptical. "Well... I suppose, but *why*

now? Why after all these years does he suddenly need you back in Egypt?"

"That is true, Alexander," Claudius joined in. "Your father has managed his estates fine until now. And, if you leave, who will manage his office here in Rome? ... Perhaps, you can write to your father and explain to him why you must stay."

That was a good thought. Alexander pressed his lips together and considered, but then slowly shook his head with resignation.

"No. I want to, but I can't. My father takes his role as the head of the family very seriously. I could not disobey when his instructions were so clear. Besides, there isn't time to get a letter to Alexandria and back."

"What do you mean *'No time'*? When must you leave?"

"Next month. My ship will sail from the port at Ostia on the seventh. My father has already arranged my passage."

Rutilus scrunched his forehead as he did some quick calculations. "But today is already the ides of July. That means that you have only ... twenty-three days!"

"Indeed," Alexander replied softly. "Just twenty-three days."

The three friends fell silent. This was going to be a big change, for *all* of them. Claudius and Alexander had become close friends soon after Alexander had arrived in Rome. At just aged ten, he had joined the Jewish prince Agrippa in the circle of Claudius. Rutilus was a couple of years younger, but had shared the same tutor as them for awhile. He was naturally cheerful and this had drawn him to the other boys whose home life had encouraged a more dour nature.

Absently, Rutilus tugged at the folds of his toga that were beginning to slide off his shoulder again. Suddenly, he brightened and looked up.

"I know," he announced. "If Alexander must leave us, then there is only one thing to do."

"And what would that be?" Claudius asked suspiciously.

"We must *drink*! Truly, you must also hear that amphora of wine that is calling to us? It is a ... siren's call. We *must* follow it." Rutilus broke into a broad smile. "Now, don't give us your serious look, Alexander. You have the rest of your life to act responsible. You only have twenty-three days left to have *fun* with *us*!"

Alexander thoughts had already started racing through all the things he was going to have to get done if he was going to be leaving Rome for good. Disappointment tore at him as he realized that he really, really did *not* want to go.

Claudius tapped Alexander on his arm to draw him from his reverie. "Rutilus is right, you know. You don't need to start planning everything today. Spend some time with us. It may be a long time before you return to Rome."

Alexander's thoughts vacillated through competing senses of despair and duty ... and friendship. The last thought won. He shook his head and smiled in defeat.

"Oh, all right you two. I suppose there is no work that *must* get done today. Where shall we go?"

Rutilus laughed with delight and exclaimed, "I know just the place."

He paused and glanced from man to man as if he was building up something momentous to say.

"... *the Venus House!*"

2

THE VENUS HOUSE

THE Venus House was Rome's version of a high-class brothel being a three-story structure located half-way up the Palatine Hill. It was perfectly situated to serve Rome's elite after a weary day of orating in the Senate's *Curia* or the *Forum*.

Mainly, though, the Venus House was famed for the exotic experiences available on its third floor – not that many visitors had ever seen the third floor. It was reserved for customers with the largest purses. But people could *imagine* and they could talk, and there was a lot of that when it came to speculation about the *"Third Floor."*

Rutilus stared wistfully up at the Third Floor. Would he ever discover its secrets? It didn't seem likely, especially now with Alexander leaving. Alexander was his only friend who could actually afford the high price of visiting that floor. But in this, his friend totally lacked his own sense of adventure. In fact, when it came to the Venus House, Alexander was quite dull; always the second floor, always the same woman.

The three friends had stopped a short way from the entrance to the Venus House. They often talked before going in to plan their visit – what they would drink, how long they would stay, when they would meet up again after they had separated to different rooms.

Rutilus settled himself on the edge of a public fountain and raised his eyebrows to Claudius and then Alexander.

"How about it? This time, the third floor?"

Alexander smiled and shook his head. "No, Rutilus. I don't think so. I think the usual is good enough for me."

"But why, Alexander? *Why?* Always the second floor. Always Electra. It is just too dull. There *must* be a reason why you won't ever try someone new."

When Alexander didn't answer, Rutilus turned to Claudius. "There *is* a reason isn't, there? Something happened?"

Claudius glanced at Alexander before confirming, "Something happened. … when we were younger."

Alexander visibly winced at the memory. There were certain events in his life that served as reminders that he was … *different* from other Roman citizens. Sure, he had the tri-part Roman name, *Gaius Julius Alexander.* He wore a citizen's toga, had a citizen's haircut; he even physically looked a lot like a native born Roman.

But occasionally some event would occur reminding Alexander that, in fact, he was not like other Romans. Rutilus' question recalled one of the more embarrassing of those times.

Claudius was surprised that after all these years, Alexander was still so bothered by that one event.

"Come on, Alexander," Claudius chided. "That happened years ago; we were just kids. It didn't mean anything then and doesn't mean anything now. Besides Rutilus knows what it means to be a Jew … or at least that part of it."

"If it doesn't mean anything, Claudius, then it is not worth speaking about now."

Rutilus perked up at this. "Then there *is* a story behind this. It may not be much of a story, but you are my friend, Alexander, and I must know. You can't leave Rome without telling me."

"You see how Rutilus is, Alexander. He is not going to stop asking until someone tells him. If you won't tell him, then I will," Claudius said.

"Go ahead then," Alexander sighed.

"Oh, good," Rutilus smiled and scooted over to make space on the edge of the fountain. Claudius eased himself down next to him and began the tale.

"Hmm, this is something that happened about eight years ago when Alexander and I were just fourteen. As you know, my father died when I was little, so I always looked up to my big brother Germanicus. That year, I had not seen much of my brother because that's when he was adopted by our uncle Tiberius.

"Let's see ... I guess Germanicus would have been about nineteen then. Anyway, back then Germanicus was one of the most popular young men in Rome."

"What do you mean *back then*?" Rutilus snorted. "My mother is thrilled that I spend time with you, just because he *is* your brother. Now that Germanicus is a Consul for the Senate, I think he must be one of the most popular men in all of Rome."

"True," Claudius smiled fondly. "But this is back when we were still young, before Germanicus had become so active in public life. You know that he's always been a good brother, even after he was adopted by Tiberius. Every few months, Germanicus would arrange to spend some time with me. Sometimes he would invite me and some of my friends to the chariot races, to a play, or sometimes gambling with his friends. ... But *this time*, he told us he was taking us to visit our first brothel."

"Ahhh," Rutilus nodded. "So it was Germanicus who brought you to the Venus House the first time. I wish *I* had an older brother like that. Was Agrippa with you, too?"

"Not that time. Agrippa usually was with us, but that day he was out of Rome. And, of course, *you* were still too young then.

So it was just Alexander and me."

"*Hmm*, Germanicus brought you and Alexander to the Venus House. So where is the story, Claudius?"

"I'm coming to that. Anyway Alexander and I were both pretty shy that first time. So Germanicus made the arrangements for us, and some girls came and took each of us up to her room. But, what none of us had realized was that a brothel in this neighborhood did not attract many Jews. The girl with Alexander had never seen a Jew before, at least not in *that* way."

"Oh no," Rutilus gasped. "Alexander, was it just like all those strange looks you get when we go to the baths?"

"*Worse*," Alexander replied through clenched teeth. "She laughed. She laughed at me."

Rutilus was appalled for his friend. "What did you do?"

Alexander remained silent.

"He tried to leave," Claudius answered for him. "But then Germanicus came and he summoned the owner. Germanicus had some pretty strong words for the man. Then the owner brought Electra. She's from … Alexander, what's that region called?"

"Samaria," Alexander replied shortly.

"That's right, Samaria. It's next to Judaea. She knew all about circumcision because some of her people do it, too. And ever since then, Alexander only asks for Electra."

Rutilus looked disappointed. "Is that all?"

"I told you the story was not worth telling," Alexander responded with an exaggerated shrug.

Rutilus jumped up and clapped his fellows on the back. "Let's go then. It's time to sample their fine wines!"

An hour later, Alexander descended from the second floor and found Rutilus having a cup of wine in the reception area.

"Did you see Claudius?" Rutilus asked.

Alexander shook his head.

"I wish he would hurry. I'm getting hungry." Rutilus was known for his good humor, but not particularly his patience.

Alexander ordered a cup of wine and the two young men reclined on a couch as they waited.

"Claudius is taking too long," Rutilus finally announced. "I'm going to go up and tell him to hurry."

"Don't bother," Alexander replied. "That big ex-gladiator is the hall guard today, and there's no way he'll let you disturb a paying customer."

Rutilus rested his cheek on his hand with a bored stare. Just as quickly his look brightened into a devious smile.

"I know," he whispered. "I will go up the back stairs, the ones reserved for the third floor customers. Look, the usual guard isn't there right now. There is no one to stop me. If the door on the second floor isn't locked, I should be able to get to Claudius without that ex-gladiator seeing me."

With that, Rutilus jumped from his couch and then tried to appear as if he was casually lounging against the wall. When he saw the moment was clear, Rutilus slipped down the short hallway, then disappeared up the third floor stairwell.

Still sipping his wine, Alexander kept a casual eye towards the staircase where his friend had disappeared. After awhile, a hooded figure descended the staircase and hurried out the front door without so much as a glance around. A few minutes later, the figure was followed by Rutilus and Claudius, both obviously bursting with something to tell.

"What is it?" Alexander asked. But Claudius shook his head and whispered, "Wait until we get outside."

Once outside, Claudius and Rutilus began to snicker as they

walked.   Alexander finally paused and sat on the edge of the nearby fountain.

"All right. Out with it," he demanded. "The two of you are cackling like a hen in the market."

Claudius and Rutilus looked at each other conspiratorially and then burst out laughing. Finally, Claudius pointed to Rutilus and gasped, "You tell him."

Rutilus caught his breath and looked at Alexander. "Did you see the man who came down the stairs just before us?"

"Yes," Alexander replied puzzled, "but his head was covered. I have no idea who he was."

"Well, *we* do," Rutilus hooted.

"You are making something up," Alexander complained. "Men go to brothels every day. There is nothing remarkable about this."

"Go on, Rutilus, tell him," Claudius urged.

"Alright. As you know, I sneaked up the back stairs to the second floor to find Claudius. He was done so I told him to get dressed so we could go eat. While I was waiting for Claudius, I decided to climb the stairs up to the *third floor* and have a peek."

Rutilus paused for effect, but he already had Alexander's full attention. The third floor of the Venus House had long been a subject for their speculation.   Since the second floor already provided anything that *they* knew of, it left much to the imagination as to what could be left to be done on the exclusive third floor. Once, they had thought they heard a goat bleating up there and that had led to weeks of increasingly hilarious theories.

"Go on," Claudius urged Rutilus again.

"I opened the door and looked in, but there was an attendant blocking the way so I couldn't get in. I climbed back down to the second floor level to wait for Claudius in the stairwell,"

Rutilus continued.

"Then I heard the door to the third flood open and a man started coming down the stairs. He had the hood of his cloak pulled so far over his face that he didn't even see me until he had run right into me."

"Tell him *who* it was," Claudius butted in.

"It was Lucius Servilius – as in the *Augur* Lucius Servilius!" Rutilus laughed. "And was he upset that I had seen his face."

"So what?" Alexander shrugged. "There's no law that says an *augur* can't use a brothel."

"*Now*, tell him the good part," Claudius insisted.

"Well," Rutilus paused and glanced around to ensure that they were alone. "I climbed back up to the third floor and bribed the door attendant to tell me what the man who had just left had been doing. He could not have known the man was an *augur*, or he never would have told me for so little."

He paused and grinned again with anticipation, "Guess what the honorable *augur* was doing on the third floor?"

"*Romulus and Remus!*" Alexander snapped. "If you're going to tell it, then *tell* it."

"*Men*," Rutilus declared. "Big, hairy, sweaty men. At least two of them. And the attendant said that Lucius Servilius likes it when they put him on his knees."

Alexander whistled. This was almost better than the goat. While the Greeks had accepted homosexuality as just another aspect of life and pleasure, this was *not* the Roman way. Especially *now* under Augustus's moral reforms. Every man of rank was expected to marry and sire many children. Indeed, men were fined if they didn't marry, and fined again if they didn't produce children. At least, that was how Augustus decided men should behave and the Senate went right along with him.

Of course, everyone knew that these Greek-style relations still went on, just not openly anymore. And *not* by one of Rome's highest priests who was supposed to exemplify the new moral code. More so than that even, it was the role that the *augur* chose. Taking the passive position on his knees? Indeed, *catamitus* was one of the most vicious insults one man could make to another in this Roman society.

If the proclivities of the *augur* were to become known, it could mean a serious loss of face in society.

Alexander, Claudius, and Rutilus considered the implications of their new found knowledge.

"Such a man might do much to keep his secret," Claudius commented.

"A nice little bribe to keep my mouth shut would be nice," Rutilus observed.

"Better not," Alexander warned. "Men like that could become very dangerous. Do you think he recognized you?"

"No," Rutilus replied. "Without career or money, there would be no reason for the *augur* to have learned my face. And since he was not in his *augur's* toga and his head was covered, he may also have assumed that *I* did not recognize *him*."

He paused then added, "There is no reason for him to think that I would have bribed the door attendant for his secret. In fact, he probably thought that I was just another customer ascending to the third floor. Usually, the guard is there and that stairwell is kept only for their use."

"Let us hope so," Alexander replied. "There is no point in making an enemy of a powerful man like him. I suggest we keep this matter to ourselves."

"Agreed," said Claudius. Both men looked at Rutilus who was obviously still considering how he could spend the potential bribe money.

"Come on, Rutilus," Alexander coaxed. "We don't want to see you get hurt over money that will quickly be lost on wine and women."

"That's easy for you to say," Rutilus shot back. "You're both rich."

"Let it go, Rutilus," Claudius offered, "and I will treat you to dinner tonight."

Rutilus turned a calculating eye on Claudius and then on Alexander. "Two," he bargained. "Two dinners before Alexander goes. One from each of you."

"Very well," Alexander replied.

The grin was back on Rutilus' face. "Now, that's what I call friends," he announced. "Come, let us go get something to eat now. I'm starving."

The three friends shoved off their post on the fountain and headed down the Palatine towards the Forum.

For the moment, at least, the affair of the *third floor* appeared to be forgotten.

3

FIGHT IN THE FORUM

"**WE'RE** *going to cut you, you thieving, barbarian Jew.*"

Alexander froze in mid-step as the angry, snarling shout tore into his thoughts.

He had spent the morning visiting business associates advising them of his upcoming departure from Rome. As he passed through the Forum, his mind had been busily itemizing and prioritizing the many things he had yet to do.

Absently, Alexander had noticed that a crowd had gathered on one side of the path to watch some sort of spectacle -- perhaps an orator or some sort of performer? He decided to skirt around the other side of the Forum to avoid the gathering. No, he certainly didn't have time for that today.

But suddenly both his thoughts and his steps had stopped dead as the words from the angry shout finally registered in his consciousness.

"We're going to cut you, you thieving, barbarian Jew."

The menacing words had not been directed at *him*; he knew that much. No one was even looking his way.

Alexander's eyes sought out the source of the now increasing level of taunts and jeers. They came from the small crowd he had just noticed gathered outside the offices of the Basilica Julia on the south side of the Roman Forum.

For a moment, Alexander considered walking on. Getting

involved in a Forum fight was definitely not a good idea even at the best of times.

He let that thought pass. Like it or not, he knew he had to get involved. Alexander was one of the few Jews in Rome who held the Roman citizenship. Because of that, many of the other Alexandrian Jewish merchants considered him their patron. Well, considered *his father* to be their patron, actually. But he was his father's representative here in Rome. And that came with certain obligations.

Edging up to the back of the crowd, Alexander first looked around to gauge the situation. There appeared to be four instigators loosely circled around one man whom they currently were shoving back and forth between them. The gathered crowd had the look of idlers just hoping for a good show.

Alexander next studied the target of the attack as a hard shove turned the man's face toward his direction. He didn't recognize the man, but he was definitely a Jew. He wore fringes on the four corners of his tunic as prescribed by the Law of Moses. It was unusual in Rome to see the fringes worn for daily wear, although some Jews had similar tunics that they wore for prayer services. Most were like Alexander and had the fringes sewn on a separate shawl that he carried with him to services.

The man had probably recently arrived from Judea. This was not a young man either, probably in his fifties, and not a fighter. His face was drawn in fear and he was whimpering that he had done nothing.

Turning his attention to the four assailants, Alexander made a quick assessment. Bullies, he concluded. They were easy to spot as they lacked the cool detachment of a professional fighter. Instead, they kept looking to each other for encouragement. No doubt these men were cowards who would never have acted alone, or, if their victim hadn't been so helpless.

Alexander stepped back slightly and considered the situation as he saw one of the men land a kick on the Jew's leg causing him to sprawl face first into the dust. The kicker then lifted his hands expectantly at the crowd waiting for their cheers as if he had just performed some athletic feat.

His first thought was of going for the Urban Cohorts who policed the Forum. But Alexander quickly ruled that out. It might take a while to find them, and he sensed the situation was about to escalate. That left him with two choices: *fight* or *bluff*. These were choices he knew well, since he had gotten into his share of fights as a youth. But at least five or six years had passed since he had last been in any type of physical fight.

Once again, he studied the four thugs. They may not have been professional fighters, but there were still four of them to his one. And most likely one or more of the men had a knife on him and Alexander carried no weapon. Not only that, because of his business meetings this morning, he was wearing his toga. If he removed the toga, he couldn't bluff, but if it came to a fight, the toga would quickly become an encumbrance.

The man who had just kicked the Jew drew out a knife and began tossing it back and forth between his hands, pausing to grin at the encouraging cheers from the crowd.

Alexander made up his mind. He would bluff.

Straightening his shoulders to use his height and posture to best advantage, Alexander roughly shoved the crowd aside and stepped into the circle. At the sight of him, the thug with the knife hesitated, momentarily thrown off guard. Alexander calmly walked up to him, looking him straight in the eye and didn't stop until he was a few inches closer than usual for normal conversation. He had learned that moving close into a bully's comfort zone usually caused him to fall back. Sure enough the man took a step backwards.

"Well, now," Alexander drawled. "These hardly seem like

fair odds. Let's see, there seem to be...one, two, three, ... four. Yes, four of you," he confirmed as he turned slowly seeming to note the others for the first time.

Alexander glanced down at the Jew cowering in the dust. He may not have recognized him, but the man seemed to recognize Alexander. He made to speak, but Alexander gave him a slight wave of warning to stay silent.

Then he turned back to the first man whom he had already guessed was their leader.

"Did this man really have the gumption to pick a fight with all *four* of you?" he asked incredulously. "Hmm, now that took nerve. I would not have guessed him for the type."

Alexander shrugged indifferently and continued, "Well, I'm not laying a bet till I know what it's all about. A man likes to know the odds before betting on a fight."

He leaned in and gave the thug leader an expectant look as if a full explanation should soon be forthcoming.

The bully lowered his knife and licked his lip as he looked Alexander up and down appraisingly. He could see the man taking in his fine clothes and proud bearing that went well with his cultivated Latin accent. Too bad there was no purple stripe on his tunic indicating nobility. That may have clinched it. But at present, Alexander knew the man was startled, but not cowed.

The bully spat on the ground. "This Jew stole a statue of a Roman goddess," he sneered.

"*Really?* Where is it?" Alexander replied, peering around as if expecting to spot a statue standing in the the midst of the crowd.

"It ain't here," the bully growled. "But we're going to find out where it is, right now." He waved his knife around grinning as the crowd gave the anticipated cheer in response.

"Ahhh," said Alexander appearing unruffled. "Then you

must be with the Urban Cohorts, or, I suppose, Augustus's Praetorian Guard. Which is it? I don't recognize you without your uniforms."

The bully gaped for a moment and then his face turned ugly. "No, we ain't with the Cohorts. 'Not the Praetorians either, but we know how they feel about these god-hating Jews. Thieves the lot of 'em. And maybe we're gonna throw the filthy lot out of Rome."

He gave a barking laugh and his fellows chimed in. This seemed to give him courage, but Alexander pressed on.

"Well, this *is* confusing isn't it?" Alexander scratched his head in apparent puzzlement. "Everyone knows that Augustus has decreed that the Jews are permitted to live in Rome. But *you* say you are going to throw them out?"

Alexander tapped his chin and appeared to consider this for a moment.

"Huh. I guess this must mean that you are with one of the factions that oppose the First Citizen. How interesting. Which one is it?"

The bully stared back at Alexander, the lines in his forehead working as he struggled to keep up with what Alexander was saying to him.

"This is it," Alexander thought. "He's not going to start any trouble now that I've made this about Augustus. If I can just keep his eyes on mine, we can end this here." Carefully, Alexander kept his stance as non-threatening as possible, praying that his face revealed nothing beyond mild curiosity.

But suddenly, the bully's expression turned mean.

"Here now. What's this to you anyway? "Does this Jew owe you money or something?"

The crowd chuckled and the bully swaggered over to the crouching man and gave him another kick.

"Now, my boys here and I are gonna *question* this here Jew until he tells us about the statue. If he don't have it, we're gonna cut him until he tells us who does. He's bound to know. Everyone's seen how they pack together." A number of heads in the crowd nodded in agreement.

He swaggered back over to Alexander and this time he was the one glaring straight into Alexander's face. His voice regained its original menace.

"Now I suggest you get out of my way. Because if you try to keep us from finding this statue, I'm gonna *cut you first*. Now move."

His bluff had failed. All Alexander could hope for now was to get the poor man and himself out of this alive. When the lead bully had walked over to kick the crouching man, Alexander had taken note of the positions of the other three. Already, he was calculating the odds. He knew which man would strike first and undoubtedly the next closer man would come second. Even if he could take them both, that still left two more.

The bully must have expected Alexander to back off because his face flushed bright red when Alexander didn't retreat.

"I said, *MOVE!*" he roared.

"I'm afraid that won't be possible," Alexander replied mildly.

"And why's that?" the lead bully sneered.

"Because, unlike you, *I* am not a coward."

The crowd gasped and murmured their approval. Oh, it looked like there would be a good show for them today.

Alexander's taunt had been deliberate. If there was going to be a fight, Alexander wanted it started on his terms and well before the other three thugs had a chance to close in on him. And so it played out.

The lead bully gave a strangled cry and lunged forward, his knife held tightly in his right hand in the classic stance used to thrust a blade into the opponent's belly.

But Alexander was ready. He swung his right hand around at waist height grabbing the other man's wrist and forcing the knife off to the side. Still grasping the wrist with his right hand, Alexander swiveled to his left and then brought his left fist up hard behind him exactly finding other man's groin. He shoved the bully's right arm with the knife aside as the man grunted and collapsed.

Alexander didn't wait for him to hit the ground. Already the second man was running at him from just ahead on the left. Alexander assumed a stance as if to meet him head on. Then at the last moment, he stepped to his right, too late for the bully to check his forward motion. As he lunged by, Alexander leaned back on his right foot and kicked out his left smashing into the other's kneecap. Another man down. His timing had been perfect and he felt a moment of exultation.

But even as the second man went down clutching his knee, Alexander knew that he had gravely miscalculated. His body had been thrown forward as it had followed through with the kick. Alexander was leaning away from the last two thugs with his toga twisted around his legs. The wads of loose wool entangling his body meant he could no longer maneuver. He was helpless and could feel them closing in behind him.

In his mind, he could see the third man running in with his knife pulled back to plunge into his lower back. Vainly he grabbed his toga and yanked it away from his legs knowing he could never turn back in time.

"Thwack!"

Clutching the gathers of his toga to his waist, Alexander managed to swivel in time to see the third bully's face turn to astonishment as a long board collided with his middle. At the other end of the board was Alexander's own slave, Amarantus, who gave him only the barest nod before swinging back toward the fourth man.

Still facing the third, Alexander noted that the bully had made the error of an amateur. Instead of holding his knife down at his hip to thrust upward, he had raised it above his head intending to strike down into Alexander's shoulder. The motion took precious extra seconds and left his whole body exposed. As the bully buckled forward with his arms instinctively clutching his middle, Alexander took a step toward him grabbed the back of his head and brought his knee up hard into the man's chin. He dropped like a rock. Three down.

Alexander turned in time to see Amarantus swinging his board smack into the back of the fourth man who had apparently tried to flee, but couldn't get past the crowd. The man fell forward and the crowd gasped with delight. But then, Amarantus swung the board back and made like he was heading for the crowd and the idlers began to scatter like rats running from water.

Three men were still down, but the first bully who Alexander had punched in the groin was struggling to get back up. Calmly, Amarantus strode over and brought the board down on top of his head. This time, he fell back unconscious. Amarantus turned back to Alexander.

"Are you alright, Master?"

Alexander was still panting, but managed a nod in return. "Your timing couldn't have been better, Ranti. Where did you get the board?"

"Oh, I ... *uh*, borrowed it from that man over there."

Amarantus pointed at yet another man who was lying unconscious on the pavement and shrugged. "He didn't want to share."

Alexander grinned. "We'll talk about this later, but for now

I think we had better get out of here before anyone official takes an interest in this fight. I don't need that kind of trouble right now."

He walked over to the older Jew who was staring up at him in some mix of relief and admiration.

"We need to move on," Alexander whispered urgently. "Can you walk?"

The man nodded, but when Alexander tried to help him up, the leg that had been kicked gave way. Alexander and Amarantus each pulled an arm around their shoulders and hoisted him to his feet. With only a fleeting glance at the bullies still sprawled where they had fallen, the three hobbled off and turned onto the first side street.

Glancing up, Alexander realized that they had stopped in front of the door that led into the Cloaca Maxima, the huge underground sewer that passed through the Roman Forum.

"Let's rest here," he panted. "If any of them decide to chase after us, we'll duck inside the sewer."

He smiled at the immediate looks of consternation on the other men's faces.

"A few minutes in there won't kill us. I have a good friend, Rutilus, who told me that when he was a boy, he used to explore the sewers for fun. He said that when the Tiber was low the smell wasn't that bad." Alexander chuckled. "Well, I guess that would make more sense if you'd ever met Rutilus."

Fortunately, the men were not forced to explore the sewers for themselves. After a couple minutes without hearing pounding feet or raised voices, it was clear that no one had followed them. Amarantus was dispatched to bring back a litter to carry the injured man.

In the meantime, Alexander learned that the Jew's name was Elias. He was a silver merchant from Jerusalem visiting the large Jewish community on the other side of the Tiber River. Elias had been passing through the Forum on business and had been completely dumbfounded when he was accosted by the bullies and accused of stealing a statue.

Alexander expressed his surprise as well. It seemed quite inexplicable. True, there were some Romans who resented that Jews didn't worship the Roman gods. And there were lots of Romans who didn't like so-called barbarians –anyone not from Rome-- at all. But incidents like this were mostly uncommon.

Amarantus returned with a *sella* litter, a chair set on two carrying poles. They coaxed Elias into it, in between his profuse expressions of gratitude. Alexander paid the bearers to take him all the way back across the Tiber.

As the litter moved safely on its way, Amarantus stepped up and calmly began to remove the toga that now hung about Alexander like a blanket. Now that the panic of the incident has passed, Alexander paused to consider their situation.

"I can't believe that whole fight just happened right there in the Forum and the Urban Cohorts never knew."

"They *knew*, Master," Amarantus replied quietly.

"What? How?"

"Master, I was headed for the office when I thought I saw you coming in the distance. I leaned up against a wall and waited for you.

"I saw two Cohorts patrolling the Forum. But just before the fight started, several of the Praetorian Guard showed up and insisted on buying them a drink. They went into a tavern right across from where I was standing so I could see them. When the fight started the Cohorts made to get up to check it out, but the Praetorians pushed them back into their seats and waved for more wine."

"You mean," Alexander asked skeptically, "that some of Augustus's own Praetorian Guard deliberately kept the Cohorts from coming to Elias's aid?"

"Master, I could not hear. But, yes, that's what it looked like to me."

"But this whole thing makes no sense," Alexander mused. "Why would those bullies attack some poor Jew who was just passing through the Forum? Why would the Praetorians interfere? Why keep the Urban Cohorts from doing their job?

"... Well, for that matter why would the Praetorians want to drink with the Cohorts in the first place? They're not exactly known for their good relations."

"I don't know, Master, but I don't think you should go to the office looking like this."

Alexander looked down and grimaced at his sweaty tunic and then at the toga bunched up in his slave's arms.

"No, I suppose not. But let's take the side roads back to the Capitoline. I think it would be better to avoid the Forum, at least for the rest of today."

They set out in silence, then, Alexander turned to Amarantus and smiled. "You didn't do so badly back there, Ranti."

"Neither did you," Amarantus responded with a bemused expression. "Master, I did not know that you knew how to fight.... like that."

"Like a street thug?" Alexander laughed. "I learned as a boy. A lot of the sons of rich Romans liked to pick on the little Egyptian boy, or so they called me. And sometimes I'd fight for Claudius, too."

"Claudius? But, Master, he is one of the imperial family."

"Well, you see how much good that's done him so far," Alexander frowned. "Most of the kids that picked on him were the sons of Senators so they expected they could get away with it. And that bum leg has always made Claudius an easy target."

"Still, it seems unwise to pick on the great nephew of the First Citizen."

"Indeed. Claudius may not have much influence now, but no one can know the future. And Claudius is not one to forget his friends, *or* his enemies."

Roman citizen draped in a toga.

Source: Harper's Dictionary of Cassical Literature and Antiquities / edited by Harry Thurston Peck, 2nd ed. (New York, Cooper Square, c1896.

4

THE GOSSIP

MORNING broke, a day later. Hovering between sleep and awake, Alexander struggled to hold on to a dream … or a memory, rather.

It had been but a few months ago. Alexander had arrived early at a friend's house and was waiting for him in the garden. Strolling aimlessly, his mind was still focused on work as he mentally reviewed that morning's business transactions. Then, as he passed a thicket, a small hand slowly extended through the bracken and grasped his forearm.

That was when everything changed.

Alexander had regarded the slender arm as the hand tugged him closer. The grip wasn't tight and the tug wasn't strong, but he found himself willingly stepping into the direction in which he was being pulled.

And there she stood; her eyes gazing up at him were wide with hope … and fear. He knew her, of course. He had known her for years. But … she was just a child, wasn't she? Now it was a young woman who stood before him. When had she grown up? Alexander didn't know. But he was surprised by his own physical response as they stood just inches apart in the shelter of the foliage.

"Alexander," she had whispered. "I have watched you for so long now, wanted to be near you. Yet I can tell that when you look at me, you don't really see me. Please, look at me.   Can you not care for me?"

Her final words tumbled out as rapid, deep breaths caused her shoulders to quickly rise and fall. Alexander felt his breath quicken as well. Her hand was still on his arm and he felt it tighten. She took a step forward, so close to him now. Almost unconsciously, he reached out and placed his hands lightly covering her upper arms.

What more may have happened that day, he did not know. For in the distance they heard her mother calling her. Immediately, they broke apart, eyes darting warily around them to see if they were exposed.

"Go," she whispered. "I'll walk behind the bushes to the new plantings in the back. Mother will find me there."

Alexander didn't know what he should say, so he said nothing. He just headed back for the garden path. But before he stepped out through the shrubs, he turned and looked back. She was looking back, too. Their eyes met. No words were spoken; no promises were made. But ever since that day, Alexander found that all of his thoughts and hopes were only for *her* ... only for *Rutila*.

Alexander was fully awake now; time to start the day. With a grunt of impatience, he kicked off the coverlet and reached for his tunic.

As he did every morning, Alexander draped a fringed prayer shawl over his shoulders as he prepared for morning prayers. He wrapped his left hand and arm with the leather straps of the *phylacteries* in the prescribed manner. Attached to the leather straps was a tiny box holding a small parchment inscribed with words from scripture. By tying the box to his hand he brought the words of the Lord closer to his flesh and therefore closer to his heart.

"... *You shall have no other gods before me. You shall not make for yourself a graven image, or any likeness of anything that is in heaven above. You shall not kill. You shall not commit adultery. ...*"

Alexander concluded the Ten Commandments that the Lord had given to his people through Moses. Then he began the *Shma*, the most holy prayer for a Jew.

"Shma O Yisrael Adonai elohenu Adonai echad."

"Hear, O Israel, the Lord our God. The Lord is one."

He spoke in Hebrew, although he did not really know Hebrew. Like most Alexandrian Jews, Alexander used the Greek translation of scripture. But, his father had insisted that his sons learn the basic rituals in Hebrew, the language of the patriarchs and the prophets.

As Alexander finished folding and storing the prayer shawl with the *phylacteries*, he heard the sound of his slave, Amarantus, behind him.

"Breakfast has been laid out, Master. Will you be going to the office today?" Amarantus asked as he approached the wardrobe chest.

"Yes, but I have a few stops to make first. Meet me there in mid morning.

"… Oh, and I will be dining with Rutilus this evening so take out one of my better tunics."

Alexander ate and then let Amarantus help him into a toga. Both his tunic and toga were white and of a fine, soft wool woven thin for the summer weather. Only a Roman citizen was permitted to wear the toga, and this set Alexander apart from most other Jews. Relatively few Jews in Rome, or anywhere in the Empire for that matter, had been granted the citizenship.

Still, Alexander knew that the plain white tunic he wore under the toga meant little enough to other Romans. No, a Roman would only be impressed if under his toga he wore a tunic with purple stripes, the mark of nobility.

"I guess it's too late for that now," Alexander thought as he headed for the door. He had hoped that before he ever had to leave

Rome, he would find a way to raise his family's status as Romans. The equestrian class was Rome's top businessmen. Alexander's family certainly qualified financially, but they would need some noble act to move them up with the elite.

After stopping to see several business associates, Alexander headed to his favorite barber for a trim and shave. His slave, Amarantus, could shave him if needed, but like most men in Rome, Alexander went to the barber's for the *"news."* He rarely joined in; but, Alexander listened attentively to every tall tale or innuendo. After all, a good businessman needed to know who may have fallen into debt, or out of favor, or whose star was on the rise.

As Alexander approached the barber, he recognized two Forum wags lounging around the barber's stand, clearly looking for an audience. He had never heard their names, but tended to think of them as "Bushy Brown" and "Grisly Gray" in reference to their unkempt hair and beards -- an irony for men who spent so much time loitering around a barber.

Today the usual fare of politics mixed with a little adultery, bribery, and unpaid loans had been preempted by, of all things, *religion*.

"Are you sure? Did they look everywhere?" asked the current resident of the barber's folding stool, a local merchant.

"Of course, they did," answered Bushy Brown. "It's not like there was any place the old priest could hide it. The temple only has the one room."

"But, what about the *augur*? There are many places he could have put it. Maybe he just forgot," the merchant insisted.

"I told you," Bushy Brown answered. "He says he *don't* have it, never took it in the first place."

With his shave finished, the merchant pushed himself up out of the high stool and paused to give Bushy Brown a disdainful glare.

"Well, I don't believe it," the merchant said. "No Roman would ever do such a thing. That's sacrilege and something a Roman just wouldn't do." He stalked off.

Bushy Brown stared at the departing merchant with raised eyebrows and pursed lips and waggled his head back and forth, the usual face a poor plebian made to an uppity citizen – although never to his face of course.

"Well, maybe it wasn't a *Roman*," he shouted after the man.

Alexander took the vacated stool, asked for a trim and a shave and then tried to assume his usual calm demeanor of indifference to the local wags. Instead, he almost immediately winced as the barber tried to run a comb through his unruly mop of curls. His hair was cut in the Roman fashion – more or less, but no barber had figured out how to make Alexander's curly hair fall into the loose waves that was the current style.

The barber mistook the hunch of his shoulders as a sign that Alexander was leaning forward out of interest in the previous exchange between the wags and the merchant.

Knowing every Roman's penchant for gossip, the barber decided it was time to winkle out a coherent story. If the gossip was good, he knew he would get a bigger tip for it. After clearing his throat, the barber then knitted his brows in confusion.

"I didn't hear all of it, so tell me again. What did you say happened?"

Bushy Brown heaved an exaggerated sigh of exasperation, as if he didn't secretly revel in being asked to tell the story again. He would be repeating this one for the rest of the day, for sure; maybe the rest of the week if nothing more exciting happened.

"Like I *told* you," he began. "It's Victory. She's gone missing. Not the goddess, of course, but her statue. 'Taken from her temple right up there on the Palatine Hill."

"Huh. When did that happen?"

Bushy Brown scratched at his beard. "She was taken on the ides, so they say."

The barber looked up frowning. "But that was *three* days ago. How is it that you're just telling us about it today?"

"Because everyone just *found out* today ... well, apparently Augustus and his people knew before that. But, it took a day for the rest of us to hear about it." Bushy Brown responded sarcastically. "Now just *listen* and I'll tell it to you again.

"According to the old priest at the temple, three nights ago, there came a loud banging on the temple door. He got up and went to see what it was all about. There, he says, was the *augur* Lucius Servilius saying that he had come to fetch the statue of the goddess as she was to be there for a procession and sacrifice on the morrow."

Bushy Brown took a deep breath and plowed on.

"Well, the priest told the *augur* that there wasn't no procession planned. But the *augur* said it was Augustus himself that ordered it. He said that there would be a special sacrifice and Augustus wanted the *augur* to interpret the signs for Rome. Well, we all know how the old man feels about Victory, so that part wasn't any big surprise."

"Besides," he continued, "the priest said that the *augur* had the cart and everything all ready. A team of men bustled in and quicker than boiled asparagus they had the statue wrapped, crated, and on the ox cart driving off."

There was a lull in the story as the wag turned to look at Grisly Gray who nodded back. Apparently they had heard the same version of the story, at least so far.

"And then what happened?" the barber prompted.

Bushy Brown shrugged. "Well, the priest says he just went back to bed."

"No, no," the barber said impatiently. "I meant when did the statue go missing?"

Bushy Brown raised eyebrows at Grisly Gray who scratched his stubbled chin, then continued on with his fellow's story.

"Well, that's the odd part. The old priest says he got up early the day after the ides and took himself down to the Forum so he could see the goddess go in the procession. But he said she weren't there. There was no procession. He went to the temple of Jupiter to see if there was sacrifice. Nothing. He came back and started asking the around the Forum, but no one knew about any procession.

"I guess the priest assumed it had all been canceled for some reason. So he went back to his temple on the Palatine and waited all morning for the Victory statue to be returned. But they say neither the statue nor the *augur* ever showed up."

Now the barber was curious. He stopped part way through Alexander's shave and looked to the wag. "So, *what* did the priest do?"

Grisly Gray expelled a long breath and rolled his eyes as if the barber had asked a silly question.

"Same as *anyone* would do," he replied sarcastically. "He went to the home of Lucius Servilius and asked after the statue."

"And?" the barber asked wondering why gossips liked to pretend the information was somehow being dragged out of them.

"Apparently, Lucius Servilius refused to even see the priest. 'Told his door man to say that he didn't know nothin' about a statue. When the priest put a fuss over it, the steward had him tossed out in the street."

"Wait. One moment now," the barber broke in. "You say the priest said it was Lucius Servilius, the *augur*, who came and took the statue."

"That's right," Bushy Brown replied. "Said he recognized

him from when he saw him before. Said he was wearing his toga *trabea,* you know that maroon toga with the purple stripes like only the *augurs* wear? And he said that wrinkled face and bald head couldn't have been any of the others."

"But, now you say that Lucius Servilius claims that he wasn't there. … How does the *augur* explain that the priest says he saw him?"

"From what I gather," Grisly Gray responded, "He didn't try to, just told his men to toss the priest out on his ear."

"Then what happened?" Bushy Brown took up the questioning. "I didn't hear nothin' after that."

Grisly Gray seemed to puff up with self-importance.

"According to *my sources,* the priest went up to the palace and started wailing until they took him to see the *Pontifex Maximus* himself. At first, Augustus didn't believe him, but he sent a couple of his Praetorians over to inspect the temple. The servants say that when the Praetorians reported back that the statue wasn't there, Augustus was in a fury. His servants were scared to even be in the same room with him."

"And then what happened?" the barber pressed. "Did Augustus arrest the priest? Is he going to question the *augur*?"

"Don't know what's been going on now," Grisly Gray admitted holding his palms up and shrugging. "But there sure are a lot of messengers running back and forth and not a one of them will stop for a friendly hello. They say that Augustus is having a fit over this one."

"*What's this?! Augustus?* What's happened?" demanded a new Forum wag who had ambled up to join the group.

Before either wag could puff up and launch into their gossip again, Alexander paid his barber and retreated down the hill. The main road that passed through the Forum was the quickest way to get from the barber's on the Capitoline Hill to his family's office near the banks of the Tiber.

"A curious little mystery," Alexander mused as he walked. A goddess statue disappearing from a temple was certainly unusual. But that particular bit of gossip was of little use to him professionally ... or personally. Sure, a lot of Romans would be upset. But as a Jew, he felt nothing personally over the disappearance of a statue of a goddess.

For a moment, Alexander pondered the coincidence that yesterday the Forum bullies had accused the Jew, Elias, of stealing a goddess statue. He dismissed the thought. As the two wags had said, no one in the Forum would have known about the missing Victory statue until today.

5

RUTILA

"MASTER, I wish you would let me come with you tonight. It may not be safe for you to go out alone."

"I don't think that will be necessary, Ranti. I'm sure that what happened in the Forum yesterday had to be an isolated incident. Relations between Jews and other Romans are not that bad."

Amarantus didn't look convinced, but kept his silence as he expertly rolled the inside hem of his master's toga into folds and placed them over his left shoulder.

When he was done wrapping the toga, Alexander stepped back. He was a little taller than most other men and the toga showed his height to his best advantage.

"How do I look?"

"Excellent, Master, as always. ... I'm sure she will think you very handsome."

Alexander looked up sharply at his slave.

"*She?*"

"The lady Rutila, Master. Will she not be at dinner tonight?"

Rutila. Just hearing her name said aloud returned Alexander back to his thoughts of that morning.

Rutila was the younger sister of his dear friend Rutilus.

Alexander had known her since they were children when he used to visit Rutilus at home. But back then she was just the little girl who always tried to interfere with the boys at play.

Ever since that day she had touched him in the garden, everything seemed to make him think of her. What would she think of this, how would she like that, and most importantly, how could he arrange to see her again?

But he had thought that he had kept those feelings to himself.

"Have I been so obvious, Ranti? Do you think others have noticed?"

"I think that maybe your friend Rutilus has, Master. It seems to make him happy."

Alexander hesitated, thought he should act reserved, but then blurted all the feelings that he had been trying to hide for months.

"She is beautiful, Ranti. And graceful and dignified. She's a patrician, too. Not many of Rome's old nobility are left these days."

"Master, is she poor like her brother?"

"Hmmm, indeed she is. I believe there is a small dowry that was left by her late father. Their stepfather, Sextus Fadius, however, has refused to adopt or even sponsor either of them. If Aemelia had not had the good sense to invest in a slave who could weave and sew, I think that she and her children would be practically dressed in rags.

"But really, Ranti, what do I care about a small dowry? My family is rich. We don't need the money. An alliance with a patrician family should mean more to us than money."

"Master, ... *is she a Jew?*"

Alexander blew out a long breath.

"No, Amarantus, she is not a Jew. And *that's* a problem. I

don't know how I will ever get my father's approval."

"But, Master, other men at your synagogue have married women who were not Jews. Many of the women have converted."

"True. But none of them have my family's position. It may not mean much in Rome, but to Jews back in Egypt fealty means everything. My father is the Alabarch, descended from both High Priests and Judean nobility. There are few left alive who can claim our lineage. Every Jew in Egypt looks up to my family.

"Back in Egypt, a marriage to Rutila would be thought beneath me. ... and now my father has recalled me to ... that world. I just don't think I belong there, not anymore."

"Master," Amarantus said very softly. "What of your father's letter?"

"Letter," Alexander snorted. "You mean the betrothal? My father should not have done this without consulting me. Oh, I'm sure the girl is respectable and all that, but for all I know she could look like a crone. I'm going to have to convince my father that is not the right match for me -- just as soon as I get back to Egypt."

***

Alexander's sense of anticipation grew as he headed through the Meat Marketplace so he could take Victory's Incline up the Palatine Hill. As he stepped onto the Incline, his thoughts were drawn back to the gossip that he had heard just that morning at the barber's about the temple statue.

Why would anyone take a temple statue? And why Victory who was thought to bestow her blessings on only a very few?

And, most curiously, could that have something to do with yesterday's fight in the Forum? The thugs had accused the Jew, Elias, of stealing a statue, although he didn't recall them ever saying which one. He had assumed that even if the thugs really did know about a stolen statue, it would have had to be something small. For one man to steal a statue, it would have had to be small enough to fit in a pouch or under a tunic.

By the time Alexander had reached the top of the Palatine, all musings on stolen statues and lost goddesses was quickly replaced in his mind with a happier vision of this young man's idea of a 'goddess.' This one was very human with a fair oval face, large green eyes and red-gold tresses. She had the beauty and the grace that dreams were made of.   At least, for months now, Alexander's dreams were.

After a few minutes, Alexander had crossed to the east side of the Palatine, a distinctly less fashionable area of the hill because it faced away from the Forum, the heart of Rome. Yet few who were not wealthy had a house anywhere on the Palatine Hill, and this was certainly true of the master of the *domus* before which he now stood.

Rutilus' stepfather, Sextus Fadius, had bought the house many years earlier after acquiring a fortune through foreign investments in wine and olive oil. Sextus Fadius was an ambitious man and his newfound wealth only made him determined to join the ranks of the Roman elite.

Seeing an opportunity for advancement, Sextus Fadius married the recently widowed and financially bankrupt Aemelia Scaura, mother of Rutilus and Rutila. Aemelia was not only of the patrician Aemelius Scaurus family, but the young mother had already earned a reputation as an ideal Roman matron for virtue and dignity. With Aemelia's contacts and a few generous bribes, Sextus Fadius had made it into the Roman Senate. Not that Fadius had ever given his wife much credit for her part.

Alexander pulled his thoughts back to the present and rapped on the door. The old door steward, Hermias, responded shortly.

"Gaius Julius, good day to you."

He had addressed Alexander in the formal manner, but

there was the warmth in his voice of one who had known a young man since he was a boy. Hermias had been with Aemelia since her childhood, long before even her first marriage. He had always shown a special care for her children, especially now that their stepfather had no consideration to spare for either of them.

"Ah, Hermias. I am here to dine with Rutilus."

"Alas, the young master has not yet returned from the baths, but I expect him shortly. Would you care to wait in the garden? I, *umm*, believe the young mistress may also be awaiting him there."

Was that a glint in the old man's eye? Once again Alexander wondered whether his feelings for Rutila were quite as secret as he had thought.

Rutila was in the garden, but, to his disappointment, she was not alone. She was sitting next to her mother and they were unrolling a small scroll. Both women looked up as Hermias announced him.

After a few polite greetings, Alexander took a seat on a bench opposite theirs.

"Mother has just received a letter from my stepfather. He is on his military legate duty in Gaul," Rutila informed him. "We were about to read it."

Aemelia glanced at him inquiringly. Alexander knew that she was likely to be curious about the letter's contents, but would consider it rude to read it with a houseguest present.

"Please, go ahead and read it," Alexander said and then lied. "I would be interested to hear how Sextus Fadius is doing."

Aemelia unrolled the parchment and studied its contents. Unlike many Roman women, Aemelia was fully literate, but Latin letters were difficult to read at a glance since no spaces were placed between the words. After a few moments, Aemelia wrinkled her brow and whispered, "Oh dear."

"What is it, Mother" Rutila asked leaning over her shoulder as if she could read the Latin sideways.

Aemelia sighed softly. "It appears that your stepfather has acquired a collection of 'booty' that he is sending home. It is primarily artwork."

"Oh dear," she repeated. "You know what dreadful taste Sextus Fadius has in art. Remember that horrible carved alabaster urn he insisted on exhibiting in the atrium? Or that silver platter with the nymphs that looked like men that he insisted we use at dinner parties?"

Rutila giggled. "That was a truly wretched platter. How did you ever convince him to stop using it?"

The smallest mischievous smile crossed Aemelia's usually prim countenance. "I informed your stepfather that I thought I had observed Senator Metellus greatly admiring the platter. After that he felt obliged to send the platter to the Senator as a special gift."

"Oh Mother, you didn't!" Rutila cried.

She looked at Alexander and they started laughing. Alexander remembered the platter with the men-nymphs well. Rutilus had once brought it out and used it as the butt of a dinner party's humor. His imitation of a nymph who looked like a man 'pretending' to run from a satyr had left the diners shaking with laughter. Sextus Fadius, of course, had not been present.

"But Mother," Rutila continued. "He's not here. Maybe we can take the lot and put it all in storage."

"I'm afraid not, dear," Aemelia responded, then pointed to a spot in the letter. "It says here that he's arranged for his agents in Rome to accept the shipment and personally deliver it to the house. He's even provided specific instructions for the disposition of a number of the items within the house. Apparently some of the pieces are quite large."

"*Oh, noooo,*" Rutila drew out in mock agony.

"Yes," her mother replied. "He mentions specifically a painting, a large jar for mixing wine, and it looks like at least one or two statues."

"I may never be able to invite a friend home again," Rutila sighed.

Aemelia lowered the letter and she, Rutila, and Alexander each looked from one to the other until they all burst out laughing.

"Alright, what am I missing?" demanded Rutilus as he finally made his belated appearance in the garden.

Between their laughter his sister filled him in on the upcoming art booty and reminded him of the now infamous silver nymph platter. Catching the spirit, Rutilus began to regale them with impressions of some of his stepfather's other art treasures until Hermias came to announce that dinner was ready to serve.

Because of Amelia's meager household budget, meals with Rutilus and his family were usually a simple affair. Today, Alexander barely noticed the food. As an old fashioned matron, Aemelia rejected the modern practice of women reclining on the dining couches like men. So Rutila sat in a chair across from Alexander and Aemelia sat in one across from her son. The conversation was jovial and Alexander managed to touch Rutila's hand more than once as they appeared to reach for the same serving dish.

Afterward Rutilus invited his sister to join them in their stepfather's study to see a new scroll from the poet Horace he had just borrowed from Claudius. And so they passed a pleasant evening talking, reading, and laughing.

Walking home later by moonlight, Alexander only had thoughts of Rutila. He could see now that she shared his feelings. For a moment, he wondered that no one had raised the subject of his impending return to Egypt. Then he realized that Rutilus had probably asked his family not to mention it in order to keep the mood light.

In fact, when he thought about it, Alexander realized that Rutilus might have orchestrated a good part of the evening, arranging to be late from the baths and have his sister 'by chance' be waiting in the garden. It was probably just an unexpected coincidence that the letter from the stepfather had arrived and Aemelia had sought out her daughter in the garden.

Alexander wondered if Rutilus had been trying to give Alexander and his sister a chance to talk in private. No doubt, Rutilus would be delighted at a betrothal between his only sister and his close and wealthy friend.

"Poor, Rutilus," Alexander thought. "He sees me only as a Roman and not as a Jew as well. It would never occur to him that his patrician sister might not be considered 'good enough' for me."

Alexander felt a moment of shame that he had held back the news of his betrothal. If I am a man, should I not tell them of the betrothal? But what if she loses hope and marries someone else before I can convince my father?

Alexander concluded that he could not do anything that would risk him losing Rutila. He silently vowed to himself that he would find a way to prove to his father that Rutila would be a worthy match. It might mean turning his back on part of his Jewish heritage, but Rutila was worth it. The moment of indecision passed as Alexander once again recalled Rutila's beautiful face and imagined how he would fight to have her.

It was in this preoccupied mood that Alexander arrived home only to be met at the door by the somber face of his servant Amarantus.

"Master, I am glad you have finally come," Amarantus said as he let Alexander in. "There are two men waiting in your study. I think something terrible has happened."

Unlike some slaves, Amarantus had never been prone to

exaggeration or hysterics so Alexander knew at once that the matter must be serious. He quickly wiped his evening fancies from his mind and assumed the demeanor of the young man he had become, a no-nonsense businessman who represented his father's interests in Rome. Silently he gestured to Amarantus who straightened the folds of his toga and brushed off the dust from the street.

Thus composed, Alexander mustered his dignity and strode into his study and to whatever awaited him inside. Two men jumped up as he entered. He recognized them at once, Apollonius and Saul, Jewish merchants from Alexandria. Both men were clients of his father's. That meant that, by extension, Alexander functioned as their patron while they were in Rome.

Per custom, Alexander spoke the opening greetings to his clients and then offered them some refreshment. Both men shook their heads. Saul, who was clearly the more agitated, began to pace the small study.

"Alexander, you have got to help us. No one else can. Oh Lord, what shall we do?!"

"Saul, calm down," Alexander ordered. He may have been the younger man, but his position carried all the authority he required. "Tell me what has happened."

Saul tried to answer, but the words that tumbled out were unintelligible. Apollonius walked over and laid his hand on his friend's shoulder to calm him. Then he turned to Alexander.

"It's about Theon," he said and waited for Alexander's nod of acknowledgement. Theon was a Jewish art dealer, also of Alexandria, and a client of his father's.

"Go on," he said.

Apollonius hesitated a moment and then blurted out, "Theon has been arrested for sacrilege against a Roman god!"

6

THE ARREST

SACRILEGE .... *Sacrilege?*   Usually the charge was heresy – unfounded of course.

Every Jew knew that Augustus had confirmed the religious freedoms granted to Jews by his adopted father Julius Caesar. The Jews of both Alexandria and Palestine had been instrumental in Caesar's victory in the Alexandrian War. Caesar, in turn, had been unstinting in his display of gratitude, at least in this respect.

Alexander's own family had benefited from it. Caesar had sought out Alexander's grandfather as one of the most illustrious Jewish leaders in the Alexandrian community and bestowed upon him the Roman citizenship as a bond of goodwill between Jews and Rome. Beyond that, Caesar had decreed that all Jews in Alexandria would have Rome's protection to follow their ancient beliefs and practices. Alexander remembered how as a boy in Alexandria his father had taken him to the heart of the city to see Caesar's decrees for the Jews inscribed on a great column in the square.

Not only were Jews free to follow their traditional religious practices, they were exempted from observing those of the Romans. No Jew ever had to prostrate himself or make sacrifice before a pagan idol or give money to a Roman temple. Such rights of religious practice were reserved for Jews alone and no other people had ever acquired such privileges under Roman law.

But with privilege came envy. Although Caesar's, and later

Augustus's, decrees had ensured Jewish religious freedoms, they had also ensured that a certain portion of the non-Jewish population would despise them for having this distinction. Indeed, there had been occasional incidents in the Roman provinces where government officials had tried to charge Jews with heresy for non-observance of local gods. Other provincial magistrates had tried to requisition the Jewish tributes for their Temple in Jerusalem. Some even tried to install pagan statues in local synagogues as if Judaism were like any other 'barbarian' religion.

No matter what the nature of the offense or where, Augustus had consistently sided on behalf of the Jews. In friendship and gratitude, some of the Jews of Rome had even named their place of prayer after him, the Synagogue of the Augustesians. Augustus's endorsement for Jewish rights was well known and official pronouncements against Jews inside Rome were virtually non-existent. Alexander couldn't even remember the last time a Jew had been accused of non-observance of Roman gods.

Now, an arrest of a Jew? And a charge of sacrilege? Just the thought was almost preposterous in Rome in this day and age.

Alexander stared back at Saul and Apollonius.

"What do you mean *sacrilege*? This must be a mistake," he spoke with an easy confidence. "Surely, this must be some new magistrate looking to make a name for himself; someone who has not been in Rome long. Anyone of sense would know that Jews are not required to sacrifice to Roman gods. Tell me the details because I'm sure this wrong can be quickly fixed."

Alexander looked expectantly at his visitors waiting to hear the tale of some new Roman official attempting to flex his magisterial powers. But Saul just gaped at him. Even Apollonius seemed to be moving his jaws as if he had something to say, but couldn't quite get it out.

"What is it?" Alexander asked completely perplexed. "Was

Theon arrested for not honoring a Roman god? Is there more that you haven't told me?"

Saul and Apollonius looked at each other, and then both began to blurt out their stories in a tangled rush of words.

"It was only a jest. He was angry when he spoke."

"The priest said he wasn't there."

"No one could hide a Phidias."

"He said he'd seen it, but he would never touch it."

Alexander thrust out his hand forcefully with palm forward in a sign for silence. Apollonius ceased talking as Saul began to rock back and forth softly intoning some prayer. Despite their mangled delivery, understanding was beginning to dawn upon him and Alexander did *not* like what he was beginning to think.

"Apollonius… and *only* Apollonius," Alexander added as he saw Saul take in a deep breath for another outburst. "Tell me now, with *what* exactly has Theon been accused?"

Apollonius took only a moment to collect his thoughts before replying, "The charge is sacrilege and it is for stealing the statue of the goddess Victory."

Alexander held up his palm again as Saul appeared about to elaborate.

"And now, Apollonius, tell me who has arrested and charged Theon?"

"He was arrested this afternoon by the Urban Cohorts and charged by the Urban Prefect."

"And where is he now?" Alexander prompted.

Saul answered before Apollonius could get the words out. "The Carcer," he said grimly. "The prison."

Indeed there was no other way but grimly to speak of the Carcer. It had long existed as a dungeon for prisoners about to be executed. But ever since Augustus had established the Urban

Cohorts as a police force, the Carcer had seen increased use. The Carcer was now Rome's first real prison.

Alexander swayed physically as his mind struggled to digest these astounding facts.

"I think we had better all sit down," he said quietly. "I believe some wine is required."

Alexander waved his visitors to their seats, then called for his servant Amarantus to bring wine and water. When the two men moved to speak, he shook his head and indicated that they were to wait for the refreshment. Alexander took his own seat behind his desk and placed his chin on his fist as he stared down at the polished wood.

Was it just that morning that he had heard the tale of the stolen statue? How or why a Jew became involved, he would have to learn from further interrogation of his overwrought visitors. But if the Urban Cohorts had already made an arrest, there could be little doubt that the matter was very serious.

Alexander thought that the creation of the Urban Cohorts several years earlier was one of Augustus's more laudable attempts to bring peace and security to Rome. Before that, there had never been a true police force in Rome and any notion of civil justice had been a mockery. For the wealthy, retribution for real or imagined injuries had been meted out by hired thugs and street gangs. Since the time of the Dictator Sulla, decades before, there had been criminal courts. But like most things in Rome, money and rank influenced any outcome.

Augustus had created three Urban Cohorts, with 1,000 men each, and an Urban Prefect to manage them. These men were trained and dressed like soldiers. It was their job to keep the streets safe and arrest any wrongdoers. One could count on them to break up a street fight, beat their way past any number of hired ex-gladiators to make an arrest, or toss a house so efficiently that no secret was left unearthed. They were tough, aggressive, efficient, and, utterly lacking in *finesse*.

And that was the problem, Alexander thought. The Urban Cohorts were trained as soldiers. Just as with any soldier, they waited for someone to point out "the enemy" and then they ruthlessly went to work. But perhaps what Rome needed was someone trained as a jurist; someone who understood the fine points of the law such as seeking out evidence, examining the credibility of witnesses, assembling the disparate pieces to make the whole case. …someone like….. well, Cicero.

As part of his education, Alexander had studied the records of many famous trials with some of Cicero's being foremost among them. His teacher had always emphasized fine oratory and the speaker's ability to sway an audience. Alexander, however, had been more interested in how the case had been built. How did the advocate manage to step back and find the bigger picture and then begin to assemble the blocks that would fit it all together?

That's what the Urban Cohorts need, he thought; not just soldiers who could shout loudly, bang heads, and basically intimidate anyone they questioned. By the time Urban Cohorts came on the scene the deed was usually done and the perpetrators vanished. What the guard of the Cohorts needed then was *subtlety*. Who should they interrogate and how much should they believe? Who had something to gain, or perhaps, nothing to lose?

Alexander's musings were interrupted as Amarantus returned with goblets, a flask of wine and a pitcher of water. He raised an inquiring eyebrow at Alexander as he raised the flask to pour.

"Let's have the wine well-watered, Ranti," Alexander confirmed. "I think we will need our wits about us tonight."

After Amarantus had served the wine and left, Alexander turned his attention back to his visitors.

"Now," he said. "I think we had better have the whole story."

"But that's just it!" Saul cried. "We don't know it. We weren't there when the guards came to take him and now they won't let anyone near him."

"But surely, you know something," Alexander replied. "If I'm not mistaken, you are his friends, are you not?"

He glanced at each man in turn and both nodded miserably.

"Well, that's a start then," Alexander continued. "Now, as his friends, can you think of any reason why the Urban Cohorts would descend on a Jewish art dealer from Alexandria for the theft of a Roman goddess statue?"

Each man gave the other a somewhat guilty look, but said nothing. Neither would meet Alexander's eyes.

"By the blood of Abel," Alexander shouted in exasperation. "A man's life is in danger; perhaps many men's lives. Will you just sit there and say nothing?"

Apollonius gave Saul a searching look and then turned toward Alexander, clearing his throat awkwardly.

"It's just that Theon may have made an indiscreet remark," he said haltingly. "He didn't really mean it, and besides we didn't think that anyone had heard it anyway."

"It would appear that someone did," Alexander sighed. "Start at the beginning. I think I had better hear it all."

Once Apollonius had gotten that much out, the following words seemed to gush forth. He related how the week before the ides the three of them had paused in front of the temple of Victory; how Theon had been angry with the Senator Gnaeus Pulcher for commissioning a statue and then refusing to pay the agreed price. Finally, he related how Theon had revealed that some art collector had offered him a considerable sum if Theon could acquire the statue of Victory.

Alexander leaned forward listening intently, but chose not to interrupt Apollonius now that he had gotten him to tell the story. After the words had finished tumbling out, Alexander leaned back and gazed at him and then Saul intently.

"Now, think carefully, who might have heard Theon say this?"

Saul and Apollonius both shrugged and shook their heads.

"We don't know," Saul said. "We had stepped onto a side path to escape the crowds, but I suppose we were still close enough to Victory's Incline to be overheard."

Apollonius added, "We did glance around and there didn't seem to be anyone staring at us. Then we just decided to walk away from there as quickly as we could."

"And do you remember seeing anyone you knew on Victory's Incline that day? Anyone at all who may have recognized any of you?"

Again the men shook their heads.

"We talked about it afterwards, but we had been so intent on our conversation that nothing short of an entire Urban Cohort marching past would have drawn our attention." Apollonius winced at his inadvertent reference to the guards that had arrested their friend only that morning.

"Since that day, have either of you mentioned Theon's, *uhhh, unfortunate remark* to anyone? Family? Friends? Other merchants?"

Saul looked shocked. "Never," he said. "As you could see, we could barely tell it to you. Words like that could get a man cracked on the head and thrown in the Tiber."

Alexander looked at Apollonius who emphatically nodded his concurrence with Saul's statement.

"And what about Theon? Would he have repeated it?" Alexander asked.

Both men looked startled and then looked at each other inquiringly.

"We don't think so," Apollonius finally replied. "But he was so angry. This business with Gnaeus Pulcher could ruin him. He wasn't thinking right."

Alexander looked at his visitors appraisingly as he attempted to digest the information imparted thus far. He felt he was forgetting something important…. ahh yes.

"Did Theon give either of you any indication of the identity of this mysterious art collector interested in the statue of Victory?"

They indicated that he had not, but Apollonius added, "If one had to guess, Gnaeus Pulcher himself would be the obvious person who comes to mind. His particular passion is sculpture and his methods are known to be, *errr*, one might say, *unscrupulous*."

Alexander made a tight smile. For Gnaeus Pulcher, unscrupulous was almost an understatement. He was a very powerful man in Rome… a man who was unafraid to use that power when it suited his own purposes. If Gnaeus Pulcher was involved in this matter in any way, things could get very dangerous, very fast.

"And now, I have to ask you one thing more," Alexander said. "I assume you have come to me because my father is your patron." He paused and both men nodded.

"And as his son, I am his agent in Rome. Therefore by extension I can and must act as your patron." Again he paused and waited for them to nod their agreement.

"Therefore, as your patron, I demand that you answer me now and answer me honestly. Do you have any information, anything at all, to cause you to suspect that *Theon* may have stolen this statue?"

Both men seemed taken aback.   Perhaps they had not expected such directness from one so young. Apollonius recovered first.

"No," he said firmly looking Alexander straight in the eye. "I have known Theon since we were boys, and I do not believe he would have done such a thing."

"Nor I," Saul added. "I am older than he, and, before I knew Theon, I knew his father. They fear the Lord. He would not have done this thing."

Alexander sat back and nodded. "I believe you. It fits what I know of Theon. He may have a temper, but he is an honest man."

"And now," Alexander continued, "tell me what you know of the arrest."

Despite further questioning, Alexander found that Apollonius and Saul knew little else. The Urban Cohorts had shown up at Theon's home in the afternoon, searched it thoroughly and then taken him into custody. A neighbor had sent a messenger to inform Saul, who had immediately contacted Apollonius.

Saul and Apollonius had gone to the Carcer and attempted to intervene. But they had been repulsed at the entrance to the prison without being permitted to speak to either Theon or a tribune of the Urban Cohorts. It had been the door guard who had told them about the charge of *sacrilege*, but with no further information than that.

By the time they had finished their story, it was already the second hour into the night. If the men did not leave soon, the streets would be too dangerous to pass. Alexander showed the men to the door and promised to look into the matter the first thing in the morning. Saul and Apollonius looked much relieved as they spoke the traditional parting phrases for good evening and good health.

It was clear that both men knew that as Jewish merchants

from Alexandria, there was little they could do to intercede for their friend.   An accusation of this magnitude in Rome could only be addressed by a man of consequence.   Alexander may be a young man, but he was a citizen, a respected businessman from a very wealthy family, and with close social ties to some of Rome's elite.

Of all the Jewish men currently in Rome, Alexander was possibly the man with the greatest influence … *well, except for one other*.

7
THE CARCER

THE fourth hour of night must have already passed, Alexander reckoned, as he studied the brightly colored patterns painted on his bedchamber's walls. Not that he could actually see them. Like most bedchambers in Roman apartments, his had no window and the small oil lamp he had extinguished had left the room in absolute darkness.

Silently he pondered what he could do about the arrest of Theon.

Alexander was not naïve. Soon many Romans would hear the rumor that a Jew had stolen the statue of Victory from her temple on the Palatine hill. Romans would be angry and it was unlikely that anger over the theft would stay focused on the arrest of a single Jew. The attack on the Jewish merchant, Elias, in the Forum made that abundantly clear.

Alexander would have to act quickly to clear Theon's name before further repercussions were felt in the Jewish community.

But how? Alexander struggled to construct a plan just as he imagined the famous advocates would have done. But Alexander knew he was no Cicero, and certainly no particular helpful revelations had sprung forth out of the dark corners of his bedchamber. He yawned widely as he determined that he would just start at the beginning and let tomorrow decide where he would go from there.

The first thing in the morning, he would visit Theon in the Carcer prison. Hopefully, Alexander's status as a citizen and patron would warrant a face-to-face visit. Then he would find out what Theon knew of the matter. At the very least, Theon could tell him the name of this mysterious collector of statuary. That is, if such a person truly did exist. The thought of anyone seriously coveting a statue of a goddess from a temple on Rome's Palatine Hill was almost too preposterous to contemplate.

With another huge yawn Alexander turned his thoughts to a far more pleasant topic, the one he thought about nearly every night before falling asleep. He closed his eyes and the temple goddess was supplanted by a different type of beauty with large green eyes and red-gold tresses.

Alexander finally drifted off to sleep knowing how it felt to covet something very precious, something seemingly unobtainable.

***

Morning broke and Alexander awakened once again feeling warmed by the vestiges of a fond dream -- until he remembered the task that lay before him that day. As he spoke his morning prayers he hesitated as he recited the commandment, *"Lo tignov -- Thou shall not steal."*

Could a Jew have broken the Lord's commandment and stolen the statue? Of course he could have. As much as Alexander didn't want to believe it, he knew that he had to treat Theon as a suspect. Even the most devout of men experienced moments of weakness. And Saul and Apollonius did say that Theon was facing financial ruin.

As Amarantus served breakfast, Alexander related to him some of the events of the day before. Alexander knew that many people treated their slaves as if they were no more than domesticated animals. They would talk about them as if they weren't even in the same room.

This was never the case with Amarantus. Amarantus was more than a house slave; he was also Alexander's personal secretary. Alexander had quickly discerned that his slave had a keen intellect and found himself consulting Amarantus on business matters with increasing frequency.

So it was with some expectation that Alexander related to Amarantus the tale that the Forum wag he called Bushy Brown had related at the barber's on the previous morning. He shared it all; about how the temple priest had sworn the *augur* had come and taken the statue, but the *augur* had denied it when it was never returned.

Then he continued with the previous night's account of Theon's injudicious words and subsequent arrest. When done, Alexander looked at Amarantus expectantly hoping for some clever hint of how to go about solving this mystery.

Amarantus appeared to consider carefully then said, "Master, you must discover how much of what this Bushy Brown said is true. You will speak with this Theon, of course?"

"I intend to visit the Carcer as soon as I've eaten," replied Alexander, suddenly remembering the cheese and bread laid out before him. "Then I suppose I must question some of these other men."

"Master, if this Gnaeus Pulcher and the *augur* are involved, that could be very dangerous."

"Yes, it could be," Alexander sighed. "But how else am I to learn the truth?"

Amarantus' lips twitched into a small smile as he answered, "Master I do not believe that one who questions those men should expect to receive the truth."

Alexander glanced up sharply and then smiled in return. "I suppose not. What do you suggest?"

"Master, I would question their slaves. There are few slaves who do not know the measure of their master. And, if I guess correctly, the slaves of such men could be encouraged to speak freely."

Alexander gazed at Amarantus thoughtfully. "You are right. I have often seen that the more exalted the man, the less likely he is to take note of his slaves. They may well see and hear many things without him even realizing it."

"Shall I add some extra coins to your purse, then?" Amarantus queried.

"Yes, that would be a good idea; and bring my toga. Oh, and Amarantus. I think you had better come too. It would not appear dignified for me to walk up to the prison with no attendant. Wear one of your better tunics. It's time I got this little investigation started."

The Carcer was only minutes away from Alexander's apartment on the Capitoline Hill. It stood at the foot of the hill in the northwest corner of the Roman Forum, and was easily recognizable since it was one of the few buildings that had not been faced with marble. Alexander had passed it many times, but had never been inside.

As he descended the hill, Alexander thought back on what he knew about the prison. There was an older, lower level that was legendary. It was called the Tullianum although he was not sure if anyone remembered quite why. Few people had ever seen it, but everyone knew that it was a small round dungeon with no doors or windows; just a hole in its ceiling through which prisoners were thrown. Those consigned to the dungeon were awaiting only one thing – execution.

Another structure had been built over the Tullianum dungeon which was called the Carcer proper. The Carcer had always been used as a detention area. Prisoners awaiting trial who might seek to escape would be held in the Carcer until their fate was finally settled. In this respect, the function of the Carcer had not changed under Augustus. What had changed was its frequency of use. Alexander had heard that at one time, the City did not even keep a regular guard at the Carcer. But since Augustus had created the Urban Cohorts to police the city, the prison had seen a steady increase in use.

Alexander paused before he reached the prison entrance and had Amarantus straighten the folds of his toga. Then he sucked in a deep breath, threw back his shoulders and stalked to the entrance with as much confidence as he could possibly project.

A guard wearing the uniform of the Urban Cohorts stood at the entrance to the prison. "I'm here to see the prisoner Theon," Alexander announced.

Unfazed the guard looked at him coolly. "And who would you be?"

"Gaius Julius Alexander," he began and tried not to wince when the guard smirked at his obviously foreign name. Gaius and Julius were Roman enough, but the Greek Alexander gave him away immediately as a man from the provinces.

Alexander made a show of ignoring the slight and continued.

"The art dealer Theon is my client. As his patron, I demand to see him to determine the appropriate litigious action."

The word 'patron' did get the soldier's attention. The rights and responsibilities of the patron were an integral part of the Roman social structure. It also meant that Alexander was probably richer and more influential than the soldier had initially assumed.

Still the guard hesitated. Alexander began to fear that he might be turned away.

With a flounce, Amarantus stepped forward and with a great show of snobbery stared the soldier up and down. Then he announced with a sarcasm usually found only in the slaves of the very powerful, "My Master *is not happy* to be delayed when on the business of *his patron,* the First Citizen Augustus."

Alexander straightened his face to hide his own astonishment at Amarantus' rather outrageous proclamation. It *was true* that Augustus was his patron, but Alexander was confident that Rome's First Citizen barely knew that he existed. A couple of times, Augustus had sent Alexander messages to deliver to Jewish leaders in Rome, but Augustus certainly had never entrusted him with any important State business.

The mention of Augustus, however, was enough to get the attention of the soldier. He flashed a quick look at the man who had spoken and saw a slave wearing a tunic of a quality that would have cost more than he could ever afford on a Cohort's salary. And, now that he noticed it, the Master's tunic and toga also were of the highest quality. Perhaps this young citizen was more than he had initially seemed.

The soldier scrunched his eyebrows together in what would pass in a Cohort as deep thought.

"Augustus is your patron?"

"He is," Alexander replied.

"And you are the prisoner Theon's patron?"

"I am."

"Well, I suppose that's different then," the soldier replied. "Wait here please, *err,* Citizen."

As the guard left them at the entrance to fetch the keys, Alexander turned on Amarantus.

"What was that about?" he whispered. "I am not here on the First Citizen's business."

"I did not say you were," Amarantus' eyes twinkled back. "I merely said that *when* you are on the First Citizen's business, you don't like to be delayed. And you don't do you?"

Alexander's initial attempt at a severe expression quickly shifted into a smile. After all, Amarantus had gotten them in, hadn't he?

But whatever secret delight he'd felt at being escorted so respectfully into the prison was quickly subdued when the guard led them to Theon's cell. The interior of the prison had no decoration, not even a coat of plaster, and the exposed *tufa* block lent a primitive texture to the prevailing gloom. All around him, Alexander smelled the sickly, stale air. Sweat, vomit, urine, blood assailed him, and … something less palpable… fear. Alexander liked to think of himself as a brave man. But the atmosphere in the prison knotted his stomach.

In silence, he followed the guard to a wooden door and waited as it was unlocked and the bolt was drawn. The guard took a small oil lamp from a shelf, lit it and handed it to Alexander.

"The door will have to remain open," he said. "I'll be waiting out here."

Alexander nodded and motioned to Amarantus to remain outside as well. Raising the lamp, he stepped inside.

It took awhile for Alexander's eyes to grow accustomed to the gloom inside. At first, the chamber seemed empty except the eerie shadow thrown by the light of the lamp. Gradually, he made out a lump on the floor and realized it was a man lying on the bare stone.

"Theon!" Alexander cried and bent to help the man into a sitting position.

Alexander could barely make out the once successful art dealer in the creature who now cowered before him. The man was filthy, his usual tunic had been replaced with a rag; his feet were bare. And he had been beaten. His face was puffed and darkened. One eye was swollen shut and the other seemed to stare without

"Theon!" Alexander cried again and then gently turned the man's chin until the one blank eye stared back at him. Was that a flicker?

Striding to the door, Alexander practically yelled at the soldier.

"This man needs water. Show my slave where he can get some."

The soldier seemed to start in surprise, but turned and muttered something to Amarantus.

Alexander returned to Theon and squatted next to him until the water arrived. Taking the pottery bowl, he lifted it to Theon's lips and helped him to drink.

The water, or perhaps it was just the kindness, seemed to spark something in Theon. He gasped and began to look more alert.

"Theon, do you know who I am?" Alexander asked.

Theon nodded.

"I am your patron and I have come to try to help you. Do you understand?"

Again, Theon nodded.

"Can you talk?"

Theon motioned toward the water bowl and Alexander helped him to another drink.

"Thank you, Alexander," Theon rasped. "How did you...?"

"Apollonius and Saul came to see me last night. They had tried to see you yesterday, but were turned away."

Theon nodded.

"What has happened to you, Theon? Have you been tortured?"

"No, not tortured. *Not yet.* Just beatings. Lots of beatings. And lots of questions."

"I will see the Urban Prefect today and speak to him about your treatment. Surely, I know someone who can call in a favor. Perhaps I can get you transferred into my custody."

"Don't bother," Theon countered. Then at Alexander's obvious surprise, "It's not in his hands anymore."

"Explain."

"Do you know the charge?" Theon asked.

"I understand it is theft of a Roman temple statue," Alexander replied.

"No, the *exact* legal charge?" Theon asked, but didn't wait for an answer.

"*I know*, because it's been repeated to me over and over since they brought me here yesterday. I am charged with being a *sacrilegus*, one who plunders public sacred places. But that's where it starts to get tricky. Sacrilege is covered under the *Lex Julia Peculatus*. It's a new law created by Augustus himself."

"I know this law," Alexander replied. "It's what makes it illegal for anyone to plunder our tithes to the Jerusalem temple. But I thought it was basically aimed at thieves who stole money or other offerings for temples."

"And that's the catch," Theon grimaced. "No one ever thought it would be used for a theft this ... *spectacular*. It appears this incident had the noses of the good Roman jurists stuck in the law scrolls trying to determine jurisdiction. It may be the only reason I haven't been tortured yet."

"And has the jurisdiction been decided?" Alexander pressed.

"Yes, the last guard who came in said that it has been decided that this charge of sacrilege falls under the jurisdiction of the *Pontifex Maximus,* and you know *who* that is."

"Augustus," Alexander gasped.

"Yeah, him. First Citizen and head priest, too. Apparently now they're waiting for him to send someone to question me."

In an instant, Alexander's heart had leapt into his throat. So the guard outside had been waiting for someone to come to see Theon on the First Citizen's business. Suddenly, Amarantus' clever little ploy to gain entrance didn't seem so funny anymore. In fact, it started to feel a lot like trouble.

Setting that thought aside, Alexander turned to Theon.

"If I am to help you, I must ask you some questions. Will you answer?"

Theon nodded his head in the affirmative.

"And do you swear that all your answers will be true and complete?"

"I do," Theon rasped.

"Did you steal the statue?"

"No."

"Do you know who did?"

"No."

"Is it true that you made a statement outside the temple that you had a buyer for the statue?"

Theon closed his one good eye tightly and bowed his head before mumbling, "Yes."

"Did you make that statement at any other time to any other person?"

With head still bowed, Theon shook it from side to side, "No."

"Was this statement the reason for your arrest?"

"Yes. They had no other evidence."

"Then who turned you in?"

"I don't know!" Theon cried. "Do you think I haven't thought of it over and over? There was no one else. At least no one that I saw, but I was very upset."

"Do you suspect either Saul or Apollonius?" Alexander asked.

Theon jerked his head toward Alexander. *"Never!* Never. I've known these men all my life. They would never do such a thing."

"Calm down. I agree," Alexander said softly. "But I shall have to find out the identity of this mysterious informant who can blend into a hillside path without being seen. Now, Theon, about the statement itself; was it true?"

Theon hesitated and a look of fear crossed his face.

"It was true, but more the fool I was. To even say his name is more danger than where I sit now. Dangerous to you too, Alexander, if I tell you."

"Nevertheless, I think you must. I understand that we are probably dealing with a powerful man? ... a ruthless man?"

Theon nodded in response, but said no more.

"Is this man Gnaeus Pulcher?" Alexander demanded.

"Yes," Theon croaked. "The man collects statues. It's not just a passion with him; it's an obsession. Many times in the past year, he's mentioned how badly he wants to add an original work by Phidias to his collection. And once ... just once ... he said how much he would like to possess the beautiful Victory in the temple."

Alexander raised his eyebrows. "He said he would *like to possess*? Doesn't that sound more like wishful thinking than anything criminal?"

"You have to know the man," Theon replied. "It wasn't just

what he said, but how he said it. I knew exactly what he meant and he knew that I knew. I have never seen his art room myself, but I've heard from some pretty reliable people that a good part of Gnaeus Pulcher's collection is stolen."

Alexander pursed his lips and thought this one through.

"A man like that would have many visitors to his house. How could he have so many stolen works and no one has reported it?"

"Because," Theon replied, "he has a room, a special room in the back of his house that is always locked. That's where he keeps them. At least, that's what I hear."

"Then Gnaeus Pulcher could have taken the statue," Alexander mused. "Not personally, of course, but what he said to you, he may have said to others. Perhaps one of them wanted the money badly enough to take the risk. It seems incredible, but the statue *is* gone. Did you tell the guards about Gnaeus Pulcher? Did you give them his name?"

Theon was adamant. "No! And I won't. No matter what. As things stand, there's a chance that I may get out of this simply because I didn't do it. But if I so much as breathe his name, I'm a dead man... and, Alexander, maybe my family, too."

Alexander nodded in agreement.

"Theon, is there anything more you can tell me? Any hint of how I can pursue this investigation?"

Theon shook his head ruefully. "Nothing. I was caught completely by surprise when the Urban Cohorts busted down my door and took me into custody. Alexander, my family; what's happened to them?"

"They are safe. Apollonius moved them to his home, and I have advised him not to let them go out until this matter is settled."

Theon let out a sigh of relief and Alexander added, "It is

good that you kept no slaves, for surely, they would have been tortured by now."

Theon winced as the mention of torture, then whispered hesitantly, "And me, Alexander? Can you help me?"

"I'll try. I think the best thing I can do is find out who took the statue. Until we have the real thief, it will be difficult to prove your innocence."

Theon fixed the one good eye in his hideously swollen face on Alexander. Even through the dirt and the gloom, Alexander could see the gratitude that shone in it.

"Alexander, I don't know how to...." But Alexander stopped him before he could complete his sentence.

"Not necessary, Theon. I am your patron .... and a fellow Jew. It is my duty."

"Then may the Lord go with you," Theon replied. "I shall pray for you."

Alexander rose and left for there was nothing more to say. Every day since he was a boy, Alexander had said his prayers to the Lord. He hadn't spent too much time considering whether the Lord was listening or not. But now, he sure hoped the Lord would hear the prayers that both he and Theon would be saying tomorrow.

8
THE EYEWITNESS

"MASTER, what is it?"

Alexander could feel Amarantus' worry as he fell into step behind his master, but he did not stop walking until he was well out of the sight of the Cohort guard at the prison door. Then he staggered and leaned against a nearby wall. The stench of the Carcer seemed to cling to him.

Amarantus knelt down and gazed up worriedly into his face.

"Master, was it so… so very bad?"

Alexander just nodded mutely, but after a minute seemed to find his voice. He related to Amarantus what had transpired in Theon's cell. Amarantus listened attentively. He didn't seem quite as shocked as Alexander had been by the beatings. Then Alexander recalled the old scars on his slave's back. Under his former Master, beatings for Amarantus had been just another part of life.

But his slave was truly horrified when Alexander told him the part about how the soldier had been waiting for someone to come to see the prisoner on the First Citizen's business.

"Master," Amarantus cried with genuine anguish. "I never meant to say something that would bring you trouble. If the guards come, you must tell them that I am a disobedient slave. Then you must beat me."

Alexander placed his hand on his slave's shoulder to stem the flow of words.

"Nonsense. It *was* a good idea, Ranti. There is no way you could have known about these other… *uh*, circumstances. Besides, I went along with it, and that means any fault lies solely with me."

Amarantus seemed to want to discuss this further, but Alexander just waved a hand and told him he wasn't up for a debate on the matter. They walked down a side road off of the Forum until they found a small tavern facing west away from the morning sun. While Alexander found a seat, Amarantus was sent to haggle with the tavern keeper for the better vintage wine.

Amarantus returned with the wine to find his Master deep in thought.

"Master, you are worried because of what I have done?"

"*Hmmm*… No, no, Ranti. My thoughts have been a bit more productive than that."

Alexander turned to his slave. "So, Amarantus, you are worried about this morning. How would you like to make it up to me?"

Amarantus looked puzzled, but was quick to agree to whatever his Master wished him to do.

"That's good," Alexander replied. "Because I wish you to become a *spy*."

He laughed softly at Amarantus' surprised expression. "Let me explain. I have been thinking about what you said this morning. And about what Theon told me as well. I think it would be too dangerous for me to approach the Senator Gnaeus Pulcher. If I even approached his slaves, they would likely report that to him as well. Therefore, I want *you* to do it. Not directly of course. Everyone says slaves love to gossip. So find one of his slaves and see what you can learn."

Amarantus nodded slowly. "This I can do. And, Master, I will be discreet. He will never know that I am seeking information for you."

"Good," Alexander replied. "And while you pursue your investigation, Ranti, I shall pursue mine. I believe it's time I had a little chat with this temple priest."

Alexander headed through the Forum back towards the steps cut into the side of the Palatine Hill. It was mid-morning and already the July sun was burning down on the streets of Rome. He contemplated removing his toga, but decided it was better to leave it on until after his interview with the priest. Once removed, he would never be able to put it back on by himself, at least not properly.

When he finally arrived at the Temple of Victory, Alexander realized why he had never taken note of it before. The little temple was overshadowed by the grander one that stood next to it, called the temple of the Magna Mater or the Great Mother Cybele.

Pausing on the temple path that led off of Victory's Incline, Alexander took a moment to study the exterior of the temple of Victory. It was clearly one of the older temples and quite modest in contrast to the ones found in the Forum or on the Capitoline Hill. He could not tell if it had been built of wood or stone for the front had been faced with marble. Several decades earlier, Augustus had sought the goodwill of the gods for Rome by restoring all of their temples. Not out of his resources, of course. Augustus had strong-armed private citizens into funding the renovations.

Alexander climbed the steps to the portico and entered the double doors of the temple. The darkness of the interior was broken by only a few small oil lamps. It was a small room, perhaps no more than 20 feet deep.

Alexander could see the large plinth toward the back on which the statue must have stood. But other than that, the temple appeared deserted.

"Hello," he called. "Is anyone here?"

Moments passed, then an old man emerged from a dark

corner.   One look at the man and Alexander knew that he had better proceed slowly.   The old priest was haggard and it seemed probable that he had barely eaten or slept for days.   As he came closer, Alexander could see the anguish in his eyes.

"Are you the priest of Victory?" he asked.

The priest appeared to be struggling for words.

"She's gone," he mumbled. *"She's ....just ... gone."*

"I know," Alexander replied.   "I have come to see if I can help."

The priest tilted his head and looked at Alexander through bleary eyes. "You've come from the palace?"

"No," Alexander answered firmly.   "But I am the patron of the man who was arrested yesterday, and I have promised to investigate this."

"You mean the Jew?" the priest asked.   Alexander nodded.

"It wasn't a Jew that took the statue.   I wouldn't have given her to a Jew."

"Good," Alexander thought.   "An eyewitness that can state that Theon wasn't there.   It's a start."   He turned to the priest.

"Would you tell me your name?"

"Vatinius," the priest mumbled.

"Well, Vatinius.   You look tired and I bet you haven't had much to eat in days.   How about if I buy you a meal and you tell me what happened?   I swear to you that I will do everything in my power to get the statue of Victory back to you."

Alexander had expected the priest to react with hope or even suspicion, but the poor old man just seemed numb.

"Can't leave the temple," he shook his head back and forth. "What if they brought her back and I wasn't here to greet her? Can't leave."

"Of course, you are right not to leave." Alexander replied in what he hoped was a soothing voice. "I will go buy some food and wine and then we can sit on the temple steps and eat."

The priest seemed to nod, so Alexander hurried off. Although he was tempted to stop at the first stand he passed, he decided that some extra effort might pay off. He descended Victory's Incline all the way to the *Forum Boarium*. This area was known as the meat market, but, in fact, there was a stall for almost every type of food.

Alexander stocked up on enough food that the priest would have a little left over for the following day. He selected carefully some meat and vegetable rolls, fruit, and a skin of simple wine. It was good fare, but not so good that it would seem like a bribe.

As he shopped he considered what he had learned of the priest already. *Was he honest?* The priest did seem genuinely distraught. But could the statue have been taken without some collusion from the priest?

Alexander returned to the temple of Victory, took the priest gently by the elbow and led him out to the steps where they sat down in the shade from the roof. At first the priest took the food reluctantly, but after a few bites Alexander noted some color beginning to return to his face.

They ate in silence for a while, then Alexander finally said, "Tell me about the statue, Vatinius. Is she beautiful?"

The priest seemed flabbergasted. "You mean you've never seen her?"

"No, but I've heard she was particularly fine."

Not surprisingly, talking about the statue seemed to be the priest's favorite topic, and it took only a little prodding to get him to open up. At first, the priest seemed to begin with ancient history, but Alexander just let him talk. The priest told how many centuries before, the great sculptor, Phidias, had been commissioned to build the Parthenon in Athens. Alexander, of course, had heard of this temple to Athena Parthenos, as it was known as one of the architectural marvels of the Greek-speaking world.

For the center of the temple, Phidias had sculpted from gold and ivory a nearly forty-foot statue of the goddess, Athena, who held a smaller six-foot statue of the winged Victory in her outstretched hand. Except, the priest noted, the Athenians called the goddess *Nike* not Victory as the Romans did. Before the final statue was created, it was said that several slightly larger than life versions of each Athena and Nike had been sculpted in marble in order to determine which style would best suit the final design for the temple.

"I see," said Alexander. "So, our Victory is one of the original models sculpted for the Parthenon?"

"Exactly, but *not* the one that was selected."

"No?"

"No. That Victory, simply stands straight up with both feet on the hand of Athena Parthenos. Ours is one of the descending Victory's, but with the detail and expression of the classic Phidias style."

Alexander nodded. He was no art connoisseur, but even he knew that the Greeks had asserted that Phidias had gazed upon the countenance of the gods. Phidias alone had been empowered to reveal the gods to humanity through his art. Although his sculpted gods resembled humans, they retained a certain reserve, an air of nobility that lent them an ethereal quality never found in statues of mere mortals.

"Go on, tell me about her," he prodded. But Vatinius needed little prodding.

"Well, she's about 6 ½ feet tall and sculpted of white marble. She is descending from the sky with outstretched wings and the right foot has landed on the base. Her posture is straight and reserved with both arms held out, but slightly downward as if she is reaching out for the petitioner. In her left hand is a laurel wreath. Her face also looks downward at the petitioner with such an expression of …. Well, I can't quite describe it, but if you stand at the base of the statue and look up, it seems as if she is gazing down *with eyes only for you*, and a *laurel wreath only for you.*"

"She sounds beautiful. She's painted, of course?"

"Oh, yes. Of course, her hair and clothes are of the fashion worn in Athens way back in the time of Phidias. Her hair is twisted on the sides and pulled up in the back. It's painted a light brown, but tiny strokes of real gold were used to put highlights in her hair. She wears a long tunic painted in dark blue that ties only at the waist and drapes very close to the body.

"…Oh, and her legs and shoulders are covered; none of that modern half-naked stuff sculptors are doing now -- making goddesses look like Suburan whores. No, this Victory is dignified, a great lady."

"Anything else?"

"Hmmm, well her face and arms are painted, but the skin is so very pale that it's not much darker than the marble. The wings weren't painted, but left with the original white marble."

"I can see why someone might steal her," Alexander thought aloud. But then noting the shocked look on the priest's face added, "Not that anyone should, of course. It's a sacrilege. I just meant that I have known men who covet beautiful things. Ruthless men."

The priest grunted. "Yeah. I know the type. I've seen them here. You can always tell the ones who come just to see the statue. They don't care about the goddess. Half the time they don't even leave an offering. They just want to see the beautiful statue, as if she were no more than a chunk of marble."

"Anyone in particular?" Alexander asked.

Vatinius gave him a startled look, then seemed to consider it.

"Nah, no one in particular that I can think of."

"What about, perhaps, a certain Senator named Gnaeus Pulcher?"

The priest raised his eyebrows, but responded. "No, not *him*. He used to come here a lot to look at the statue, but he hasn't been in the temple for months."

Alexander stared down at the steps of the temple trying to think of what else he could ask, but apparently Vatinius wasn't finished.

"Of course, it's not just the art collectors who come to be so obsessed with this Victory. The soldiers are just as bad."

"Really?"

"Oh yeah, I think it's on account of the way the goddess seems to be looking straight at you and holding her arms out towards you. There are other statues of Victory in Rome, but *this* is where the soldiers come, the important ones at least. They look up into her face and they're sure that the goddess is telling them about their own victory."

"Yes," Alexander recalled. "I remember a friend telling me that his stepfather Sextus Fadius had sacrificed at many of the temples before assuming his duties as military legate in Gaul. He must have come here."

"Sextus Fadius!" the priest snorted.

"You know him?"

"Couldn't help but know him," the priest replied. "He was in here many times; kept bringing finer and bigger offerings to the goddess."

"Is that typical?" Alexander asked.

"*Naah*. This temple is lucky to get one visit since Senators can make small offerings at the statue of Victory in the Curia building. But this Sextus Fadius kept coming back. He said he'd had a dream that Victory had come to him, descending out of the sky and handed him a laurel wreath just like the one our Victory is holding."

"A most auspicious dream," Alexander remarked.

"Indeed," Vatinius responded. "And most men would have been happy with that and a single sacrifice of thanksgiving. Sextus Fadius, however, became like a man obsessed with the goddess. He kept bringing her bigger and bigger offerings and demanding that she appear to him again. ...As if any man could hope to *control* a goddess."

The priest snorted again in derision.

All along as they had been talking, Alexander had kept passing the priest the wine flask without taking much himself. Whether it was the wine or the fact that they had been talking about the priest's favorite topic, he didn't know, but old Vatinius seemed to have opened up. Knowing that he was unlikely to get a better chance, Alexander cleared his throat and spoke softly.

"Can you tell me about the other night? ... the night the statue disappeared?"

Instantly the priest was suspicious. "What's it to you? Who did you say you were?"

Patiently, Alexander explained to the priest again who he was and about his client Theon who had been arrested. Again he repeated his honest desire to help recover the statue.

Vatinius stared at him a few moments and then shrugged.

"Well, nobody told me *not* to talk about it, so I guess there's no reason why I shouldn't tell you."

And then he related the full account ... how the *augur* Lucius Servilius had come late at night and demanded the statue for the procession, how the procession had never happened and the statue hadn't been returned. And then the priest told about his visit to the home of Lucius Servilius who had refused to see him, but, through his steward, had denied ever taking the statue. In fact, the whole story was remarkably like the account the Forum wag Bushy Brown had told at the barber's on the previous morning.

"Are you sure it was Lucius Servilius?" Alexander asked.

"Of course, I'm sure. He stood right there in the temple, didn't he? A priest ought to recognize an *augur*, shouldn't he? And I could see that he was a real traditional one, too. I'm not a fool."

"I meant no offense, Vatinius, but you have been serving here for very many years, haven't you?"

"Nearly thirty," the priest confirmed.

"It's just that, I was wondering, is your eyesight as keen as it once was?"

"*Huh*," the priest scoffed. "You young bulls come around here and think you know everything. Well, I'll tell you, my eyesight is as good as the next man's."

"No offense," Alexander held out his palms placatingly. "I was just wondering. Can you tell me now about Augustus?"

But Vatinius began to break down as he spoke of that and the anguished look returned. Not surprisingly, Augustus had been very hard on the priest, had questioned him thoroughly, accused him of neglect, stupidity, and then of plotting to steal the statue.

"Still you were not imprisoned," Alexander commented. "He let you return to the temple. Do you think he believed you?"

Vatinius could only shake his head and shrug.

"Did Augustus send for the *augur* Lucius Servilius?"

"If he did, he did it after he sent me back," Vatinius shrugged again.

Seeing that he would get little else out of the priest,

Alexander thanked him and pressed some coins into his hand.

"For the goddess," he said. "For when she is safely returned."

Alexander had much to ponder as he climbed down the Palatine steps heading home towards the Capitoline. A statue stolen. A Jew arrested. Another Jew attacked by bullies who may have been spurred on by Praetorians, the First Citizen's own personal guard. And the only suspect at present was, Gnaeus Pulcher, one of Rome's most powerful senators.

Alexander shook his head in resignation. This was no longer just about a patron helping a client who happened to be Jewish. The theft and arrest could now affect the welfare of other Jews, perhaps many Jews, perhaps even *all* Jews in Rome. This was too great for him to handle alone. Alexander knew he needed to bring this matter to the attention of a higher authority.

He needed to bring it to… Alexander groaned … to *Agrippa*.

9
AGRIPPA

MARCUS Julius Agrippa. He was the grandson of King Herod the Great, and, along with his older brother Herod, an heir to the throne of Judea. That was assuming there would ever be a Jewish king in Judea again, now that it had become a Roman province.

Agrippa and Alexander had known each other since Alexander had first arrived in Rome years earlier. They had grown from boy to manhood together. They had even lived in the same house. Agrippa's mother Berenice had raised Alexander in Rome after Alexander's father had brought him here from Alexandria at age ten.

Because of Berenice's friendship with the imperial lady Antonia, both boys had studied and played in the circle of Antonia's son Claudius. The three boys, Agrippa, Alexander, and Claudius, had grown up close, practically inseparable.

But by the time the boys were finishing their schooling, Agrippa had started to change. He stopped spending so much time with Alexander and Claudius and began to curry favor with a new crowd, the political crowd. His new companions were the sons of Senators and he carefully chose ones with the greatest influence.

Alexander did not begrudge Agrippa his efforts to run with a more influential crowd. For someone in Agrippa's position, forming powerful alliances was a political necessity. It was just that Agrippa had become so *irresponsible*.

While Alexander had settled in and begun to learn his father's business, Agrippa had been gaining a reputation for dissolute behavior. He stayed out late, drinking and gambling. What little inheritance he had was squandered and now Agrippa was racking up debt with the moneylenders. The only time Alexander saw him anymore was when Agrippa dropped by to borrow money.

For the most part, Berenice kept matters in check. Her influence over her son was still very great, and she kept him out of too much trouble. But she couldn't stop things she didn't know about. And so Agrippa would borrow from Alexander knowing that, out of friendship, Alexander wouldn't report the loans back to Berenice.

Once, just once, Alexander had suggested that Agrippa should try to work for a living rather than continuously borrow money that he could never hope to repay. Agrippa had been completely astonished at the suggestion, and patiently pointed out to Alexander that he was a prince and that princes did not work.

Claudius had agreed with Agrippa on this point. "I couldn't work either," he had said. "There are some classes where that is just not done. --Unless, of course, the work is public service such as an appointment from the Senate. But that doesn't seem to be an option for either Agrippa or me right now."

Alexander had found it easiest simply to avoid Agrippa as much as possible. The present situation, however, called for someone with higher rank than Alexander.

Berenice's oldest son Herod no longer lived in Rome. In any case, he had never shown the political acumen – or ambition – of his younger brother. So as the grandson of King Herod the Great and the only Jewish prince in Rome, Agrippa was indisputably the political head of all Jews in Rome. Any matter that affected the Jewish community was a matter for Agrippa.

Alexander sighed. There was nothing for it. He would have to go to Agrippa and take along a suitable gift … *like a bag of silver.* Given the urgency of the situation he would have preferred to go that evening. But it was already getting late, and it was almost a certainty that Agrippa had already left for that night's dinner party, wherever that may have been.

Instead, Alexander sent off a quick note asking for a meeting the next day at mid-morning. To his surprise, a reply came back with the original messenger. When he opened it, he saw the reply was from Agrippa's mother Berenice confirming the appointment and offering her assurances that her son would be home for the meeting.

Satisfied that he had accomplished all he could that day, Alexander settled himself down for a late dinner. Afterwards he pushed back his plate and summoned Amarantus.

"So, Ranti, tell me about your day as a spy."

Between the interview with the priest and composing the message to Agrippa, Alexander had nearly forgotten that he had commissioned his slave to spy on Gnaeus Pulcher. But as it turned out, Amarantus had learned very little. No slaves of any note had left the house. However, Amarantus assured him that since the following day was market day, the odds were very good that he would succeed in talking to one of the household slaves then.

***

The next day, Alexander presented himself at the home of Agrippa at the appointed time. Not surprisingly, Agrippa had not yet risen, having been out quite late the night before. After only a moment of waiting, Berenice appeared and greeted him warmly.

"Come into the garden and sit with me, Alexander. I would like to have a word with you."

Alexander followed her into the garden and she chose a

quiet spot on a marble bench under some shade trees. She patted the bench next to her for Alexander to sit down.

"I hear that you have been betrothed," she began.

Alexander started visibly. What with everything else that was going on, the betrothal had passed clear out of his mind. After all, he had only learned of it himself three days ago and he had told no one but Amarantus. He gave Berenice an inquiring look.

"I have had a letter about it; *several in fact*," she smiled. "One was from your father, a rather *short* one. Alexander, I have long wished your father would stop writing in the Alexandrian style. It's impossible to understand what he is really trying to say half the time."

Alexander let out a half snort. "I received one of *those* letters myself several days ago. All he said was that he had betrothed me to the younger daughter of the High Priest. Not even a name to go with that."

"It is as I suspected," Berenice replied. "Your father is a good man, but he does tend to overlook the social niceties. Well, I can help you a little. As you know, over the years I have endeavored to stay in close touch with the people and events happening in Jerusalem. Of course, the High Priest and his family will always be considered of critical importance to the community and so are much talked about."

She paused and Alexander nodded.

"Unfortunately, a *younger* daughter does not get discussed as often, but I can tell you that her name is Miryam. Her friends and family call her Miri for short. She is regarded well, as she is known for being both clever and having a sweet disposition. Naturally, being raised in the High Priest's household, she is very familiar with all of our customs and will bring dignity to your home."

"*Dignity to my home?*" Alexander sighed.

Berenice studied him carefully. "Alexander, what is it?"

"It's just that …. Is she pretty?"

"This I do not know," Berenice replied. "But in all the letters that have ever mentioned her, she was never described as such. People do tend to mention that about girls when it is so. You must prepare yourself that your wife may be known for qualities other than her beauty."

Alexander grimaced and stared at the ground shaking his head.

Leaning forward, Berenice put her hand on his arm and pulled gently until Alexander turned to look at her.

"Alexander, this is *a good match*. Your father has done very well for you. It is important that the alliance between the Jews of Palestine and Alexandria be kept strong in these times. I am happy to be a Roman; you know that. But as a people we must not lose ourselves to Rome. I fear that we may have already lost too much."

"Yes, yes, I know about *duty* and all that. But my father should have asked me first. Maybe I had other plans."

Berenice looked worried. "Alexander, I feared this. Have you made a promise to another girl?"

"Well, no, not in so many words, but we are meant for each other. I know that we both feel that."

"And would this girl happen to be Aemelia's daughter? … the one called Rutila?"

"Yes, it would," Alexander replied feeling uncomfortable. Apparently, Berenice still didn't miss a thing. "I love her. She means everything to me."

"I know of this girl, and I have heard that she is of good character, a credit to her mother. But Alexander," Berenice said sadly. "She is not a Jew. This can never be. You must let go of this fantasy because that is all it could ever be. To continue it will only be hurting yourself and the girl."

"But it could work," Alexander protested. "I've thought about it. She is patrician and marriage to a patrician would help raise our family's status in Rome."

"And what good will that do you back in Alexandria? Most of Egypt cares little enough for Rome and, I suspect, even less for one patrician girl."

"But I love her," Alexander insisted stubbornly. "Why should I marry some pig-faced girl I've never met just to make my father happy? What about my happiness?"

Berenice leaned closer. "Listen to me, Alexander. I have known you since you were a boy and I have loved you like a son. You know that I would not wish to see you hurt. But if you defy your father in this, he *will* disown you. As Alabarch he would have no other choice. If this happens, I cannot help you. No Jew could help you, for it would be a grave insult to our High Priest. You will be cut off, on your own, and without a denarius to your name."

To his surprise, Berenice embraced him tightly and kissed his cheek. "Think about it, Alexander. At least you have time."

"*Time?*"

"Yes, time," Berenice answered with surprise. "Indeed, your father really did not tell you much, did he? Miryam is only fifteen years old and her father does not wish her to be married until she is seventeen. Promise me, Alexander, that you will go back to Alexandria and think this through."

Time, yes, time. That was what Alexander needed. A lot could happen in two years. Perhaps he could convince his father that the Roman patrician alliance would be much better for the family. Maybe he would let Alexander return to Rome once the affairs on the estates back home were settled.

Absently, Alexander nodded his agreement to Berenice as a servant came in and announced that Agrippa had risen and was waiting for him in his study.

Alexander leaned down and gave Berenice a kiss on the cheek and a smile as he headed for the door. But, suddenly remembering something she had said, he paused.

"You mentioned that you had other letters besides my father's about the betrothal. Who wrote those?"

Berenice's eyes twinkled as she replied. "Those were from two of Jerusalem's biggest gossips. They wrote to inquire if you are handsome ... apparently you are quite the talk of Jerusalem now."

Agrippa was taking breakfast in his study as Alexander entered and presented him with the little bag of silver containing his "*gift*." Agrippa accepted it with a smile and invited Alexander to sit down and join him.

As they munched on stuffed rolls and fruit, Alexander filled Agrippa in on all that he knew. He began with the arrest of Theon and his visit to the prison, told him of his interview with the priest, and finally of the fight in the Forum where the bullies had attacked a Jew.

Agrippa listened attentively. He may have been a drinker and gambler, but he was quick and apparently took his responsibility as head of the Jewish community in Rome very seriously.

"This is troubling about the *Praetorians*," Agrippa mused thoughtfully, when Alexander had finished. "I had heard some rumors about some anti-Jewish sentiment among the Praetorians. - - Not all of them, of course, not even most of them. But there's supposed to be a small clique of them that want to stir up trouble. Have you ever heard of a Praetorian named Aelius Sejanus?"

When Alexander shook his head, he continued. "Well, if you hadn't yet, you would have soon. His father is Lucius Sejus Strabo. I'm sure you've heard of him, the Praetorian Prefect, head of Augustus's personal guard. By all accounts, Sejanus is a man to watch. He's climbing up the ranks fast and no one would be surprised if he replaced his father as Praetorian Prefect someday. The problem for us, however, is that this Sejanus is a power hungry little *mentula*."

Alexander started when he heard Agrippa use the street slang for the male genitalia, and unconsciously checked over his shoulder to see if Berenice was nearby. It was one of Berenice's least favorite words, and he recalled a time when she had overheard the boys using it. They had to drink warm vinegar for a week as their punishment.

"Yes, Yes," Agrippa waved his hand, as he misinterpreted Alexander's expression. "I know half of the men in Rome are power hungry *mentulae*. The difference is, Sejanus is vicious. He doesn't just want power. He wants power so he can use it to hurt anyone that annoys him. And, apparently, for some reason, Jews annoy him a great deal."

He paused and pointed a finger at Alexander. "If any Praetorian is involved in making the theft of this statue a Jewish matter, it would be Sejanus, or perhaps one his cronies. I'll make some inquiries and see if I can learn anything."

This news about the Praetorian Sejanus was disturbing, but Alexander felt some reassurance now that Agrippa was involved. If any Jew was in the right position to track down anti-Jewish sentiment among the Praetorians, it would be Agrippa.

"And now ... what to do about Gnaeus Pulcher," Agrippa continued with a grimace. "I know him and he's an even bigger *mentula* than Sejanus. It sounds like we've got to find out if he has the statue, and that won't be easy. *Hmmm*, I wonder if it would be possible to ...."

Before Agrippa could finish, there was a knock at the door and a servant announced that Amarantus had requested to see his master.

"Excellent," said Alexander. "Show him in." He turned to Agrippa, "I've had him spying on Gnaeus Pulcher's slaves. Maybe he has learned something that could help us."

Amarantus came sweeping in wearing one of Alexander's own best tunics over his slave's tunic with the long sleeves. His hair was heavily oiled and Alexander could detect a distinctively expensive scent, although he was sure it was not one of his own. He blinked at the transformation of his slave *into a ... into a ... well*, no one seeing Amarantus like this would doubt that this man was a most favored slave from an extremely wealthy house.

"Ranti, have you learned something?" he asked eagerly.

"Yes, Master. Gnaeus Pulcher has a Phidias statue hidden inside his house."

"What?!" Agrippa and Alexander both jumped up and began shouting questions at him at once.

"Wait, wait," Alexander said finally. "This is too fast. Amarantus, slow down and start from the beginning. Tell us how it came about that you should learn this interesting, and I may add, highly confidential piece of news."

"Master, it was not hard. I waited out of sight until I saw the house steward leave. I followed him discreetly until I saw the right time when the steward was making a purchase in the Forum. Then I elbowed him out of way and announced that *I* was there to make a handsome purchase for *my* master, Theodosius, *the most respected collector of statuary in Rome.*

"Master, if there is one thing a snobbish slave cannot stand, it is an even more snobbish slave. Immediately, the steward informed me that *his* master, Gnaeus Pulcher, was the most celebrated sculpture collector in Rome, and not *my* master, Theodosius. I told him that I had heard of this Gnaeus Pulcher, but by all accounts *his* collection could not compare to *my master's.*"

Alexander sat back and smiled. Truly, Amarantus was a shrewd judge of human nature. "Go on," he encouraged.

"Well, I told him that *my* master Theodosius had recently traveled to Rhodes and obtained an original Agesander. Then he said *his* master had a Leochares. So I said *my* master had bested five senators at an auction and acquired the original Neptune sculpted by Periander."

"Wait," Agrippa frowned. "I don't think I know of that sculptor."

"I don't believe he exists, lord, but that steward wasn't going to admit that *he* didn't know that. Then he told me that his master had *a something* and *a something*; I don't remember their names. So, I dropped my voice very low and said that *my* master had a Praxiteles which he kept locked away for only very private showings. That's when the steward triumphantly told me that *his* master *had recently acquired a Phidias*, and he dared me to top that."

"A Phidias, you say? You're sure he said Phidias?"

"Definitely, Master."

"But he didn't say which one?"

"Alas, no, and it didn't seem a good idea to inquire too closely about the missing Victory."

"No, of course not. But Romulus and Remus, how will we ever discover if Pulcher's got the stolen statue?"

"I suppose you can determine that for yourself when you see it, Master. We are invited to see it tomorrow night while Gnaeus Pulcher is away at a dinner party."

Both Alexander's and Agrippa's jaws dropped open.

"Amarantus, how on earth did you manage that?"

"It was *easy*, Master. *I called him a liar*."

"You … called him a liar?"

"Well, I suppose you might say that the language I used was much more colorful, but, that is essentially correct. I said that he was just making up the story about the Phidias to make himself feel important. But that *I* had the keys to my master's locked room containing his most select sculptures; and *I* was prepared to prove that everything *I* said was true. After that, he had no choice, but to either prove the existence of the Phidias or be scoffed out of the market."

Agrippa burst out laughing. "Remind me never to place bets against you, Amarantus."

"And so, Ranti," Alexander pressed. "We have been invited to see this famous Phidias?"

"*Weeeell,* at first he only wanted me, but I insisted that my master would have to come since it was likely that he would just show me some copy and try to pass it off as an original. I assured him that my master possessed many *very private* works of art, and that he would be completely discreet since he has no desire to draw attention to his own collection either.

"Master, I assume you will come tomorrow night? -- as the collector Theodosius of course, not as yourself. But there is just one thing. This 'Theodosius' is an experienced collector of sculpture, and the steward may become suspicious if you don't act the part. ... So, Master, *do you think you can become an expert by tomorrow night?*"

This time, Agrippa threw back his head and roared with laughter.

"Really, Alexander, your man is just too good. You must sell him to me when you leave for Egypt."

Alexander joined Agrippa and laughed too. Neither man seemed to notice the change that came over Amarantus' face.

10
THE PHIDIAS

AGRIPPA and Alexander decided that if Alexander had only one day to become an expert on something, there was only one place to go .... to see Claudius.

Claudius was the recognized scholar among their peers with an immense library. So Alexander sent Amarantus home, while he and Agrippa headed off for the home of Claudius.

Agrippa had insisted on coming along saying that he was part of this now, and he had a responsibility to help find the statue as well. Alexander was glad for his support, although he privately wondered if Agrippa saw the theft as much as an adventure as a potential crisis for the Jewish community.

They were fortunate to find Claudius at home in his study and eager to help once he learned of the circumstances.

"I wish that I could go with you tomorrow night," Claudius bemoaned "but I'm afraid that even as one of the lesser members of the imperial family, my face would be too recognizable."

Agrippa was quick to agree. "And I, too. How I would love to see the look on old Pulcher's face if he ever found out how easily he was duped."

"But he's *not* going to find out, Agrippa, agreed?" Alexander asked nervously, starting to worry more that Agrippa might not be taking the inquiry seriously enough.

"No, of course not," Agrippa replied. "Although, I would

surely love to be there with you Alexander; but, I think my face would be too easily recognized as well."

He clapped Alexander on the shoulder, "I'm afraid you'll have to do this one on your own, Alexander -- at least you will have that wily slave with you. I promise that I'll be waiting outside for you. If the statue is there, we will go see Augustus together. I suspect that it may be a bit easier for me to get an audience with him than it would be for you."

Both men looked up as Claudius let out a sudden hiss, then followed his gaze to the door of his study which was now cracked open. Alexander distinctly remembered closing it before he and Agrippa had disclosed the private nature of their visit. Agrippa stalked to the door, threw it open and gazed out in all directions before turning back. He shook his head in response to their unspoken query.

"I thought I heard footsteps and maybe a door close, but I was too late to see anything."

"Who was it, Claudius? Do you know?" Alexander asked.

Claudius grimaced. "*Sp-sp-sp-spuh,*" he stammered and then paused to take a deep breath and calm down. "Spies," he continued. "I'm always watched in this wretched house."

Alexander was shocked. "Spies? Claudius, why have you have never told me this? Who is having you watched?"

"I know I've never said anything, Alexander," Claudius stared down miserably. "It's just so damn embarrassing. As to who ... could be my mother or Livia, perhaps even my "loving" wife Urgulanilla. I would hope that my great Uncle the First Citizen would have better things to do than track the movements of the family fool."

There was a long silence. Alexander tried desperately to think of something consoling to say to his old friend, but no words would come to mind.

It was Agrippa who broke the silence. "I have an idea."

The other two men looked up expectantly.

"I seem to recall that the stepfather of Rutilus has a rather fine library although, no doubt, Sextus Fadius was not the one who assembled it. Let's gather up whatever scrolls on sculpture you have, Claudius, and go there. Between the four of us, we should be able to make our dear Alexander an expert by tomorrow night."

Alexander and Claudius enthusiastically nodded their agreement, but Agrippa was not done.

"Between you and me," he murmured, glancing toward the door and then turning back with a wink, "I rather suspect that my mother's having me watched, too."

All three men broke out in laughter and cheerfully began to collect whatever scrolls Claudius directed them to take. Alexander was happy to see Claudius looking much relieved.

And so, a short time later the three friends found themselves at the door of the house of Rutilus' stepfather Sextus Fadius, who thankfully was still well away in Gaul. The old steward Hermias raised an eyebrow at the sight of the young men gathered rather jovially at the front door, but invited them to wait in the garden while he inquired after the young master.

Alexander secretly suspected that he had sent them to the garden because Rutila was there, but, when they arrived, it was her mother Aemelia who was sitting there reading. Aemelia rose and greeted the young men fondly. She was beginning to make the polite inquiries to Claudius and Agrippa about their families, when both Rutilus and Rutila walked in together. Apparently, Rutila had been visiting friends and Rutilus had stopped by to escort her home.

Rutila looked lovely, Alexander thought. Her face was slightly flushed from the walk home in the summer sun, but that only made her more radiant. She was wearing a gown that

Alexander had not seen before. It was a light yellow with a purple stripe on the hem and matching *palla,* or shawl. He thought it worked beautifully with her light complexion and red-gold hair.

The family could never afford a dress of such costly fabric were it not for their family seamstress. Ephigenia would hoard bits of dye and fabric from their paying customers so that she could dress her mistresses in style. Mentally, Alexander vowed that someday he would buy Rutila the best, so that she would not have to rely upon scraps from customers.

It was Agrippa, the social charmer, who was quick to bow to Rutila and ask her if that was a new gown she was wearing.

Delighted at the attention, Rutila smiled and twirled around to show off her new dress. But suddenly she stopped still with her face aghast.

"Oh, Mother, *what* is that? It's *horrible!*" she cried.

As one, the others turned to see what had caught Rutila's eye. There, standing at the far end of the garden, partially hidden beneath a large shade tree, was what had to be the ugliest statue in Rome. The figure appeared to be thrown off balance, as if she was about to topple over drunk. The folds of the faded and water-stained tunic seemed to fall unnaturally about the body. And behind her were spread oversized wings with a large crack running across one as if it had been broken off in the middle and then inexpertly cemented back on. The worst was the face with heavily rouged cheeks and bright red lips that curled in a permanent sneer.

Alexander was doubly aghast because not only was the statue a mockery of art, it was unmistakably a replica of the beautiful statue of Victory by Phidias. It was just as the priest had described it on the previous day a goddess descending on one foot with spread wings and arms reaching out holding a laurel wreath. Except, there was no doubt, that *this* statue had *not* been sculpted by the hands of a master.

Behind him, someone sighed and Alexander turned back to see Aemelia with a pained expression on her face.

"Well, my children, as you can see, your stepfather's collection of booty has arrived from Gaul."

"*Jupiter*," said Claudius softly. "It looks like a great flying whore."

Instantly, the garden came alive with laughter. Between gasps for breath, Rutila told Claudius and Agrippa of their stepfather's letter announcing the collection of "art" that he was sending home from Gaul. Rutilus once again began to regale an audience with tales of his stepfather's mistaken treasures.

In between the laughter, Rutila turned a questioning look on her mother. "But, Mother, why *this* statue? My stepfather has never favored the female gods. He's always preferred the male gods of war and wealth like Mars and Saturn."

"I can answer that," Alexander replied. All eyes turned on him. "When I interviewed the old priest at the temple of Victory on the Palatine Hill, he said that Sextus Fadius had recently become a frequent visitor. Apparently, Victory had appeared to Fadius in a dream and he had become almost obsessed with propitiating the goddess."

This seemed to surprise all of the family members. "He never mentioned it," Aemelia remarked, and her son and daughter shook their heads to concur. "But then I saw very little of him in the weeks before he left for Gaul. Still, I am surprised. As Rutila said, my husband never had much time for the female deities."

"Well, perhaps this was his idea of erotic art," Agrippa quipped making the group laugh again.

Aemelia shook her head trying to maintain some sense of dignity despite her mirth. "I told you," she said, "that poor Sextus Fadius does have rather bad taste in art. At least I was able to convince his agents that the statue would be ruined by the sun unless it was placed far back under that tree."

She sighed, "I suppose we'll just have to keep our visitors out of the garden."

Still joking over the "great flying whore," the four young men removed themselves to Sextus Fadius' study now being used by Rutilus in his absence. Alexander was the last to leave having delayed to cast a wary glance at the statue. The coincidence of this monstrosity appearing just as the original disappeared seemed odd. Could it be possible that Sextus Fadius had ...?

No, that couldn't be. For one thing, the letter Sextus Fadius wrote to Aemelia from Gaul announcing the travelling art collection had to have been written weeks ago. Plus, the original *was a Phidias*. This statue *was not*. Even from here across the garden, Alexander could see the track of a huge old crack running horizontally through one of the goddess's wings. Alexander doubted if the original had such a crack. Even if did, it would never have been so inexpertly repaired ... or hideously painted. He smiled at himself and shook his head. Sometimes a coincidence *was* just a coincidence.

Alexander turned to follow his companions and caught the eye of Rutila still standing in the garden. He realized that she must have been watching him and was gratified when she blushed and smiled at him shyly through long upturned lashes. He thought to move towards her, but realized she was sitting near her mother. Instead, he smiled then followed his friends to the study.

For the rest of that day and much of the next, the four men worked on art and statuary. They went over drawings and descriptions. Alexander was quizzed on how to recognize this sculptor or that, all of his major works and all their known locations. Not only that, but apparently, Agrippa had mastered the art of appearing to recognize a statue without giving away that he hadn't a clue.

"I'm a royal prince," Agrippa shrugged. "A lot of people expect a prince to know everything, just because you are a prince. You have to learn to side-step, deflect, or get others to reveal information in a way that makes it look you knew it all along."

Thus, Alexander was taught a number of tricks for soliciting the name of an artist while appearing to know it all along.

On the second day of their studies on statuary, Claudius took Alexander aside.

"Alexander, you have heard about this Gnaeus Pulcher, haven't you?"

Alexander nodded.

"Well, I have heard things, too. Bad things. The man will stop at nothing if he feels insulted or challenged. I mean *nothing*."

Claudius took a breath. "Alexander, you must *not* be caught in Gnaeus Pulcher's house. Do you understand me? You must not."

Alexander smiled and promised his friend that he would be careful. He was pleased by Claudius' concern, but the warning did make him anxious. He hadn't thought much about the consequences if he was caught. For a moment, he thought about canceling their plans, but only for a moment. He had to know if the statue was there. Other lives than his depended on him succeeding tonight.

After a few more hours of tutoring, Alexander felt that he was as ready as could be expected given the time involved. He returned home for dinner; then, he and Amarantus dressed up in their Theodosius, the rich collector, and his pampered steward costumes. Shortly after dark, Agrippa came by to meet them.

"I still wish I could come in with you, but I guess I'll just have to wait here for the news," Agrippa sighed as the three men stopped nearly a block from Gnaeus Pulcher's residence to wait.

Alexander studied the house from a distance. It was difficult to tell the layout, because the entire home was surrounded by a seven-foot wall. But Alexander guessed it was likely to be a traditional villa with rooms on all four sides, bordering a large atrium in the middle. The back rooms opposite the entrance should be the dining room and Gnaeus Pulcher's office. He guessed that the secret art stash would be near the latter. Behind the main house would be a garden and the kitchen and slave quarters beyond that.

After awhile, a palanquin litter and slaves appeared at the entrance. Shortly thereafter, they watched Gnaeus Pulcher exit his home and then recline in the litter. The bearers lifted it onto their shoulders and moved away in the opposite direction until it turned down a side road. The men let a few more minutes pass, then Alexander and Amarantus presented themselves at the entrance. Gnaeus Pulcher's steward was waiting there and gave them a long appraising stare before escorting them in. Amarantus somewhat obsequiously introduced his master, Theodosius. The steward eyed Alexander's rich clothing then bowed and gave him a deferential greeting. However, Alexander noted the steward's attempt to snub Amarantus with a brief disdainful glance.

The steward led them back into the house, stopping periodically to point out a statue on display along the way.

"*Good so far,*" Alexander thought as he easily recognized the pieces and announced the sculptor's name in a bored voice.

But then the steward stopped in front of a life-sized statue of a male nude and looked up at Alexander slyly.

"What do you make of this one?" he asked.

Alexander knew at once that this was a test. If he didn't make it past this one, he was never going to get into the locked-room to see the Phidias. Adopting his best imitation of an expert, he examined the statue critically. It was a beautifully sculpted bronze of an athlete, obviously Greek and old judging by the style. He carried a spear, and, though he was depicted in motion, his body was in perfect balance. Alexander circled the statue noting that the physical detail continued on all fours sides of the form, unlike some works where the sculptor devoted his attention to the front and the back was finished more quickly.

Alexander had no idea of the sculptor's name. So he smiled and jerked his head once in a knowing nod, then turned haughtily toward Amarantus.

"So, tell me you recognize this sculptor," he demanded.

Amarantus looked back in surprise and murmured that he didn't know.

"Oh, come now, man. Have you learned nothing from me? Look at it. Note the exact proportions of the body, realistic carving of the musculature, the reserved expression, the fact that the detail goes all the way around the body."

He looked at Amarantus expectantly, but Amarantus looked back dumbfounded. Alexander could see that the steward was enjoying Amarantus' discomfort immensely.

"I'll give you a hint. It's Greek, it's an athlete and it's hundreds of years old. Now who was known for his bronze athletes?"

Amarantus stammered that he wasn't sure. The steward was getting more excited as Amarantus grew more distraught.

"Guess, man," Alexander demanded.

Amarantus looked miserable, but said hesitantly, "Is it a Myron?"

"*Hah!*" sneered the steward. "Not so uppity now are you when you can't even recognize a simple Polycleitos."

"*Ahh, a Polycleitos,*" Alexander thought with relief. Good, that was one that he had studied.

"Indeed," he responded. "Apparently this steward pays more attention to his master than you have. Polycleitos sculpted a series of athletes in Argos over 400 years ago. He was known for using mathematics to determine his human proportions. I myself have seen his Hera that still stands in the temple at Argos, but I believe all of his athletes have gone to private collections."

He turned to the steward. "Your master was fortunate indeed to acquire this piece. It is splendid."

"But, come now. This is not why I came," he added impatiently. "Show me a Phidias. Now *that* will impress me."

Clearly he had passed the test, because with a look of contempt at Amarantus, the steward led the way to a door farther back in the house. With a flourish, he withdrew a key from his tunic and unlocked the door.

As the door swung open, Alexander tried not to appear overly eager. At last he would know. If the Victory was here, it would all be over. Theon would get out of prison and any trouble for the Jews would end.

The steward bowed slightly as Alexander started to enter the room, but stopped at the entrance. It was a wonder; statues and paintings were everywhere. The room was way too full for everything to be displayed properly, but just what he saw took his breath away. It must have been a fortune in fabulous art that had come from all over the world. Alexander sucked in his breath as he beheld what must have been the spoils of looted temples, bribes, blackmail and, no doubt, stolen treasures.

He started to enter into the room when a ruckus broke out at the front of the house. Even towards the back, they could hear the banging and the swearing. The front door must have been opened because the volume suddenly increased.

"Where is she?" a drunken voice bawled. "I know she's in here. Portia! *POOOORRTEEEAAH!*"

Alexander knew that voice. Agrippa. Amarantus had recognized it, too, and he now looked worriedly back at him.

"Master, there appears to be trouble. Perhaps we should leave."

"*I KNOOOOW SHE'S HERE.* I won't tolerate my wife sleeping with another man. Pooooortia. Where is that scum Lucius?"

"Master," Amarantus whispered urgently. "We must leave this place. You could not stand another scandal. Remember what happened in Baiae."

"*LUUUUUCIUS.* You can't hide from me. Come out and face me like a man!"

They both looked at the steward who kept looking fearfully at the unlocked door, clearly agitated.

"*Luuuucius! What?! Gnaeus Pulcher? What's he doing in Lucius' house? POOOORTIA!*"

"Now, Master, now!" Amarantus cried. Grabbing Alexander's arm he propelled him towards the entrance at the front of the house. But he didn't have to push hard. Alexander could guess what Agrippa was up to. Claudius' words came back to him as his heart began to pound. *"You must not be caught ... he would stop at nothing if insulted."*

The sound of Agrippa's voice had now grown fainter as other slaves must have joined the first and ejected him back onto the street. Their pretense of rich art collector and fancy steward was completely forgotten as Alexander and Amarantus hurled through the atrium, but drew up short as they saw a slave hurrying to open the front door.

"This way," Amarantus gasped and led a mad dash back through the atrium into the dining room. There was only one slave there who gaped at them in astonishment.

"Quick, man," Alexander said in an urgent voice. "Where is there another door?"

But even as he spoke, they heard Gnaeus Pulcher in the atrium roaring for his steward.

"No time, no time," Amarantus whispered.

Grabbing Alexander's arm he dragged him to the window, lowered his shoulder and shoved his master through it before he could think. In a moment, Amarantus had tumbled through the window after him, and both men were running toward the garden wall. Somehow they managed to push and pull each other over the seven-foot wall and then stopped panting, lurking in the shadows on the other side.

A litter stood before the front door of Gnaeus Pulcher's home surrounded by half a dozen slaves holding torches. It appeared that Pulcher had forgotten something and had returned home to get it. After a while, Pulcher himself reappeared and kicked the nearest litter attendant who had squatted down for a rest.

Alexander and Amarantus watched silently until the litter had disappeared down a cross street. Then a new dark figure emerged out of a doorway and made its way toward them.

"*Ha, ha*" Agrippa laughed. "How did you like my little warning? I did know a woman named Portia once, but I believe I was the one who cuckolded the husband and not the other way around."

Alexander stared back at Agrippa's grinning face with his heart still beating hard in his chest. He couldn't decide whether he wanted to punch Agrippa or kiss him.

Agrippa lifted his eyebrows and tilted his head in query. "*Well?*" he asked.

"*Weeeell,*" he repeated when Alexander did not reply at once. "Was it the statue or not?"

Amarantus was also watching him anxiously.

"I- I think there was a Phidias," Alexander said slowly. "I

only got a glimpse."

Both men stared at him expectantly.

"But, it was one of his early bronze heroes. It was *not* the Victory."

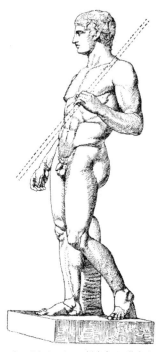

Copy of the Doryphorus of Polyclitus. (Naples.)

Drawing of a 5th century B.C. bronze sculpture of a young spear-throwing athlete by Polyclitus.

Source: Harper's Dictionary of Cassical Literature and Antiquities / edited by Harry Thurston Peck, 2nd ed. (New York, Cooper Square, c1896)

11

SEJANUS

ALEXANDER and Amarantus accompanied Agrippa back to his home where they knew Claudius and Rutilus would be waiting to hear about the night's adventure.

Once in the atrium, however, Alexander delayed long enough to ask Agrippa to assign a couple of his slaves to escort Amarantus home. Amarantus was still wearing his *"pampered steward of the rich collector Theodosius"* costume and Alexander had serious doubts about his safety walking home alone.

Then the two friends went into Agrippa's study where they found Claudius and Rutilus well into their second flask of wine. Although they were disappointed when they learned that Alexander had not found the missing statue, they were eager to hear every detail of the night's encounter.

Alexander was quizzed thoroughly on what statues he had seen and how he had recognized them. He was congratulated heartily as he described how he had used one of Agrippa's sly tactics to trick the steward into revealing that Polycleitus was the sculptor of the bronze athlete.

For Claudius and Rutilus the night's outing had been no more than a vicarious adventure. Nevertheless, they consumed more wine and congratulated themselves on how well they had tutored Alexander to play act an art collector.

Agrippa quickly diverted their attention to himself as he

regaled them with his daring rescue of Alexander who was trapped in the house with Gnaeus Pulcher's litter fast approaching.

As more wine flowed, the young men's notion of humor became sillier. Agrippa paraded through the room rerunning his performance of a drunken brawler looking for his wayward wife. Then they insisted that Alexander show them how he had played the arrogant collector Theodosius. Alexander made Rutilus stand up and pose like the nude athlete while he critically inspected him.

No one said it aloud; but it was as if everyone knew that with Alexander leaving soon, this may be one of their last chances to all be together again. The night grew late, but not one of them had any thought of going home. And so the friends laughed and drank into the night until each one passed into sleep wherever he fell.

The next morning Alexander woke with an aching head. At least he thought it was morning. There was sunlight streaming in through the room's only window, and that seemed a pretty good indication. He struggled to sit up and looked around him. Agrippa had pitched forward with his head on his desk. Claudius was stretched out on the room's only couch. Rutilus was leaning next to a chair with his head resting on the seat. And, as far as he could tell, Alexander had been flat out in the middle of the floor with someone's toga spread over him.

"Huumph."

Alexander became aware of the sound that must have awakened him. Painfully, he turned his head in that direction and gazed up into the stern face of Agrippa's mother Berenice. He tried to speak, but all that came out sounded something like, *"Uurrrrghhh."* He wasn't sure what he had meant to say anyway.

Berenice tried to suppress a smile and failed.

"Oh, come along then," she laughed. "My chef's got

something that will fix that up for you."

She grabbed Alexander by the arm and tugged until he hoisted himself to his feet, and then walked him shakily to the door. Alexander paused at the exit and looked back at his fallen comrades.

"Don't worry about *them*." Berenice waved a hand dismissively. "I know my son, and he wouldn't be up before mid-morning even with half that much wine. And *those two* ... they were already half-gone long before you got back from your evening's adventure. We won't be seeing their faces before mid-day."

Berenice guided Alexander to a small table that had been set up in the garden, and soon a servant brought him a steaming drink. It looked and smelled horrible, but Alexander drank and soon his head began to clear.

"What was that?" Alexander asked, putting the empty cup down with a grimace.

"An old Roman recipe, crushed leaves and berries from the rue plant boiled in vinegar. Some people find it bitter, but personally I wouldn't know," Berenice answered with a smile.

She signaled for a servant to bring some food and urged Alexander to eat. After Alexander had nibbled a bit of bread and cheese, Berenice gave him an indulgent smile.

"I take it that Gnaeus Pulcher did not have the statue?"

Alexander did a double-take, and then instantly regretted it as he reached for his head.

"But... *how* did you know?" he asked.

"Alexander, half the household knows. You boys were not exactly quiet last night.

"Besides that I have heard about that incident with the Jew in the Forum a few days ago. Alexander, you did a brave thing.

I'm proud of you."

Berenice reached out and ruffled his hair as if he were still the young boy who had once lived under her roof. But then her expression turned somber.

"*I'm worried*, Alexander. This ... situation... is becoming serious. What will you do now?"

"I don't know," Alexander replied as he realized that indeed he did not know. He had set his hopes so high that he would learn that Gnaeus Pulcher had the statue, that he hadn't thought beyond that.

"I guess I'll go home and try to reason it through. I'm sure that Augustus has had his Praetorians tossing the city. If the First Citizen hasn't been able to learn anything, I'm not sure what hope I have."

"Well, you have something the Praetorians don't have, a good head on your shoulders. Think it through, Alexander. Stealing a temple's statue of a Roman goddess is no common crime. Why would anyone do such a thing? I have a feeling that if you can figure out the why, the rest of it may start to fall into place."

A short time later, Alexander found himself walking back to his apartment on the Capitoline Hill. Berenice had done all she could to clean him up short of a bath. His face had been washed and his hair combed. The fancy embroidered tunic from the night before had been brushed and pressed. His head even felt a little better. But, what a night. Alexander wasn't sure if he wanted to collect Amarantus and head for the office or simply fall into bed.

He tried to think about the statue on the way home, but his mind didn't seem up to it. Instead, he daydreamed about his favorite topic, Rutila. How beautiful she had looked the other day in her new yellow gown with the purple border trim. Someday, he would buy her more clothes in that alluring color.

As Alexander turned the corner and headed to the front of his apartment building, his feet suddenly turned to lead. Standing before his front door was a two-person litter and lounging around that were several members of the Praetorian Guard. Of course, the Guard might have been there for anyone living in his building, but somehow Alexander didn't think so. The timing left him with little doubt.

Alexander's stomach clenched as he quickly considered the possibilities. Gnaeus Pulcher must have learned he had been in his house and filed a complaint. ... But why send the Praetorians then? Why not the Urban Cohorts? Perhaps if someone figured the stolen statue was involved, they had notified the Praetorians.

Or perhaps it was about the fight in the Forum... or his visit to Theon where Amarantus had claimed they were there on the First Citizen's business? Maybe Augustus had just found out, and he wasn't too happy. A small voice in his head told him to turn around before anyone spotted him, return to Agrippa's house and wait it out.

With a sigh of sleepy resignation, Alexander resumed his steps toward home. He was a Julius Alexander after all. The only honorable course was to face the consequences, although he could have wished for a little more sleep and a head that was less muddied by the previous night's wine.

As he reached the entrance, Alexander composed himself and strode past the Praetorians toward the front door. But he found his path blocked.

"Are you Gaius Julius Alexander?" a Praetorian brusquely inquired.

"I am."

"You have a visitor inside. He *demands* an immediate audience."

Alexander did a quick once over gauging the Praetorian

who had spoken. The man had the condescending half sneer of one used to intimidating other men and liking it. But Alexander was not going to give him the satisfaction.

He made a slight shrug at the man and replied with equanimity, "Really? I had better go in then. How fortunate for him that I was already heading that way."

He didn't wait for the Praetorian to reply, but headed to his apartment on the second floor. Amarantus must have been listening for his footsteps, because he opened the door as Alexander reached the landing.

"Master, a man has come for you -- a Praetorian Guard."

Although he strove to maintain some dignity, Amarantus' face revealed both confusion and concern.

"He would not give his name, but insisted on being shown to your study until you returned. And, Master, I did not tell him where you were. He asked, but I said I only knew that you were out with friends."

"You did right, Ranti," said Alexander then looked down at his tunic. "How do I look?"

"Better than I had expected," Amarantus replied with a wry smile. Quickly he brushed off the street dust, looked Alexander over and then gave him a quick nod.

Alexander stepped into his study and faced the back of a man who stood gazing out of his window. The visitor turned slowly and looked Alexander up and down. Alexander took the time to return the visitor's assessment. What he saw was a man in his early thirties of average height and build, dressed in the usual Praetorian's military style uniform. If it were for looks alone, he might have been no different than a dozen others. But there was something about this man. He seemed to exude a certain confidence bordering on arrogance. Without saying a word, he gave the impression of being a superior.

The visitor spoke.

"Are you Gaius Julius Alexander?"

"I am."

"Do you know who I am?"

Alexander searched his memory, but his visitor's name was not forthcoming. After a moment he replied, "Your face is familiar, but I regret that I am unable to assign it a name. Are you from the palace?"

"I suppose you could say that. I am Lucius Aelius Sejanus."

It was only with effort that Alexander kept his face a mask. So this was Sejanus, the famous Jew hater, whom Agrippa had mentioned. But before Alexander could respond, Sejanus continued.

"And I am a very busy man. You've kept me waiting here for nearly two hours. Where have you been?" he demanded.

Alexander thought quickly. He wasn't about to implicate Agrippa or any of his friends, but his mind was too tired to think up a lie. In times like this, it might be best to tell the truth – just not the whole truth.

"Unconscious," he replied.

This was clearly not an answer that Sejanus had expected. "What? Where?"

"On someone's floor."

"You were attacked?"

"Yeah, by three jars of Falernian."

Sejanus gave him another appraising look. "You don't look like you've been drinking."

"Well, that's what the women are for, aren't they? To clean you up and send you home. Now, I'd appreciate it if you would tell me your business because my head is killing me. I think I need to find my bed."

Clearly, not what he had expected, but Sejanus seemed to like Alexander's answer. Maybe he'd been cleaned up and sent home a few times himself.

"I'm afraid that will not be possible. The *First Citizen* commands your immediate presence."

The First Citizen? Just for sneaking into a Senator's house? That seemed a bit petty for the First Citizen's personal attention. After all, they hadn't taken anything.

But when Augustus commanded, it was not for him to disobey so Alexander merely said, "Is there time for me to bathe and change into a toga? I fear that I am not dressed appropriately for an audience with the First Citizen."

Sejanus looked him over and with some satisfaction Alexander realized that he was wearing his "rich collector Theodosius" costume which was about the finest tunic he owned. Briefly, he wondered if the guard would assume he dressed like this every day.

"That will do," Sejanus clipped. "Come, I have a litter waiting outside."

So Alexander was off to his first formal audience with the ruler of most of the western and eastern world. He had seen Augustus several times before, but always in groups, never alone. Somehow, Alexander hadn't pictured his first audience with Augustus happening like this.

Sejanus climbed first into the litter and lounged back lazily on the cushions as he watched Alexander get in. Alexander stepped in and then winced and rubbed his temples when the litter lurched forward. As they moved swiftly down the Capitoline Hill, Sejanus studied his fingernails and said in a bored voice, "I haven't seen you around the palace before. What does the First Citizen want with you?"

For all of his feigned nonchalance, Alexander could sense that Sejanus was burning with curiosity. Perhaps the Guard knew nothing about the affair at Gnaeus Pulcher's home last night. The circumstances today must have been just as puzzling for the Praetorians as it was for Alexander. A group of elite Praetorian Guardsman were sent to retrieve a single man ... a man whom none of them had ever heard of ... a man who dressed in the finest clothes, but had no purple stripe on his tunic as a mark of distinction ... a man who readily admitted to spending the night passed out drunk on someone's floor.

Alexander shrugged and tried to feign equal disinterest. "I suppose we'll have to ask him that. He's my family's patron."

"Really?"

Alexander could see that Sejanus was impressed by that, although he was trying not to show it. They traveled in silence for a while, then Sejanus tried again.

"Gaius Julius Alexander. That's not a name from one of the old Roman families."

"No."

"Freedman?"

"No," Alexander responded firmly. "My family's citizenship was a grant from Julius Caesar made to seal a friendship."

"Ahh, from the provinces then."

Alexander said nothing. Sejanus was on a fishing expedition to find out what he could and Alexander was determined not to tell him any more than he had to.

"Gaul?" Sejanus prodded.

"No, Alexandria."

Sejanus seemed to ponder this for a minute before continuing.

"Would this happen to be about the missing statue? We arrested a Jew for stealing the statue and he is from Alexandria."

Alexander simply shrugged to indicate that he didn't know. But now Sejanus had started himself on what must have been a favorite topic.

"Filthy little vermin, Jew. They took a whip to him and hot irons as well, but he won't tell where he hid the statue. I'd like to have a few hours alone with him. I know how to get the truth out of his sort."

Alexander stifled a shudder. "Perhaps, he doesn't have it."

"Oh, he's got it, or one of those other god-hating Jews has. I can't imagine why Augustus tolerates them. Have you ever been to their district on the other side of the Tiber? It stinks of them. Filth everywhere. Half of the diseases in Rome are caused by that lot."

Sejanus didn't seem to be deliberately baiting him, which confirmed for Alexander that Sejanus did not know that he was a Jew. Another man might have announced his religion then, but Alexander had never felt much need to explain himself to strangers. If Sejanus asked he would confirm it, but for now it might be more useful to hear what Sejanus had to say.

For several minutes Sejanus rattled on about all the reasons he hated the Jews. Alexander had stopped paying attention, when Sejanus looked at him and grinned.

"And that's why a lot of us think this may be a good thing."

"What may be a good thing?"

"The statue, of course. If it'll get these cursed Jews out of Rome, then perhaps the theft of the statue wasn't such a bad thing, right? In fact, we just keep sending up the word that we've had a tip that the Jews have it here, or the Jews have it there. Keeps things hot, if you know what I mean."

Alexander was stunned. Had Sejanus just admitted to lying

to Augustus? The man had to be either a complete fool, or, awfully confident of his position. Alexander didn't think that Sejanus was a fool. So what did he know that made him so confident? .... Or whom?

Alexander gave Sejanus an indifferent nod. His head still ached from the wine, but his mind was clearing rapidly. Sejanus' crude boasts would bear some further thought. Was it possible that a few of the Praetorian Guard had found the statue already, but elected not to report it? Could their complicity have extended even further?

Yes, he would have to consider this further later, but at the moment the litter was climbing Victory's Incline and was not far from the palace. With each step Alexander felt a knot growing larger in his stomach as his sense of dread grew.

How had Augustus learned of last night's illicit excursion so quickly? And what was his personal interest in the matter? Perhaps Gnaeus Pulcher was a client of his and had requested some retribution beyond what he might have received in the law courts. What chance would Alexander have before such a powerful man? It was well known that Alexander's family was rich. Would money buy his way out of trouble?

Alexander lay back in the litter and tried to hide his increasing panic. Sejanus had apparently given up on getting any interesting conversation out of him and had turned to stare out the side of the litter. Alexander hoped that Sejanus had assumed that he was simply too hung over to talk.

The litter finally turned off of Victory's Incline and arrived at the palace of Augustus. Alexander expected it to stop there, but they bypassed the main entrance to stop at a partially hidden door on the south wing. A pair of armed Praetorians flanked each side of the door and saluted Sejanus as he descended from the litter. Alexander followed silently as they entered the palace.

He expected to be led directly to a waiting area, but once

inside Sejanus stopped in the deserted entrance. Alexander looked up expectantly and saw Sejanus regarding him coolly.

"Well, Gaius Julius *Alexander*, you didn't have much to say for yourself today, did you? No matter. If there's one thing you will learn about me, it is that *I don't like secrets*. Before today is over, I will know everything about you. *Everything*. Every bribe you've made, every man you associate with, every bad habit, right down to the last time you put on a clean loincloth. You got that?"

Alexander knew that he was supposed to feel intimidated, but he was too worried about his interview with Augustus to get rankled now. And he *really* hated bullies.

In response, he shrugged. "As long as you're investigating my loincloths, I'd appreciate it if you would have a word with the laundress. I think she's been swapping mine for another man's. She swears not, but I bet a man like you could find out the truth about that."

Sejanus just stared. Alexander could tell that he wasn't used to people responding like this. Alexander was supposed to be intimidated. Sejanus obviously wanted people to be afraid of him. He seemed uncertain what to do about this Alexandrian enigma. Sejanus apparently decided to let his arrogance pass, at least for now. With a tight smile he beckoned Alexander down an adjoining corridor.

"I hope your nerve holds out a bit longer, Alexander of Alexandria, because you're about to meet a man who makes me look like one of Juno's tame geese. You are about to meet *Augustus*."

12

AUGUSTUS

AUGUSTUS. Alexander was glad that Sejanus was walking ahead of him, because he knew that his face had just revealed the anxiousness he had been feeling since the Praetorians had picked him up that morning.

Every dire thought was now racing through his brain. What would Augustus do to him? Prison, torture, exile? What had he done that had angered Augustus enough to warrant this summons? Was it that his slave Amarantus had told the guard at the Carcer that they were "on the first citizen's business?" Or, was it that he had sneaked into the home of a powerful senator? Oh Lord, what would his father say? His family; why had he not considered his family before he acted?

Alexander's head ached and his steps dragged as Sejanus led him past the State reception rooms – the only part of the palace that Alexander had ever seen. Where were they going? Were there dungeons in the palace?

He became even more confused as they turned toward the private quarters in the northwest section. Sejanus turned and saw his face.

"*Hah.* I thought you knew what this was about," he curled his lip into what he probably thought was a menacing sneer. Actually, Alexander had to concede, it was a pretty menacing sneer.

Sejanus wasn't done. "Don't worry. There are new mosaics

on the floor. Augustus won't do anything that will stain them there. He likes to handle that sort of thing …," he fondled the hilt of his sword, "…elsewhere."

If Sejanus had hoped to scare Alexander further, his words, in fact, had the opposite effect. *Dignitas.* It was a Roman concept and it had been instilled in Alexander since he was a boy. Dignity before everything. A man's wealth, home, and freedom might be taken from him, but only he could relinquish his dignity.

With a deep breath, Alexander straightened his shoulders and calmed his face. Whatever he had done, he had done out of sense of duty. He was still terrified, but determined that he was not going to lose his dignity, not even for Augustus.

Sejanus led him into a small room. Alexander stared ahead barely noting the simple, yet beautiful wall fresco that lined the room. On each wall were painted two or three golden pillars with garlands of pine branches strung between them. After a moment, he realized that Sejanus had bent and was murmuring to a man lounging on a small couch against the wall.

When Sejanus straightened, Alexander could see it was Tiberius. *Tiberius?* The First Citizen's adopted son and appointed heir.   It was said that Tiberius was already sharing the responsibilities of running Rome alongside Augustus. But what was he doing *here*?

Alexander braved a glance in that direction. Tiberius returned it with the slightest nod, then he resumed reading a scroll that lay unfurled on his lap. Apparently, they were all waiting for Augustus now.

No one had invited him to sit, so Alexander stood there in the middle of the room waiting for whatever came next. About fifteen minutes passed. He observed that Tiberius kept looking up and asking Sejanus questions, apparently about things in his scroll. To Alexander's chagrin, he noted that Tiberius and Sejanus appeared to be on very friendly terms. Well, that may answer one question -- just whom Sejanus knew that made him so confident in his authority.

Another five or ten minutes passed. Alexander tried to discreetly shift his weight by softly shuffling his feet while trying not to look nervous. However, the previous night's drinking was catching up with him. If he had not been so apprehensive, he feared that his eyelids may have started to droop.

Finally, a palace servant appeared at the door, followed shortly by Augustus himself. The First Citizen breezed in with the energy of a much younger man. Alexander had never seen him this close before and was surprised to realize that Augustus was shorter than himself by more than a hand span. He was also trim, not prone to the corpulence that affected many of the great men of Rome in their older age. But any sense of diminutive size was quickly outweighed by Augustus's tremendous aura of presence. He seemed to radiate power and his expression was intelligent and alert.

Without looking at Alexander, Augustus nodded to Tiberius and turned to Sejanus.

"*Ahh,* here you are at last. What took so long?"

"He wasn't home, First Citizen; hadn't been home the whole night and his slave didn't know where to find him. He finally straggled home a short time ago, and we brought him straight to you."

Augustus raised an eyebrow to Sejanus in an unspoken query.

"He *claims* he had been lying unconscious on some unnamed lady's floor. 'Says he was attacked by three jars of Falernian."

Behind him, Tiberius guffawed and Sejanus turned and shared a common smile. But Augustus did not react other than to

stare shrewdly at Alexander. Alexander, in turn, could feel his face
heating up. Now, Augustus would think him a sot and an immoral
womanizer, in addition to whatever else had inspired him to drag
Alexander to the palace in the first place. Things just kept getting
worse.

After a moment, Sejanus stalked over and posted himself by
the door, clearly expecting to be present for the interview.

Without taking his eyes off Alexander, Augustus said, "That
will be all, Sejanus. I don't believe we will need a guard."

Sejanus looked disappointed, but obviously thought better
than to argue with the great man. With a last piercing glance at
Alexander, he removed himself from the room and pulled the door
shut behind him.

Augustus continued to hold Alexander's gaze, then broke
the silence.

"*Gaius Julius Alexander*, son of Gaius Julius Alexander. Your
family received its citizenship from my father."

It was a statement and no answer seemed expected, so
Alexander briefly bowed his head and remained silent.

"And now you are *my* client, are you not?"

"Yes, Augustus."

"Do you know why I have asked you here?"

Alexander endeavored to keep his incredulity off his face at
Augustus's choice of words: *Why I have asked you here? Asked?* No.
Alexander had been brought here by armed guards. Still, that was
hardly a point worth quibbling with the First Citizen, who was
clearly waiting for an answer. Alexander tried to think.   It could
have been because of Gnaeus Pulcher, or Theon, or the fight in the
Forum, but he didn't really know for sure.

"No, Augustus."

"*Really?* That surprises me. You see, I have learned from certain sources that you have taken it upon yourself to investigate the disappearance of the statue of Victory from her temple."

Alexander had a fleeting recollection of the door to Claudius's study left cracked open by whoever had been spying on them. *Someone* must have overheard the young men talking about the statue ... and wasted no time in repeating it. He supposed it was too much to hope for a spy who kept their mouth shut.

When he didn't reply, Augustus pressed the point. "Is this true? Do you seek the Victory?"

"Yes, Augustus."

"*Why?*"

"The man accused of the theft, Theon the art dealer from Alexandria, is a client of my father's."

Augustus raised a hand to interrupt. "Are you saying this man is a *citizen*?"

"No, sir, not a *Roman* citizen. It is a system we have developed in Alexandria. There are very few native Roman citizens there, and even fewer of them are also Jews. Therefore, those Jews who do have the citizenship have taken on certain others as clients, you see, in order to help and protect them in their dealings with Rome."

Augustus appeared to ponder this for a moment. "A bit unorthodox, but I suppose not illegal as long as they don't claim the citizenship. *Continue.*"

"Since my father is in Alexandria, I am acting as his agent in Rome. I believe that I am honor bound to assist our client, Theon, even as my father would if he were now here in Rome."

Augustus paced quickly up and down the room and then stopped immediately in front of Alexander, glaring with a fierceness that penetrated every line of his face.

"*Did he steal it?*"

"I do not believe so, First Citizen."

"Why? Why do you think not?" Augustus demanded.

Alexander considered and responded. "I have heard of his words on selling the statue and they were very foolish; more than foolish. However, I believe they were no more than words. I have inquired after his character among his friends. They have agreed with my own assessment that he is rash, prone to angry mutterings, but not criminal. I have also spoken with Theon himself. He denies taking it and I believe him."

"Which may make you a good *patron*, but not necessarily adept in *logic*. ... As you may know, we have had his home and warehouses searched and those of his known confederates. It yielded nothing. Every man who has ever worked for him, or with him, has been vigorously questioned. Every single one of them has denied any knowledge of the statue."

"Perhaps, that is because they truly *know nothing* to tell, First Citizen."

Augustus glared at him and Alexander wondered if he had gone too far. But Augustus wasn't done.

"*Huumph*. Well this Theon knows *something*. Who was this mysterious collector who offered to buy our statue? He refuses to tell."

"He is afraid, First Citizen."

"I should think that he would be more afraid *of me* than of Gnaeus Pulcher," Augustus retorted.

Alexander's mouth fell open. "Then ... *then you knew?*"

"No," Augustus smiled mirthlessly. "I *guessed*. And I believe that you have just confirmed that it was a good guess."

Alexander suspected that he had just been tricked by a master, but it didn't matter. Augustus *was* his patron and he would have told him anyway. Augustus paced the room some more before stopping in front of Alexander again.

"I have made some inquiries and have learned that Gnaeus Pulcher has a locked room filled with statuary. Much of it is stolen. Have *you* learned as much?"

Alexander was startled. For the first time it occurred to him that perhaps Augustus did not know of his nocturnal visit to the home of Gnaeus Pulcher. He started to answer cautiously, but then decided to reveal what he knew. After all, Augustus was his patron and he owed him his honesty.

"Yes, I knew this. I had also learned discreetly that Gnaeus Pulcher had recently acquired a Phidias."

Alexander quickly shook his head no as Augustus looked up expectantly. "Gnaeus Pulcher does have statue that may be a Phidias, but it is *not* the Victory."

"Can you be sure? How do you know this?" Augustus demanded.

Alexander eyes widened, but he kept his gaze on the distant wall. "Well, *errr*, you see... I may have arranged a ... *umm* ... *visit* to his house last night... when, *errr* ... Pulcher may not have *exactly* been ..."

Augustus raised his hand to stop him, but he was smiling. "*Hold.* I think perhaps you had better not say anymore. I cannot be expected to act on something I do not know about. Perhaps you are better at investigating this, than I had thought.

"Now, Alexander, just move your head to indicate yes or no. You have seen the contents of the locked room in Gnaeus Pulcher's house? ...*Yes.* And there was what appeared to be a Phidias there? ... *Yes.* But it was not the missing statue of Victory? ... *No.*"

Augustus let out an oath and began to pace again. "*Where is it?* I've had my Guard searching everywhere in Rome. Every warehouse has been examined closely, every shop that deals with art. My Guard has been investigating every sculptor, every art dealer, every auctioneer and ... *nothing*. I fear it may have left Rome by now, but where? How? I've sent agents to the port to question the customs inspectors and dock workers, but again, *nothing*."

He stopped pacing and once more stopped in front of Alexander.

"So, whom do you suspect now?"

"Well," Alexander answered nervously glancing over at Tiberius who had remained silent throughout the interview. "I'm not really sure. Clearly you have investigated this far more thoroughly than I have."

Augustus looked at him narrowly.

"You prevaricate. Alexander, do you *know* what that statue means to me? Not just the statue, but the great goddess Victory herself?"

"*Umm,* Not fully, sir; just a few stories that I've heard around the Forum."

"Then I shall *tell* you," Augustus snapped. "And then you shall see that I take this incident *very personally*, and I will brook *no further* evasion to my questions.

"*You*, Alexander, are a *Jew* and, therefore, do not worship the Roman gods. That is your right; a right given to you by my father, Gaius Julius Caesar, and confirmed by myself. But because of that, you may not know that it was the goddess Victory who delivered my defeat of Marcus Antonius at Actium. It is why I placed a statue of Victory and altar in the Senate house. We must *never forget* what the gods have done for us."

Augustus paused and looked at Alexander to see if he was following. Alexander nodded.

"The gods are not just important *to me*. The gods are

important *to Rome.* In fact, the gods *are* Rome. When Rome's devotion to the gods wavers, then the gods' protection of Rome wavers likewise. This is the reason for the terrible civil wars of recent generations. I am sure of it. Likewise, when Rome protects and cherishes the gods and their temples, Rome prospers. This is why I have devoted *my life* to protecting and cherishing the gods of Rome."

Again Augustus paused to stare at Alexander, who quickly nodded his understanding. Like everyone else, he had heard of Augustus's nearly two-decade campaign to rebuild or rejuvenate every temple in Rome. But, until now, he had no notion of the *personal fervor* that Augustus had brought to this endeavor.

Augustus continued. "And so I will ask you *again,* Alexander. Whom do you suspect?"

Much to his own surprise, Alexander blurted out, "The *augur,* Lucius Servilius."

For once, Augustus seemed taken aback. "No *augur* would do such a thing. Of this I feel sure."

"But … he might have been *forced* to do it," Alexander said hesitantly. "For example, if there had been a case of blackmail."

"You know something," Augustus said shrewdly. "Out with it. *Now.*"

Alexander was suddenly worried again that he had gone too far, but there was no hope for it now. Quickly, he told Augustus about the time that he and "his friends" had been visiting the Venus House and learned that the *augur* had been on the third floor dallying with other men. "They say he likes to be the one who is on his knees," he added softly.

Augustus listened carefully and afterwards glanced at Tiberius. They seemed to be communicating some silent message, for Tiberius nodded.

"This is all very interesting," Augustus observed then gave

a dismissive wave of his hand. "But it was *not* the *augur*. I have already cleared him. He said he was not in Rome the day the statue was stolen, and a witness has confirmed this. Do you suspect *anyone else*?"

"No," Alexander replied shaking his head. He decided not to mention Sejanus's suspicious words about the Praetorian Guard passing on false information about the statue. After all, he lacked any real evidence against them.

"Then, Alexander, I am instructing you to *continue* with your investigation. You have been trained in logic; *use* it. I think we both agree that recovering this statue is of paramount importance, both for Rome and for your client."

Alexander felt a ray of hope. "Will you release Theon into my custody? He is an art dealer. He can help me with my investigation."

"No, no," Augustus replied to Alexander's expectant look. "I cannot release your client. Until the statue is recovered, his is the only evidence we have."

"Speaking of which, sir," Alexander asked hesitantly. "Could you possibly tell me exactly how you learned of my client's unfortunate statement about having a buyer for the statue? He and his friends seemed quite sure that no one else had been present when he said that."

Augustus waved his question aside as if it was of little importance, "Just some gutter rat from what I understand. When the statue went missing, he reported it to my Praetorian Guard."

This set off alarms in Alexander's head. "Did you say he reported it to *the Praetorians*, sir? Not the *Urban Cohorts*? I thought it was the Cohorts that arrested Theon."

Again, Augustus waved his hand dismissively. "*Whatever*. My Guard told me that they got everything out of him that he knew."

Alexander glanced at Tiberius who was looking at him keenly and decided to let the matter drop. Augustus continued.

"Now, Alexander, if you learn anything about this missing statue, and I mean *anything*, I want you to report it immediately to Tiberius. Just come to the palace and ask at the gate. He will inform his secretaries that you are to be sent to him at once."

Augustus glanced at Tiberius, who nodded in acknowledgement.

"Yes, sir. I will do that, First Citizen," Alexander promised as he felt himself almost unconsciously edging toward the door. "Will that be all?"

"*No.*"

That brought Alexander to halt. *What more could there be?*

Augustus seemed to study the wall fresco for a moment before turning back to Alexander.

"I understand that you have been recently betrothed... *Oh, don't look so astonished.* I've had a letter from your father. I *am* his patron, after all, so it was right for him to consult me on this matter."

Augustus began to pace again and spoke almost distractedly. "And, as you know, *you* are to be my next Alabarch."

"*What?!*"

Alexander was completely taken aback. His face must have reflected it, for Augustus knitted his eyebrows and stared at him.

"You mean you did not know this?"

"But, but," Alexander stammered. "I thought *I* was to run my father's business here in Rome, so someone else ... perhaps my brother..."

Augustus shook his head no. "*Not* your brother. Your brother is younger than you – not by much -- but he *is* younger. More importantly, your brother has no head for the job. And he doesn't want it, anyway. He fancies himself a philosopher, does he not?"

"Well, Philo is more of a spiritual thinker," Alexander replied.

"Whatever. In any case, the Alabarch is a political appointment. I need someone I can rely upon handling my gold in Egypt. It has always been assumed you would follow your father in this. It's what he has been grooming you for."

Alexander did not know what to say. The thought had simply never occurred to him. He had always assumed that much of his training had been in business, because he would be working in the family business. If anything, he had expected to continue to be the family's representative *in Rome.*

Huh, ... no, this just didn't make sense. The Alabarch was in charge of weighing and assaying gold in Egypt. Alexander had grown up mostly in Rome. He knew that the gold mines in Egypt were important, of course, but that's about all he knew. ... *Surely,* the First Citizen could find *someone* who would be more appropriate to appoint as the new magistrate.

As if sensing his thoughts, Augustus stroked his chin as he faced Alexander.

"Did you never wonder *why* I kept *your family* as my clients when I have passed so many other clients on to other members of my family?"

Alexander had wondered that a little, but he had guessed that his family lived too far away for the First Citizen to take much note of them. Augustus dispelled that notion.

"I see what you think, and you are *wrong.* Egypt is *very* important to Rome, very important to *me.* I will not allow even the least of the Senators to travel there without my permission. It *is* that important. Egypt is not only Rome's biggest producer of wheat, it is also now our greatest source gold. ... but there's more.

... How many Jews live in Egypt?"

Alexander literally pulled back in surprise at the change in subject. *Where did that come from?* Augustus was staring at him, clearly waiting for an answer, so he collected thoughts.

"I am not sure, but some say that more than one in ten in Egypt is a Jew; perhaps more than a million?"

Augustus gave curt nod and drew him out further. "...And historically are all of these Jews *farmers*?"

Alexander tried to think quickly. "Well, many of them are, but others are artisans, shopkeepers, and *umm* soldiers."

Augustus raised his eyebrows. *"Soldiers?"*

"Yes. Well, not so much anymore now that you've brought in the legions, but historically there were multiple Jewish garrisons guarding Egypt. ... In fact, you may know that my own ancestor, Ananias, was Egypt's top general under the third Cleopatra."

Augustus nodded. "I see; *Jewish* generals, *Jewish* soldiers."

Alexander still wasn't sure that he was getting the point. By now, Augustus seemed he might be losing patience.

"Alexander, *who* leads those million Jews in Egypt?"

"Well, of course, the Prefect governs all Egypt. But, if you're speaking strictly of influence with Jews, I suppose that could be our *ethnarch* in Alexandria. ... Who is *not* a Roman citizen. ... If you're thinking of the most influential Jew in Egypt who *is* a Roman citizen, I guess that would be ... *my father* ... the current Alabarch."

Augustus gave sharp nod of satisfaction. "Indeed. The Alabarch *is* a Roman magistrate. *My* magistrate. By appointing a Jew in that position and keeping him as my client, I resolve a secondary issue.

"I certainly am *not* going to lose control of one of Egypt's wealthiest and most influential citizens. ...One who holds political sway over a million Jews in Egypt. ... Jews who, as you just pointed out, have a long history of military excellence. Egypt's Jews supported my father in the Alexandrian war, and that was the reason why Caesar chose to tie them so closely to Rome."

Augustus paused and looked at Alexander.

"By binding your father to me as my client *and* as my magistrate for gold, I have taken one more step toward securing the future of Egypt for Rome. Do you *see* this?"

Alexander pressed his lip together as he thought furiously. Well, yeah, once Augustus put it that way, he guessed it did make sense. But he had just never looked at things that way before. His father had always been, well, *just* his father. And Alexandria had just been his home far away. He had never thought of the Jews in Egypt ... thought of *his father* ... as being that *important to Rome.*

Augustus was still studying him. "Alexander, I have not spent much time with you and that may have been a mistake. And now you are leaving Rome. But the fact remains that someday you *will* take your father's place. And someday it will be *you* who is a wealthy and influential leader of over a million Jews in Egypt.

"Alexander, there is something I must know. When that happens, *will you remain loyal to Rome?*"

"Yes," replied Alexander almost breathlessly.

"Do you swear it?"

Alexander looked into the eyes of the most powerful man in the world and once again was struck with his tremendous presence.

"*Yes,*" he replied. "*I swear.*"

13

ELECTRA

ALEXANDER bowed out of the room where the interview with Augustus and Tiberius had taken place. He felt shaky, and it wasn't just the effects of last night's drunken binge. He knew that he had been completely overwhelmed by the encounter.

Just being alone in the same room as Augustus and Tiberius was enough to make any young man nervous. But there was so much more to it. So many things had been brought up. ... *the statue, his client, the Senator Gnaeus Pulcher, his betrothal, his father, and not least, this revelation that he was being groomed to become the next alabarch.* ... So much was said in such a short period of time. Too much. Alexander's head hurt. All he wanted was to go home, lie down and think.

"Well, Alexander of Alexandria, I don't see any blood. I guess the First Citizen's mosaics are safe."

Alexander made no attempt to hide his grimace at the taunting voice. Sejanus was leaning against the wall a short distance from the room where Alexander had been interviewed. Augustus may not have permitted him to stay for the interview, but clearly Sejanus had elected not to stray far. Now he shoved off from the wall and stood directly in Alexander's path looking at him curiously.

"What is it man? You look as though you've just faced a gladiator in the ring. Augustus must have given you an earful.

What did *he* say?"

Alexander was in no mood to dissemble and turned on Sejanus irritably.

"Augustus wished to speak to me about my family and my clients. If you believe you're entitled to know the First Citizen's private business, I suggest you take that up with him."

Sejanus held his hands up in mock defeat. "Fine, don't tell me. But like I told you, Alexander of *Alexandria*, I don't like secrets. By the end of today, I'll know everything about you anyway."

"That doesn't scare me," Alexander shot back. "Now, if you'll get out of my way, I have business of my own."

"Sorry, citizen. But the Guard doesn't allow strangers to walk around the palace unattended. You'll have to follow me."

Sejanus still didn't seem sure how he should treat this stranger from Alexandria who claimed to be a personal client of Augustus. He settled by simply leading Alexander to the same door where they had entered and gave him a curt nod as he exited.

Alexander stalked purposely back out to Victory's Incline and descended the short distance to the base of the Palatine Hill. At the bottom, he decided to take only side streets back to his apartment on the Capitoline, praying that he would encounter no one he knew. Alexander breathed a sigh of relief when he finally made it home unaccosted. He took the stairs two at a time to the second floor. Amarantus must have been watching for him again and threw the door open as he arrived.

"Master, what has happened? Are you in trouble?"

Alexander shook his head.

"Not, now Amarantus. I don't have time for you right now. I must think."

Amarantus' face stiffened. "Of course not, Master. Forgive me. A slave has no right to inquire after his master's business."

Alexander was too distracted to take note of his slave as he headed for his bedroom.   Amarantus tentatively stopped him before he could lie down.

"I am sorry to bother you, Master, but I must report that you have had visitors."

"Visitors?" Alexander looked up sharply. "Who?"

"Several business associates that have been trying to reach you. I have their names and messages."

Alexander waved this aside. "Later. They can wait until later."

"And there was one other … a most *unusual* message."

Alexander looked back inquiringly.

"It was a message from the prostitute Electra at the Venus House, Master. She insists that you must come at once."

"What?" Alexander asked, puzzled. "How did that message come?"

"A street urchin, Master. I told him that prostitutes do not summon respected citizens, but he was most insistent that this Electra needed to see you."

Alexander pondered this a moment. What in *Roma* could Electra be doing? But then he had a flash of inspiration.

"*Rutilus*," he said with a smile and shake of his head. "It *must* be one of his pranks to get me to buy him a visit to the Venus House. … Well, I have no time for that right now either. Come, Amarantus, help me out of these clothes. I need to lie down. I need to think."

Amarantus made no more attempt to speak as he grabbed the hem of the *"Theodosius the art collector"* costume of the previous night and lifted the gaudy tunic over Alexander's head. Alexander sat down on the edge of his sleeping couch as Amarantus knelt to unfasten the leather straps that tied his boot at the ankle and then unlaced them until he was able to slip each boot off his foot. With a sigh, Alexander lay back on his bed and closed his eyes.

***

"*I said, let me in!*"

Alexander's eyes flew open at the crash of a door being slammed back against a wall. A scuffle seemed to be taking place at the front of his apartment. He sat up alert and noted that Amarantus had left a clean tunic next to the bed. Quickly, Alexander tugged it over his head and padded barefoot towards the noise.

He wasn't quite sure what he had been expecting, but could not hold back a grin at the sight that met him. Amarantus had just toppled over onto the floor attempting to maintain a grip on a boy of about seven or eight who was squirming and wriggling like an eel.

"And *I said*, you're *not* going in there," Amarantus panted. "The Master's asleep." He rolled over and tried unsuccessfully to trap the boy beneath his weight.

"*Yes, I am,*" the boy answered writhing out of Amarantus' grasp. Amarantus reached out and grabbed the boy by the ankle and tried to pull him back by his one leg. The boy responded by twisting his body and began kicking at Amarantus with his other foot.

"*Hmm,* It's hard to tell from up here, Ranti," Alexander said dryly, "but I do believe you're losing."

The struggling stopped and two sets of eyes stared up at Alexander from the floor. With a wrench the boy jerked his foot loose and scrambled up to face Alexander.

"Master, I'm sorry. This street urchin was most persistent,"

Amarantus shrugged his shoulders as he sank back on his knees.

"I am *not* a street urchin. I am from the Venus House and I have an *important* message."

Alexander looked to Amarantus who was now raising himself from the floor.

"I take it this is the same boy who brought the message from Rutilus earlier?"

"*Rutilus?*" The boy looked confused. "No, it was *Electra* that sent me. See, I'll show you."

The boy reached down into his tunic and withdrew a small object tied onto a rough cord around his neck.

Alexander bent to inspect it. It was a small bronze ring with a miniature Venus engraved upon it. He knew it. It was the same ring that he had given Electra a couple of years earlier as a Saturnalia gift. The boy looked up at him expectantly.

"Ok. You have my attention," Alexander said. "What message does Electra have for me?"

The boy swelled up importantly. "Electra says that she has learned something that you will want to know and that you are to come at once."

"I told you that whores do not summon Roman citizens," Amarantus snarled at the boy.

"Hold on, Ranti. Let's hear what the boy has to say." Alexander turned to the lad, "What else does she say? What is this about?"

"'Dunno," the boy shrugged. "She just said to make sure you got the message *today*. She said to tell you that you *must* come *today*," he added with a glare at Amarantus. "Will you come now?"

"No, I think not," Alexander smiled. "But you may tell Electra that I will come later today. I warn you though, if this is a trick I will order my servant to beat you."

"It isn't," the boy quipped and held out his hand palm up.

"Give him a *sesterce*," Alexander instructed Amarantus. Then noting the boy's calculating look, he added. "That is enough for you until I check out your story. If I find this is worth my time, I shall leave something more for you with Electra."

That seemed to satisfy the boy who accepted his coin and scampered out the door that was still open.

Alexander blew out a long breath as Amarantus moved to shut the front door.

"What a day. Summoned by the First Citizen *and* a prostitute in the same morning. I think I'd better have something to eat, Ranti. Please bring it to my office. Oh, and, Ranti, no wine. I believe I had enough of that last night to last me for some time."

***

An hour later, Alexander was on his way to the Venus House accompanied by Amarantus who carried a wooden club attached to his tunic belt. Slaves were not allowed to carry knives or swords inside the walls of Rome, but wooden clubs were permitted if they were to be used in defense of their masters. Alexander fingered the knife attached to his own belt. He hoped that there wouldn't be any trouble, but the way things were going, he wanted to be prepared. For this reason, he had also dispensed with his usual toga and wore a knee-length linen tunic and short boots.

It was late afternoon as they descended the Capitoline and made their way into the Forum. Alexander had decided to stop first at a jeweler's shop nearby and purchase a small farewell gift for Electra. He had no idea what she wanted with him, but he assumed that for Electra to break protocol and send for him, she must think it was important.

"Master, take a look at this," Amarantus said and pulled him into a bookshop as they turned onto a side street.

"What it is it?" Alexander asked puzzled.

"I think we are being followed," Amarantus whispered as he pulled him to the side of the shop.

They waited and sure enough two men turned the corner only moments behind them. They were dressed in plain tunics, but carried themselves like military men.

"*Praetorians,*" Alexander hissed.

Amarantus nodded and unrolled a scroll widely and held it in front of them. They took turns peering out from behind the scroll through the store entrance. The two men tailing them had paused and were looking up and down the street. Finally they moved partway down the street and began looking into the taverns as they moved forward.

"Thank goodness, a Praetorian would never think to look in a bookshop," Alexander commented humorlessly.

By that time, the shop owner had finished with a customer and hurried over to see if he could assist them. Alexander started to decline and then remembered his father's letter where his brother had requested the remaining scrolls of Ovid.

At first the shopkeeper shook his head at his inquiry. Augustus had taken offense at Ovid's writings and exiled him from Rome many years earlier. Since then, shopkeepers who were smart did not keep an open stock of Ovid's works. Of course, that had only made Ovid's writings more in demand by a curious public, so an illicit trade had sprung up.

Alexander counted out a handful of *denarii* that got the shopkeeper's attention and then promised to double it if the scrolls were quietly delivered to his home within a week. He assured the man that the scrolls were about to leave Rome forever and would never be traced back to him. That and the money seemed to satisfy him and the sale was concluded.

"Well, I guess the Praetorians did us a favor with that one,"

Alexander remarked as they left the shop and turned in the opposite direction from which the men tailing them had gone. "I had nearly forgotten that Philo had asked for these. I suppose I should also purchase gifts to take to my father and a number of other people in Alexandria. We'd better make a list tonight."

They did not see the men that had been following them again as they made their way to a jewelry shop. Alexander selected a bronze bracelet for Electra with a beaded pattern on it.

They left the jeweler's and decided not to retrace their steps in case their shadows had doubled back. Their new path led them past a goldsmith's shop and Alexander wandered over thoughtfully to view the merchandise.

"Another gift for Electra?" Amarantus asked.

"No, I was thinking of Rutila," Alexander responded.

Amarantus gave him a worried look, but said nothing. Alexander selected a fine pair of gold earrings. Each had a horizontal gold bar and dangling from that were four little chains with a bead at the end of each. Alexander had seen fashionable ladies wearing similar earrings and felt sure that Rutila would like these. For a little extra, the goldsmith wrapped them in tufts of wool and placed them in a small, carved box.

"Now then," Alexander said as they left. "Let's head for the Venus House. I'd like to return home before dark."

They stuck to the side roads and reached the Venus House without incident. Fortunately, Electra was free and Alexander negotiated an hour with her as usual. He also surprised Amarantus by treating him to a visit with anyone of his choice on the first floor.

"You should finish first," he advised. "Wait for me here."

No sooner than he had entered Electra's second-floor room, than she called his name and rushed into his arms.

"Alexander, I was worried you would not come."

"I'm here now," he smiled. "Now, tell me what is so important that you would summon me."

"It's about *the Rat*," she breathed.

"A rat? What about a rat?"

"Not *a* rat. *The Rat*. That's his name, or, at least, that's the only name that anyone calls him."

"I see. Now what's this Rat done?"

"He turned in the Jew."

That got Alexander's full attention. He led Electra to the sleeping couch and sat down facing her.

"Now start from the beginning, Electra, and tell me everything."

"He came yesterday. Oh, he's come before, but always stays on the first floor. I've heard about him because all the girls hate him. But yesterday was different. This time he had a lot of money and he chose Irene in the room next to me. Last night she told me all about it."

"Go on," Alexander urged.

"Well, Irene said that he spent most of the time bragging. He said that he had been near the temple of Victory, and that he was the one who had overheard the Jew plotting to steal the statue of Victory. After the statue went missing, he tried to go straight to Augustus to report it. The Praetorians wouldn't let him in the palace, but he said they treated him *real good* when they heard what he had to say. He said they gave him a lot of money and told him to first go tell the Urban Cohorts. Then he was to spread the word all around the Forum about how the Jews had plotted to steal a Roman goddess."

That may explain a few things, Alexander thought. "Electra, is there anything else?"

"Yes. Irene said that he kept bragging that very soon he's

going to be getting a whole lot of money, and then everybody is going to treat him with respect."

"Did he say where he was going to get all this money? Was it from the statue?"

Electra shook her head. "He didn't say. He just said that he had a plan and that he was going to be getting the money soon."

"That doesn't sound too good. 'Could have something to do with the statue; especially since he already appears to have some connection to its disappearance. Can you tell me where I can find this Rat?"

"Not usually. The girls think that he just lives in the sewers. That's why I had to see you *today*. You see, yesterday, he kept talking about the races. You know the races they're having for the *Neptunalia* tomorrow?"

Alexander nodded.

"Well, Irene said that the Rat had been drinking a lot and then he kept talking about the *fifth race*. He kept saying that he was going to put his money on race number five because he *knew* who was going to win that one. Each time he said it, he would burst out with this cruel laugh like he knew how to put a hex on the horses or something. Irene said he frightened her."

Alexander thoughtfully rubbed his chin. "So, it sounds like I need to talk to this Rat and that I can find him at the Circus Maximus tomorrow. That's a big place. Electra, how I can recognize this man?"

"Oh, that's easy. He really does look like a rat. He's small and his hair is flat and greasy and his eyes are dark and beady. He's very dirty and he always wears the same tunic. It may have been white at one time, but now it's gray, and it hangs down below his knees like it's way too big for him. ... Oh, and, of course, there's *the smell*."

"The smell?"

"*Ich,* yes. It's why all the girls hate him. We get dirty, stinky men in here all the time, especially down on the first floor. But this one is different. We don't know if it's something he eats or maybe he has a disease of some kind, but he always smells horrible. We're pretty sure he must live in the sewers. He's got *that* stink on him, too. I bet he could take a dozen baths and he couldn't wash that smell off of him."

Electra scrunched up her face and nodded agreement at her own words. "Really, Alexander, it's like nothing you can imagine. You can smell him from at least ten feet away, maybe more. So, you see, all you have to do is walk around and if you suddenly smell the most horrible thing that you can imagine, then you've found the Rat."

Electra vigorously nodded her certitude.

Alexander chuckled. He suspected that Electra had probably never been to the Circus Maximus and didn't realize how big it was. Nevertheless, he nodded back at her.

"Then I guess tomorrow I'll be going to the races. While everyone else is looking at the horses, *I'll* be trying *to smell a Rat.*"

Electra gazed up at him through her long, dark lashes. "Alexander, did I do right to send for you? You're not angry about it, are you?"

"Definitely not," Alexander replied. "The man who was arrested for the theft is a client of mine. For days now, I've been working to prove his innocence and I had run out of leads. Electra, you may have just helped me very much."

He pulled the new bronze bracelet out of the pouch tied to his tunic belt.

"In fact, Electra, to thank you, I have brought you a little gift."

"Oh, Alexander!" Electra cried slipping the bracelet over her hand and then holding it back to admire it. "No one has ever given me a gift so fine."

"You deserve it. Oh, and before I forget," Alexander took several bronze sesterces out of the pouch and placed them on the table next to the sleeping sofa. "That's for that little scamp you sent for me. He was most persistent to make sure I received your message."

"Alexander, how can I ever thank you?" Electra asked still admiring her bracelet.

"Well ... we do still have some time left."

14

THE RAT RACE

"IT appears that precocious little messenger was correct, Ranti. The information was worth the trip. I now have a new lead for finding the statue."

After reaching home from the Venus House, Alexander had dashed off messages to Agrippa, Claudius, and Rutilus to meet him the next morning at their customary place in front of the Circus Maximus. No message came back from Agrippa, who, no doubt, had already gone out for the evening. But Rutilus sent a reply back with the original messenger that he would be there.

A message also arrived from Claudius saying that he would come if he could get permission. Alexander frowned at this. Although 22 years old and married, Claudius suffered the humiliation of being forced to remain under the guardianship of a man selected by his mother and grandmother Livia. Because he was a member of the imperial family, Claudius was required to seek permission before appearing at any type of public assembly. It had to do with Claudius' deformed leg that caused him to walk strangely and his stutter that grew worse when he was nervous. Augustus found it politic to keep Claudius out of sight, so as not to expose the family to public ridicule.

Before going to bed that night, Alexander sat down and made a list of every event connected with the theft of the statue. So much had been happening that he was having trouble keeping it all straight, especially when his own personal life kept intervening at the most unsettling moments.

***

Morning broke with the promise of another hot July day. Leaving Amarantus behind to handle some pressing correspondence, Alexander left early for the small wine shop where he and his friends usually met before the races. Rutilus was there already standing in front waiting for him, wearing his usual grin.

"Alexander, what a *wonderful* idea. Truly, you've been working too hard. This will be an excellent distraction."

"Don't get too excited," Alexander shrugged his apology. "We're here on *business* – at least I hope you'll help me. I need all of the eyes and ...*errr...* noses that I can get."

Just as he was about to explain, a litter stopped next to them and Claudius got out.

"Claudius! I was worried that you would not be able to come."

"It took a little persuading, but I'm here. I am told that I am not to appear near any of the magistrates who are presiding over the race, and I am not to sit in the section with the Senatorial class so that I won't be recognized."

He gestured at his tunic and shrugged. Alexander noted that Claudius was wearing a plain white tunic, instead of his customary white one with the purple stripe. Before Alexander or Rutilus could respond, Claudius changed the subject himself.

"So, Alexander, what do you have planned for us today? Your message was a bit *mysterious*, asking us to bring our 'eyes and noses' to the chariot races."

"I wondered about that myself."

The three men turned toward the new voice as a sleepy-looking Agrippa walked up to join them.

"Agrippa! I thought this might have been a bit too early for you."

Agrippa snorted. "You can thank my *mother* for this. Apparently she became concerned that your message might be important and took it upon herself to open it for me. Your wording was cryptic enough that she decided it must be urgent, so she sent for me to return home early."

"Jupiter," Claudius commented. "Even *my* mother wouldn't do that."

Both men shared a wry smile. Their mothers had been close friends for many years, and both young men had learned what it meant to grow up under similarly strong-willed Roman matrons.

"So, Alexander," Agrippa continued. "We're all here now. I'm guessing this has something to do with the missing statue. Is our new suspect a gambler on the races?"

"Well, not exactly." Alexander related to them his meeting with Electra and her story about the Rat.

Agrippa clearly was not impressed to have been dragged out of bed so early to look for a smelly street rat.

"Really, Alexander, what could you *possibly* want with the man? I'm sure the Praetorians got everything out of him that he knew."

"Perhaps, but I'm not sure that the Praetorians have been revealing all they know of the matter." Then he quickly told them about his meeting with Sejanus and his crude boasts that the Praetorians had been sending up bad information to implicate the Jews.

Agrippa frowned and shook his head. "I told you that I've been worried about this Sejanus."

But Claudius was more interested in the part of the story that Alexander hadn't told.

"You were summoned *by Augustus*? Really? What did he want? Was it about the statue or your betrothal?"

Alexander winced at the mention of his betrothal. Why did everyone seem to know about it even though he had told no one except Amarantus? He quickly answered that one for himself. Agrippa's mother, Berenice, was close friends with Claudius' mother Antonia. Of course, Berenice would have mentioned the betrothal since Antonia also had known Alexander since he was a boy. After that, it would have been only natural for it to come out in dinner conversation or a dozen other ways. Alexander chose to ignore the mention of his betrothal and respond to the other part of Claudius's query.

"The statue, Claudius. He said that he had heard from *certain sources* that I was looking into it. Do you suppose those *certain sources* had anything to do with whoever was spying on us in your office that day?"

"Probably," Claudius replied sadly. "I'm sorry, Alexander. You know that I would never have caused you trouble deliberately."

"Don't worry, old friend. There was no trouble. In fact, Augustus wanted a report on my progress. I told him about Gnaeus Pulcher having a Phidias, but not the right one. I also told him that I suspected the *augur* Lucius Servilius because of blackmail, and then I told him what Rutilus had learned about his visits to the third floor. But he said that he had cleared the *augur* because he wasn't in Rome the day the statue was taken.

"Then he told me that I was to continue with the investigation and inform Tiberius directly if I learned anything."

"Jupiter," Claudius said for the second time that morning. "You said *all* that to Augustus? Were you scared?"

"A little," Alexander admitted. "Augustus does have a lot of … presence … well, you know. Talking to him is like …. Well, as if your Roman Jupiter had come down and addressed me himself."

"He *is* a great man," Claudius agreed. "And he has often been kind to me. I sometimes think that if it weren't for Mother and Livia, that he would have given me my chance."

"You're... you're *betrothed*?"

Everyone stopped and turned to Rutilus who was standing there looking bewildered. "Alexander, why did you not tell us that you were betrothed?"

Alexander suddenly felt a little sick. This was *not* how he had wanted Rutilus ... and therefore *Rutila* ... to find out what his father had done. He knew that perhaps he had been a little cowardly to not face them before. There was no choice now but to tell his friend who he knew must have been hoping for a betrothal to his own sister.

"Because I've only recently learned of it myself, Rutilus. ... And because I am *not* happy about it.

"Rutilus, my father recently arranged for the betrothal *without* consulting me. I have ... other plans. When I return to Alexandria, I will speak with my father and ask him to cancel the betrothal. She is only a child and there is plenty of time for them to find someone else for her."

Now Agrippa joined in. "*Cancel* the betrothal? What are you talking about Alexander? It's a good match. Not just anyone gets betrothed to the daughter of the High Priest."

"Oh, not you, too, Agrippa," Alexander was frustrated. "I'm *sick* of everyone telling me about my *duty*. I'll settle this when I return to Alexandria."

"A High Priest? Is he rich?" Rutilus asked.

"Very, and very powerful," Agrippa replied.

"*Enough* of this!" Alexander cried. "I don't want to hear any more about that pig-faced girl or any of her relatives. Now come on, we have a Rat to find."

Without a backward glance, he strode off towards the Circus Maximus leaving the other three men standing in front of the tavern exchanging puzzled looks. With a shrug Agrippa, set out after Alexander and the other two fell into step beside him. Alexander led them to the Arch of Stertinus which served as the main entrance into the Circus Maximus, then paused to suck in long breath before he turned back to face his friends. He should not have lost his temper with them. After all it wasn't their fault that he had been betrothed. They were only curious.

Shoving thoughts of his betrothal from his mind, Alexander turned to his friends and proposed that they station themselves next to the entrance and watch for the Rat entering with the rest of the crowds. They then spent much of the next hour watching the people that passed through. There were thousands of them.

"This is *hopeless*," Claudius said at last. "How are we to spot him in this crowd? For all we know he may have entered hours ago. You know that many people arrive well before dawn just to get a good seat."

Alexander had to agree, but at the moment he couldn't think of what else to try.

"Oh, let's go in and take a seat," Agrippa said finally. "We can at least watch the races while we look for him. Perhaps if he smells as bad as you say, he'll reveal himself for us -- the only man sitting with a whole section to himself."

The others laughed and agreed to go watch the races until Alexander could think of some other way to catch the Rat.

"Speaking of getting there early," Claudius commented, "by this time most of the good seats have probably been taken. We'll be stuck up in the third section."

Agrippa sniffed. "Clearly, you have forgotten with whom you're dealing."

"What do you mean, Agrippa?"

"Remember, I got Alexander's message last night. One of my slaves should have arrived here to hold seats for us hours ago."

"Only *one*? Will he be able to hold seats for all four of us?"

"You'll see," Agrippa replied. "He should be in the lower section not far from the starting gates."

The three men followed Agrippa to that section and sure enough one slave was waiting there. Space on the wooden bleachers for four men had been covered with ...

"*Tyrian purple!?*" Alexander laughed. The seats had been covered with a long mantel of the finest linen cloth died with Tyrian purple. The color of kings. No wonder the slave had been able to save the space for four men. After all, who was going to try to take seats that had so obviously been reserved for royalty?

As the men sat down, Alexander shot a quick look at Rutilus. That was definitely not the way he had wished his friend to learn of his betrothal. He should have told him sooner, should have been more honest with him. It was true that they had never actually *discussed* it, but both men knew that Rutilus had hoped for a match between Alexander and his sister. But if Rutilus was upset by the news, he did not show it now.

The third race had just ended so there would be a lull while horses and course were being set up for the next race.

Alexander studied the course carefully, realizing that it may be a long while before he got to see it again. The Circus Maximus was Rome's largest race course, and certainly its busiest. A glance around showed Alexander that most of the stadium's seats were full. The *Neptunalia* was a minor festival for Neptune and was unlikely to have top rate entertainment. Rome in July, however, tended to be a very dull place so the stands were packed with people who, no doubt, were happy for some relief from their hot summer routines.

Down on the field, men were raking out the sand of the racecourse. It took a dozen of them to smooth the long track that was nearly 100 feet long and wide enough for twelve chariots. In the middle of the track was the *spina*, or the long walled strip around which the chariots circled. On the end of the *spina* where they were seated was the elevated stand with the seven eggs for each of the seven laps in a race. As each lap was completed, an egg would be removed. On the other end were the seven dolphins that served the same purpose. And in its middle, towered the 60 foot red granite obelisk that Augustus had brought from Egypt.

"Alexander, *look*."

Rutilus nodded towards a large gold-plated statue that stood on the *spina* near the finish line. It was a statue of Victory holding a victor's palm branch and wreath.

"Do you think the thief might have been a charioteer?" he said with a wry smile. "A goddess is about the *only* thing that could help the Reds this year."

Alexander had forgotten about the Victory statue at the Circus Maximus. It wasn't quite like the one that had gone missing. At least not as he had heard the statue described. Surely, it was just a coincidence that Victory was an integral part of award ceremonies for victorious charioteers.

A series of public criers began to make their way through the stands announcing the names of the charioteers for the next race. The spectators quickly responded by making their bets, using runners dispersed through the crowd.

Agrippa leaned towards Alexander and whispered, "I don't suppose you could loan me..."

"Say no more," Alexander stopped him with a smile. He opened his pouch and removed three small bundles that he handed to each of his friends. "It's a gift for helping me."

With silver in hand, each of the men placed a bet. Claudius

inevitably went for the Blue team and Agrippa for the Green. Normally Alexander went for the Greens also, but he had seen the charioteer for the Whites perform quite well in the past, and decided to take the long shot. Rutilus put a small bet on the Blues.

The crowd started getting antsy as the time for the race grew near.

"I wonder who is officiating today?" Agrippa wondered aloud. "Ah, look Claudius. It's *the Consul*."

Claudius' older brother Germanicus was one of the two Consuls that headed the Senate that year. Now they could see Germanicus moving forward in his box indicating that the race would soon begin.

The crowd was still muttering about the race, but many scooted to the edge of their seats as they saw the Consul step forward. Excitement filled the air. All eyes were on Germanicus who raised a white napkin in the air. The stands fell silent. Then Germanicus let the napkin drop and thousands of eyes turned to the starting gates.

As the napkin fell, the gates sprang open and four teams of horses rushed out vying for the lead position. There were just four teams in this race, one each for the Greens, Blues, Reds, and Whites. Each charioteer wore a tunic in his team colors and stood in a lightweight chariot consisting of little more than two wooden wheels under an open basket about knee-high in front. The reins for each of the four horses were wrapped firmly around the charioteer's waist so he could use his whole body to direct their movements.

The crowd roared as the chariots came out fast. The charioteer in the red tunic had drawn the place on the inside track closest to the *spina* and he was clearly determined not to lose it. All four chariots were almost side-by-side as they headed into their first lap. But most bettors knew that races were often won or lost on the narrow turn around the end of the *spina*. The crowd held its breath as the Red driver appeared to be taking it too fast, but somehow he made it around. The other drivers had to swing a wider arc to make it around and were now shouting and cracking their whips to make it up on the longer stretch.

Again the Red driver made it around the narrow turn on the other end completing the first lap. But the White driver was only inches away from his side as the Red pulled into the long stretch.

Alexander's heart was pounding as he began shouting for the Whites. Next to him, he was aware of his friends shouting encouragement for the Greens and Blues. Now in the second lap, the Red driver made it again around the far end of the *spina*, but slowed too much as he completed the lap at the other end. With a shout from the crowd, the White driver pulled out in front of him and took his place as the driver hugging the *spina*. Having slowed too much for the turn, the Red's horses could not regain their speed fast enough and were quickly passed by the Green and the Blue drivers who had chosen wider arcs that maintained their speed.

Now it was the White driver trying to hold on to his lead.

"It *won't* work," Agrippa shouted. "Those horses will never be able stay on the inside track."

Alexander could see his point. The horses moved well enough together in the straight run, but lacked the synchronized motion to take the tight corners at a fast pace. Yet the Blue driver was giving them little choice. He was crowding them from the side, forcing the White's horses to keep moving closer and closer to the *spina*. The White driver should have pushed his way out and not allowed the Blue to press him so closely. It was simply a matter of technique.

Somehow both the White and Blue chariots made it around the corner at the far end. But as they were turning around the near end of the *spina* to complete the third lap, the Blue driver hugged the turn tightly forcing the White's left-most horse into the sharp corner of the low marble border along the wall of the *spina*.

With a shriek of pain, the horse stumbled with a bloody gash running across its side. The cry only frightened the other horses who tried to run faster. The chariot tipped to the left and smashed into the wall, throwing the driver whose head struck the same wall that had taken his horse. Blood spurted from a head wound, but the White driver clearly remained conscious as he tried frantically to untangle himself from the reins wrapped around his waist. It was no use. The frightened horses kept running although the right three were thrown off pace by the wounded fourth and the tipped and shattered chariot. There was nothing the White driver could do. The reins held him fast and he was dragged behind his struggling horses.

With the Red's chariot still lagging behind, the Blue driver pulled out in front. He was attempting to stay inside, but not hug the *spina* so closely that he couldn't make the turns. Now the Green driver was coaxing his horses, trying to force the Blue driver inwards toward the *spina*. They spun around into their fourth lap, but the White's horses were still running the inside track blocking the way for the Blue. With a shout from the crowd, the Green's chariot pulled ahead as the Blue driver had to slow as he tried desperately to avoid a collision with the White's driver still being dragged behind his broken chariot.

Now the Red's chariot bypassed the flailing White's and surged forward. It still trailed the Green's driver as he was able to take a wide arc around the *spina*'s end to maintain his speed. The Blue driver fought to regain speed, but neither he nor the Red were able to catch up as the Green's chariot shot through the sixth lap and finally the seventh. As the Red's and Blue's chariots thundered in behind the Green's, the White's crew rushed out and grabbed the bridles of the still running horses. The crowd cheered the Green driver who now took a victory lap, but most eyes returned to the White's charioteer who lay behind his team in a blood streaked heap.

Quickly, his crew came out with a stretcher, cut away the reins and carried the man from the track.   The driver wasn't moving, and no one could tell if he was alive or dead.   The horses were unfastened and the three good ones were led away.   It took two men to lead off the frightened injured horse which was neighing and rearing wildly.

"That shouldn't have happened," Claudius said shaking his head.   "That horse shouldn't have been forced into that sharp corner.   The ends of the *spina* should be rounded so that it slows them down but doesn't injure them."

"Well, Claudius, that can be your gift to Rome someday when you're a famous public benefactor," Agrippa remarked, "rounded ends on the *spina*."

Alexander couldn't tell if Agrippa was being sarcastic or not, as he slid past them to collect his winnings.

"It *is* a good idea, Claudius. I hope someday that you can do it," Rutilus added softly.

Agrippa returned jingling his winnings.   "And now comes the *big* race. Everyone was talking about this fifth race last night. Apparently, it's a grudge match and both the Blue's and the Green's are putting up their top charioteers. A lot of money is going to be bet on this one."

Agrippa's words pulled Alexander's thoughts back into the present. "What race did you say?"

"The *fifth*. This is the really big one for the day," Agrippa replied.

"But that's it!" Alexander cried. "The fifth race. That's the one that the Rat bragged that he knew who would win. Now, how would he know that?"

"Well the race isn't *fixed*," Agrippa said.   "I've been

following these two charioteers for a long time, and they hate each other. I can't imagine anything that would incite either of them to throw a race; certainly not for anything this Rat could offer them."

Alexander accepted this but..."Weeeell, how else could someone like that fix a race?"

Now, Claudius was interested.

"Maybe he's going to try to injure one of the horses."

Rutilus wrinkled his brow, "Do you think he could be putting some sort of hex on a driver or the horses? You can still buy things to do that out on the Field of Mars. I heard that's what happened when the Greens lost the big one last year."

"Well, whatever it is," Alexander decided, "he's not going to be doing it up here. He'll be down near the chariots. Come on, let's go…. *Oh, come on, Agrippa.* There is no point in placing a bet on a race that may be fixed."

The four young men rushed out of the stands and back down the stairs. Outside they found a side entrance that led beneath the stands where the charioteers and their staff prepared for each race. Not surprisingly, the entrance was guarded by a couple of large men who blocked their way.

"We have to get in," Alexander whispered urgently. "We have…"

Before Alexander could say more, Rutilus pushed in front of him with a stricken look and half stumbled up to the door guards. *"The driver for the Whites!* He's my father's freedman. I have to see if he's *alive."*

The guards looked at each other awkwardly. They had obviously already heard about the accident in the previous race, but must have had their orders against letting in people from the crowd. Rutilus continued to look anguished.

"*Now,* Man! My father needs to know at once about his freedman. He can't come himself; he's sitting with the Consul."

The two guards took in the two wide purple stripes on Rutilus' tunic and looked back at each other. One spoke slowly.

"Well, we're not *supposed* to let anyone in."

Alexander stepped forward pulling out his pouch.

"We can't keep the Senator waiting. I know you have your orders, but maybe this will repay you for your trouble."

He counted out three silver *denarii* into each guard's palm knowing it was very large tip. That seemed to convince them.

"Go straight to the Whites," the guard said. "No sightseeing. We've had to eject better men than you before."

Rutilus thanked them and rushed in with Agrippa discreetly steering him in the right direction toward the stables for the Whites. Once out of sight of the door guards, the friends stopped to reconnoiter.

"*Brilliant!*" said Claudius.

Rutilus smiled and shrugged. "It usually doesn't help me much that I'm entitled to wear the purple stripes of my father. I think it made a difference this time though."

"I'm sure of it, Rutilus," Alexander added. "But now how shall we proceed? This is a big place. Agrippa, you seem to know your way around."

"Indeed," Agrippa nodded. "I've been down here many times during practice races. I like to get to know the horses and drivers that I intend to bet on. ... Let's see, there are four of us. We *could* split up and one each go to the Blues, Green, Reds, and Whites and tell them of our concerns. But they are getting ready for the next race and there's no guarantee that they'll listen to us. After all, we only have the word of a prostitute who heard it from another prostitute who heard it from a man with no Roman name."

Alexander almost winced. Hearing it described that way made their whole search for the Rat sound rather ridiculous.

Agrippa continued. "Or, we could go to the *starting gates* and make a sweep back and see if we can locate this Rat ourselves."

They all looked to Alexander who considered the options.

"Agrippa, how long do you think we have until the next race?"

"There's a long break between the fourth and the fifth, perhaps half an hour."

"Then let's head for the starting gates and sweep back. As Agrippa said, there's no reason why the teams should believe us. If we can find the Rat, we can make our case."

Agrippa led the way as they hurried back towards the starting gates as quickly as Claudius could go with his bad leg. They passed through a series of arches and then Agrippa called back over his shoulder.

"It should be right after this one. ... *Eww,* what's that smell?"

The men slowed then stopped as they turned right after the arch. Before them stood the twelve starting gates which appeared deserted except for one man. There was no missing him, because he stood on a ladder high above the rails that marked the stall for each chariot.

"What's he doing?" Claudius whispered.

They studied him for a moment before Agrippa softly replied, "He's sabotaging the gates."

On closer inspection, they saw exactly what the man was doing. The hinges on each of the doors of the starting gates were on a spring that would throw the door open. After each race, attendants would force the doors closed against their hinges and then hold them shut by sliding a long bronze bar through slots on the inside of the doors. Attached to the end of the bronze bar was a strong cord that ran up the side of the door to a small mechanism near the ceiling. A similar locking mechanism was over each of the starting gates and through each passed a single cord. The single cord connected all of the bronze holding bars over every gate to a lever at the end of all of the gates. Each mechanism had been synchronized so that by lowering the lever, the bronze bar would be pulled simultaneously out of each set of doors and all starting gates would fly open at once.

The Rat, for it could be none other than the Rat, was on a ladder fiddling with the cord that ran along the top of one of the gates.

"He's shortening the cord so that gate will open before the others," Agrippa explained.

Up to this point, the Rat had been so intent on what he was doing that he had not heard the young men enter the room. Now he turned and saw them and jumped down from the ladder to make a run for it.

"Quick! Stop him!"

The four men moved forward forming a human wall between the Rat and the only exit. The Rat feinted towards Claudius on the far right, then turned and dashed the other way obviously hoping to pass Rutilus on the left. With a huge lunge Rutilus threw himself forward catching the Rat around the knees and tackling him to the ground.

"Oh, my Lord Jupiter!" Rutilus cried. "What a stench! Now it's all over me."

Agrippa and Alexander knelt and each grabbed one of the Rat's arms and threw him backwards into one of the starting stalls. The Rat sprawled then quickly regained his feet, but now Alexander, Agrippa, and Claudius were blocking the exit.

Each man tried not to gag as the stench wafted off of the filthy, ragged, little man who stood in front of them. Sure, smelly men were not that uncommon in Rome. There was always someone who didn't like to visit the baths; and, it was worse when it was someone who did manual labor in summer.

Nothing like that prepared them for the reek they were encountering now. It was such a cacophony of foul smells that Alexander couldn't even imagine the cause of it all. In fact, he was quite sure he did not even want to try.

"Someone had better go for a guard," Claudius said while trying not to breathe through his nose.

"You should go, Rutilus," Alexander said. "You're the only one wearing a patrician's purple stripes. They'll have to believe you."

Rutilus tried to brush himself off then headed for the exit. Alexander studied the Rat, whose beady dark eyes were darting back and forth looking for an escape.

"Well, I think it is obvious that you are the man who is known as *the Rat*. I think we should have a little talk while we're waiting for the guards."

The Rat let out an oath, but said nothing else.

Alexander continued. "According to my information, you are the man who turned in the Jew, Theon, to the Praetorian Guard … *and* to the Urban Cohorts."

"So what if I am?" snarled the Rat. "What's it to you?"

"It's plenty to me. The man, Theon, is my client and I have a personal charge from Augustus himself to investigate this theft. Now, why did you accuse Theon of stealing the statue?"

The Rat licked his lips and said nothing.

"I strongly suggest that you answer my questions," Alexander said trying to control his rising anger. "I am authorized to bring all new information to *Tiberius* personally. Of course, I would have to leave you at the Carcer while I'm waiting for an appointment with Tiberius. It also means that *I* won't be the one who *questions you*."

The Rat stared at Alexander and appeared to be stalling while he thought up some lie or new angle.

"Forget about the *Praetorians*," Agrippa admonished. "You're dealing with the *Imperials* now. You can talk here, or it's the Carcer for you. They have ways there of making you talk."

"*'Heard him say it*," the Rat said finally. "I was near the temple of Victory, and I heard him tell his friends about how he knew someone that wanted to buy the statue."

"And how did you know his name?"

"'Followed him, across to the other side of the Tiber. First he went to his friend's house and then home. I asked the locals what his name was."

"That was quite *energetic* of you. The Trans-Tiber is a long way from the temple. *Why* did you follow him?"

"I collect … *information*," the Rat cracked with a hoarse laugh. "People pay a lot of money for me to tell my information, or, for me *not* to tell it."

"Blackmail," Claudius scoffed.

"Indeed," Alexander nodded. "And so you thought to blackmail Theon, correct?"

The Rat nodded.

"But you did not. Why?"

"Asked around. The locals said he had no money. Sometimes I save my information until I have the right buyer."

"Ahh, and that's where the Praetorians come in. What did you tell them?"

"Same as I told you."

"He's lying," said Agrippa.

"No, I ain't. 'Didn't need to tell the Praetorians any more than that. That Guard was happy just as soon as I told him it was a

Jew."

"And was the Praetorian you spoke to named *Sejanus*?"

The Rat nodded.

"And did Sejanus give you money, and tell you to go tell the Urban Cohorts and spread it around the Forum?"

"So, what if he did? Like I told you, I sell information. It ain't my concern what people do with it."

"Yes, you're a regular businessman, aren't you? Are you sure you didn't say anything more to the Praetorians? Maybe, add a little bit to make the information more valuable?"

"Like I said, I didn't need to. As soon as I told 'em it was a Jew they were happy. 'Didn't really ask me anything more after that."

"Do you *know* anything more?"

The Rat looked cagey.

"I'll *pay*," Alexander said.

The Rat looked suspicious. "How much?"

"That depends on the information. If it leads to the recovery of the statue and my client being freed, then I'll pay you a lot. My name is Gaius Julius Alexander, and, if you ask around, you'll learn that my family is very well off."

The Rat seemed to be vacillating. Alexander couldn't tell if the man actually knew anything, or, was just trying to think of a good lie so he could cheat him out of some money. Suddenly, the waves of reeking odor reminded Alexander of something Electra had said. Something about how she thought that the Rat lived in the sewers. He decided it was worth a try.

"I understand that you sleep near the temple of Victory. Would that be in the *umm passage* beneath the Clivus Victoria?"

That seemed to unsettle the Rat. "How did you know that?"

"I have *my* sources. Were you there the night the statue was removed? Did you see anything?"

Again the Rat looked calculating. Alexander jingled the coins in his money pouch. The Rat stared at the pouch looking like he was about to blurt something out, but then seemed to change his mind. "*Nah,* I wasn't *there* that night. 'Had business *elsewhere.*" He added a hoarse laugh.

"What do you think?"

Alexander had posed the question to Agrippa and Claudius, but before they could answer they heard Rutilus' raised voice.

"This way, we have him trapped in one of the stalls."

The Rat's look turned desperate and he eyed the three friends as if planning his chances to slip past them.

"Don't even think about it," Alexander said firmly to the Rat. "We've all trained on the Field of Mars."

The Rat swore and began to back away. Just then Rutilus came around the corner with two guards and apparently a few of the charioteers' staff in tow. The three friends each took their eyes off of the Rat for a moment to glance at the newcomers.

A moment was all he needed. The Rat took a final step backwards and pulled the bronze bar out of the slot holding the doors shut. The starting gates sprang open, but instead of a chariot, the Rat emerged racing out onto the track of the Circus Maximus.

The guards looked at each other and then with a grunt took off after him. Some of the charioteers' staff wearing their team colors ran out the gate chasing after the guards. Alexander and his fellows stood there at the gate staring after the men running down the sandy race course.

Suddenly, a cheer went up from the crowd in the stadium. No doubt the spectators were delighted that the long break between chariot races was being filled in with this new and unexpected race.

"Ten silver ones on the Rat," Agrippa said dryly.

"Done," Claudius replied.

Circus Maximus. (Restoration by Benvenuti.)

Reconstruction of the Circus Maximus showing the long oval track and the *spina* down the middle around which the chariots raced. As emperor, Claudius had marble end posts installed on the *spina* (Suetonius, *Claudius*, 516)

Source: Harper's Dictionary of Cassical Literature and Antiquities / edited by Harry Thurston Peck, 2nd ed. (New York, Cooper Square, c1896)

15
THE BATHS

"**WELL,** I can't go back up into the stands now," Rutilus declared. "*Yech*, I smell like sewer filth. I was the one who got stuck tackling the Rat, and now his slime has rubbed off on me."

"We noticed," Agrippa said waving the air away from his nose and making an overly obvious attempt to lean as far away from Rutilus as possible.

The four young men had exited the charioteers' area under the stands and were now standing outside of the Circus Maximus. The Rat had indeed managed to outrun the guards until he had found an opening and scrambled over the side of the track, disappearing into the stands. Agrippa had been quick to collect on his wager.

"That's got to be it," Claudius suddenly blurted out. The others looked at him. "The *sewers*. That's must be why the Rat stinks so badly. We've all smelled sweaty, stinky men before, but this is different. He must spend a lot of time slinking around in the sewers and then never takes a bath. The smell seems have permeated every pore of his being."

"That makes sense to me," Rutilus agreed. "A man doesn't get that way just by missing a few baths." Scrunching up his nose, he grabbed his tunic with thumb and forefinger and held it away from his body as if that could somehow diminish the exposure.

"About going back into the races, you know there's going

to be a long delay before the next race," Claudius pointed out. "After what the Rat did to shorten the cord, they will have to spend some time checking and re-synchronizing the starting gates. The next race may not be for quite awhile."

"Then I have a suggestion," Alexander proposed. "Let's go to the baths. Agrippa and I handled him, too, and now I feel like I've got pig *merda* all over me."

"Careful, Alexander," Agrippa cautioned slyly. "Rome's sewers do serve everyone. It could be *patrician merda* on you, too. ... But perhaps not; I've heard that *it* doesn't stink." He raised his eyebrows innocently to Claudius and Rutilus, as they all groaned at that old, worn-out joke.

"Really, Agrippa," Claudius chided. "That joke was old in my father's time. Usually, you've had a bit more wine before you start in on the low humor. Today, you've won a couple of bets and you've already become insufferable."

"To the baths then?" Alexander asked.

"To the baths," the friends agreed.

Agrippa called over his slave, who had remained at a discreet distance ever since they had relieved him of the seats he had been saving in the stands. He instructed the man to run home to fetch his bathing kit and clean clothes, and to send messengers to the others' homes for the same. At Alexander's request, they had decided in favor of some smaller baths on the far side of the Palatine Hill where they had a better chance of talking privately.

It would take a little while for their servants and clean clothes to catch up to them. To stall for time, the friends took a slight detour through the *Forum Boarium* market place and stopped for some meat-filled pastries at an outdoor stall. They stepped away from the hustle of the market, then stood in a small circle munching their pies.

"So what now, Alexander?" Agrippa asked.

"Well, I was hoping we could all talk. Last night I made a list of every event connected with the theft. We're educated men, right? Trained in law, rhetoric, and logic? Perhaps if we go through it, we will think of something that I may have missed."

"Makes sense. So, talk."

"Let's begin with the Rat. Did you believe him?"

Agrippa rubbed his chin. "*Hmm,* well what he said did agree pretty much with what you already knew."

"Yes," Claudius added, "but what about what he didn't say? When Alexander asked him if he knew anything else, he got pretty cagey." Claudius took a moment to fill Rutilus in with what had been said while he had been away summoning the guards.

"So he didn't really add anything new?" asked Rutilus. "But he acted like he *might* have known something more?"

"That is one problem," Alexander replied. "He did *act* like he knew more about the missing statue, but it may have been just an act. He might have been just thinking up some lie in order to get some money out of me."

Rutilus shook his head. "Surely, he would have guessed that you would have checked out his information before paying him."

"Which is why he may *not* have told us anything. He may have weighed the chances of cheating me against the possibility of getting caught, and decided not to risk it."

"On the other hand," countered Agrippa, "he *may* have known something, but decided that there was too much risk that you wouldn't pay up. After all, we had just threatened to take him to the Carcer to make him talk. ... Also, he did say that he sometimes holds on to his information until he finds the right buyer. Maybe he didn't think *you* were the *right buyer*."

Alexander let out an oath. "I shouldn't have let him get

away."

Rutilus put his hand on Alexander's shoulder. "Alexander, you did tell him your name, right? Your full name? Yes? Then if this Rat knows anything, he is going to track you down.

"Think about it. You had him trapped in one of those starting stalls with guards coming to take him away. They would have beaten him, had him arrested, and certainly taken away any money that you might have given him. From *his* perspective, it would have been foolish to tell you anything while he was stuck in that stall."

Claudius nodded. "He has a point."

"Trust me, Alexander," Rutilus added. "If the Rat has any information to sell, *he will* find *you*."

And with that settled, the men headed for the baths.

When they got there, Agrippa's man had already arrived and was waiting with his bathing kit. At Agrippa's query, he assured them that messages had already been sent to each of their other homes, so their kits should be arriving shortly.

"Let's not wait," Agrippa said. "I'll share my oil with you, so we can start. Your slaves should arrive with your kits and sandals before we get to the hot room."

The four men placed their tunics, undergarments, and boots in the little cabinets in the dressing room. As they were waiting for Rutilus to finish, Agrippa looked around the corner towards the cold bath.

"Look, there were only two men and they're leaving now. Come on, we have the cold water plunge to ourselves."

Rutilus whooped and ran ahead of them and jumped in. The others lowered themselves more gingerly into the cold water that felt shocking after the heat of the July weather outside.

Alexander waited until they had each settled for a short

soak before returning to the subject of the stolen statue.

"What about the thief's *motivation*?" he asked. "I've been thinking about something Berenice said. She told me that stealing a Roman goddess statue was no common crime. *'Find the reason why someone would do such a thing,'* she said *'and the rest will start to fall into place.'* I think we can rule out simple burglary."

"Why is that?" Claudius asked.

"Because a common thief is going to take something that he knows that he can sell like jewelry, silver dishes … things that are easily taken and disposed of. What is the market for a stolen temple statue? None. The thief must have known that he had a definite buyer, or it never would have been worth the risk to take it in the first place."

"Well, it's too bad we've had to rule out the obvious buyer, Gnaeus Pulcher," said Agrippa. "Although I suppose there could be some other over-zealous art collector that may have done it. Did the temple priest hint at anyone else?"

"No, he didn't mention any other art collectors specifically. However, he did say that many of the men who visited the temple were obviously more interested in a Phidias statue than in the goddess Victory. He also said that a large number of the supplicants were military men. Remember that he mentioned *your stepfather* in particular, Rutilus, as being almost obsessed with the goddess."

"Sextus Fadius? I guess that would have made him the primary suspect if it weren't for two, no, *three* things."

The others looked at Rutilus expectantly. He held up his fingers one at a time.

"First, Sextus Fadius is in Gaul not Rome. Second, he has no taste at all when it comes to art. One statue of Victory would have been just as good as any other; which leads me to the third point. He had already acquired his statue of Victory when he looted some house in Gaul and sent it back with his other art booty. Surely you remember *the great flying whore?*"

The men laughed at that, but had to concede Rutilus' points.

"And most military men with enough rank to care about Victory's blessings would either be in the Senate or *trying* to get into the Senate," Alexander added. "Stealing a temple goddess statue would be a huge risk for someone hoping to advance their political career, especially when there are replicas of this statue available."

"How about an *enemy of Rome?*" Claudius asked. "Could someone have done it as an insult to Rome?"

"*Hmmm,* that's something I hadn't thought of," Alexander admitted. "But it doesn't seem like a very effective insult unless they actually take credit for it so Rome knows *who* has insulted her. So far, no one has taken credit. Plus, if insult had been the goal, it does seem like there would be better ways to achieve that, such as, say, defacing the statue of Jupiter on the Capitoline."

The others nodded their agreement. Agrippa looked thoughtful for a moment.

"How about someone who was looking to discredit Jews?"

That one stunned Alexander. Would someone enact a crime of that magnitude just to cast blame on Jews? But after a moment's thought, he shook his head.

"I don't know, Agrippa. That theory would only work if someone knew in advance that a Jew would be blamed for the theft."

"What about Sejanus and his Praetorian friends? The Rat says that he told the Praetorians about Theon saying that he had a buyer *after* the statue was stolen, but what if the Rat reported it to them *before* it disappeared? What if *the Praetorians* heard about his words and then *they* took it."

"*That* would make some of the Praetorian Guard guilty of sacrilege," Rutilus gasped.

"*Sshhh.* We'd better be *very careful* here," Claudius said nervously glancing around. "Accusing the First Citizen's personal guard without any evidence is a *very bad* idea."

"Still, after what Alexander has learned from Sejanus, we must acknowledge it as a possibility," Agrippa insisted. He tilted his head in thought. "*I* don't personally know any Praetorians, but I think I may know a way to make an inquiry, very discreetly of course."

"Be careful, Agrippa," Claudius warned. "Don't let it get back to them that you've been the one asking."

Agrippa winked. "You know me. *I'm* the picture of discretion."

The other three men guffawed at that.

"So let's see where that leaves us," Alexander summarized. "It could be an art collector, a military legate, an enemy of Rome, or an enemy of the Jews. "

"Or, how about a charioteer?" Rutilus asked. He continued after seeing their skeptical looks in response. "Not an actual charioteer, of course. Most of *them* are slaves anyway. I mean someone higher up, like the men who own the colors, such as the Reds for example. Or, it could even be someone who bets heavily on the races. You know how seriously people care about their team. And the goddess Victory *is* particularly associated with the winners of chariot races."

"Rutilus is right about that," Agrippa nodded. "Really, can you think of a single other thing that can get Romans riled up faster than competition between the colors? … And didn't Rutilus remind us just today about that scandal last year when some people tried to put a hex on the Blue team's horses? If you think about it, trying to use a goddess to get an unfair advantage for a charioteer isn't that much different from that."

"I don't know," Alexander shook his head. "That still

sounds like a stretch to me, but we'll leave it in for now. So then, that leaves us with the possibilities of an art collector, a military general or legate, an enemy of Rome, an enemy of the Jews, or someone trying to get an unfair advantage for one of the chariot teams. ... Well, that doesn't narrow it down much. Let's try looking at it from a different angle."

"Good idea," said interjected Claudius. "But let's move to the warm water bath first. I think my toes are turning blue."

Since their servants had not arrived yet with their towels and sandals, Alexander, Claudius, and Rutilus climbed out of the pool naked and shook themselves off, before padding barefoot after Agrippa to the next room. Agrippa looked back at them from around the arch that separated the two rooms.

"Good news. It's just those same two men here and they look like they're about to leave."

Again, Alexander waited until his friends had settled into the warm water pool before returning to the investigation. He was glad that the time was still before noon. By afternoon the bath would be packed with bathers, and there would have been no chance to talk privately.

"Let's consider *'where'* the statue could be," he started. "Augustus said that his Praetorian Guard had searched every warehouse, studio and shop where the statue might be hidden and found nothing. He thinks it's left the city."

"But how could they have gotten it out of the city unnoticed?" Rutilus asked.

"The sewers," Claudius said suddenly.

The other men looked at him curiously.

"It's something that I have been thinking about since our encounter with the Rat. What if he really did see something, but it was down in the sewers? Think about it. Some of Rome's sewers are quite large, large enough for a small boat. The thieves could have lowered the statue onto a boat and floated it out of the city through the underground sewers. In fact, it could be hidden in the sewers even now. I bet that's one place the Praetorians haven't looked."

Alexander looked frustrated. "I suppose it's possible, but how could we go about investigating it? The sewers cover a lot or area under Rome."

"Well, don't look to *me*," Agrippa said. "I've come with you this far, Alexander, but I draw the line at descending into the sewers."

The others laughed, but nodded their agreement. Alexander tried a new tack.

"As I said earlier, last night I made a list of everthing we've learned so far. How about if I recite it now and see if any new ideas materialize?

"Good idea, Alexander," Claudius nodded. "These events are harder to keep straight than a toga in the wind."

Alexander closed his eyes for a moment to organize his thoughts. Then he opened and began to recite from memory the list he had created the night before.

On the fifteenth day of July, the Ides, a man who appeared to be the Augur Lucius Servilius arrived at the temple late at night and insisted on taking the statue for a special procession to be given on the next day. He had a slave and a freedman with him and a team of professional art handlers who quickly packed up the statue and took it away on an ox cart.

"Stop there," Claudius held up his hand. "You're sure the priest said these men were professionals?"

"Yes," Alexander replied. "He said they had all the right

equipment for lowering the statue from its plinth, wrapping it, crating and transporting it. Apparently, they worked very quickly, which seems to suggest that they do this kind of work often."

"*Hmm*, even if they were professionals that could still cover a lot of people like sculptors and art dealers." Claudius noted. "There must be hundreds of those in Rome."

"And auctioneers. There are a lot of them, too." Agrippa added.

"And that's a problem," Alexander noted. "Augustus told me that the Praetorian Guard had been identifying and investigating every sculptor or other type of art handler in Rome. If the Praetorians have been unable to uncover anything, what hope have we? Does anyone here have a contact in the art world?"

The others shook their heads no.

"Well, that fact doesn't help much now, but it might later," Alexander concluded. "Our suspect must be someone with access to professional art handlers who have their own equipment and supplies. Let's come back to that one later.

"What do you think of the priest's identification of the man as Lucius Servilius?"

Claudius leaned forward. "Are you sure the priest said the man who took the statue was wearing a toga *trabea*, the maroon and purple striped toga of an *augur*?"

"Yes, that's what he said. He seemed quite sure of it. I asked him about his eyesight, but the priest insisted that it is still keen."

"Well, his eyesight wouldn't have to be that good to tell if the man was wearing an *augur's* robe," Rutilus added waving a wet hand for emphasis. "Now, *that's* a toga of a different color. There aren't going to many of those in Rome."

"The evidence does seem to point back to the *augur*," Claudius admitted. "Not that I think he would take it for personal reasons, but there *is* that chance of blackmail."

"I agree," Alexander nodded, "but Augustus said that he had cleared the *augur* because he wasn't even in Rome that day."

Rutilus looked pensive and held up a hand palm facing out. "Wait a moment. Something's wrong here. What day did you say the statue was taken?"

"The Ides."

"But, Alexander, that's the day we went to the Venus House -- the day I saw Lucius Servilius coming down from the third floor."

"Rutilus, are you sure?"

"Yes, I'm sure and you should be, too. Remember? You had just gotten the letter from your father saying that you had to return on the *nones* or 9th day of August. And, remember, *I* said 'Today is already the Ides' and then I counted how many days we had left."

Claudius knitted his brow. "Rutilus is right. I remember it, too, now that he says it."

Alexander shook his head looking perplexed.

"Then somebody is mistaken. Either Rutilus and the temple priest are mistaken about seeing the *augur* in Rome that day, or, Augustus is mistaken about the *augur* being out of Rome that day." He lowered his voice. "Do you think Augustus would cover for the *augur* for some reason?"

"*No*," Claudius said firmly. "Not with the statue involved. If Augustus said that Lucius Servilius was out of Rome, it could only be because Lucius Servilius provided him with some evidence indicating that it was true."

Alexander gazed at nothing for a moment pursing his lips. "Do you think Lucius Servilius *was* away from Rome and the man the priest saw was an *imposter*?"

"That would be difficult," Claudius replied. "The priest said that he wore the toga *trabea*, the maroon toga with the purple stripes. That could only be worn by an *augur* and there are *only sixteen* of them in Rome. It would *not* be easy to obtain one of their togas without someone noticing.

" ... And, you did say that the priest recognized him, right? Plus Rutilus recognized him. That's *two* men who say that Lucius Servilius *was* in Rome on the ides."

Alexander smacked his flat palm against the water. "Well, the man could not have been *both in* and *out* of Rome on the same day. We must discover which one it was, and he's not likely to talk to us. Any ideas?"

The friends had only begun to weigh ideas, when they had to quickly fall silent as three men with towels wrapped around their waists entered the room. Each remained lost in his own thoughts about how to find the statue.

Too late, they realized that they should have paid more attention to the men who had entered. One of the toweled men purposely squatted down behind Alexander.

"What are *you* doing here, *Jew*?" he sneered as he grabbed the back of Alexander's head and forced it down under the water.

Rutilus had been the first to realize what the man was up to and, as quickly as he could, he pulled himself up out of the water and ran to his friend's aid. One of the other two toweled men, a good head taller than Rutilus, met him half way there. He shoved Rutilus back, then slammed his head hard against the wall. Rutilus crumpled onto the floor unconscious.

Alexander was struggling with all of his might to free himself, but the man had him bent forward in the water and he couldn't swing his arms back far enough to make contact.

Both Agrippa and Claudius were now out of the water, but two toweled men blocked their way. They were big and muscular and carried themselves like soldiers.

"*Praetorians*," Agrippa hissed.

"Hey, look this one is a Jew, too," one of the men shouted pointing at Agrippa's naked form. Agrippa visibly winced.

The squatting man lifted Alexander's head out of the water and he came up sputtering and gasping for breath.

"We hear that you've been going around asking a lot of questions and making trouble, Jew. We don't like that and we're going to teach you a lesson."

He shoved Alexander's head under the water again. Agrippa began shouting and the man that blocked his way took a menacing step toward him. Suddenly, a strong authoritative voice rang out through the room.

"Let him up, *now*."

All three of the toweled men turned a surprised look on Claudius.

"My name is Tiberius Claudius Nero, member of the Imperial family. I *order* you to let him up now, or feel the anger of my family."

The two standing men looked to the third, who was still holding a thrashing Alexander under the water. He seemed momentarily taken aback, then his look turned ugly.

"Claudius, the fool. We've heard what Tiberius thinks about you. Don't give us any trouble or you'll join your Jew friend here."

"I don't care about Tiberius," Claudius replied. "Let him up, or you'll hear from my brother *Germanicus*."

The two standing men sucked in a breath. Germanicus was not only this year's Consul of the Senate, but he was also widely respected for his sense of fair play. They might not have feared Claudius, but messing with Germanicus was asking for trouble.

Claudius glanced down at Alexander who had ceased to struggle.

"Germanicus will *not* overlook this attack on his childhood friend, just as *Augustus will* retaliate for this outrage on *his client.*"

"Client?" the squatting man said as he pulled Alexander's head out and dropped it on the edge of the pool. "Nobody said anything about him being a client of Augustus."

"Well, *Sejanus knew,*" Agrippa shouted angrily. He thrust the toweled man in front of him aside and rushed to Alexander, who had started to slide back down into the pool.

The three toweled men stood there for a moment, apparently looking for a way to save face. But Claudius limped over and stood in front of the leader, his naked and dripping body shaking with anger.

"*Get. Out. Now.* And don't think that you've heard the last of this."

The toweled men turned and left.

"Hurry, Claudius. Help me pull him out. I don't think he's breathing."

Agrippa and Claudius each took an arm and pulled Alexander out onto the floor.

"I've got Alexander," said Claudius. "Go check on Rutilus."

He swung his bad leg over Alexander's prostrate form to straddle him and began to push hard on his chest and slap at his face. "Come on, Alexander, you're going to make it. You have to."

Finally, Alexander began to cough and spit up water.

"He's breathing!" Claudius yelled. "How's Rutilus?"

"Hit hard, but there's no blood. I think he's starting to come around."

For long minutes, Claudius and Agrippa sat next to their friends as they struggled to regain their composure. Alexander finally dragged himself over and leaned his back against the wall next to Rutilus.

"What happened?"

Agrippa filled him in on Rutilus' valiant effort and then Claudius' bold rescue.

"Thank you, Claudius," Alexander said quietly. "And you too, Rutilus." Rutilus mumbled something back through his hands.

"After all the times you've saved me, Alexander, I'm glad that I could finally help you in return." Then Claudius' face clouded. "But it almost wasn't enough. We nearly lost you, *both* of you. I meant what I said. Germanicus will hear from me this afternoon. Praetorians attacking a patrician and one of the First Citizen's own clients; this will *not* go unanswered."

Suddenly, the men were alerted by the sound of approaching footsteps and looked up apprehensively. But it was only their house slaves carrying towels and their bath kits. Amarantus was clearly disturbed to find his master on the floor looking pale, but said nothing in front of the others.

Alexander was tempted to forget the rest of the bath and go home, and he could tell that Rutilus was of the same mind. Claudius, however, insisted that they couldn't let thugs scare them off, so they finished their bath. While Agrippa's man continued to stay with their clothes in the outer room, the others three slaves stood guard as their masters went on to the sauna room where they hired staff from the baths to scrape the oil and sweat from their bodies.

No one brought up the Praetorians or the statue again until they were all dressed and ready to depart. Outside, Claudius agreed to hire a litter and take Rutilus home since he was still feeling groggy from the blow to his head. Agrippa also hired a litter to take him home. But Alexander decided that he and Amarantus would head home on foot in hopes that the exercise might help to clear his head.

As he was stepping into his litter, Agrippa turned back to Alexander. "So what do you plan to do next?" he asked.

Alexander still felt nauseated from choking on the dirt filled bath water. He looked at Rutilus who was being helped shakily into the litter, and then to the worried look on his servant's face.

"My plans," he replied, "are to go home and forget the statue."

His three friends stopped and looked back at him in surprise.

"At least for today," Alexander sighed. "I've had enough."

16
LAYING PLANS

"AMARANTUS, I think I will lie down while you're out buying food. Before you do that, I have a little errand I would like for you to run ... at the Venus House."

A couple of hours later, Alexander was awake and feeling more alert than when they had left the baths. He settled down to eat the dinner of stewed lentils that Amarantus placed in front of him.

"Any problems at the Venus House, Ranti?"

"No, Master, everything happened just as you directed."

"Good. In that case, I think that this afternoon I shall turn my attention to some of these messages from business associates that have been accumulating. These messages on top," he gestured at a pile of small papyri, "are men who I shall visit personally. You had better come with me. After this morning, I know I'll feel better if I have someone to watch my back."

Before they could leave, a messenger arrived bearing a scroll with Claudius' seal.

Ti. Claudius Nero to G. Julius Alexander. I wrote to Germanicus at once about the affair at the baths and he wants to discuss it with us personally. Germanicus has invited us to dinner tonight -- all of us, you, me, Rutilus and Agrippa. I knew my brother wouldn't let us down. Write back at once and assure me that you feel well enough to attend dinner tonight.

While the messenger waited, Alexander wrote back a reply indicating that he was honored by the invitation from the Consul, and that he would be there.   Once the messenger hurried off, Alexander turned back to Amarantus.

"We should leave at once before anything else happens to detain us."

But as luck would have it, the next detour was already at the door. As they started to leave his apartment, Alexander found the way blocked by someone preparing to rap on his door.   He recognized the man immediately as Agrippa's slave from the baths.

"Alexander," the man said. "Agrippa sent me to find you. He requests that you come to his house at once. I believe there has been some kind of trouble."

Trouble. Alexander blinked once then turned around and walked back into his apartment.   Couldn't he get through *one* afternoon – just one – in peace? Would that this cursed statue had never been stolen.

"Alexander?"   The slave's worried voice broke into his thoughts. "The prince is waiting. Will you come?"

Amarantus was giving him a worried look as well.

"Master, are you well?"

Alexander forced a smile. "I am. It's just that too much is happening right now. I have what fifteen or sixteen days left in Rome and they seem to be consumed with the trouble caused by this cursed missing statue. It is ... *trying.*"

He took a deep breath and nodded to Agrippa's slave. "Very well. I will go and hear what the prince has to say."

It was now mid-afternoon and the July sun that burned down on Rome had warmed the cobblestones under their feet as they made their way down the Capitoline Hill. As usual, Alexander had chosen to walk rather than take a litter, so Amarantus had divested him of his toga to make the going more bearable. As they walked along, Alexander noted that Amarantus kept lagging behind then quickly appearing at his side. After the third such time, Alexander turned to Amarantus as he trotted to catch up with him.

"Anyone following me?"

Amarantus shook his head. "I don't believe so, Master. If someone is tracking you today, he is very good at it. But I don't think there is anyone there. Still, after what happened at the baths, I don't want to take any chances." He reached down to his waist and his hand settled on the short club tucked into his belt.

Suddenly realizing his own lack of foresight, Alexander knew that he should have armed himself, too. But then, he glanced down and saw the knife that Amarantus had remembered to tuck into his own belt. Thank the Lord that Amarantus was keeping his wits about him. Alexander gave his servant a nod of approval and resumed walking.

They reached Agrippa's house on the Quirinal Hill without incident. Alexander, wearing his toga again, was ushered into the atrium to wait while he was being announced to Agrippa. He had hoped for a quick greeting with Berenice, but learned from the steward that she was out of Rome visiting Agrippa's older brother Herod.

The original slave returned and escorted Alexander into Agrippa's study. Alexander jerked his head to Amarantus motioning to follow him in case he may be needed in his role as Alexander's private secretary, or as a messenger even.

Agrippa's servant had mentioned trouble and had pressed Alexander to come at once, so Alexander entered the study expecting to find the prince looking worried. Instead, he was surprised to find Agrippa almost negligently reviewing some papers and looking quite complacent. Agrippa rose and smiled as Alexander entered.

"Ahh, Alexander. How about this dinner with the Consul? And it's not even Claudius' birthday for another week. This should do much for our reputations."

Alexander frowned in return. "Agrippa, *what has happened*? Your man says there's been some trouble. He said that I should come at once."

"Oh, slaves, you know how they over-dramatize," Agrippa waved his hand in dismissal. "We *have been summoned*, however. Apparently, there have been several unfortunate incidents over in the Jewish quarter across the Tiber. It started out small, but it seems that things are escalating and the people are getting scared. The leaders of the synagogue have asked us to come meet them tomorrow night to discuss this situation."

"Which synagogue?"

"The one sponsored by my namesake, the Synagogue of the Agrippesians. But that's just the meeting place. I have an impression that several congregations will be joining us there."

Alexander furrowed his brow. "Agrippa, what do they expect from us?"

"Umm, I think some reassurance that something's being done to resolve this situation. ... Don't shake your head, Alexander. I know that you haven't found the missing statue yet, but you have made progress. You've eliminated some suspects and identified a few more. These are *our people* and they're looking for a little hope, Alexander. Don't deny them that."

Alexander let out a long breath. "I understand, Agrippa. It's just that I'm getting so frustrated, and I'm running out of ideas."

Agrippa tilted his head. "Huh, I *may* have something new on that, but first can we go through everything again? You started to do that at the baths before we were so rudely interrupted by those Praetorian *merdas*. I want to make sure I understand everything before we meet with Germanicus or head for the Synagogue."

Alexander started to shake his head no. "I wrote it down, but I don't have it with me."

"I have it, master," Amarantus said softly as he pulled a papyrus scroll out of his pouch. He returned his master's questioning look. "I thought you might need it. Plus, I was not sure that this should be left on your desk. Remember that when he came to your apartment, Sejanus insisted on waiting for you in your office. What he *did* in there... I don't know."

Agrippa slapped his palm on the top of his desk in delight. "Really, Alexander, I've said it before. Your man is just too good. I need someone just like that. I bet he could figure out how to keep my mother out of my affairs. I may have to *insist* that you sell him to me before you leave Rome."

Alexander was already intently perusing the scroll and ignored Agrippa's little outburst. Amarantus, stepped back and fixed his eyes on the floor.

"I think I have it," Alexander said as he looked up at Agrippa. "Most of the words are abbreviated in the Greek style, but I can remember it all now. It's a summary of what happened each day since the ides. Why don't I just read it aloud?"

> On the fifteenth day of July, the Ides, a man who appeared to be the Augur Lucius Servilius arrived at the temple late at night and took the statue of Victory.
>
> The next day, the 16th, there was no procession with the Victory statue and it was not returned to the temple. Lucius Servilius refused to see Vatinius, so the priest went to Augustus.

The 17th. *Some thugs attacked the Jew, Elias, in the Forum and accused him of stealing a statue. However, the disappearance of the Victory was not general knowledge yet. Obviously, someone knew.*

The 18th. *That morning word spread throughout Rome of the statue's disappearance. That afternoon, my client Theon was arrested.*

The 19th. *I visited Theon in prison and learned that the Senator Gnaeus Pulcher may have been interested in owning the Victory statue.*

The 20th. *I asked you, Claudius, and Rutilus for help and we planned to sneak into the home of Pulcher which I did the next day with no luck.*

The 22nd. *The Praetorian Sejanus took me to see Augustus. Sejanus hinted that he may have been passing bad information to implicate Jews.*

Augustus said that the augur Lucius Servilius could not have taken the statue because he had not been in Rome on the ides. But Rutilus reminded us that he had seen the augur at the Venus House on the ides. Augustus ordered me to continue my search.

Today. *We found the informant called the Rat at the chariot races, but didn't really learn anything new from him. Some men who probably were Praetorians attacked us in the baths and tried to warn us off the search for the statue.*

Alexander frowned at the papyrus in his hand as he came to the end of his list. "Not much to go on, is there? I hope you have something else, Agrippa."

"Well, Alexander, that's the other reason why I wanted to see you. I may have a lead for more information, but I'll need your … *uhh, errr* … help. Sit down."

Alexander pulled up a chair. "So, will we be breaking into some other art collector's house?"

Agrippa smiled. "No, nothing like that. Do you recall at the baths this morning I said that I may know someone who can get us some inside information about the Praetorian Guard? Or, more particularly, that little faction in the Guard that seems to have some problem with Jews?"

"Yes, I remember. Have you found someone?"

"I have. At least, I've found someone who is willing to try … for a *price*."

Alexander sat back and crossed his arms. "I see. Who is this man?"

"Unfortunately, I can't tell you. He insists on that. No one may know his identity, but myself. He's scared, Alexander. Those Praetorian Guardsmen are mean as you have plenty of reason to know. If he gets caught spying on them, he's a dead man."

Alexander shrugged. "So you're suggesting that a little silver will bolster his courage?"

Suddenly, Agrippa seemed very interested in a design painted on the far wall. "*Well,* … not silver exactly."

"Then what?"

"Gold. Two pieces."

"What?!" Alexander was out of his chair leaning over Agrippa's desk. "Two pieces of gold? And I suppose you expect *me* to pay it, no doubt. Why in the Greek Hades should I pay some man who I don't know that kind of money?"

Agrippa leaned forward and this time he met Alexander's eyes.

"Listen, Alexander, answer me this. Do you believe those Praetorian Guard are mixed up in this somehow, particularly Sejanus?"

Alexander thought for a moment. "I do. I don't know if they took the statue, are covering up for who took it, or are just plain looking to start trouble for Jews. But, yes, I believe the Praetorians are in this somehow."

"I agree" Agrippa nodded back. "And, Alexander, *if we* try to pursue the Praetorians ourselves, you know that we'll be lucky to escape with our lives and still be none the wiser. *We* don't have a way to spy on the Praetorians. This man is our best chance to find out what's going on, and *I* can *vouch* for him personally."

Alexander sat back and considered for a moment, then gave a curt nod. "You're right. Bribery is about the only thing we haven't tried yet. We haven't even known whom we should bribe. … And as you know, I *can* afford it. But I don't want to give him both coins up front. We'll give him one now, and he'll get the other if and when he brings us some useful information. Agreed?"

"Agreed," Agrippa confirmed. "It's the right thing to do, Alexander. We had run out of ideas."

"No," Alexander replied softly. "I am pursuing one other."

Agrippa looked at him questioningly, but Alexander said no more.

Home, once again, and Alexander sought out the blissful solitude of his office. But soon he found that quiet time was not what he needed; he really needed to talk. So he called Amarantus into his office and talked about his meeting that day with Agrippa.

Much to his surprise, Amarantus very delicately asked if Agrippa could be trusted with the gold pieces. Alexander laughed out loud.

"A good question, Ranti. I don't expect to see a return of any money I've ever loaned to Agrippa so far, but, yes, I believe that Agrippa can be trusted with this gold. He may not be terribly responsible about much else, but Agrippa *does* take his responsibilities as a Jewish prince very seriously. And if any of us would know the right person to bribe for information about the Praetorians, it *would be* Agrippa. I shall take him the gold when we dine with Germanicus tonight."

Alexander tilted his head in further thought. "Agrippa *is* our Jewish prince. I suppose I had better come up with a suitable farewell gift for him before I leave Rome."

He did not notice as his slave's eyes widened in alarm.

17

GERMANICUS

FORMAL dinners in the Summer-time always began slightly later than in Winter, because of the longer hours of daylight. So nearly five hours after noon, Alexander presented himself at the home of Germanicus. Alexander was the first to arrive and the steward showed him to a seat in the atrium. Within minutes, Claudius and Rutilus walked in together with Agrippa no far behind them.

Claudius looked at Alexander and saw the strain of the day showing on his face and spoke softly.

"Alexander, I have a good feeling about this dinner tonight. If my brother Germanicus can't help with this problem, then I don't know who can. Oh, and Alexander, his wife Agrippina has gone to Antium to get away from the Summer heat. So it's going to be a business dinner, men only."

Now Alexander genuinely smiled. He knew how much Claudius hated to attend dinners with his wife Urgulanilla. It had been an arranged marriage and there was no sense of love, or even companionship, between the couple. No doubt, Germanicus had thought of this as well when he had arranged the men-only dinner. A good man, Germanicus. Perhaps he could help at that.

As they relaxed in the atrium, Germanicus put in a quick appearance and greeted them warmly.

"Claudius and friends, I apologize for the delay, but

something has come up, a matter of State. I must take a few minutes to address it before I can join you. But I did want a quick word before the other guests come. Yes, yes, I know," he said at Claudius' look of disappointment. "I had hoped to keep it private, too; but, you know the demands of a Consul," he shrugged.

"There are four others coming to give us the standard nine diners. But I'm sure they will eat and leave early, since I told them that we would be forgoing the usual entertainment. I want you to stay behind so we can talk after my social duties to these other guests have been satisfied. Agreed?"

The four friends murmured their agreement and Germanicus hurried off to complete his Consular duties.

"I wonder who else will be coming?" Agrippa thought out loud. "You know, I do believe this is my first dinner where the host was also the Consul and the host's immediate family were not present. It will be interesting to see where Germanicus places each of us on the couches."

"Well, I don't care if I am put at the end of the third couch," Rutilus responded. "I'm just glad to be here. Mother was absolutely ecstatic when she heard that I was dining with one of this year's Consuls. She said that my stepfather, Sextus Fadius, was never invited to dine with the Consul Germanicus. She seemed so happy that I didn't point out to her that Sextus Fadius left for Gaul shortly after Germanicus took office."

Before long, they were joined by one of Germanicus' freedman, then a Senator who had brought along a young man whom he was obviously sponsoring in Roman society. The Senator looked around the gathering with ill concealed distaste.

"It was my impression that the Consul was dining tonight with his boyhood friends."

Claudius sucked in a breath and reddened.

"Well, let's just say that the Consul was fortunate to have an interesting childhood," Agrippa quipped back with a bland smile.

They were soon joined by Germanicus and an overweight and perspiring Senator whom Alexander recognized as one of the senior Metellii.

"Ahh, good. We're all here," Germanicus remarked. "Have we all met each other?"

He went around making introductions. When he came to the snobbish Senator, the man introduced his protégé with a great deal of pomp. The young man instantly went into action praising Germanicus, his house, and was beginning to flatter his family when Germanicus cut him short with a curt, but polite acknowledgement. Alexander smiled to himself. If Germanicus' cooks put as much honey into their desserts as the young man had oozed into his words, they would all be going home with bellyaches tonight.

Germanicus clapped both hands together. "Well, friends, I hope you have come hungry. Shall we begin?"

The guests followed their host into the dining room and waited to be assigned their places. The three dining couches were arranged in the usual horseshoe pattern. The couch at the head was usually reserved for the Consul and his most distinguished guests with the one to his right designated for the host's family and the left for the lesser guests.

"Since my esteemed fellow Consul is not with us tonight, I believe I shall take the place of the Consul. Claudius, as the next senior family member would you please take the place on my right and help me to play host?"

Claudius smiled gratefully at his brother and moved to his place.

"And Senator Metellus you'll be at my left, of course."

Germanicus seated Alexander on the family couch next to Claudius and his freedman on the end. The unpleasant Senator, he placed on the other end of the head couch. Agrippa was first on the guest couch and, in a surprising move, Rutilus was placed next to him in the center with the flattering young man on the end in the least distinguished position. Alexander noted the unpleasant Senator frown at this and knew that he had taken it as a slight.

After the slaves had washed each diner's hands and feet, Germanicus called for the aperitif of *mulsum*, the honeyed wine served in a shallow double handled bowl. The bowl was passed around and each guest took a sip to clear his palate. Then a slave set up the central serving table and the starters began to arrive.

Germanicus may have called this a simple business dinner, but he had not spared on the delicacies that were now being placed before them. Besides the usual quail eggs and bowls of black and green olives, the servants brought out roasted fig peckers in herb mayonnaise, cucumber salad marinated in vinegar and honey with mint, and roast leek and cabbage rolls.

"Delicious," Agrippa remarked appreciatively.

"I'm glad you are enjoying it," Germanicus responded. "Oh, Agrippa and Alexander, there's no pig on the menu tonight. I had my chef consult yours Agrippa. I think everything he serves should be suitable."

Agrippa and Alexander both expressed their sincere appreciation at his thoughtfulness. Few Roman hosts cared about the particular dietary requirements of Jews, so Jews invited to Roman homes had adapted in different ways. Some simply ate what was placed before them, but both Agrippa and Alexander had learned to discreetly select their helpings so as to stick to vegetables and fowl and other dishes that appeared safe.

"You don't eat pig?" the unpleasant Senator asked. "Then you must be Jews. I couldn't tell from your names."

Before either man could answer, the Senator's young protégé decided it was time to slip in what he thought was a witty remark.

"*Jews, ehhh?* I sure hope you're not with the ones that stole the statue. Otherwise, I guess the Consul here had better be checking his art collection when the dinner is over."

He grinned at his fellow diners waiting for their chuckles, but the room had suddenly grown completely silent.

"*Y-y-you* ...," Claudius began to stammer in anger, but Germanicus reached out and squeezed his brother's forearm and turned himself to the end of the couch.

"Young man, not only have you just insulted my guests, but as their host and friend you have insulted *me* twice over."

The young man eyes widened and he made to speak, but Germanicus cut in.

"I'm going to assume that you spoke out of ignorance and not malice, so allow me to *educate* you.

"Marcus Julius Agrippa here, that is *Prince* Agrippa, is the grandson of Herod the Great, who was a very close friend of Augustus's. Agrippa's family was pivotal in ensuring Caesar's victory in the Alexandrian War several decades ago, and since then they have been recognized as loyal friends to Rome."

Germanicus shifted on the couch as he waved his hand in a gesture towards Alexander.

"Gaius Julius Alexander comes from a distinguished and noble blood line. His family was also important to Caesar's success so Caesar gave them citizenship as a token of Rome's friendship. Augustus has *personally* chosen Alexander here to succeed his father as his *Alabarch* in Egypt.

"And so you see, when you insult these men, you not only insult *them* and *me*, you also insult their *patron* Augustus. I hope you will bear that in mind before you offer such opinions so freely again."

The young man appeared utterly devastated as he mumbled an abject apology.

"That's it!"

Startled, all eyes turned to Senator Metellus, who continued as if it were part of the normal flow of conversation.

"That's *why* I'm here tonight. 'Couldn't remember at all until I heard the word 'patron' and then it popped right into my head. I asked the Consul to invite me here tonight because he told me that *you* would be here, young Rutilus."

"Me?" Now all eyes turned onto Rutilus, who appeared completely flabbergasted by the comment.

"Yes, *you*. It's about that man of yours, that sculptor Achilles. Can't you do *something* about him?"

"Why? What has happened, sir?"

"It's what *hasn't* happened; that's the problem. We commissioned a new sculpture from him for the garden, some Greek hero or another. It's a big piece. My wife had the garden completely redone to show it off to its best advantage. The problem is that he promised it no later than two days after the Ides, in time for the big Metellii family ceremony, and it never arrived."

Rutilus frowned. "That doesn't sound like Achilles. He's usually very reliable for an artist."

"That's why I hired him. He's done work for my family in the past and he's always been excellent. So yesterday, I sent a man around to check on him and he had cleared out. Packed up his whole shop and left town. Oh, he left some story about having to attend to his sick mother, or something like that. So tell me, son, *where* is he and what are *you going to do* about this?"

"Well sir, I, uh, don't know," Rutilus stammered.

"You're his patron aren't you? He shouldn't have left town without notifying you."

"No, actually I am *not* his patron. My stepfather Sextus Fadius is."

"I thought *you* were. Isn't he the freedman of your grandfather on your mother's side?"

Rutilus looked embarrassed. "He is, and he served our family long and well. When my father died, the patronage did fall to me. But you see, my … *errr* … father did not leave me in the best position, *errr*, financially. I found that I could do little to help Achilles, so I passed him to my stepfather. Sextus Fadius is a Senator and can do more to help a client."

"I see. Sextus Fadius still in Gaul?"

"He is. I'm sorry that I can't be of more help Senator Metellus. I'll be happy to check and see if Achilles left any word with my mother. He was quite close to her family when she was young, and may have thought to leave word with her."

"*Jupiter's balls,*" Metellus exclaimed, and then, "Oh good, here comes the main course."

The rest of the meal passed uneventfully. The unpleasant Senator was the first to leave, taking his rather subdued protégé along with him. Senator Metellus followed not long after, and then Germanicus' freedman left, as well.

"*Phew,* alone at last," Germanicus said. "When Agrippina left for Antium three days ago, I thought that things would slow down around here. Rome is usually so quiet in the Summer."

"How is Agrippina?" Claudius asked. "When is the baby due?"

Germanicus smiled. "I suppose you all have heard that Agrippina is with child again. She's due in about a month. This will be our third."

Alexander, Agrippa and Rutilus expressed their congratulations.

"What will you name it?"

"I think it's going to be a boy," Germanicus said. "And if it is, we're going to call him Gaius. I've got a feeling about this one, Claudius. This boy is going to be special. I can feel it. Speaking of children, it sounds like it may be your turn soon, Alexander. I hear you're betrothed."

"Oh, don't mention it to him," Agrippa cut in. "His father set up the betrothal without telling him and he's still sulking."

Germanicus nodded. "I understand. Arranged marriages can be difficult." He gave a small sideway glance at Claudius. "Agrippina and I have been lucky. ….. So how about you, Agrippa? Isn't it time that you started making another generation of little princelings?"

"Me? I'm still waiting for my bride to grow up," remarked Agrippa.

That got everyone's attention. "What? Agrippa, are you betrothed?"

"Yes, I am -- more or less. If you think it's hard for you imperials to find a suitable spouse, you should try being the grandson of Herod the Great. Fortunately, my Aunt Salampsio and Great Uncle Phasael have finally come up with a wife for me. Her name is Cypros and she's, well … I forget how old, but she's still a child. I've got a few years left as a bachelor," he grinned.

After a bit more catching up on family and friends, Germanicus turned the subject to the missing statue and the Praetorian Guard.

"I was very concerned when I received Claudius's letter, but it was a little short on details. What's happening? I want to hear everything."

The four friends took turns telling Germanicus everything that had happened from the arrest of Alexander's client, Theon, to the attack in the baths. Germanicus listened carefully, occasionally stopping them with questions. When they were done, he leaned forward on his couch resting his chin on his fist in thought.

"Hmmm, I know you're just trying to help your client, Alexander, but this is a dangerous game you've been drawn into. The good news is that Gnaeus Pulcher has been cleared and he doesn't seem to know who you are. If Pulcher had decided that you should be drowned in the baths, *he* would have succeeded.

"The immediate threat appears to be that particular group within the Praetorian Guard, for whatever reason they have. Here is my problem: *'Where's your proof?'*"

"*Proof?*" Alexander and Claudius looked blankly at each other. "What do you mean proof?"

"First you tell me that Sejanus said that some of the Praetorian Guardsmen are deliberately trying to implicate the Jews. Where's your proof for this?"

Agrippa cut in. "Sejanus told Alexander in the litter."

"So where are your witnesses?"

Alexander jerked back in surprise at the question. "There weren't any. It was just the two of us in the litter."

"Exactly," Germanicus said with a nod. "Now, take the incident at the baths. Your attackers were naked except for towels. How do you know they were Praetorians? Did they identify themselves as such? Did you recognize any of them? ... No?"

Claudius looked crestfallen. "Germanicus, don't you believe us?"

Germanicus put his hand on his brother's shoulder. "Of course, I believe you. I would believe any one of you, long before I'd believe a single word from Sejanus. It's simply a question of proof. Remember, we are speaking of the First Citizen's personal bodyguard and Sejanus *is* the *son* of the Praetorian Prefect. I can't do anything officially without proof."

"What about *unofficially*?" Agrippa asked shrewdly.

Germanicus appeared to ponder this for a while. "Difficult. I don't see that there's much I can do right now, but I'll keep thinking. ... Claudius, I see that you're disappointed, but you must realize that my position is not as strong as you might think. Consuls have no real power anymore. The real power resides with just two men, Augustus and Tiberius.

"Augustus is a good man, but he's seventy-four years old. He won't be around much longer, and then all the power will go to Tiberius. Yes, Tiberius is my adopted father, but, remember that he did not *want* to adopt me. Livia and Augustus forced it. Tiberius doesn't want *me* as his heir. He wants his own son Drusus, but Drusus is younger than I am. Right now, *I'm* standing in *his* way."

"Germanicus!" Claudius cried. "Are you in danger?"

"No, no, that's unlikely. I'm too popular with the people and, of course, Livia supports me. My point was simply that right now *I* don't have that much influence in the right circles. On the other hand, *Sejanus has*. Tiberius respects him and places a lot of trust in him."

Germanicus shrugged and smiled almost sheepishly.

"I'm sorry Claudius, Alexander, Agrippa, Rutilus. I haven't given up. I'll think about it and see if I can find a way to help you unofficially. Bring me some proof and I'll do all I can to help you officially as well.

"... Until then, I must advise you most strongly, '*Watch your back*.'"

18

A SCULPTOR

"I can't believe that Germanicus couldn't help us," Claudius shook his head sadly.

The night was still young, so the friends had decided to meet back at Agrippa's house and discuss their conversation after dinner.

"I suspect it may be more of the case that he couldn't *promise* to help us," Agrippa suggested.

"What do you mean?"

"Claudius, *we* know your brother better than most men do, having grown up with him. And Germanicus the *man* is very much like Germanicus the *boy*."

The others looked back at Agrippa in confusion.

"Think about it. Would Germanicus the boy have overlooked a violent attack on his brother and his brother's companions?"

It was Alexander who answered. "*No.* No, he would not. Claudius, remember all those fights we got into when we were boys? Most of the time Germanicus left us to handle them ourselves, but a few times we lost; we lost badly. Whenever that happened, the boys who had beaten us would turn up a couple of days later pretty battered themselves. Germanicus never said anything, but I always knew he had done it. Those same boys would never mess with us again."

A look of realization dawned on Claudius face. "You're right, Alexander. I guess I always assumed that Mother had said something to their parents, or maybe Livia had. But how could they have? We never told them about it."

"Exactly," Agrippa confirmed. "That was his style. Germanicus has always had a sense of fair play. He didn't like bullies then, and I doubt he cares much for them now. Look at how he stuck up for Alexander and me at dinner. You know that was meant for that sour faced Senator just as much as it was for his little snot companion."

"You're right," Claudius nodded to Agrippa. "Germanicus is a good brother, isn't he?"

"*The best.* And Claudius, a Consul may not be able to make a show of calling out Rome's newest bullies, but I would be very surprised if Germanicus sat back and did nothing at all."

The other young men considered and then nodded in agreement.

That seemingly settled, Alexander brought up the topic that had been on his mind for much of the night.

"So, Rutilus, what about this sculptor?"

Rutilus rolled his eyes. "That was so embarrassing, wasn't it? It's bad enough being Rome's poorest patrician without having it thrown in your face at your first important dinner party."

"No, I mean can you tell us about him? Did you say his name is Achilles?"

"Yes, Achilles. He was born to a slave in my grandfather's house."

Agrippa grinned at this. "You mean your grandfather named his slave Achilles? After the hero?"

Rutilus smiled and nodded. "Yes, it was my grandfather who named him that. It seems that when Achilles was still crawling, he got angry when my grandfather wouldn't give him a bite of honey cake. So he bit him on the back of his foot. Grandfather named him Achilles after his own vulnerable heel."

The others chuckled at that.

"So how did your grandfather's slave become a sculptor?" Alexander prodded.

Rutilus rubbed his chin.

"Well, from what I understand, early on, Achilles showed a particular liking for painting. The problem was that he did his painting on the walls. And since his mother worked in the kitchens, his paint tended to be whatever sauce they were having that day.

"My grandfather got fed up with the mess and gave the child some old wax tablets to draw on. When Achilles started showing some real talent, Grandfather apprenticed him to an artist. He had hoped that Achilles would learn to paint wall murals, but it seemed his real talent lay in sculpting. Achilles stayed with my mother's family until he was about thirty and had earned enough to buy his freedom. Then he opened his own shop. … Why do you ask?"

"I'm not sure. It's just that we're looking for a missing sculpture and tonight we hear about a missing sculptor."

"Oh, Alexander, *not* Achilles. He would never get involved in something like that. Besides, you heard Senator Metellus. His work is excellent and he is in demand by many of the best families. Achilles didn't need the money."

Alexander shrugged. "I know it's a stretch. But we do know that there were professionals involved with moving the statue. Perhaps Achilles has *heard* something. I'm sure sculptors must gossip amongst themselves the way they do in other professions."

Rutilus looked suspicious. "I'll ask Mother if she's heard anything about where he's gone, but really, Alexander, there's nothing strange about a man leaving Rome for awhile to take care of his sick mother. You have no reason to be suspecting my family's freedman."

"I know, I know, Rutilus, and I am sorry. I guess I am just getting desperate for leads. Still, if you don't mind, I'd like to pursue the gossip angle. Do you know where Achilles' shop is located?"

"Sure, it's down in the Subura."

"Are there other sculptors in the area?"

"Yes, at least one or two right on the same block."

"In that case, Rutilus, would you take me there tomorrow? I'll bring some extra silver and we'll see if anyone knows anything they might be willing to sell us."

"... *All right*, Alexander. As long as you're not trying to accuse our freedman, I'll be happy to help if I can."

"Excellent," Agrippa added with a nod towards Claudius. "Let us know what you learn."

The young men parted company a short time later with Alexander confirming his appointment to meet Rutilus the following morning for a trip to the Subura. Before leaving, he picked up his servant Amarantus who had been waiting near the kitchens. On the way back to his apartment on the Capitoline, Alexander filled Amarantus in on the night's events.

They had walked in silence for awhile when Amarantus asked hesitantly, "Master, does it surprise you that Rutilus never mentioned that his family's freedman is a sculptor?"

Alexander frowned slightly, creasing his forehead. "Yes, yes, it does a little. It seems this Achilles might have been able to offer us some insight into Rome's art world. But perhaps Rutilus did not think of him because he gave him up as a client to Sextus Fadius years ago. Or perhaps, he did not want to bring his grandfather's freedman into this.   If word got out that we had questioned a sculptor, no matter how innocently, it might have caused trouble for the man."

Alexander seemed to consider it a moment longer. "Well, in any case, it's not worth puzzling over. It's not like I suspect Rutilus of stealing the statue. He's done nothing but try to help me since this whole mess began, and at the baths he suffered for it, too."

***

The following morning, Alexander presented himself at the home of Rutilus. He had hoped for a glimpse of Rutila, but she was nowhere in sight.   Instead, it was Aemelia who accompanied Rutilus into the atrium. After their initial greetings, Aemelia came directly to the subject that was on her mind.

"Alexander, Rutilus has told me that you have been inquiring after Achilles. Do you suspect him of something?"

"No, Aemelia, not at all. I was simply hoping that he might be able to give me some general information about art collectors in Rome. My investigation is not going well, and I was hoping a little insight might give me some new ideas."

Aemelia let out a sigh of relief. "I hope you mean that. Achilles is a good man. I would be very sad to see him, and thus indirectly my family, drawn into this scandal. ... In any case, as you have already learned, Achilles has left Rome for awhile to care for his mother."

"Did he contact you then?"

"Yes, briefly. Since Sextus Fadius is out of Rome, Achilles sent me a short note explaining his absence. ... It was a good time for this to happen. I'm afraid my husband can be a rather demanding patron and may not have allowed him to go."

"No?"

"Perhaps. Perhaps not. You know that my husband is an ambitious man, and having one of Rome's more favored sculptors as a client has enabled him to strike deals. I'm afraid he has insisted that Achilles take on a few jobs that he did not want, this statue for the Metellii for example."

Alexander was not surprised to hear that Sextus Fadius would use his own client ruthlessly for political advantage. Achilles had probably been happy for a chance to get out of Rome for a while.

"Did Achilles happen to say where he was going?"

"Oh yes, he's gone to his mother's farm out in the country. He has always been close to his mother."

"Where in the country? Perhaps, if it is not far, I still may be able to interview him, discreetly of course."

Aemelia looked thoughtful. "I'm not sure. When my father died, he freed Achilles' mother in his will. She married a retired soldier and they moved to Ostia. Sometime after that, I heard that they had bought a small farm in the country, but I don't recall where exactly."

"Oh well," Alexander shrugged. "It was just a thought. Rutilus has probably told you that we're headed down to his block in the *Subura*. There are other sculptors there; perhaps questioning one of them may give me a lead."

"Well, I wish you both luck, but, Alexander, please remember not to say anything that would cast aspersions on Achilles. My family has very little left, but we still have our respectability."

"I understand, Aemelia, and I promise I will be very careful what I say."

With a smile and a quick peck on her son's cheek, Aemelia

was gone. The two young men, with Amarantus following, crossed to the west side of the Palatine. The quickest way to the *Subura* was to head down to the Forum, then pick up a road that led northeast toward the valley that lay between the Esquiline, Viminal, and Quirinal Hills.

The young men chatted about the previous evening as they walked.

"Alexander, that was really impressive what Germanicus said about you last night. I didn't realize that your family was so important, rich of course, but not that important. And you are to follow your father as Alabarch?"

Alexander shrugged. "That's what Augustus told me, but I had no idea of that until he said it. I guess I assumed my father would keep me here to look after the family's interests in Rome."

"What exactly is the Alabarch anyway? Is he some sort of tax collector?"

"*The Lord forbid*," Alexander countered with a smile. "Tax collectors are about as well liked in Egypt as they are elsewhere in the Empire. You should read my brother Philo's opinions on tax collectors. If my father were one, I think it would cause a family rift."

"I'm sorry, Alexander. I didn't mean to imply that..."

"No apologies needed, Rutilus. People sometimes make some interesting assumptions about the meaning of the Alabarch since it is a word that simply doesn't exist outside of Egypt.

"*.... Hmm*, I'll have to ask my father if he knows what the original meaning of the Alabarch was. It's the '*chief of the alab,*' obviously, but what is the *alab*? I think there is a village in Egypt called *Alabaston* ... and, of course, there is considerable mining of *alabaster*. ... but I'm not sure what either of those would have to do with testing gold.

"You see, that is what the Alabarch does, Rutilus – assays

gold. As you may know, there are important gold mines in both Egypt and Nubia. Augustus had to appoint someone to test the gold purity and then stamp it so everyone would know they could trust the quality of his Roman gold."

Rutilus gave Alexander an appraising look. "So, you're telling me that your job as Alabarch is going to be to sit around and handle *gold* all day long?"

Alexander laughed. "I doubt there will be enough gold to keep me busy *every* day. Most of my time will probably be spent on the family estates. As you know my family grows a lot of the wheat and dates that we eat here in Rome."

"Still, Alexander, spending time getting to handle all of that gold is a job *I* sure wouldn't mind having. I never understood that was what an Alabarch does."

Alexander shrugged. "I guess not many people do. Augustus doesn't allow his family or the senators to get anywhere near Egypt's gold supply. And since there is no Alabarch outside of Egypt, people tend to just guess what one might be. I've heard people guess tax collector, census taker – even Jewish lord as if such a thing existed in Egypt."

Alexander smiled and jabbed a finger towards Rutilus. "Oh, I should tell you my personal favorite. I was at some sort of public lecture and overhead a *would-be* philosopher declaiming that since 'alabarch' rhymes with 'arabarch,' then they must be the same thing."

Rutilus shook his head. "That is … *stupid.*"

Alexander laughed. "Indeed it is. It just shows how little Romans understand of the provinces. Now the *arabarch*, or the '*chief of the Arabs*,' really *is* a tax collector and there are lots of them. They're not just in Egypt; they're in provinces all over the region. Most of *the arabarchs* are *not* Roman citizens."

Alexander wrinkled his nose making it clear what he thought of *arabarchs.*

"There is only *one* Alabarch at a time," he continued "and he is *always* a Roman citizen appointed by Augustus directly."

Rutilus thought about that. "Isn't Egypt Rome's largest source of gold right now?"

"I believe it is. There is supposed to be gold in the mountains of Spain, but I think they are still figuring out to mine for it."

Rutilus blew out a long breath. "*Wheew*, I guess you would have to be a pretty important person for Augustus to want you to become his Alabarch."

Alexander returned a rueful smile. "I know it sounds grand, Rutilus, but it doesn't really mean anything here in Rome. Here, I am just an ordinary citizen with a provincial name and not even so much as a narrow purple stripe on my tunic to indicate nobility. Look at you, on the other hand. You are descended from patricians and Senators. In Rome, *that* is all that matters."

"I suppose," Rutilus answered slowly. "But without money, my noble ancestry doesn't do me much good." He grinned at Alexander. "I do believe that I would rather have your family's money over my ancestry any day. ...

"... *Hey look*, we're almost there."

The two young men had been walking at a good pace and now found themselves in the tangled maze of streets and alleys of the valley that lay between Rome's Esquiline and Viminal Hills. The Subura was Rome's most densely populated region encompassing a wide range of artisans, foreign businessmen and Rome's urban poor.

Rutilus and Alexander stopped talking in order to concentrate on weaving their way through the throngs of people bustling through the narrow streets – all the while keeping a look-out for cut-purses. Although both men had abandoned their togas for the day, the fineness of their tunics and Rutilus' red patrician boots were a dead give-away for anyone looking for a likely by-passer to rob. Alexander was glad that they had Amarantus following behind them bearing a stout club.

"Are you sure you know the way, Rutilus?" Alexander asked gazing around at the tumbled mass of multi-storied tenements and portable vendor stalls.

"Sure, I do. My father used to bring me here as a boy. Achilles has kept the same shop for nearly 20 years."

Alexander nodded and then moved to follow directly behind Rutilus with a wary Amarantus falling into line behind him. After a few minutes, Rutilus turned onto a little side street, if one could call it that since it ended after about ten buildings.

The street looked like much of the rest of the Subura, except that there were no temporary stalls set up. In fact, the block looked a bit more upscale than most. It was lined with the usual apartment buildings ranging from three to five stories high. Most sported fresh coats of paint and many of the apartments had cheery colored flowers on the balconies. The first floor of every building seemed to be devoted to shops with counters and the telltale pallets of supplies spilling out into the street.

Rutilus looked around him with a smile. "This is it. I used to have a lot of fun when Father brought me here. Achilles would let me chisel on broken pieces of marble and pretend I was sculpting scenes of heroes and gods. Then I would get into the paints and by the time I was done my work was a true monstrosity. But Father would always nod and make some comment like 'Ah, it is much like the Parthian style.'"

"A happy memory," Alexander laughed. "Have you been here recently?"

"No, not for many years. I don't think I've been here since my father died. The block looks almost the same as I remember. I bet a lot of the same shops are here, although I doubt anyone would remember me after all this time."

Alexander made a decision. "Let's begin with the shop of Achilles. Perhaps he has returned, or sent a man to run it in his absence."

But the shop of Achilles was closed and appeared to be locked up tight. To be sure, Alexander had Amarantus bang on the door and shout for the owner within.

At the noise, a man came hurrying out of the next shop down.

"Here, here, what is all this noise? This is an honest neighborhood and we don't tolerate…"

He stopped as he caught a good look at the young men. "Oh, it's you, young Rutilus. What brings you around here today?"

Rutilus looked back at the merchant in surprise. "So you recognize me then?"

The man gave him a quizzical look, "'Course I recognize you. Why shouldn't I?"

Rutilus just shrugged in response. "Alexander, this is Diogenes. He's a sculptor, too. 'Guess you've had your shop here about as long as Achilles' has, haven't you?"

"Longer, I'm the senior man on the block now that the old Egyptian on the corner has passed on."

"Then perhaps you can help us," Alexander said. "We were hoping for a word with Achilles. Can you tell us where he is?"

The sculptor waved a hand as if shooing a fly. "Gone. He left some days back. Said he was going out to the country to stay with his sick mother. That's why I've been looking out for the shop for him."

"Did he say when he would be back?"

"No, but I doubt it will be soon. 'Packed up the whole shop

and took all his tradesmen and apprentices, too."

"Wasn't that unusual?"

"Oh, yeah. I can't remember the last time Achilles left for more than a week. But he must have been planning to set up a temporary shop somewhere. He even took the big pieces he's been working on. I saw no less than three large crates in the ox carts. Now, taking big pieces overland is risky business. Too much chance that the cart may tip and the marble gets broken. You don't do that unless you're planning to be gone awhile."

"I suppose not," Alexander replied. "Can you tell us where in the country Achilles has gone? We may need to speak to him about some business."

Diogenes screwed up his face. "Nah, not exactly. He just said out to his mother's farm. Don't recall where that is, if he ever said it."

Suddenly, the sculptor's look got suspicious. "Say, you're not the fellow that sent that smelly man round here are you?"

"Smelly man?"

"Yeah, one of Rome's true vermin. 'Came by a few days ago asking a lot of questions about Achilles and where he'd gone. 'Got real nasty, too, so I had some of my boys toss him back out into the Surbura. 'Gave him a few knocks to remind him of his manners."

The old sculptor grinned as Alexander and Rutilus shared a startled look.

"Diogenes," Rutilus asked, "Would this smelly man happen to look like a rat with beady little eyes, greasy hair, and a filthy tunic that looks way too big for him?"

"Yeah, that's the one. Do you know him?"

Rutilus grimaced. "Our paths have crossed. He's known as the Rat."

Alexander decided it was time to be more direct.

"Diogenes, I want to be honest with you. I've been charged by Augustus to look into the missing statue of Victory. We came down here because I was hoping to have a word with Achilles. I thought that maybe he could give me some ideas on where to look."

Diogenes raised his eyebrows. "Augustus, you say. You know the Praetorians have already been by here and questioned every sculptor on the block."

"This is a separate investigation. Augustus is my patron and the man who was arrested for the theft is my client. I've been working ... different angles ... than the Praetorians, so Augustus told me to continue. Both sides are reporting our findings to Tiberius."

Diogenes gave Alexander a long appraising look, glanced at Rutilus, then seemed to make up his mind.

"Alright, I'll help you if I can. What do you want to know?"

"Well, I understand that the workers who lowered and packed the statue were real professionals. I figure that sculptors have their own goss... err... trade network like the other artisans. Has there been any talk, anything at all, that might give a hint who might have done the packing?"

Diogenes shook his head. "Nahh, and that's surprising. You're right we do have our own *gossip* network and we haven't talked about much else for days. This theft has been bad business for us all – makes sculptors look untrustworthy. We've even checked out some of our own people -- you know, the ones who are known to be a little *flexible* in what jobs they take. But they've all been cleared. I don't see how it could have been a sculptor. Not even one of the auctioneers. We all do business regularly and we know each other too well. I don't see how any of us could been involved without others knowing."

"But," Alexander asked, "Isn't that surprising? Wouldn't it

have been obvious if a sculptor and his men were out in the middle of the night crating up statues?"

Diogenes gave a barking laugh. "You haven't bought much art work lately have you?"

Alexander shook his head.

"Of course, there's nothing unusual about sculptors being out moving statues in the middle of the night. Remember, that our statues are heavy. The only way to move them is by ox cart, and the ox carts aren't allowed in Rome until after dark. It is only at night that sculptors, or their men, are out delivering statues, picking some up for restoration, or just plain getting supplies like big slabs of marble and paints. In fact, the very night that statue was taken, practically *every man* on this block was out on business, *legitimate* business."

Alexander felt deflated. Now that Diogenes said it, he realized it made sense. Once again he had put too much hope into finding another lead to help him find the statue.

"Hey, Alexander!" Rutilus' voice broke in. "Smell that. *Ummmm.* Diogenes, does that Gaul still run that bakery three doors down?"

"He does indeed," Diogenes smiled. "And he still makes those spice cakes you used to beg for as a boy."

Rutilus was already headed that way. "Come on, Alexander. You have to try these. There's nothing in the world like them."

Alexander laughed. "Go ahead, Rutilus. I'll be there in a moment."

He paused to thank Diogenes and pressed a couple of silver coins into his hand.

"I've heard that a few people have been worried about Achilles and his mother, so if he comes back, would you please send someone around to let me know?" He gave him his address. "Oh, or if you remember where his mother's farm is, let me know that, too."

"Yea, guess I will," Diogenes replied, "being as how you're a friend of Rutilus and all – only … it is the oddest thing." He screwed up his face in thought.

"What is?" Alexander asked.

"Achilles' mother. I could have sworn she *died* nearly three years ago."

An entrance to the *Cloaca Maxima* sewer in Rome.

Source: Harper's Dictionary of Cassical Literature and Antiquities / edited by
Harry Thurston Peck, 2nd ed. (New York, Cooper Square, c1896)

19
THE CLOACA MAXIMA

"I'M sorry, you didn't learn anything helpful," Rutilus said through a mouth half full of the Gaelic bakery's spice cake.

"Still it was worth the trip just for these, wasn't it?" He waved the other half of the cake still in his hand. "Aren't they wonderful? I wondered if they would taste as good as they did when I was a boy, and they do."

Alexander agreed as he munched on his own cake, but was starting to question if this trip had been completely fruitless. Why would a sculptor of Achilles' caliber have risked taking large marble pieces with him in ox carts? He must have planned to quit his lucrative practice in the City for a very long time. But why? And why did no one seem to know anything about Achilles' mother? ... where she lived, or, indeed *if* she still lived? And most puzzling of all, what had the Rat been doing there asking questions?

Alexander glanced over at Rutilus, who now seemed to be lost in his own thoughts. Perhaps, his friend was reminiscing on these now revived memories of his childhood. He decided not to raise his questions about the missing sculptor to Rutilus. After all, Alexander had given Aemelia his word that he would say nothing to implicate Achilles, or through him, her family. He couldn't break it now without some kind of evidence. There really was no evidence of anything; just Alexander's own suspicions, or curiosity, at least.

What had the Rat been doing at the sculptor's shop? Could it possibly be a coincidence that both Alexander and the Rat had sought out the same sculptor at almost the same time?

Looking back over his shoulder, Alexander made eye contact with Amarantus who nodded back gravely. The same questions had probably occurred to his servant. Amarantus had been standing behind Alexander during the interview with the sculptor and would have heard all that he had heard.

When the young men finally made their way back from the Subura to the Forum, Rutilus moved to part company and return home. Suddenly, Alexander felt an impulse to try something else. He didn't act on impulse very often, but Alexander had a feeling he should do it now.

"Wait! Rutilus."

Rutilus turned back and raised his eyebrows, "Yes?"

"Would you be up for one more adventure this morning?"

Rutilus tilted his head studying Alexander and then let out a laugh. "I *might* consider it, if it includes lunch and some decent wine. What are you thinking, Alexander?"

Alexander rubbed his chin. "Well, you're not going to like this, but I'm not sure who else could help me."

"You're making me suspicious, Alexander. What is it?"

"*Hmmmm*, it's just that I looked off to the side there and noticed the door to the *Cloaca Maxima*."

Rutilus frowned. "Now, you've really stumped me, Alexander. If you need a toilet, there are better options that using the sewers directly."

"No, no," Alexander laughed. "I'm thinking back to the day of the chariot race when we caught the Rat. Remember how badly he smelled?"

"*Ich*, who could forget that? It was unnatural."

"*Exactly*, Rutilus. That's it. Unnatural. Remember what we were thinking at the time, that perhaps the Rat was living in the sewers?"

"Umm... yes, I remember that. ... Oh, yes, and didn't Claudius suggest that might be how the Rat got his blackmail secrets – by standing under sewer covers and listening."

"I suppose that could work for a blackmailer," Alexander nodded. "The sewers lie under many parts of the city. And who is ever mindful of what they are saying when they are standing near a sewer cover? A man who could bear to spend that much time in the stench could overhear a lot. *In fact, ...*"

Alexander paused, furrowing his brows as he thought for a moment. "I believe my clients did mention that they had stepped to the side of Victory's Incline to get away from the smell coming through a sewer cover. ... Rutilus, do you think the statue could have been taken down into the sewers?"

"I suppose, but they couldn't have gotten the statue into the sewers from anywhere on the Palatine. The sewers there are not large enough; not even close."

Rutilus snapped his fingers and grinned. "But they wouldn't have *needed* a sewer on the Palatine, would they? You said they had an ox cart and that the statue was already laid out horizontally and boxed. Think about it, Alexander. They would simply need to move the ox cart to the nearest large entrance to the sewers ... like that one you just pointed to over there."

Rutilus nodded towards the large entrance to the *Cloaca Maxima* located off the side of the Forum.

Alexander whistled. "You have a point. But would it really be possible? Rutilus, you told me that you used to explore the sewers when you were a boy. Would it be possible to get a statue out of Rome that way? ... or even just hide it for awhile?"

Rutilus screwed up his face in thought. "Well, that was a

long time ago when my father was still alive. I explored the sewers near our house which was on the Viminal Hill then, not the Palatine."

"Yes, I understand that, Rutilus, but were the sewers that you saw big enough? Would it be possible to fit a boxed statue into them ... maybe on a small boat?"

"I guess so, Alexander; probably not in any of the side sewers. But the *Cloaca Maxima* there would be big enough, especially if the Tiber was running low."

Alexander gazed speculatively at the entrance to the *Cloaca Maxima* for a moment and then shook his head.

"No, that doesn't feel quite right. The Forum is a busy place, even at night. It is hard to imagine that these thieves could have driven an ox cart right up to the *Cloaca* here in the Forum and carried a huge, heavy box in through that sewer door without anyone noticing. That would have been so odd, that surely *someone* would have remembered seeing that."

"But, they wouldn't have *had to*, Alexander. There's another door to the *Cloaca Maxima* just down there." Rutilus waved vaguely in another direction. "You must have seen it, by the meat market. It is how all the blood and offal from the butchers gets washed out to the Tiber. And no one goes to the meat market at night. All the shops are closed."

Alexander looked at his friend in amazement. "But that's just minutes from here. Let's go take a look."

Rutilus hesitated. "*Umm*, I don't know. I haven't been in the sewers since I was very small. The sewers ... near the meat market ... in July? That's going to be *rank*." He grinned. "You're my friend, Alexander, but I'm sure that I like you *that* much."

Alexander realized he could relate to that.   "I know, I know. I don't want to go in the sewers either. But we're so close to it right now and I'm desperate for any clue on this statue. ... Why don't you show me where it is, and then you can wait outside while I go in and have a quick look? It will just be a couple minutes. I want to go in long enough to see if it would be possible to get the statue out that way."

Rutilus pursed his lip and gave Alexander a squinty look. "Just a quick look? … And then you will buy lunch … with a particularly good wine?"

"With a *very* good wine," Alexander confirmed. With a smile and nod, Rutilus led the way toward the *Forum Boarium*, Rome's meat market.

***

Standing before the entrance to the sewer, Alexander was struck by three things. First, Rutilus had *not exaggerated* about the rankness of a butcher's sewer in summer. Second, the entrance to the sewer was easily large enough to fit a box holding the marble statue. Third, the *Clivus Victoria*, the path that led from Victory's Temple down the Palatine Hill, ended not far from here. If someone had used the sewers for the statue, this entrance would have been almost … convenient.

He turned to his two companions, Rutilus and his servant, Amarantus, who had quietly shadowed him throughout the day.

"I have to see this for myself, although I *will* try to be quick. Rutilus, why don't you wait over there? Ranti, you don't have to follow me in, but I want you to wait by the entrance. If there is any trouble I will call out to you."

Alexander took several deep breaths, pulled his tunic up until it covered his lower face, and entered the sewer. Inside was a high arch consisting of closely fitted tufa blocks. The stones were wet and covered with some sort of thick sludge. It was revolting.

"Hoop, hup," he gagged aloud as his senses rebelled at the odor that seemed magnified in the close quarters of the sewer.

Taking a shallow breath through his mouth, Alexander stepped forward and noticed that he was standing on a ledge that ran the length of the sewer. It was probably there for maintenance, especially when large pieces of refuse clogged up the passageways causing waste to back up into the city. Someone would have to go into the sewer and use long poles to get the sewage flowing again. The ledge was easily wide enough for a man to walk along the inside of the sewer. A shorter man like the Rat, or even Rutilus, would have been able to stand upright. But, Alexander was too tall and had to walk stooped over.

As Alexander's eyes began to adjust to the dimness inside the sewer, he noted that it was not quite as dark as he had expected. At various intervals light filtered down from the ceiling. Aha, that must be light coming in through the sewer covers. Despite the near overwhelming stench, Alexander was curious. He shuffled forward until he was under the first sewer cover. Much to his surprise, he could hear voices. In fact, he could hear them quite distinctly, since the walls of the sewer were creating almost an echoing effect.

"Anything interesting?" someone whispered behind him.

With a start, Alexander turned and saw Rutilus standing on the ledge next to him. He was also holding his tunic up to cover his lower face. Silently, Alexander pointed up towards the sewer cover and both young men cocked their heads and listened until the voices drifted away. Then, they turned to each other with wide eyes.

"So *that* is how you bribe an *aedile*," Rutilus said shaking his head.

"I'm surprised at how little it took," Alexander replied in disgust. "Nevertheless, that exchange does seem to have confirmed one point for us. If someone could *stand* to stay in these sewers for very long, they might overhear information that could be used for blackmail. ... I wonder."

Even as he spoke, Alexander became aware of a soft scuttling in the distance.

Rutilus scrunched his nose, even as he sucked in a short breath to hold back his gagging. "*Ick*, let's get out of here, Alexander, and leave the sewer to that rat."

Alexander glanced toward the other end of the sewer tunnel and saw a figure in the distance. There wasn't enough light to make out details, but it was definitely a man.

"No," he responded softly. "Not *a* rat. I think it is *The* Rat. *Quiet now*, let's grab him and force him to tell us about the statue."

Alexander set off on the ledge along the side of the sewer heading toward the oncoming man. Hunched over, he had to set his feet down carefully on the sludge coated surface, but the sludge also blocked any sound of his footsteps. Fortunately, the figure ahead seemed to be shuffling slowly and staring at his feet, completely oblivious to the fact that he was not alone in the sewer.

Carefully, Alexander stepped closer and closer. Just as he was nearly in arm's reach, he yelled "*Got you now!*" and lunged forward to grab the other man's tunic.

... except, his body didn't lunge forward. Just as he started his forward momentum, Alexander felt a strong tug on his tunic yanking him backwards. His feet slid in the sludge causing him to throw out his arms in an attempt to keep his balance.

Behind him, Alexander could see Rutilus's arms pin wheeling wildly as he tried not to fall into the sewer. One of Rutilus's hands grasped at Alexander's tunic as he fought to regain his balance. In turn, Alexander reached out and dug his fingers into a crack between two of the tufa blocks trying to steady himself. But it wasn't enough. The momentum had started and he could feel both Rutilus and himself wobbling back and forth near the brink of the sewage flowing just below them.

Alexander closed his eyes. "We're going in," he thought. "Dear Lord, I am about to be drowned in *merda*."

Even as Alexander wavered on the brink of toppling into the flowing sewage, he suddenly felt a solid shape press firmly against his abdomen pushing him back. He glanced down and in the dim light recognized the club that Amarantus carried as protection. Apparently, his slave had followed them in and held out his club to keep both men from falling into the raw sewage. Alexander let out a long breath; his sense of relief was palpable.

"Ranti," he began, but before he could continue Rutilus broke in.

"I'm sorry, Alexander. I slipped and reached out to grab at the wall, but I caught your tunic instead. I didn't mean to throw you off balance like that."

Rutilus looked over Alexander's shoulder down the tunnel of the sewer. By that time, the figure they had seen had disappeared.

"Shall we hurry? Maybe we haven't lost him yet."

Alexander turned back and looked down the length of the sewer. His shoulders slumped. "I don't think so, Rutilus. The Rat knows these sewers far better than we do. I think he's long gone by now."

Alexander forced a smile at this friend. "He got away this time. I don't think the Rat can avoid me forever." But his face fell and he realized that he'd taken in too deep of a breath. *"Hoop, hup."*

Alexander covered his mouth and gently pushed his companions back towards the entrance. Once he had shuffled his way out the door of the sewer, he promptly leaned over and vomited. He could hold back the gagging from the stench no longer. Alexander was not at all surprised to hear the two others retching beside him.

20
WHEN A LADY SUMMONS

AFTER the sewer, Rutilus had to admit reluctantly that he had lost his appetite. He was unsure if he could even hold down some wine, no matter how fine. They agreed to part company for the moment, but Alexander promised he would make it up to Rutilus with a good meal and a good wine in a few days. After all, how many men had a friend good enough to follow him into Rome's sewer?

Instead, he stopped briefly by his office to check on a new shipment of grain. With a scroll containing the ship's inventory tucked under his arm, Alexander and Amarantus headed home for a quiet afternoon of checking on accounts. That evening, he and Agrippa would be going to the meeting at the synagogue, so this afternoon Alexander planned to work at home in peace.

... But, once again, he found that he had little control over his interruptions.

Upon reaching home, Alexander learned that a messenger boy had been waiting for him most of the morning. He immediately recognized the blue and green livery worn by the slaves of the house of Claudius. But when he opened the scroll, it turned out that the message was not from Claudius, but from his mother Antonia.

> *Antonia Minor to Gaius Julius Alexander. Please call on me this afternoon. I have a matter of some importance to discuss with you.*

Another mystery. What could Antonia want with him? Had she heard about Claudius' role in catching the Rat at the Circus Maximus or the conflict at the baths? Could she possibly be summoning Alexander to warn him to keep Claudius out of it? But that made no sense. If Antonia was unhappy, surely she would speak to Claudius himself, or, to Claudius' guardian even.

"This afternoon," she had written. *Hmm,* he and Rutilus had gotten an early start to visit the sculptor in the Subura. Even with the detour to the *Cloaca Maximus,* it was still just barely noontime. Good. Alexander needed time to collect his thoughts and change his tunic which had absorbed foul odors, even from the short time he had spent in the sewer.

Alexander sent the messenger back indicating that he would be there at mid-afternoon. Then he scrubbed down with a wet cloth that Ranti had brought him and changed his tunic. He couldn't help but smile as Amarantus dramatically carried away the soiled tunic pinched between thumb and forefinger on an outstretched arm.

Then Alexander retired to his office to work. But, instead of his business accounts, Alexander began to ponder what Antonia might want from him. She was the daughter of Marcus Antonius and Octavia, the beloved sister of the current First Citizen Augustus. Antonia's husband Drusus had died within a year after the birth of their third child, Claudius. She had chosen not to remarry. Instead, she had taken her place as a member of the imperial family and one of Rome's leading matrons. One might argue that, aside from Augustus's wife Livia, Antonia was one of the most powerful women in Rome. She didn't usually involve herself in politics as Livia was said to do. But when Antonia felt there was a need, she presented her views to Augustus; and, it was said, that her advice was usually taken.

Of course, Alexander had known Antonia since he was a boy, having grown up in the circle of Claudius. He had always been a little afraid of her, especially when he saw how coldly she treated her younger son.

Antonia had never been unkind to him personally. But then, neither had she been particularly warm. That was to be expected, though. Antonia was old-blood Roman nobility, and the niece of the First Citizen. What use would she have had for a little Jewish boy from the provinces?

With a sigh, Alexander let the thoughts pass. He had no idea what Antonia wanted with him and would simply have to wait until that afternoon to find out. He smiled wryly to himself. At least this was *one* mystery that would have a sure solution and soon. Now, if only the goddess Victory would provide him with a little help in her own recovery. But then, Victory probably had little use for Jews as well.

Alexander's head was buried in the ship's manifest, when Amarantus came to inform him that a messenger wished to speak to him. Looking up distractedly, Alexander expected to see the young boy in the blue and green livery again, and was quite surprised when he beheld a grown man with a bald head. He quickly recognized the slight form and familiar crinkled smile of Hermias, the door steward at the home of Rutilus.

"Hermias!" Alexander exclaimed. "This is a first. When did you get demoted to messenger boy?"

Hermias spread his hands in a mock deprecating manner, "*Ahh* the life of a slave; we only live to serve."

"And how do you serve today?"

Hermias' face turned a bit more serious. "I am here at the request of the lady Rutila."

That explained that. For a young, single woman to contact a young, single man was considered most inappropriate in Roman society. No wonder she sent Hermias personally, rather than entrust a private message to some other.

"And what is the message of the lady Rutila?"

"Simply, that she asks that you visit her this afternoon. Her mother has called upon a sick friend and is not expected back for another two hours."

Hermias paused and studied Alexander's reaction. "Will you come?"

Alexander considered what Rutila may want which led to a moment of panic. *Rutila, Rutila, what have you heard?* Did she know of his betrothal? Suddenly, the meeting with Antonia seemed much less urgent.

"Of course, I will come. I will accompany you back to the house now. … Ranti, fetch my toga, but I won't put it on until later."

A brisk walk through the Forum, up the steps of the Palatine, and then across to the other side of the hill and Alexander, Amarantus and Hermias were at the home of Sextus Fadius. Alexander motioned for Amarantus to wait in the atrium and headed for the garden. With a slight bow, Hermias indicated that he would go to fetch his mistress.

Alexander strode quickly into the garden and kept walking until he reached the end of the path. Absently, he stared up at the gross replica of the Victory statue nestled back under a group of trees. His heart ached. Surely, Rutila must know of his betrothal. Why else would she summon him? How could he explain it to her? He touched the small box in his pouch that held the gold earrings that he had bought for Rutila two days before. Perhaps the nice gift would distract her.

The afternoon sun broke through the leaves and from the head of the statue came an answering glint. Alexander blew out a breath. Gold. How ludicrous. Some probably half-drunken artist had sculpted this monster, and then the painter had tried to dress it up by painting a few streaks of gold in its hair.

It made Alexander consider his current situation. The artist could paint all the gold he wanted on the statue, but it was still just *"a great flying whore."* No, he could not present Rutila with a bit of gold and hope that it would cover up a difficult situation. He would be honest with her … about the betrothal … and about how he felt.

"Alexander."

Alexander turned at the sound of the familiar, sweet voice and sucked in his breath. How beautiful she looked. Her red-gold tresses lay unbound over the shoulders of another new gown, soft pink with maroon borders at the top and hem. How well it suited her. She looked every inch the noblewoman she was.

"Alexander, come sit with me. Here on the bench."

Alexander crossed the garden in an instant and seated himself on the bench, without ever taking his eyes off her. Rutila returned his gaze for a moment and then looked down and blushed.

"I know it's not proper for a young woman to summon a man," she began tentatively.

"I'm glad you did," Alexander replied. "I came as fast as I could."

Rutila hesitated and then seemed to find her courage. She looked up at Alexander and her gaze was steady.

"Alexander, I know it is also not proper for a woman to say what I'm about to say. But we may have only a short time alone together. I must say this now while I have the chance."

She faltered and swallowed. Alexander reached out and took both of her hands in his.

"Alexander, I love you. I have loved you for a very long time."

Alexander ached to answer, words gushing forth with all

the love that was in his heart. With effort he remembered the self-promise he'd just made by the statue to tell Rutila the whole truth. Before he could respond, she continued.

"I have heard that you are betrothed. Is this true?"

"It is." Alexander almost choked on the words. "But, Rutila, I knew nothing of this until I received a letter from my father just a few days ago. He did this without asking me about my wishes in the matter."

"So, Rutilus told me. He also said that you are not happy ... that you do not love her."

"I do not."

"Do... do you love me?"

"I do."

Rutila sighed and squeezed his hands.

"Rutilus said that I must be practical. Marriages are rarely made based on love. He said that her father is very rich. ...Oh, Alexander, it is *my dowry* isn't it? If it were larger, then would we have a chance?"

"No," Alexander replied softly. "It is *not* the dowry. Rutila, you must remember that I am a Jew. A Jew must marry a Jew. It is our religion."

Rutila gave a dismissive wave of her hand. "Oh, no one marries for *religion*, Alexander. One god is as good as another. I can worship your god, too. I'll learn all the rites."

"It doesn't quite work that way, Rutila. Ours is a jealous god. We may worship no other god but him."

"Then I will worship only him, Alexander. I promise."

Alexander gazed down into her earnest face, suddenly aware that she was only seventeen years old. So young. How little she understood of the world outside of her small circle in Rome.

"Rutila, there is much more to being a Jew. It is in our

blood. It is about a promise, a promise made long ago by our God to my people. We must live our lives according to his ways and place our faith only in him. Every day, we must thank the Lord for his guidance and his protection."

Rutila looked puzzled. "Don't be silly, Alexander. The gods don't care that much about mere mortals. Anyway, I could learn it -- all the prayers and whatever else you think your god needs. I learned all the rites of the Bona Dea in just one day. I can learn your god's, too."

She hesitated and sucked in a breath. "Alexander, stop trying to distract me. I am *not* a child anymore. It *must* be the money. After all, I am patrician. What more could anyone ask except for the dowry? What if my dowry were bigger? We could talk to Sextus Fadius and Mother and I can give our jewelry."

Alexander sat back unaware that he had released Rutila's hands.

"Rutila, please try to understand. It is *not* the dowry. Jews are *not* like the Romans, the Greeks, or any other people you know of. For us, religion *is* that important. Our relationship with our God defines who we are ... who *I am*."

Rutila looked up at Alexander with her eyes filling with tears. The appealing look on her innocent little face tore at his heart.

"Then, Alexander, what can we do? Is there no hope that we can be together?"

"I ... I don't know. Perhaps. It may be possible for you to convert to my religion. Would you be willing to consider that?"

"Yes, Alexander, anything. Only, please don't leave me. Don't marry that pig-faced girl."

Alexander smiled as he took her hands again. "Rutila, I swear to you that I will try. But I *will* have to speak to my father. In fifteen days my ship will sail for Alexandria. When I get there, I will face my father and I will speak to him of you. I will tell him of your beauty and character and your patrician blood. And I will tell him that I think you would make a very, very good Jew."

***

Alexander was completely distracted as he returned to the atrium and found Amarantus waiting for him. He gave no response to his servant's questioning look except to say, "We should call on Antonia next."

Alexander headed quickly out the door and nearly ran into a little man standing just outside who staggered back in surprise. As Alexander wrinkled his nose in disgust, he knew in an instant who it was. Unfortunately, he had no time now to try to chase down and tackle the little villain. Already, the man was edging away, getting ready to bolt.

"You've been following me, haven't you?" Alexander said to the Rat. "Why?"

The Rat seemed taken aback, and then his eyes began to dart around furtively concealing whatever had been on his mind.

"Come on," Alexander demanded. "If you are here, then you must have been following me. You must be thinking that you have information to sell. My offer stands. If the information is good, I'll pay you for it."

Still, the Rat hesitated.

"If the information leads to the release of my client and the return of the statue, I will pay you handsomely. Since you've been following me, then by now you must know that I mean it. My family is very rich."

The Rat got that same torn look that he had worn while trapped back in the stall at the *Circus Maximus*. Alexander couldn't tell if the Rat knew something, but wasn't ready to sell it. Or, did the Rat know nothing, but was trying to find a way to cheat him? It must be the latter, he decided. He was offering good silver, and if the Rat knew anything, surely he would have grabbed at it by now.

"Oh, let's go," Alexander said to Amarantus in exasperation. "He doesn't know anything."

Still, what if he did?

As he was walking away, Alexander turned and spoke over his shoulder to the Rat. "Again, my name is Gaius Julius Alexander. I live in an apartment complex on the northeast side of the Capitoline Hill, just east of the public fountain. Second floor. If you decide that you have information to sell, come find me."

Amarantus fell into step just behind Alexander and, for a few minutes, they walked in silence. He seemed to sense that his master was troubled, but dared not ask what had passed between him and Rutila. Instead he chose to distract him.

"Master, do you think this Rat may come to see you?"

"What? Oh, I don't know. You saw him. It's impossible to tell if he knows anything or not. Why do you ask?"

"Only that I will need to go shopping, if he is coming."

Alexander stopped and looked at Amarantus curiously. "Shopping?"

"For incense, Master. Lots and lots of incense."

Alexander chuckled. "I take your point. If he does come, I had better interrogate him outside."

Fortunately, the house that Claudius shared with his wife, Urgulanilla, and mother Antonia was also on the Palatine Hill and just a few minutes' walk away. Amarantus had succeeded in distracting Alexander momentarily, but still his thoughts kept returning to Rutila. How beautiful she was and how much he wanted her. When she looked at him that way, he felt that he would do anything, anything to have her.

And yet … how could she have known him all of these years and have formed no concept of what it meant for him to be a Jew? And could she possibly understand what she was agreeing to when she promised to become a Jew, too? *Rutilus*, Alexander concluded. He must discuss this with Rutilus. Perhaps Rutilus could speak with his sister and explain these things to her.

With that next step firmly settled in his mind, Alexander found himself being ushered into a private sitting room where Antonia sat doing needlework with a servant. With a nod, Antonia dismissed the girl and then turned to him.

"Alexander," she said warmly. *Antonia, warm?* "Thank you for coming to see me."

"It is an honor to be invited," Alexander answered politely although puzzled. "How may I be of service to you?"

"As my note said, I have a matter of some importance to discuss with you. But first, I am afraid that I must give you a … warning."

"A warning?"

"Yes," replied Antonia. She tilted her head and seemed to be considering her words.

"I have learned from Berenice that you are investigating the matter of the missing statue."

Alexander nodded.

"It appears that my daughter, Livilla, has taken some interest in your investigation."

Now Alexander was really perplexed. He knew Livilla, of course. She was the middle child born after Germanicus, but two years before Claudius. Livilla had openly shared her mother's contempt for her younger brother, so Alexander had learned to dislike her thoroughly. Livilla was married now to Drusus, the son of Tiberius, and Alexander virtually never had occasion to see her.

Antonia was studying him.

"I'm afraid this is very sensitive, Alexander, and I must ask you to repeat it to no one. It seems that Livilla had stopped by to visit me several days ago and ...accidentally ... overheard a conversation about your investigation being held by you and Agrippa in my son's study."

Well, that was one little mystery solved -- the spy at Claudius' door. Alexander said nothing.

"It also seems," Antonia continued, "that Livilla has formed a small *friendship* with a certain *Sejanus* of the Praetorian Guard. I disapprove, of course. The man is beneath her. But Tiberius, for whatever reason, thinks highly of him. Since my daughter's husband, Drusus, *is* Tiberius' son, this Praetorian apparently has found a way to be often in their company."

Still, Alexander said nothing.

"Livilla has told this Sejanus what she overheard about your investigation. Apparently, he is not supportive of your efforts. I only learned this yesterday when she visited me." Antonia paused and shook her head. "After all these years that I have been friendly with Berenice, I can't imagine why my daughter would think I would sympathize with the prejudices of some guardsman. Of course, I told her as much.

"But, Alexander, I have learned that this Sejanus is no friend to the Jews of Rome. Therefore, I have decided I must warn you. Sejanus may decide to do something to impede your search for the statue."

Alexander nodded sharply. "He already has."

Antonia looked at him questioningly.

"Three of the Guard attacked me in the baths. I was nearly drowned." He decided not to give her any more detail than that.

He wasn't sure how she would feel about Claudius' involvement, so it was best to leave him out of it.

Antonia looked upset, so he quickly added, "As you can see, they did not succeed. And now that I am forewarned, I will go nowhere without an escort."

Antonia nodded reluctantly. "Be careful Alexander. Be very careful. This man, Sejanus, is dangerous and I would hate to lose you. … which brings me to the reason why I have asked you to come."

She paused while a servant set up a small table with refreshments, then continued.

"No doubt, you are aware that I have extensive land holdings in Egypt."

Alexander was momentarily taken aback. Of course, he had known that. It just wasn't something that he had ever spent much time considering. He responded with a few verbal observations to indicate to Antonia that he did have some knowledge of the extent of her estates and that they were primarily devoted to wheat. The wheat crop in Egypt was critical to Rome since it was the primary source for the bread that fed rich and poor alike.

Antonia seemed satisfied with his answer. "Good. I was hoping that you would be familiar with the situation in Egypt. What you may not know is that my holdings are being supervised by one of my family's freedmen. In the past few years, there have been a number of irregularities in the accounts. Oh, the man has always had an explanation for them all … a drought here, a fire there, a blight on the crops, whatever. But honestly, Alexander, I strongly suspect that I am being cheated."

"I understand," Alexander replied and he did.

Many Romans had land holdings in Egypt and seldom, if ever, had the opportunity to visit them. It had become common practice for the overseers of their estates to skim a little off the top before profits were shipped back to Rome. A small amount of graft was usually taken for granted and overlooked. There must have been some rather large discrepancies for Antonia to be expressing concern now.

"If you give me a letter, I will be happy to look over your estates and the accounts when I return to Egypt. But I must advise you, if your freedman has any suspicion of my purpose in advance he may make it very difficult for me to uncover anything."

"I know," Antonia replied, then, looked at him shrewdly. "And that is why, Alexander, I am now asking you to become the *epitropos* for my estates in Egypt."

Alexander barely kept his mouth from falling open in shock. Her *epitropos*? This was more than a simple manager of the estates. The *epitropos* would be empowered to act as her legal guardian in practically all matters. Antonia was essentially asking him to take full charge of her affairs in Egypt. To speak for an imperial would be a very powerful position. Alexander did some quick calculations in his mind. His family already had considerable land holdings in Egypt. If he also became responsible for Antonia's extensive estates, that would put his family in control of more land than, well, almost any other single person in Egypt save Augustus.

"Antonia, do you realize what you are proposing? The implications?"

"I do."

"It is such a great responsibility. Perhaps you would prefer my father?"

"I would not," Antonia smiled. "Alexander, I have watched you since you were a boy and I have seen the man you have become. You are smart, ambitious and, most importantly, honest. I know that you appreciate a shrewd business deal. But I've never heard of you deliberately cheating anyone. I have consulted Berenice on this, and she shares my assessment of you. It is *you* I want for this. No one else."

"I don't know what to say, Lady Antonia. I am deeply honored."

"Then you'll do it?"

"Of course."

"Good. I expected as much, Alexander. I've taken the liberty of having my advocate draw up the contract already."

She walked across the room and pulled a scroll out of a small chest and handed it to him.

"Please take your time to look it over and, be sure you agree to my terms. Before you leave, I will provide you with a letter for the freedman who is currently managing my estates. You may deal with him as you wish. However, if my suspicions are correct, then I would encourage you to send the man back to Rome."

Alexander thanked Antonia and stopped in the atrium to ask a slave to summon Amarantus. He would have liked to take time to visit with Claudius, but knew he had to hurry home.

Tonight he was going to the Synagogue of the Agrippesians.

21
SYNAGOGUE OF THE AGRIPPESIANS

AGRIPPA came by well before dark to collect Alexander for their short trip over to the Trans-Tiber district. When Alexander descended the stairs to the street level to join Agrippa, he was initially surprised to find Agrippa waiting in a litter that was surrounded by a half a dozen family slaves carrying clubs. As Alexander stepped into the litter, he gave Agrippa a questioning glance and nodded at the armed slaves.

Agrippa shrugged. "There is no point in setting ourselves up as targets," he explained with a gesture towards his tunic.

Alexander noted that Agrippa, like he, had traded his Roman-style tunic and toga for a longer length tunic with fringes on the four corners. For his morning prayers, Alexander typically draped a shawl with the four fringes over his shoulders, and then packed it away when done. But for a prayer service in a synagogue, it was considered more devout to wear the fringes on one's primary garment. Alexander knew that Agrippa would also have a small pouch at his belt that held his *phylacteries*, the small box containing scripture that each man would later tie to his hand during prayer.

"It is a wise precaution, Master."

Alexander looked back to see Amarantus nodding his head in approval. "Remember the fight in the Forum."

Indeed, it was only a few days earlier that Alexander had fought the bullies who had attacked the Jew in the Forum. That man had become a target by wearing his fringes in public.

"I suppose you're right," he admitted to Agrippa, as the litter set off with the slaves falling into place around it. "We couldn't do much to calm the fears of the Trans-Tiber Jews, if we ourselves were attacked on the way to see them."

The two men settled into idle conversation as they made the trip to the synagogue. The litter passed through Rome's marketplaces to the Sublician Bridge, then across the Tiber River to the Trans-Tiber district. Alexander and Agrippa were the rare Jews who had homes in the areas typically occupied by Roman citizens of greater financial means. A number of Jews who practiced particular trades were settled in the Subura area, but the vast majority lived across the Tiber.

Although the Trans-Tiber was sometimes called the Jewish district, in fact, Jews were just one of dozens of foreign peoples that had settled in that area. The district was primarily populated by unskilled labor and its residents were often marked for their poverty. Still, the various groups who made the Trans-Tiber region their home had developed a sense of community. They were the *Transtiberinis*. Here, an attack where locals singled out Jews, or any group, was rare.

After crossing the bridge over the Tiber, the litter turned northwest and soon reached an attractive one-story building nestled into a good location opposite the wharves. Nearly thirty years earlier, Augustus's friend and step-son Marcus Vipsanius Agrippa had founded the synagogue as an act of beneficence to his clients who were Jews. Vipsanius Agrippa had spent time in Palestine where he became well acquainted with Herod the Great and many of his family. Alexander's current companion, Agrippa, had been named for the family friend.

A group of men had already gathered in front of the

Synagogue of the Agrippesians. Agrippa and Alexander stepped out of the litter and the heads of two synagogues quickly hurried over to greet them.

"Prince Agrippa and Alexander, too. We are so grateful that you could take this time out of your busy schedules to meet with us. As I mentioned in my note to Agrippa, these recent attacks have our congregations quite concerned."

Agrippa looked around at the gathering. There were many men of all ages, some also wearing tunics with fringes, but, many others wearing a tunic that looked to be the only garment they owned.

"No women tonight?" Agrippa asked the synagogue leaders. "Won't there be a prayer service?"

"Yes, but the Elders of both synagogues discussed it and decided this was best. Many families in our congregations live far from here. There was no way to ensure their safety both coming and going. So it was decided that there would be no women or under-aged boys here tonight ... well ... except for Sarah," he concluded with a grimace.

Alexander and Agrippa bit back their smiles. Sarah was famous among Jews all over Rome. She had served for years as the *"Mother of the Synagogue"* for the Agrippesians. Some women who held this title chose to become the ideal for Jewish motherhood and spent their time working with families and practicing acts of charity.

Not Sarah. Sarah had chosen instead to use her title to insinuate herself into every realm of synagogue management. She never failed to express her opinion on everything ranging from weddings to repairs of the synagogue building, and, used her substantial personal fortune to ensure her opinions were well noted. It was no surprise that Sarah would assume that a general ban on women at tonight's meeting could not possibly apply to her.

As if on cue, a litter stopped directly in front of where the synagogue leaders stood with Agrippa and Alexander. An elderly woman stepped out and proceeded to pull her shoulders back in a straight stance that would have been the envy of any legionary. For a moment, she gazed about her at the assembled men with her head tilted back looking slightly down her nose. Finally, she turned to the synagogue leaders.

"Ah, good. I see that you all have made it. Well, now that I am here, we might as well get started. Come along, then. We have a problem to solve." Without looking back, Sarah started up the steps leading to the front entrance.

The leader of the synagogue looked at Agrippa in horror and started to stammer an apology, but Agrippa only smiled and waved away the perceived insult.

"*And we thought my mother was tough,*" he muttered to Alexander as they followed the leaders into the synagogue.

Alexander had not been in this particular synagogue in years. He looked around him as they walked in. There wasn't a lot physically that distinguished one synagogue from another. They were usually one-story buildings with a double row of pillars running down the length of the main room that was used for services and occasional meetings. Sometimes there was a large entrance area before entering the main room or office at the front or back.

The biggest difference among them was that some synagogues had built in a separate gallery where the women would sit during services. Men were always seated in the front, but the women would be placed in the back of the room, or in a balcony, with a curtain separating them from the view of the men. The Synagogue of the Agrippesians, Alexander noted, made no attempt to sequester women from men during services. No doubt, this fact had assisted Sarah to grow her position as Mother of the Synagogue.

The leader of the synagogue led them to the head of the main room. In a small roped off area stood the ark, the cabinet that held the sacred Torah scrolls. Several chairs had been set up near the ark. Agrippa and Alexander were shown to two of the seats, as the leaders of both synagogues took the others. Alexander noticed that Sarah had already seated herself in one of the head chairs. Behind them, the rest of the congregation filed in and took the benches that lined both sides of the length of the room.

With a solemn dignity, the head of the synagogue called the meeting to order, introduced his colleague from the other synagogue, and then Agrippa and Alexander. The meeting proceeded much as Agrippa and Alexander had thought it would. The head of each synagogue spoke briefly about recent attacks on their congregations and the accusations against Jews for stealing the statue of Victory.

Then Agrippa spoke reminding the people of the close relations that had existed between Augustus and his grandfather Herod the Great. He reiterated the rights of the Jews that had been created or confirmed by Julius Caesar and Augustus. He assured them that if the situation were not resolved soon, he would personally lead a delegation to Augustus to request relief from the current affliction.

"However, we must remember," Agrippa warned, "that the First Citizen has limited choices for addressing a volatile situation in the Trans-Tiber district. The *Vigiles* of the 14th district are the primary force for keeping the peace. They lack the numbers to address these isolated and sneak attacks. Augustus may have to consider more drastic measures such as banning public meetings, setting curfews or restrictions on our movement. Since we are outside the walls of Rome, he might even think of bringing in the legions and setting up soldiers on every corner."

That brought loud mutterings from the assemblage and Agrippa waited for it to settle down.

"I like this no more than you," Agrippa continued. "But you must realize that, even with his resources, Augustus would not have many options. Therefore, I am asking you to look out for each other. Go nowhere alone, be careful of strangers and, above all, say *nothing* against Rome."

"And now, I wish to put forward the man whom Augustus himself has charged to investigate this matter. Alexander will tell you of the many great efforts he has made, and in peril of his own life, to resolve this crime and free the Jews from these false accusations. I hope each of you will do as I have done and add Alexander to your daily prayers, in hope that the Lord will guide him in his path."

Alexander was more than a little surprised to hear that Agrippa had added him to his prayers, but he knew Agrippa would not lie about a thing like that. It was with great trepidation that he got up and faced the assembled congregations.

Just as he began to speak, Alexander was interrupted by a loud noise at the other end of the room. All eyes turned toward the entrance where a young boy had thrown open the doors and stood there ashen and trembling.

"Father, Father where are you? The men … they are coming to kill us."

In a moment, a man was kneeling by the boy talking to him softly as everyone looked on. Then he straightened and faced the leaders at the head of the room. "There are strange men coming, more than he can count, and all carrying weapons or torches."

The meeting turned into chaos as every man pushed and shoved his way out into the street where they stopped still with horror. Since they had been at the opposite end of the synagogue, Alexander and Agrippa were among the last out. About fifteen feet away stood Amarantus and Agrippa's six slaves holding their clubs, forming a loose barrier across the width of the street outside the synagogue. At the other end of the street, dozens of armed men were advancing toward them. They filled the breadth of the street and stood at least three or four men deep.

Alexander felt a hand on his shoulder and he and Agrippa turned to face the leaders of the two synagogues.

"Our congregations are asking us what they should do."

"Flee," Alexander said without hesitation.

"We cannot. Why else would they be carrying torches when there is still daylight? They mean to burn our synagogue, and, if we run, others will follow us and burn our homes."

"But we are unarmed," Alexander objected. "No man among us would have brought a weapon into a house of the Lord."

But even as he spoke, Alexander felt a motion next to him and looked down as an aged and wrinkled hand placed a wooden club into his own. He looked up and met the steady gaze of Sarah, the Mother of the Synagogue.

"They were in my litter," she spoke almost defiantly. "I had a premonition that this would happen, so I had them placed under the cushions."

Alexander looked around and saw Sarah's litter bearers moving through the congregation distributing clubs. It was better than having no weapons, but he doubted that there would be enough for every man. He looked back at the approaching men and saw that they had stopped a short distance from where Amarantus and Agrippa's men stood and were waving their weapons and shouting threats.

"That's no mob action," Agrippa muttered. "They're waiting for the signal to attack."

"What should we do?" the leader of the synagogue repeated.

"What we must," Alexander replied. He pointed to the two leaders. "You and you, take a few men and save the Torah scrolls.

The rest of us will hold them off while you get them away. If we can, we will save the synagogue, but the scrolls must survive. But first, tell your men to follow me."

The leaders murmured their acknowledgement and were off.

"You cannot stay here," Alexander said to Agrippa. "We cannot risk losing an heir to the throne and friend to Augustus, not even to save a synagogue. You must go. *Now.*"

Agrippa hesitated a moment then nodded. Alexander continued. "When you see me advance, call back your men and leave. Try to make your way to the headquarters of the *Vigiles* and send help."

Agrippa said nothing, but held out his arm. Alexander grasped it below the elbow as Agrippa grasped his firmly in return.

Then Alexander turned toward the men from the congregations and yelled, "*All men to me.*"

Dozens of faces turned to him, many of them very old or very young, and in their eyes he saw confusion and fear. These men were not trained fighters. Their chances were slim and they knew it. And Alexander knew it as well. He could feel his own jaw clenched with tension. Yet he knew that he must not let it show.

Whenever he was threatened, Alexander's instinctive response was to throw back his shoulders making full use of his six foot height. He did this now, and forced himself to relax his clenched jaw endeavoring to project the confidence that he did not feel. Then he stepped towards the gathered men.

"We are not gladiators in the ring," he yelled. "We must fight them *any way* we can. Form yourselves into groups of two, one closely behind another. The man in front shall block his attacker's blows while the other strikes hard at the kneecap or groin. When the enemy falters, strike his head. Those without clubs, take the weapons of the men who fall. Understood?"

He heard a number of yeahs and saw the men pair up and began to form a line where he pointed. To Alexander's relief, he saw the bigger men take the front. They might not have been trained fighters, but many of these men were laborers and strong. If only they were not so greatly outnumbered.

Alexander strode to the center of the line and held his club up.

"Walk with me!" he called and slowly the line marched forward until they stood abreast at the place previously held by Amarantus and Agrippa's men. The latter began to fall back as he expected.

Suddenly, their attackers let out a huge shout and lunged forward. Alexander barely had enough time to react when the lead man was upon him. He struck the man's knife away and from the corner of his eye he saw a club swing up from behind him into the other man's groin.

As that man collapsed, he stepped into the next attack. In his own line, he could hear cries of pain and knew that many of his fellow Jews were falling. An eternity of seconds elapsed. Alexander could sense that his own line was starting to be pushed back. With a cry the man to his left went down. In his place appeared a huge black Nubian man with a club in one hand and knife in the other. Alexander had no time to wonder at this, but continued to block and parry the onslaught of blows.

Long moments passed filled with more cries, then, unexpectedly, the fighting began to slow. With many shouts, their attackers began to break and run.

"Alexander, do we follow?" a voice cried.

"No! Stay with the synagogue," he yelled back. Behind him he could hear other men take up the cry, "Stay with the synagogue."

And suddenly all was quiet. Their attackers had fled.

Alexander leaned forward placing his hands on his knees, panting for breath, feeling his heart racing. A thickly accented voice came from next to him.

"*You fight well.* I think you have trained on the Field of Mars."

Alexander glanced up and saw a Parthian standing next to him with the strangely curled hair and beard of that people. The man looked back and smiled. Puzzled, Alexander looked about him. All around him were Jews... *and* Greeks, Germans, Gauls, Parthians, Nubians, and he couldn't guess what others.

Alexander turned back to the Parthian and stammered, "*Who? ... what... I...*"

".. don't understand?" the Parthian finished for him. "Don't act so surprised. This is *our* home, too. We're all *Transtiberini* and we don't much care for these strangers crossing the river and threatening our homes and businesses."

"You mean they weren't locals?" Alexander asked.

The large Nubian appeared next to the Parthian and let out a grunt of disgust.

"No," the Parthian answered. "Fighting is one thing. But no *Transtiberini* would carry torches like that. Look over there at the wharves and warehouses. They're mostly wood. If they caught fire, nothing could have stopped the spread to the whole district."

The Nubian spoke a few words that Alexander couldn't understand.

"*He* is correct," the Parthian nodding at his companion. "The Praetorians should have known better."

Alexander jerked back in surprise. "Praetorians? You mean the men we were fighting were part of the Praetorian Guard?"

"No, no, not them. The men who were *behind* them. There were two of them -- at least that we saw. 'Brought those strangers over across the bridge, then they started handing out money. The fools. Don't they realize that the food in those warehouses is what feeds them, too?"

Praetorians, again. Alexander felt disgusted. A nearby groan brought him back to the present. He turned back to the Parthian.

"I should help with the wounded. But first, how can I thank you? You have saved many lives today, including my own."

The Parthian shook his head. "We don't *want* your thanks. Like I told you, we *Transtiberini* stick together. And in case you've forgotten it, *you* are *not* one of *us*." He gave Alexander a mock salute, then, he and the Nubian quickly disappeared into one of the alleys that led away from the river.

Alexander turned to help his fellow Jews, who had already begun carrying their injured into the synagogue. A man pointed to the fallen among their attackers.

"Alexander, what shall we do with *them*?"

"Leave them. The *Vigiles* should arrive soon and they can deal with them. *We* will not help the men who tried to burn a house of the Lord."

Amarantus appeared at his side and Alexander noticed with relief that his servant appeared uninjured other than a bruise on his cheek.

"Master, the old woman inside is asking for you."

Sarah, the Mother of the Synagogue. She was another person Alexander needed to thank. If she had not hidden those clubs in her litter, the congregations would not have had even a fighting chance.

He found her just inside the entrance of the synagogue issuing orders and directing men as the wounded were brought in. No one seemed to question Sarah's authority to take charge, and Alexander could see that she was handling the situation well.

Sarah eventually seemed to notice his presence and motioned him over to join her.

"I've sent for our healers," she said. "They should start arriving soon. Until then, we'll do what we can."

"How bad is it?" Alexander asked her.

"It could have been worse. We've got one man dead. Another took a knife in the shoulder, but I think he might live if the healer gets here soon. Other than that, we have some broken bones and a few bad cuts and bruises. They'll all live, but a few of them won't be able to work for awhile and that will be hard on them and their families."

Sarah gave Alexander one of her defiant looks. "Can I *assume* that you will be making a *generous* contribution for the congregation to help them?"

Alexander smiled for the first time that night. "Yes. You can. I'll have my banker send it over tomorrow. And …. Sarah … a lot of us would be dead tonight, if it hadn't been for you. Not a single man thought to bring weapons. You saved us from being slaughtered and the synagogue burned."

Sarah gave a little harrumph and pretended to wave it away, but Alexander could tell she was pleased. Then her look turned serious.

"I will tell you that I didn't think much about the leaders of the synagogue asking you boys here tonight. *'We don't need those Roman boys,'* I told them. *'We can look after ourselves like we always do.'*

"But here you came and, Alexander, you did well leading our men into battle. You defeated the heathens and you saved our Torah and synagogue. You must be a true son of God."

Alexander blinked and looked away in embarrassment. Jews only used the expression *'son of God'* for describing the most devout of men. He felt that he hardly qualified. But when he looked back, Sarah had fixed him with a piercing look.

"You *fix this*, Alexander. You're the only one who can. I *know* this. I've had another one of my premonitions."

And as Alexander stared back with his mouth fallen open, Sarah the Mother of the Synagogue bustled off to minister to the wounded.

22

MURDER

"LOCAL tavern fight," Agrippa spat. "Drunken dock workers having a fist fight. Honestly, Alexander, I tried, but that fool tribune of the *Vigiles* refused to believe what I was telling him."

Alexander had dropped by Agrippa's home the morning after the fight for the synagogue to confirm that he had made it home safely.

The previous night, Agrippa had made it unharmed to the headquarters for the *Vigiles*, but had found their tribune to be very slow to respond to Agrippa's pleas for help. After much unseemly delay, the tribune had finally sent a few men to check it out. They had reported back that they had found evidence for no more than a *scuffle* between a few locals. They called it a tavern fight that had spilled out into the streets.

Agrippa was still livid, but Alexander was not surprised. He told him what he had learned from the Parthian about the two Praetorian Guards who had incited the attackers.

"The Praetorians, again?" Agrippa had responded. "They are growing bolder."

"Indeed. ... Shall we take it to Germanicus?"

Agrippa shook his head. "Once again, *where* is the proof? Even if you could find this Parthian again, what are the odds that he would testify ... or that anyone would believe him? He's obviously not a Roman. His word wouldn't count for much."

Agrippa hesitated as his eyes fell on Amarantus who had been waiting quietly a few feet away in the garden where the men were talking.

"I heard that slave of yours, Alexander, did pretty well last night. He seems a useful sort to have around. Yes, I could use a man like that. "

Alexander waved a casual hand. "Yes, yes, but tell me this. What is happening with that mysterious source you said you have, Agrippa? The one with my gold piece? When is he going to start to earn it?"

"*Hmm,* I've had no word from him yet. I'll put some pressure on and see if we can discover what these Praetorians are trying to accomplish."

Alexander gave him a dubious look. "Let's hope he comes up with something helpful before any more Jews have to die. ... Listen, Agrippa, I think it's time to regroup. Let's get Claudius and Rutilus together and go over the facts again. Maybe some new ideas will turn up."

"Good idea. The baths again?" Agrippa asked with a wry smile.

"I think not; too dangerous. Why don't you three come to my home for dinner? I'll have Amarantus order from a local tavern and pick up some good wine. Will you send word to Claudius and Rutilus for me?"

Agrippa nodded his agreement.

"Consider it done. And, Alexander, be careful. I would hate to hear that the next death is *yours.*"

***

Alexander stopped at his banker's on the way home and

arranged for a sizable gift to be delivered to the heads of both synagogues. It was a generous sum, but he felt sure his father would agree with the amount given the circumstances. Last night, Jews had been cut down in the street, many hurt so they would not be able to work. At least one woman was now a widow.

He then visited a silversmith's shop and selected a handsome serving dish and arranged to have it delivered to Sarah. Such were the manners that Berenice had instilled in him as a boy. But Alexander doubted that he would have needed Berenice's teachings to remember to thank the woman who had probably saved his life – many of their lives. He did not even want to think what would have happened if Sarah had not thought to hide so many clubs in her litter.

As they headed for home, Alexander found his thoughts preoccupied by the mystery of the missing statue and the previous night's events. Once again, he had cause to be thankful for his servant's vigilance. It was Amarantus who placed a restraining hand on his shoulder as they turned a corner onto the street that led to his apartment.

He glanced back and gave his slave an inquiring look. "What is it?"

"Look, Master," Amarantus responded gesturing homeward.

Alexander turned back and took in the situation at once. In front of the door to his apartment building, lounged a couple of men in military-style uniforms. Immediately, he thought of the Praetorians and was nearly seized with a sense of panic. Amarantus pulled him back into a recess of the nearest building where they could observe the men more closely without being seen.

Surreptitiously, Alexander leaned forward to sneak a glance, then let out a breath as he leaned back.

"They are *not* Praetorians."

"No, Master?"

"No. They're not wearing red tunics and the crests on their helmets are wrong. Those are two of the Urban Cohorts, Augustus's daytime police."

Amarantus gave him a puzzled look. "What could they want with you, Master?"

"I'm as mystified as you, but I do think you are right – they *must* be looking for *me*. With all that has happened, it seems most unlikely that they are waiting for anyone else in our building."

Amarantus shook his head back and forth. "I don't like this, Master. I think we should leave."

Alexander stole another glance at the waiting men of the Cohorts.

"I don't like it either. But I don't see that I have much choice, except perhaps never going home again … We could slip out of the city in the middle of the night and catch the first boat out of Ostia.

"… No, no, Ranti, I am not serious about that. I think that I had better go face them and learn what they want."

He laid a hand on Amarantus' chest and gently shoved him back into the shadowed recess where they had been standing.

"*Not you*, Ranti. You wait here. *No* protests. You're the only one who will know where I am. If things go wrong, if the Cohorts arrest me or seem to take me against my will, go straight to Agrippa and tell him everything. Do you understand?"

Amarantus looked unhappy, but nodded and held back as ordered. Alexander stepped out into the street and resumed walking home, in what he hoped appeared to be a normal stride. As he reached his door, the two men of the Urban Cohorts stood up straight.

"Are you Gaius Julius Alexander?"

"I am."

"We've been sent to request your assistance with an investigation."

Hmmm. Urban Cohorts standing respectfully and politely requesting his assistance? Whatever Alexander had expected, this was definitely not it.

"What kind of investigation?" he asked.

"Murder, Sir."

"Murder? Is it a Jew?"

"Not that we know of, Sir."

"Then why come to me?"

"Because of this, Sir."

The soldier held out a small broken shard of pottery and Alexander took it. On it was scratched *G Iul Alex – Capitol – E foun.* The words were abbreviated, but their meaning was clear. He read them aloud.

"Gaius Julius Alexander, Capitoline Hill, East of the fountain."

"That is you, isn't it, Sir?"

"It would seem to be. Where did you get this?"

"The dead man had it in his pouch. When we saw that it was your name, we realized that we should come to you at once."

Alexander tilted his head and regarded the soldier. "And why is that?"

"Orders, Sir. One of the Consuls sent a request to the Urban Prefect that the Cohorts should offer you every possible assistance."

One of the Consuls. He must mean *Germanicus.* So Agrippa had been right that Germanicus would find a way to help them after all. He couldn't take on the Praetorian Guard, so he enlisted the support of the Urban Cohorts, the city police, instead.

Alexander began to relax as he realized these men were not there to arrest him. He glanced back and saw Amarantus stealing a peek around the corner and waved him over.

Turning back to the Urban Cohorts he remarked, "So a murdered man had my name and address in his pouch. Isn't it unusual for a murdered man to still have his pouch?"

"Most unusual, Sir, and there were a few coins in the pouch as well. The motive couldn't have been robbery."

"And you're sure he wasn't a Jew?"

The second man broke into a grin as he spoke for the first time. "Well, if he was a Jew, he was a *really smelly* one," he guffawed until the other gave him a stern look and he straightened back up.

That was a description that Alexander recognized.

"Smelly, you say. Is he a small man who looks like a rat with greasy hair, beady little eyes, a filthy oversized tunic that was once white and a smell so horrible that it could knock you out from ten feet away?"

"Can't say about the eyes, Sir, because that part of his head was smashed ... and I would put the smell more at 15-20 feet, but that sounds about right. Do you know him?"

"Well," drawled Alexander, "not intimately." He grinned as the second Cohort failed to hold in a derisive '*huh.*' "But I do know of him. He is known only as 'the Rat' and he's an informer and a blackmailer."

"Is that ... *errr*... how he came to have *your* name, Sir?"

"*No!* No, at least not directly. As you must be aware given your orders, I am investigating the disappearance of the statue of Victory. There were indications that this Rat may have had some information regarding its disappearance. He was cagey about it though. I told him where I lived and offered to pay him for his information, but he never came forward to collect the money. I had assumed that was because he had nothing to sell, but now ... I wonder."

He looked at the spokesman for the Cohorts. "Where is the body?"

"At headquarters, Sir. Would you care to see it?"

"I would. We should confirm that the body really is this Rat who has kept popping up during my investigation. Let's go now and you can fill me in on the details as we walk."

Alexander turned to Amarantus now standing behind him and motioned for him to follow. As they headed for the headquarters, the senior man of the Urban Cohorts began to fill him in. The Rat appeared to have been killed sometime the night before and his body had been dumped in an alley on the Palatine Hill.

"The Palatine, you say? Was he near an entrance to the sewers? ... perhaps the one near the Forum Boarium?"

"I don't think so, Sir."

"How about a sewer cover? Was the body near a sewer cover?"

"*Hmm*, 'Can't say how close to a sewer cover without taking another look at the scene. Is it important?"

Alexander shook his head.

"Probably, not. It's just that my searches have indicated that this Rat spent a lot of time in and around sewers. Apparently, lurking under sewer covers was how he could overhear private conversations and later use that information for blackmail. ... What makes you say that the body had been dumped?"

"No blood, Sir. At least, not enough. If he had been killed where he was found there should have been more blood ... and bones and brain splatter. You'll see."

The guard from the Cohort explained that the Rat appeared

to have been killed by repeated heavy blows to his head. They had crushed his skull and smashed his upper face. Normally the *Vigiles* who had watch duty at night would have discovered him, but it had been a busy night and the alley had been dark. He and his fellow Cohort were the ones who had discovered the body during their morning patrol of the Palatine. When they had examined the contents in the Rat's pouch, they found the pottery shard with Alexander's name and decided to have the body removed to their headquarters.

"If it weren't for that shard with your name on it, we wouldn't have bothered with him. He was clearly a man of no consequence and we don't have time to investigate the death of that sort. Normally, we just would have had him hauled off to a pit outside the city walls."

"I'm glad you did come to me," Alexander replied. "No doubt, a man like that would have had a dozen enemies happy to give him a good knock on the head. But somehow, I have a feeling that this Rat holds a missing clue in the mystery of the statue."

They arrived at the headquarters for the Urban Cohorts and Alexander started for the front door when the senior Cohort gave him a sheepish look.

"Not in *there*, Sir. The smell was too bad. We've got him out back."

They circled the building toward the back where Alexander saw an old shed and walked toward it. The senior cohort cleared his throat.

"*Ehem*, not in there either, Sir. The smell again; the supply master wouldn't allow it."

Alexander looked back with a bemused expression. "Then where in Romulus's domain have you put him?"

"Over there, Sir."

The senior Cohort pointed to a spot on the grounds at the

very farthest edge of the enclosure around the headquarters. Alexander could make out what must have been a figure lying on the ground and headed toward it.

"*Wheeow,*" came a cry from behind him. He looked back to see Amarantus with his tunic pulled up to cover the lower part of his face.

"Master, it's even worse now than before."

"I guess that comes from being dead," Alexander smiled back. "You can wait here, Ranti."

He took a few deep breaths and tried to hold the last one in, as he and the senior Cohort approached the figure alone.

It was the Rat all right -- no mistaking that -- lying on his back in the open. Alexander studied him. His upper face and forehead had been crushed, but enough was left to identify him. There was something more, though. The Rat's tunic was as filthy as before, but there appeared to be some new spots. Alexander squatted down to study them, then looked up at the senior Cohort.

"These stains appear to be new." He touched one of them and a residue of blue paint came off on his finger. "He seems to have rubbed up against something that has been recently painted. Look, the paint must not have been completely dry. And what do you make of this?"

"Chalk," the Cohort replied, looking at the place where Alexander pointed. "It's mixed in with the paint, although, I can't imagine what he might have touched that would have been covered with paint and chalk together. See, it's on his hands, too."

"Curious," Alexander commented. "I know he was down in the Subura harassing some sculptors, but I don't think they would have let him get close enough to touch their work. And why chalk? Sculptors wouldn't apply chalk to a statue. What do you make of the wound?"

With a grimace, the Cohort wedged his boot under the Rat's

head and shoved it to the side so Alexander could see it better.

"'Definitely hit with a blunt, object like rock or club. Hard to say for sure, but I'm guessing this was the first strike.'"

He pointed at an injury to the left side of the head just above the jaw. The Rat's long, greasy hair was stuck in a bloody wound that was nearly horizontal with only a slight upward angle. Again, Alexander looked up expectantly at the Cohort.

"When someone smashes a man's skull, isn't the blow higher up and vertical?"

"Indeed it is, Sir. Usually the assailant will hold his club up over his own head with both hands and then bring it smashing down on the victim's head – the momentum gives the blow extra force. But this blow looks like the assailant held the weapon at his side and then swung it around and up into the head."

"Can you guess why that would be?"

"Difficult to say, Sir. It could be that the weapon was something heavy and the man wasn't strong enough to heave it over his head. So he simply swung it from his side. ... Did you notice that it's near the front of his head. I'd say that whoever struck was standing right in front on him. ... which would explain these follow-up blows."

Alexander now had his hand covering his mouth, fingers pinching his nostrils and he looked as the mess of smashed bone and brain tissue that spanned from the nose to the forehead. Again he looked up at the senior Cohort.

"This looks like repeated blows to face. Many of these strikes would have happened long after the man was already dead. What would cause someone to keep striking like that?"

"Rage," the senior Cohort replied. "Uncontrolled rage."

"*Huh.* Yes, that would make sense," Alexander replied as he stood back up. "I think I've seen all there is to see here. Let's get away from this smell."

Alexander questioned the Cohorts further, but was unable to discover anything more that might be useful. Still, he had the distinct feeling that he had just uncovered an important clue even though he couldn't make sense of any of it yet.

He thanked the two men from the Cohorts and insisted that they accept a few coins for their trouble. Then he and Amarantus puzzled through the Rat's evidence on the way home trying to make up different scenarios that would account for the paint, chalk, and nature of the wound. They were unable to come up with anything that quite worked.

***

After they returned home, Alexander sat down in his office and pulled out the scroll he had begun several days earlier with the sequence of events surrounding the theft of the statue. He added everything new that he had learned, then sat back staring at it for a long while.

While he worked, Amarantus had bustled around setting out a light lunch on the desk before him. At some point, Alexander realized that his servant had been keeping up an almost non-stop stream of muttering. That was not like Amarantus. Furrowing his brows, he listened without looking up.

"I just don't know what's happening to Rome. Guards forcing their way into people's homes. Prostitutes summoning decent citizens. Slaves being sold; no reason at all."

"Ranti, is something wrong?"

Amarantus looked up feigning surprise that he had been overheard.

"Oh no, Master. What could be wrong? After all, I am just a slave. Slaves have no feelings, anymore than they have any say what happens to them. We're just here to serve, until the master decides to beat us ... or sell us to foolish young princes."

"Ranti, this is not like you. Now, I'm *sure* something's wrong. What's this nonsense about getting beaten and sold?"

Amarantus looked petulant.

"It is not for *me* to say, Master. After all *I* have no say over what you do with me. I'm only a worthless burden. There's no reason for *you* to care what happens to *me*."

Alexander cast about for some explanation for Amarantus' strange behavior. Amarantus had always been like a rock for him; someone he could always count on. He had confided in his servant and trusted him. He had certainly never beaten him. Suddenly, Alexander latched onto Amarantus' words *"foolish young princes"* and understanding dawned.

"Sit down, Ranti."

But Amarantus had gotten himself too worked up to comply. *"Sit?!* A slave sit in the presence of his master? Many are the slaves who have been beaten for sitting in the presence of their masters."

Alexander bit back a smile. Amarantus must be truly upset to be behaving like this.

"Amarantus, I said *sit*. That's an order."

Amarantus immediately collapsed into a huddle on the floor.

"On the *stool*, Amarantus, on the stool," Alexander laughed. "Take that one there and pull it closer. Do it *now*, Amarantus. No more histrionics."

Amarantus begrudgingly pulled forward the stool Alexander had indicated and sat down on the edge trying to look as uncomfortable as possible.

"Truly, you missed your calling as an actor," Alexander smiled. "But, Ranti, now I need you to sit back and talk to me like a man. I think that it's time that we had a serious talk."

To his surprise, a look of fear flashed across Amarantus' face, but then his servant sat back and masked his expression.

"Now, Ranti, I suspect all of this drama has something to do with the somewhat flippant remark by Agrippa that I should sell you to him when I leave for Alexandria. Is this correct?"

Amarantus nodded.

"I have no intention of selling you to Agrippa or to anyone else."

A look of relief came over Amarantus' face.

"If anything, I should consider freeing you. Not only have you been a great help to me, you have saved my life on more than one occasion. Was it just yesterday that you kept me out of the *merda*?

"And so, Amarantus, I shall give you a choice. I can free you before I leave Rome, or you can stay with me and accompany me to Alexandria."

Amarantus considered for a moment and responded, "I should like to go with you to Alexandria."

"You are sure?"

"Yes, Master. I would like to be freed someday, but if you free me before you leave I will be left in Rome with no job and no patron. Besides, I think that *you* will *need me* in your new home."

Alexander felt strangely relieved. He had been too busy to think much about going home, at least not consciously. But after Amarantus' words, he realized that he had been feeling a growing trepidation about returning to the home that he could barely recall.

"It is settled then. You will return with me to Alexandria."

Amarantus looked pensive.

"Master, you know of the man who was my previous master?"

"I do," Alexander replied thinking of the old scars that

marked his slave's body. "And it shames me to know that I walk the same streets as that animal."

Amarantus nodded. "Things were ... were... bad then. Master, I never knew that life could be good like it is with you."

Alexander searched for something to say in return, but Roman men just didn't show their emotions, not in matters like this.

"I understand," he said softly and was relieved when Amarantus jumped up and began rearranging the food laid out before him.

"Fetch a little more and a plate for yourself," Alexander ordered. "I have much to tell you before our company arrives for dinner tonight."

***

The time for dinner came and Claudius and Rutilus arrived from the Palatine Hill sharing the same litter. Agrippa, however, sent a slave with a brief note saying that he had been unavoidably detained. He suggested they begin dinner without him. To this, he had added a postscript that they should be sure to save some wine for when he joined them. In characteristic Agrippa style, the urgent request that they save some wine for him had been longer than the message itself.

Alexander's apartment did not have a kitchen, of course; no apartment did for fear of fire. Like most apartment dwellers, Alexander ate most meals out, or, had his slave pick up food from local taverns or food stalls to eat in. That kind of food was not suitable for entertaining guests, so Alexander had an agreement with one of the nearby houses that had its own kitchen and chef. As long as he gave notice, and, paid a rather hefty price, the chef would have a full meal prepared for Amarantus to pick up and serve.

Alexander's apartment had a main room in its center and

tonight three couches had been arranged in typical dining fashion.

While the men dined and waited for Agrippa to arrive, Alexander related to Claudius and Rutilus the events of the past two days. Rutilus had been there for part of it, so he chimed in with whatever details he could remember. Claudius, then, lay back on his couch and scrunched his brow and rubbed his chin in concentration. Finally, he seemed to come to some conclusion in his mind and rolled back over to face his friends.

"I know that some of these events seem important, and perhaps they are in some way. By that, I mean the Rat's visit to the sculptors, his murder, and also these attacks by the Praetorians. However, to my mind, it keeps coming back to the role of the *augur* in all of this.

"After all, the temple priest reported that it *was* Lucius Servilius who took the statue. The response of Lucius Servilius was that he couldn't have taken it because he was out of town. But we know from our own eyewitness, Rutilus, that he was not. There *must* be some way to determine once and for all 'Did Lucius Servilius take the statue?'"

"I agree," Alexander replied. "And that's why I ..."

Alexander was interrupted by the approach of Amarantus who was leading a familiar-looking young boy.

"He is there now?" Alexander asked the boy simply.

"He is," the boy answered with a triumphant smile.

"Excellent. Pay him, Amarantus."

Alexander turned back to Claudius and Rutilus. "Friends, can I persuade you to join me on a trip to *the Venus House*?"

23
THE THIRD FLOOR

"**YOU** did what?" Rutilus asked.

"Bribed the boy," Alexander responded. "He works at the Venus House running errands and doing small chores. No one takes much note of a slave boy, so I paid him to be my eyes for me."

"But, why?"

"To catch Lucius Servilius in an awkward position. Like Claudius, I also believe that we must determine the role the *augur* played in the disappearance of the statue. I couldn't very well go to his home and ask him if he took it. -- any more than I could have gone to the home of the Senator Gnaeus Pulcher and asked him if he had stolen any statues lately.

"But at the Venus House, Servilius is vulnerable because he is acting contrary to the moral reforms of the First Citizen. As one of Rome's top priests, Servilius is expected to set an example. He is supposed to be producing a new generation of baby patricians; instead he's behaving like a Greek. If we can catch him at it, maybe we can force him to talk to us for fear that we might tell everyone what he is doing.

"Then I'd like to have you Rutilus, if you will, face him with the evidence that you saw him there in the Venus House the day the statue disappeared."

"Brilliant," Claudius enjoined enthusiastically.

"And it gets even better," Rutilus added with a grin. "Do

you realize what else this means? … We're finally going to get see what happens on the third floor!"

Before setting out, the three men put their heads together to plan their approach. The biggest problem was going to be sneaking up to the third floor, then getting past the door guard who, no doubt, was some big, burly ex-gladiator.

They decided that Claudius could not join Alexander and Rutilus when they faced Lucius Servilius. Since he was a member of the imperial family and Servilius one of the senior *augurs*, they felt that Claudius shouldn't risk any political repercussions. Instead, he would be their first decoy. They would all enter the Venus House together and Claudius would engage a prostitute on the second floor. The other men would stay on the first floor and take some wine and pretend to be waiting for him. But as soon as they had a chance, they would sneak up the back staircase that led to the third floor.

The next part, the most dangerous, fell to Amarantus. It would be his job to get the guard to leave the floor long enough for Alexander and Rutilus to slip into the room with Lucius Servilius. The three friends debated how Amarantus could accomplish this for a while, but came up with no sure ideas. So Alexander called Amarantus over to join them and asked him how he thought he could manage it.

Amarantus thought about it for a few moments talking softly to himself and occasionally shaking his head as he appeared to be considering and then discarding different options. Finally, he looked up and nodded.

"I think I can manage it, Master. I'll go up the back stairwell with you, but I will enter before you. At first, I'll walk calmly past the guard saying that I'm the slave of a man in one of the rooms and that I need to speak with him. Once the guard gets over his surprise, he will try to prevent me from interrupting a guest.

"When he does, I'll begin to scream that this proves that '*the man'* is there and that I am going to inform on him. Then I'll race down the hall toward the public staircase on the opposite end yelling over and over that I'm going to inform. The guard should chase after me to try to stop me, and I will lead him down the staircase. That should give you some time to find Lucius Servilius."

Alexander shook his head. "That's no good. If the guard catches you, you'll be severely beaten, perhaps even killed."

"Then I will have to make sure that he does not catch me, Master."

"No, Ranti, it's too dangerous. He could catch you."

"Then he'll say he's with *me*," Claudius said. "It's still a little dangerous; but, if Amarantus is caught, he'll simply have to yell that he is a slave of the imperial family. Even an ex-gladiator has brains enough to know that it is risky to beat or kill a slave of the imperial family. That should bring the management around and they'll most likely summon me. I'll take charge of my *naughty* slave and assure them that I'll see to his punishment personally."

They looked at Alexander expectantly and he reluctantly agreed. "That *should* work. But, Ranti, when you encounter the door guard on the third floor, save the yelling about *"informing"* until you reach the staircase. We don't want to alert Lucius Servilius."

Claudius had left his litter waiting nearby. Since he was partially lame in one leg, he usually rode unless he was only travelling a short distance. His litter was a *sella*, a sedan chair that could hold two, but there were three of them.

"Rutilus, you should ride with Claudius," Alexander said. "I am too anxious to ride, anyway. I'll walk ahead of you; perhaps, the exercise will calm me down."

Claudius' litter caught up with Alexander and Amarantus at the Venus House on the Palatine Hill. The young men soon set their plan into motion. Claudius left with the prostitute, and

Alexander and Rutilus settled onto couches and ordered wine. Amarantus hovered nearby, ever the attentive slave.

After about ten minutes, the manager was called away and Amarantus joined Alexander and Rutilus as they slipped up the back staircase. Amarantus' part seemed to go off as planned, but Alexander felt a knot in his stomach as he looked through the cracked door and watched an extremely large guard chasing his slave down the hall.

"I hope he makes it," he breathed softly.

"That is definitely *not* the same door guard that I bribed that day we found out about Lucius Servilius," Rutilus whispered back. "I don't think *that* one would have taken my bribe. In fact, I doubt I would have had the courage to try."

"Come on, then, we don't have much time," Alexander said as they stepped in and closed the door to the stairwell softly behind them.

Alexander and Rutilus gazed down the hallway. There appeared to be fewer rooms than on the second floor and each one had a wooden door.

"Which door was it?" Alexander whispered.

"I don't know. Remember, I saw him when he was already exiting in the stairwell. It could be any of them."

"Romulus's balls, I should have asked that boy before we came up."

Suddenly, an odd sound came from the first door on their right. It was like a goat bleating, but not quite that. Rutilus grinned and shrugged.

"Guess we'll have to try each door until we find him."

Before Alexander could reply, Rutilus knelt down with his hand on the latch and slowly cracked the door open. Alexander crouched over him and stared in through the crack. He immediately knew it wasn't the right room, but neither of them could pull themselves away from the sight that had met their eyes.

The room had been converted into a pastoral scene with greenery everywhere. To the side was a small fountain dressed to look like a pool, and, next to the pool, stood the god Pan -- sort of. A fat, florid faced man stood there completely naked except for goat's fur leggings wrapped around each leg ending in what looked like little round boots shaped like hooves. On his chin was a fake beard and a pair of horns had been strapped to his head. A scantily clad *"nymph"* knelt in front of him playing his pipe. As they watched, the god Pan threw back his head and let out another goat-like bleat.

Alexander felt Rutilus suck in a breath and quickly clamped a hand over his friend's mouth as he gently pulled the door shut. Rutilus looked up at him and let out a soft cackle.

"Alexander, wasn't that ..."

"Yes," Alexander interrupted. "And if you're smart, you will forget that you ever saw that. Come on, let's keep looking."

He was trying to sound stern, but Alexander could hardly hold back his own laughter. They crept over to the first door on the other side of the hall. Again Rutilus knelt down and Alexander crouched over him as they opened the door a crack.

There was no pastoral scene here. Instead the room was bare of all water and greenery and was strewn with sand and rocks. In the center of the room was a huge boulder, although Alexander suspected it had probably been fabricated from paint and plaster. Chained outstretched to the rock was a nude man whom he quickly deduced was 'Prometheus' -- although the scrawny, gray haired man hardly conjured up the heroic figure of legend. Standing over him was a woman wearing an elaborate headdress. The headdress was in the shape of a vulture, but the few tight leather straps that covered the rest of her resembled no costume that Alexander recognized from art.

Prometheus let out a groan and cried, "It was I who stole the fire to benefit all of mankind. If this has angered the gods then you must punish me for my crime."

The woman-vulture held a lit oil lamp over him. "By fire you have sinned against the gods and by fire you shall be punished." Then she tipped the lamp and spilled a few drops of the hot oil.

Alexander reached for the latch and pulled the door shut as Prometheus writhed and cried, "*Punish me, O gods!* You must punish me more."

Alexander and Rutilus stared at each other in astonishment. Then Alexander said softly, "Yes, that *was* who you think, and you had best forget that you ever saw that one as well."

With a growing fascination, they huddled down at the next door and peeked inside. This room was much larger and looked like it had been made from the joining of several rooms. Inside had been re-created a small village with several straw huts. A 'battle' was being waged around them. Men carrying clubs and wearing fierce expressions were scattered throughout the room beating back other men -- probably slaves of the brothel -- who didn't appear to be putting up much of a fight. Women were shrieking and lamenting as the victors grabbed them and threw them to the ground.

Alexander's blood rose as a man nearby knelt over a girl with a look of pure terror on her face. Without thinking, he half-rose to go to her aid, but this time Rutilus grabbed him with a hiss and held him back. The girl must have heard them for she glanced over to the door and gave them a quick smile and a wink. Then her face transformed back to one of fear as she began to beg for mercy.

Rutilus pulled Alexander back and shut the door. "It's the rape of the Sabine women," he explained. "It's one of Rome's oldest stories about how the early settlers captured their wives."

Alexander nodded curtly, but couldn't control the bile that had risen inside of him. "What kind of men require this sort of … entertainment?"

"Bored men, Alexander. Men with too much time and money on their hands. Calm down, now. Remember we are looking for Lucius Servilius. Let's try another door."

The next door was on the opposite side of the hall, and it took only a moment to realize that they had finally found the right one. And just in time too, because behind them they heard a stomping on the stairwell that must have been the door guard returning.

Quickly, Alexander pushed Rutilus into the room and closed the door softly behind them. This room was much smaller than the others and luxuriously appointed. The window was draped with silk and embroidered and beaded cushions were strewn over an intricately woven Persian rug. The main piece of furniture in the room was a large bed in the center made of carved wood that had been gilded with gold and encrusted with lapis lazuli and carnelian.

On the bed lay the *augur* Lucius Servilius wearing an embroidered silk robe that had been pulled open and draped at his sides. His head rested on the shoulder of a large, naked man as his hand slid through the other's abundant chest hair. On the other side of the *augur* was yet another large, muscular man with a well oiled physique. As they watched, an oiled arm shot out, wrapped around the *augur*'s waist and heaved him up onto his knees. The *augur* gave a little whimper of protest, but that belied the smile on his face.

Alexander was pretty sure he didn't want to see whatever was about to happen next. He took a quick step forward and cleared his throat loudly. Lucius Servilus's eyes flew open, vaguely seemed to focus on Alexander, and then instantly kindled with anger.

"Here, now. What's the meaning of this? These *boys* are mine, paid for already. You can't have either of them."

"We are not here to take your *boys*," Alexander snapped back.

"Well, I don't do groups. The management knows that. Now get out."

Before Alexander could think of a suitable retort, Rutilus pushed past him and settled himself on the end of the bed.

Fixing him with a wicked grin, Rutilus said, "Hello there. Recognize me? We've met here before, Lucius Servilius."

Now the *augur's* anger turned suspicious. He settled back sitting on his heels – although he didn't bother to close his robe. "Who are you? What do you want?"

"*The truth*," Alexander replied stepping forward. "My name is Gaius Julius Alexander and I am investigating the theft of the statue of Victory."

"So?" the *augur* replied. "I don't know anything about that. I've already spoken with Augustus and assured him that I was out of town when that happened."

"Well, now, that's not really true, Lucius Servilius, is it?"

The *augur* fixed Alexander with an angry look, but said nothing.

"You see, you may not recognize my friend here, but he recognizes *you*. It seems that you bumped into him in the stairwell on the Ides of July. That would be the *same* day that the statue was taken … the same day that the priest reported having seen *you* take it."

The *augur* muttered a curse and glared at Alexander.

"What do you *want*?" he finally demanded.

"As I have already said, Lucius Servilius, I want the truth. First, why did you tell Augustus that you were out of town that day?"

The augur looked worried for a moment and then gave Alexander a look of pure venom.

"I've never *heard of you* and I owe you nothing. What's passed between the First Citizen and me is our business, you wretched freedman."

"Now, that's where you're wrong, Lucius Servilius. I am no freedman, but I am one of Augustus's personal clients."

Alexander saw the *augur's* eyes flicker at that. He must be wondering if Augustus had sent him.

"The man who has been arrested is one of *my* clients. Therefore, Augustus has charged me with investigating the theft. In fact, he has ordered me to report immediately to Tiberius with every *new* piece of information. Shall we go there now to discuss this? Or better yet, shall we summon Tiberius here .... to *this* room?"

Alexander gestured obliquely at the two hairy, muscular men lying on the bed. He could see that Lucius Servilius was struggling between anger and fear, the desire to call the door guard and the fear that his threat to go to Tiberius might be true. In the end, caution won out.

"What do you want? Money?" the *augur* snarled.

Alexander sighed. "No, Lucius Servilius. What I *want* is the missing statue of Victory. Let's try this again. Where were you the night of the Ides?"

"Here," the *augur* answered shortly.

"Do you mean, here in Rome?"

"I mean here in this room."

Alexander did a double take. "You were here during the

afternoon. We saw you leave."

"I came back that night … with a friend who was visiting from Baiae."

"*Ahh.* And would that be the same friend who provided you with your alibi for being in Baiae that night?"

The *augur* nodded. "Check with the owner. He keeps records of all his Third Floor appointments. He can verify that I was here the whole night."

"I'll do that. Now tell me, Lucius Servilius, why did the priest at the temple report that you were there that night, if you were actually here?"

The *augur* let out a series of curse words before something intelligible finally came out.

"That old *mentula* is as blind as a bat. He couldn't identify his own mother at ten feet."

"Really, he told me that his vision was quite good."

The *augur* let out a snort. "He *told* you that he could see well? You've never spent any time as an advocate, have you? Go back and this time don't ask him, test him. See if he can recognize a stick of his own incense from five paces. Besides, he says himself that this person, if there even was someone, never claimed to be me. Ask him yourself."

"I'll do that, Lucius Servilius," Alexander nodded slowly. "But one more thing. Is anyone blackmailing you?"

The *augur* gave him an ugly look, but said nothing, so Alexander prodded him.

"Let's say, about your little visits with these 'boys;' is anyone blackmailing you? No? Not even perhaps someone like … Sejanus?"

At the mention of Sejanus the *augur* turned pale, but he shook his head.

"I may have my issues with Sejanus, but it has nothing to do with the statue of Victory. And now Alexander, whoever you are, I suggest that you remember with whom you are dealing. I *don't* like you and I *don't* like your questions. Now get out of here. And if I hear that you've mentioned a word about my visits here to Augustus, you're going to find out how unpleasant I can make your life."

Alexander shrugged. "It's too late for that *augur*. Augustus *already* knows."

He and Rutilus exited the room, leaving the *augur* staring open-jawed behind them.

24

THE PRAETORIAN GUARD

"WHEW, that was something," Rutilus panted.

After exiting the room of the *augur*, Alexander had stridden calmly to the stairwell as if he were a departing customer. Rutilus had followed his lead, but once in the stairwell, had shoved into him in his hurry to get back down the stairs.

They found Claudius and Amarantus waiting for them outside. Alexander could tell that Amarantus had at least one new bruise, but his slave looked up and grinned as he joined them.

"I would have made it, Master, except that when I started yelling the door guard from the second floor rushed out and tripped me up."

"The rest generally worked as planned," Claudius added. "The management summoned me. I assured them that my slave must have been bribed to act so disobediently, and that he would be punished. I'm not sure if they believed me, but I passed out a few coins and that seemed to settle it."

"Thank you, Claudius. I owe you. Have you been badly hurt, Ranti?"

"No, Master. I'll have a few bruises, but you know that I've had a lot worse."

Rutilus had been bouncing up and down on the balls of his feet. He could contain himself no longer. "Claudius! We found out about *the goat!*"

"What?! Tell me."

Their mission was temporarily set aside as Rutilus regaled Claudius with the tale of what they had seen on the Venus House's third floor. It did eventually come back around to their visit to the room of Lucius Servilius.

"*Huh*," Claudius grunted. "So Lucius Servilius *claims* that he was at the Venus House and could not have taken the statue? ... Do you believe him?"

"I'm not sure," Alexander replied. "But I suspect he was telling the truth. After all, if he were going to take the statue, I think he would have come up with a much better counter story than spending time with his '*boys.*'

"Let's leave this place then," Alexander added brusquely. "We have one more stop to make."

"Yes?" Claudius queried.

"Yes, at the temple of Victory."

The Palatine was a small hill. The Venus House was on its south slope and the temple of Victory was on its west. It took only a few minutes for the men to reach the temple. While Claudius and Rutilus rode in the litter, Alexander elected to walk again. He couldn't hide the troubled glances he kept giving his servant who was following a couple steps behind him.

Finally, Amarantus said softly, "Stop worrying, Master, my injuries are not serious. I *wanted* to help."

The tension that Alexander had felt since leaving the Venus House began to ease. He turned his thoughts to the next task at hand.

They paused as they reached the spot on Victory's Incline where a separate path led off to the temple of Victory. Alexander spoke to Claudius and Rutilus in the litter and described the purpose for their visit.

"The temple doors are shut, but, no doubt, the priest is inside. We shall knock until he answers, then go in and test his eyesight. Unfortunately, it is still daylight so the conditions will not be the same as the night of the theft, but we will do our best. Rutilus, I will ask you to stand 15 paces from the priest and hold up any number of fingers as the physicians do. We'll ask the priest if he can count them."

As anticipated, the men banged on the door for some time until finally the priest opened the door just enough to look through.

"Go away. The goddess isn't here. The temple has been closed."

Alexander stepped to the side so that he could be seen through the wedge in the door and addressed the priest.

"We know this. We are investigating the disappearance of the statue and are here to help."

"*Hah*," the priest scoffed. "That's what that other young fellow told me and look at all the trouble he has caused. He thought a little food would buy me off, but I won't let him in again."

Alexander looked back perplexed.

"Vatinius, it is I, Gaius Julius Alexander. I'm the man who came before and told you that I was investigating the missing statue. Don't you recognize me?"

The old priest stepped within a few feet of Alexander and squinted up into his face. "So, it is you. Do you realize how much trouble you caused me? The Praetorian Guard themselves came and threatened me if I spoke with anyone else."

At the moment, Alexander had little thought for the Praetorian Guard. "Vatinius, you told me that your vision was as good as any man's."

"And so it is," Vatinius answered gruffly.

"But you did not recognize me at just a few paces, and I was standing in daylight."

"So? What man would?" the priest responded irritably.

Alexander turned to his friend. "Rutilus, now if you will."

Rutilus placed himself about ten paces from the priest and held up three fingers on his right hand.

"Vatinius, would you kindly tell us how many fingers this man is holding up?"

The old priest squinted and peered at Rutilus and replied, "One. No, five. He keeps changing them. Hey, what sort of game are you playing?"

"We were testing your vision, Vatinius," Alexander said gently. "Apparently, it is *not* as good as any man's. Most men would have been able to see that there were three fingers held up. Most men would have been able to recognize me ... *and* the man who took the statue. Are you so sure *now* that the man that night was Lucius Servilius?"

The priest looked back confused. "Well, I thought my eyesight was good. I had no reason to doubt it, but then I do rarely leave the temple. I guess my eyes may have gotten a little old – like the rest of me. ... But the man that came that night *was* dressed as an *augur*. I'm sure of it. And he was very traditional. He was bald. I'm sure of that, too."

"Wait," Claudius broke in. "What do you mean that the man who took the statue was *'very traditional'*?"

"Well, I mean his toga of course. It was maroon and purple striped like it should be, but it was the short one – the old style toga worn during the Republic. Not one of those big ones worn today with all the extra folds."

Claudius looked astonished. "Alexander, this is *important*."

Alexander's face registered no comprehension.

Claudius sighed. "I guess *you* wouldn't understand this because you are a Jew. You don't come to our ceremonies so would not have seen the *augurs* in practice. I, on the other hand, am expected to attend virtually all important state ceremonies."

Alexander still didn't get it, "So?"

"So, Alexander, the *augurs never* wear the old Republican style toga. They wear the maroon and purple striped toga *trabea*, but it is *always* cut to the modern style – floor length, very full. And it has been that way for a long as I can remember. I can't even imagine *who* would still have a toga *trabea* cut to the old Republican style."

The old priest had been looking back and forth from Claudius to Alexander during this exchange. "B-but, who else would wear the toga *trabea* but an *augur*? Who else could it have been?"

"It may have been an *imposter*, Vatinius," Claudius confirmed. "A man disguised to look like an *augur* so that you would release the statue to him."

The priest was becoming even more distraught. "B-But he took a goddess! *What* - What kind of man would do such a thing?"

Alexander raised his eyebrows to his friends who shrugged back. "That, Vatinius, is the question that we are endeavoring to answer."

He slipped a few coins into the priest's hand and assured him that their search would continue.

***

Back at Alexander's apartment, the men returned to the dinner that had been abandoned earlier for their trip to the Venus House.

"I hate that the evidence appears to clear the *augur*,"

Claudius said with chagrin as he took another sip of wine. "He seems an unpleasant man. I think I would have liked to see him punished for *something*."

His two friends nodded their agreement.

"And *I* hate," Alexander added, "that we have lost yet another major suspect. Every time I think that we are getting closer, the solution to this mystery just seems to elude us further."

He jumped up from his couch. "Well, friends, this afternoon I added to my list of all the events surrounding the disappearance of the statue. With your indulgence, I will get it now and read it to you. Perhaps some new idea will emerge."

Alexander went to his study to retrieve the list, but as he returned to his friends, he was stopped short by a loud banging on the door. A moment later, Agrippa came in wearing a triumphant look.

"I've got it!" he cried waving a small scroll.

"What?"

"*Proof!* Here is proof that the Praetorian Guard is making trouble."

Agrippa lay down across one of the dining couches. The three friends gathered around him as he began to unroll a small, yellow sheet of papyrus.

"As you know, Alexander and I bribed a certain acquaintance of mine to spy on the Praetorian Guard. I missed dinner tonight because I received a message that he wanted to meet.

"He was a bit vague on the details, but I think he got caught at it – or, at least, he was suspected of prying. It seems to have made him very nervous and he was very afraid that he was being followed. We had to find a place where we could speak in secret. I did not dare leave until I was able to slip away in the dark over the side wall, lest they were watching the house where we met."

Alexander resisted rolling his eyes. This secret meeting and sneaking over walls seemed a bit dramatic even for Agrippa. Nevertheless, he was very interested in whatever new evidence he had brought.

Agrippa finished unrolling the scroll, which was smaller than the palm of a man's hand.

"The writing is barely legible, so I will read it to you."

> *Spurius to Sejanus. Paid 86 silver denarii to 43 men from Subura. Engagement at synagogue unsuccessful. Recommend removal of Jul Alex before future action.*

The room fell silent.

"Lord Jupiter," Rutilus whispered. "Alexander, they mean to *kill* you."

"Not if we can get this to Germanicus first," Agrippa countered. "Finally, we have the proof we needed. Claudius, do you think you can get us in to see your brother? Tonight? I think you'll agree that this matter can't wait."

Before Claudius could answer there came another loud banging on the door.

"Wait! Don't answer it!" Alexander yelled at Amarantus, but it was too late.

They could hear the door crash back against the wall. Suddenly, the room was filled with men from the Praetorian Guard, each looking ready for a fight with a drawn sword. Sejanus was not among them, but Alexander recognized the three men that had attacked them in the baths.

Alexander jumped to his feet. He could sense that his friends were also rising around him, but he was unable to take his eyes off the Praetorians. He couldn't help himself; fear gripped him. Half-heartedly, he tried to bluff.

"What is the meaning of this? I am a free-born citizen and …"

"Shut up, Jew," the Praetorian who had been the leader at the baths cut him off.

In a trembling voice, Claudius tried as well. "M-m-my n-name is T-Ti…"

"You shut up, too, Fool. We know who you are. We know who *each* of you is."

He sneered at each of them in turn as if taunting them to make a move, any move, so that he would have an excuse to strike him down. The four friends remained still.

The head Praetorian Guardsman gestured to the scroll in Alexander's hand, the one containing his list of events surrounding the disappearance of the statue.

"I believe that belongs to me. Give it to me. Now."

Alexander hesitated, but saw no alternative so he held out the scroll. The Praetorian snatched it away and then unrolled it and scanned the first few words.

"This isn't it," he said then read a bit further. "However, this Jew appears to be writing *lies* about the Praetorian Guard. He challenges our honor."

He glanced around as his fellow Praetorians stared at Alexander menacingly.

"Where is *it*?" the Praetorian said to Alexander.

"Where's what?" Alexander answered, but could not keep his eyes from going instinctively to the spot on the couch where Agrippa's small scroll had been lying.

The Praetorian followed his look, then stepped forward and shoved Alexander aside. "Look around there," he ordered the other Praetorians.

Two of them shoved the friends aside and proceeded to search around the three dining couches first overturning them and finally ripping them apart with their swords to search the stuffing.

"Nothing here," one of the Praetorians reported.

"Then search *them*," the leader said. "You others, search the rest of the apartment."

The Praetorians slammed each man against a wall and roughly began a physical search for the hidden scroll. From the other rooms came the sound of crashing and rending. No doubt, the Praetorians were smashing everything he owned as they searched it. Alexander was turned and his head banged against the wall as the search continued. Idly, he hoped that Amarantus would do nothing to interfere and get himself killed; and, then wondered that he hadn't noticed his slave anywhere around.

The search ended as each Praetorian looked to the leader and shook his head. The others returned from ransacking the rooms and shook their heads as well.

The leader grinned. There was no humor in that grin; in fact, it dripped with utter malice. Alexander's fear increased.

"Then we will have to *make* them talk." He pointed at Alexander and then at an overturned couch. "Take him there. Stretch his arm out."

Alexander struggled all he could as three Praetorians overpowered him and then forced him to straddle the side of the couch as they stretched his right arm out before him. The leader of the Praetorians stood over him tapping the flat side of his blade against his open palm.

"I'm only going to say this once. Give me the scroll, or I guarantee you will *never* be writing another lie against the

Praetorians again."

He glanced from Alexander's extended arm to his companions shoved against the wall. The three friends stared back in horror, too shocked to speak a word.

"All right, then. Have it your way." The Praetorian slowly lifted his sword up over his head grasping the hilt with both hands.

"Wait! No!" Rutilus screamed.

"Stop," came a commanding voice from the doorway.

All heads turned to see two men from the Urban Cohorts standing in the doorway. Alexander recognized the same men who had fetched him just that morning to see the Rat's body. They entered the room with their swords drawn. Behind them, Alexander saw his servant Amarantus hovering anxiously.

The leader of the Praetorians lowered his sword, but looked unperturbed.

"This is the business of the Praetorian Guard. Go on your way."

The senior Urban Cohort stood his ground. "'Can't do that. We have orders to protect this man."

The Praetorian resumed his malicious grin and once again began to tap the flat of his blade against his palm. "And how do you propose to do that? I see only *two* of you and *six* of us."

"Our orders apply to the Praetorians, as well. This man is a client of Augustus and to be protected at all costs. Those are the words of the Consul Germanicus, himself."

The Praetorian's ugly look turned into a sneer.

"Get out, now. And you can tell your sniveling Consul ..."

"He can .. tell .. me .. what?"

Again all eyes turned to the doorway.

"Germanicus!" Claudius cried.

For it was Germanicus himself who stood in the doorway with the twelve lictors, bodyguards, of a Consul crowding behind him.

"*Tell me what?*" Germanicus repeated slowly.   If the Praetorian had thought that his voice had been menacing, Germanicus had him beat twice over. It was the difference between a Roman General and a common bully.

"*Uhh,* This is a matter for the Praetorian Guard, Sir. I must ask you to allow me to carry out my duties."

Germanicus looked calm, but Alexander could sense the tension in him. He was reminded of a predator stalking its prey.

"It *may* be a matter for the Praetorian Guard. Of that we shall see. But it is *not* a matter for *you*, Spurius. I relieve you of your rank effective immediately. *Lay down your sword.*"

The Praetorian leader looked uncertain. Moments passed. Alexander thought the man was about to argue, or perhaps he would yield to the Consul. But from where he was being held, he could not see the maniacal gleam that had entered the man's eyes.

With a cry, the Praetorian lunged toward Germanicus his sword outstretched.   Blindingly fast, faster than even his own lictors could react, Germanicus stepped to the side and knocked the sword away.   Then he plunged a knife into the stomach of the Praetorian.   The Praetorian gasped, his eyes looking up at Germanicus in stunned disbelief. His sword fell to the floor.

"*Hmm,* attempting to assassinate a Consul and member of the imperial house? … For that, *the penalty is death.*" Germanicus spoke with a deadly calm.   He withdrew his knife from the Praetorian's gut and thrust it into the base of his neck. Germanicus slowly twisted his knife until blood spurted from the other man's mouth and he finally sank to the ground with his lifeless eyes staring up with surprise.

Alexander was stunned.   He had always heard that

Germanicus the General could be ruthless in battle, but it was the first time he had ever observed this side of him with his own eyes. He barely noticed that the Praetorians that had been holding him had released their grasp, and that he had slumped back to the floor.

Germanicus glanced around at the remaining Praetorians, held his arm straight out with the palm down and then slowly lowered it. The Praetorians obeyed the signal instantly, laying their weapons on the floor.

Still in the same icy calm voice Germanicus said, "This room is a bit too crowded." He turned to the two men of the Urban Cohorts. "Tie them up and take them to the Carcer. I'll sort them out tomorrow."

As if he had anticipated the order, Amarantus appeared from the ransacked rooms carrying belts and lengths of cloth that could be torn into strips for binding. Everyone else seemed to be too shocked to move or utter a word. Alexander looked over at Agrippa, Claudius, and Rutilus and saw that each man had turned white, his chest heaving as if panting from exertion. Something more had to be done.

"Wait! Don't take them yet." Alexander cried, then stopped, startled by the sound of his own voice.

"Yes, Alexander?" Germanicus asked softly.

Alexander couldn't speak for a moment, then realizing that he might not get another chance, he blurted out the words. "We suspect these particular Praetorians of involvement in the theft of the Victory statue."

Germanicus gave an exaggerated sigh, then tapped two of his lictors and pointed at one of the Praetorians. "Lean him over that couch. Stretch his arm out. Bring me a sword."

The lictors complied immediately, and the Praetorian began talking fast, protesting his innocence.

"You beg for *mercy*?" Germanicus spoke in a voice almost

without expression. "You mean like the mercy you were about to show my friend, Alexander? There is only one hope for you. Tell me the truth and tell it to me now. What do you know of this statue?"

The lack of emotion in Germanicus' voice was even more terrifying than if he had been yelling or spouting threats. The Praetorian Guardsman was not used to feeling fear. But he clearly felt it now.

"I swear to you, Germanicus. I swear on the life of Augustus himself, that we know nothing of the theft of the statue. It was Spurius. Spurius told us that the Jews had it, and that's the reason why we followed him."

Germanicus stared at the man for a long moment, then motioned for his lictors to let him up. He turned to the two Urban Cohorts. "Get these men out of here. ... and ... it's Marcus and Aulus, isn't it? You have my thanks. I will not forget your courage tonight in obeying my orders."

Nothing more was said as the body of the dead man was dragged from the room, and the other Praetorians were bound and led out with the help of several lictors. Then Germanicus motioned for his remaining bodyguards to wait outside.

All that was left were the four friends, Germanicus, and Amarantus.

"*Whew*, what a mess," Germanicus said in his old voice, looking around at the smashed up apartment.

The men stared back at him white-faced. Germanicus looked almost sheepish. "Tactics I learned while dealing with the Germans. They're not an emotional race and that was about the only thing that seemed to scare them," he explained.

The men began to relax a little.

"Germanicus, you saved us," Claudius said softly. His eyes glowed with pride in his older brother. Germanicus shrugged and smiled back. "Always, Claudius," he replied equally softly. Then he turned to the other men in the room.

"What were they looking for anyway?" Germanicus asked.

Agrippa seemed to recover first. "It was a scroll. A scroll that implicated the Praetorians in an attack on a synagogue last night."

"Yes, I just heard about that from the Urban Prefect at dinner. That's why I stopped by to see Alexander; to offer him my protection. I hadn't realized that he would be needing it quite this soon."

"The Urban Prefect?" Alexander asked puzzled. "How did he know? I didn't tell the Cohorts about the attack on the synagogue."

"But I *did*, Master," Amarantus said. "This morning. While you were talking to the senior Cohort about the Rat, I told the other. They agreed to patrol the neighborhood. That's how I knew to go fetch them when the Praetorians broke in."

"Good man," Germanicus nodded. "But what about this scroll? Where is it?"

Alexander, Claudius, and Agrippa looked around the room and then at each other in confusion. But Rutilus stepped forward and dramatically declared, "The scroll is before you."

Then he grinned and pointed to the side of his head. He had rolled up the small yellow scroll and placed it behind his left ear. Now that he pointed it out, they could see it tucked among his red gold curls.

"*Ha!*" Rutilus cried exuberantly. "They searched me everywhere I was covered, but didn't think to look there. It's a trick I learned from my step-father, Sextus Fadius. He always says that the best place to hide something is in plain sight."

Alexander swung his head toward Rutilus and stared at

him. "What? What did you say?"

"I said that the best place to hide something is in plain sight. I know it's a bit too subtle for Sextus Fadius, so it must be something he heard around the Senate. Still, it worked, didn't it? The scroll was right here all the time. They didn't even notice it because they were looking for something that was hidden!"

Rutilus presented the scroll with a flourish to Germanicus who opened it, scanned its contents, gave a nod and tucked it away. Then Germanicus turned to Amarantus.

"I can see that the Praetorians did not leave Alexander much, but, by any chance, did they leave him some wine?"

In short order, Amarantus had produced several flasks of good wine and they were drinking and laughing with the almost hysterical abandon of men who had just narrowly escaped death. The Praetorians had destroyed every piece of furniture, so they sat on the floor and leaned against whatever they could find that would still support their weight.

After they had finished off the last of the wine, Germanicus insisted that he escort Claudius, Agrippa, and Rutilus home personally.

"I'll be having a word with Augustus and Tiberius," Germanicus advised them. "After that, there should be no more trouble from the Praetorians, but *be careful* all the same. Someone has the statue, and that man must be someone very desperate."

After his friends had left, Alexander remained sitting on the floor a long while staring into nothing. Amarantus began to straighten up the mess that the Praetorians had made of the apartment, but cast frequent looks at Alexander as he continued to just sit and stare. Finally, Amarantus knelt down next to Alexander and spoke in a quiet voice.

"Master, something more is on your mind, isn't it?"

Still staring ahead, Alexander responded. "Yes. I think I

now know the solution to the mystery of the missing statue."

A few moments passed before Amarantus said, "Master, you do not seem very happy about it."

Alexander sighed. "I am not. ... But this must be done. See if the Praetorians left us any parchment and ink. I believe that I have a number of urgent messages to write."

25
THOU SHALL NOT KILL

AT mid-morning the next day, Alexander presented himself at the home of Sextus Fadius. When he was shown into the garden, he found that Tiberius and Agrippa were already there, having refreshments with Aemelia, Rutilus, and Rutila.

Tiberius looked up as he approached. "I hope you are ready to explain yourself. Your message told me very little."

Alexander knew it was not a good idea to keep Augustus's co-regent waiting and answered respectfully, "I ask you to be patient for just a little longer. There are two more who must be here."

Tiberius gave him a curt nod, but the others made no effort to disguise their curious looks. He could tell Rutilus was bursting to beg him for a hint, but was holding back in deference to Tiberius.

Several minutes later, the *augur* Lucius Servilius joined them looking very put upon. When he saw Alexander his temper flared.

"*You!* You provincial upstart. How *dare* you summon me?"

"Sit down, Servilius," Tiberius growled.

For a moment the *augur* appeared like he was going to argue, but apparently decided that a fight with Tiberius may be one he couldn't win. With an angry look at Alexander, Lucius Servilius took a seat on another garden bench.

While waiting for the last to arrive, Alexander cast a surreptitious glance at Tiberius and pondered what he could expect of the man. To some people, Tiberius appeared to be the somewhat retiring heir of Augustus -- a man with little charisma and sometime questionable character. But Alexander knew also of Tiberius' reputation on the battlefield. He was known to be a strong decisive commander capable of being both ruthless and fair. Alexander thought of the transformation that had come over Germanicus the night before. No doubt, Tiberius could turn equally cold if someone crossed him.

Suddenly, doubt and panic gripped Alexander. Oh Lord, he hoped that he was right about what he was about to propose today. Tiberius would *not* be amused if this turned into a waste of time.

Amarantus arrived holding tightly to the arm of the still-protesting priest, Vatinius.

"I'm sorry, Master. He didn't want to leave the temple. I had to … insist."

Alexander touched Vatinius on the arm and motioned him to wait. He felt so nervous that his palms were sweating as he rose and faced the group.

"I have requested that you meet me here today, because I believe that I may have discovered the solution to the missing statue."

That launched some excited muttering amongst the group, so Alexander waited a moment before continuing.

"In order to reconstruct what happened, I will need to walk through several steps to establish certain facts. I beg your patience as I go through the evidence."

Alexander looked at Tiberius for permission and received a nod to continue. Taking the old priest Vatinius by the arm, he led him over to Lucius Servilius.

"Vatinius, look at this man. Look very closely and tell me if this is the same man that took the statue of Victory from her temple."

The priest was red-faced and appeared befuddled as he stepped closer. He squinted at Lucius Servilius who scowled deeply back at him.

"No," the priest said finally. "It is not. He is not the one who took the Victory."

Vatinius turned and looked back at Alexander in confusion as some member of their group let out a startled gasp.

"And now," Alexander continued. "I ask you to look at one more thing for me."

Taking Vatinius by the arm, Alexander led him to the statue at the back of the garden – the statue that Sextus Fadius had sent back from Gaul as booty ... the statue that Claudius had once dubbed '*the great flying whore.*'

Still befuddled, Vatinius allowed Alexander to lead him back to the statue. The others stood up and followed behind them. They stopped in front of the statue. At first the priest recoiled in horror and began to jabber about cruel jokes, but Alexander prodded him forward.

"*Look* at it, Vatinius. Look very, very closely. Have you seen this statue before?"

The priest shook his head in disbelief, but walked around the statue studying it and finally looked up into her eyes. Instantly, his expression turned to shock and he fell to his knees before the statue. "Oh, my Lady. Oh, my goddess. What have they done to you?"

Most of the group erupted into excited chatter around them. Tiberius held up his hand for silence, then turned to Alexander.

"What is the meaning of this? Are you suggesting that *this* monstrosity is the missing statue of Victory?"

"I believe it is, sir, but it has been disguised." He walked over to the statue and ran his hand down the side then held it up revealing a mixture of chalk and smeared paint.

Tiberius gave Alexander an incredulous look, then he himself stepped closer to the statue, examining all sides. He ran his hand down the side to see the smeared paint and chalk for himself. Finally, he stopped in front of it and stared up into her eyes.

"My Lord Jupiter, it *is* the statue," Tiberius whispered with surprise. "I *know* her. I made a sacrifice to her before I left on every campaign. Time after time, I have stood before her as I do today. And time after time, the goddess granted me her favor in battle."

Tiberius turned back to Alexander and shook his head as if still in disbelief.

"Do you mean to tell me that days have been spent scouring every inch of Rome for the statue of Victory, and she has been here the whole time?"

"I believe so," replied Alexander. "Well, perhaps not the *whole* time, but for the last few days at least."

Anger filled Tiberius's voice. "*Who* did this?"

Alexander looked to Aemelia who was staring at the statue with a strange look.

"Aemelia, I am so sorry, but it *must* have been your husband Sextus Fadius. We know that he wanted the statue, didn't he Vatinius?"

The priest still knelt before the statue with tears running down his cheeks, but answered readily. "Oh yes, Sextus Fadius wanted her – ever since Victory came to him in a dream. He was like a man obsessed. I never thought that he would actually take her, though."

Alexander turned back to Tiberius.

"I don't know the details yet, but now that we have found the statue we should be able to learn them easily enough. My guess is that before he left Rome, Sextus Fadius arranged for the theft of the statue. It was to take place in his absence so he would never fall under suspicion. Then Fadius arranged to send home a cartload of cheap art booty and had his agents include the statue in that batch. That would make it appear that this statue had been sent all the way from Gaul."

Alexander paused and looked at Tiberius whose face had lost most of its expression. Clearly, Tiberius was withholding his judgment now that he had accused a Senator. Alexander plowed on.

"At some point, the statue has obviously been repainted in places to make it look like a poor replica. However, if you look closely, the paint has been applied superficially. Note that the 'crack' on the wing is nothing more than black paint smudged to look broken and aged.

"I have learned that a sculptor called Achilles is missing. Achilles is a client of Sextus Fadius. It seems likely that this Achilles was coerced into disguising the statue. No doubt Sextus Fadius planned to restore her once an ideal hiding place had been found."

Alexander looked at Tiberius expectantly and could tell from his face that he had proven his case.

"I had *no idea*," murmured Aemelia. "No idea that Sextus wanted this statue. Perhaps if we had ever truly lived as husband and wife, this would not have happened."

Tiberius frowned and gave Aemelia a look of pity.

"I am sorry, Lady, but you must realize that I must send someone to arrest Sextus Fadius immediately. If you can tell me the names of the agents that delivered the statue, I'll have them picked up today. And this sculptor, Achilles, too. They will need to provide testimony for the trial."

"No, no ... I don't think so," Aemelia responded vaguely.

Tiberius looked back sharply. "Do you mean that you don't think you remember the names of his agents?"

Aemelia sighed. "No ... no... I don't think that you will arrest them."

"And *why* is that?"

"Because I don't think you can prove a case against my husband. Sextus Fadius didn't do it. ... It was *I* who took the statue," Aemelia replied staring off into some unknown point in the garden.

"Mother, No!" Rutila cried. Then, turning to Tiberius. "It isn't true! You know my mother's reputation. She would never do such a thing. It was Sextus Fadius, that greedy, cold-hearted *mentula*."

The men winced at the foul language delivered so vehemently from a girl who shortly before had looked as delicate as a flower.

"No, dear," Aemelia said softly. "Sextus Fadius is not a good husband -- and he is probably not even a good man -- but he is *not* a thief. *I* took the statue."

She turned toward Tiberius and Alexander.

"You see, I *had* to have it ... for my children. Before Sextus left for Gaul, I asked him one last time if he would support my children. We are patricians, you know. Rutilus must start the path of public service soon; he is the right age. How will he become a Senator with no money? And my little Rutila, she must have a dowry so she can marry well.

"... But Sextus only laughed. He laughed and said that neither of my children shall ever see a denarius from him, not even after he is dead. So, you see, the task fell to me."

"*Money*," Vatinius spat. "You defiled the goddess for money?"

"Oh, yes ... for money."

Tiberius took Aemelia by the elbow and led her back to a

bench where they had been enjoying refreshments earlier.

"Aemelia, I think you must tell us the story now. *All of it.*"

Aemelia stared back blankly. Alexander couldn't tell what she was feeling, or if she was feeling anything at all. She just seemed numb. *He* felt numb. How could this have gone so wrong? All the evidence had seemed to point to Sextus Fadius. Nobody *liked* Fadius. Alexander never dreamed that his actions would hurt the mother of his childhood friend Rutilus.

The silence dragged on, then Aemelia sucked in a deep breath almost as if she was gasping for air. Then she began to speak.

"As I said, the task fell to me. I knew that somehow I had to find a way to provide for my children. But how? … I thought that perhaps the goddess herself had sent me the answer when, five days before the Ides, I heard them talking right there in front of her temple."

"Whom did you hear talking?" Tiberius asked.

"Just some men. They were Jews. I know that now, but I didn't know then. I'm sure they didn't see me. I was descending Victory's Incline in a litter to shop in the markets below. The Incline is steep there so my litter bearers were walking very slowly. The men weren't paying attention to my litter. They had their backs to me, looking at the temple. That's how I came to overhear them."

Aemelia paused. No one else spoke as all eyes were transfixed on her. After a moment she continued.

"The men were talking about the statue of Victory -- that it was a valuable sculpture by Phidias. One man said that an art collector would pay him a lot of money for it. That's how I got the idea. If someone would pay *him* the money, surely someone would pay *me*, too. They didn't name the art collector, but I knew it wouldn't be too hard to find out. There aren't that many men in

Rome who are that rich and that ruthless. I figured I could have an agent start with Gnaeus Pulcher; drop a few hints that the statue was for sale. If he didn't buy, there would be others. But *first* we had to acquire the statue.

"The planning was almost ridiculously simple. I didn't want to take the statue by force. It would be easier if it appeared to be taken legitimately. And who else, but a *pontifex* or an *augur* could walk into a temple and remove a statue without raising an alarm?

I decided on an *augur*. The toga is so unusual that just seeing *that* would be enough to convince someone that whoever wore it was a real *augur*. ... I have a slave who weaves and sews. I set her to work immediately making the maroon and purple toga. We only had enough dye and fabric for a small toga, but no one questioned it."

"And the boots?" Lucius Servilius asked. "Where did you get the red boots?"

"Oh, we used an old pair of my son's. He is patrician so his boots are red. They were a bit tattered, but who notices a man's boots in the dark?"

Tiberius made an impatient gesture. "Let her continue."

"Alexander was right on one thing. It *was* Achilles who helped to remove the statue. ... But you were *wrong*, Alexander, that Achilles would do such a thing for Sextus Fadius. Achilles hates him and he hates the way that Sextus has treated us. You see, Achilles is a good man and very loyal to me. He grew up as a slave in *my* house. Achilles is just a little older and he played with me when we were children. He is *my family's* freedman and was willing to do anything that would restore *my* family to its former dignity."

Aemelia paused again, but no one said a word. She shrugged and continued.

"The rest, you can probably guess. The night of the Ides our 'augur' went with Achilles and his crew to the temple and told the priest that the statue was being removed for a procession. They took it to Achilles' shop where he did his best to disguise it in such a manner that it could be restored easily. But it wasn't safe to leave it there.

"The letter from my husband that he was sending art booty home from Gaul was genuine, but it had really arrived days before. I waited until we had a witness to read it aloud,. Aemelia nodded at Alexander. "That was supposed to cast any suspicion away from our disguised statue. Then on the same day that Sextus' agents delivered the other booty, I had Achilles bring the statue here and set it up in the back of the garden where it would only be seen from a distance.

"... I got that idea from Sextus Fadius. He always used to say that the best place to hide something is in plain sight. I fear he was *not* correct in this case."

Aemelia stopped and cast a reproachful look at Alexander.

"What about the man who pretended to be an *augur* – who pretended to be *me*. *Who* was he?" Lucius Servilius demanded, his voice barely concealing an undercurrent of fury.

"Oh, just a man. No one important. I coaxed him with his lines and manners so that he could pass as Rome's nobility."

"And the maroon and purple toga of the *augur*, where is it now?" Lucius Servilius pressed.

"I had my seamstress take it apart after that night. She has been adding maroon or purple borders to every dress she has worked on since."

All eyes turned toward Rutila who was seated beside her mother wearing her new yellow gown with the purple border. Alexander expected her to be in tears or red with shame, but her look was ... vacant. "She must be in shock," he thought. He could not bring himself to turn and look at his friend Rutilus yet.

Tiberius finally broke the silence.   "So what happened, Aemelia?"

Aemelia looked up, "What do you mean?"

"The statue is still here -- not restored and not sold. And, if I understood Alexander correctly, your sculptor who was supposed to have restored it has fled Rome. What happened to your plan?"

Aemelia lowered her head and murmured, "The Rat."

Tiberius frowned. "What? A rat?"

"I think she means '*The* Rat,'" Alexander said. "He was a blackmailer and an informer. He was also the man who informed on my client, Theon, to the Praetorian Guard. Apparently, The Rat spent time under the sewer covers on the Palatine listening in on private conversations. That would include the sewer cover near Victory's temple. ... I myself suspected that the Rat may have witnessed the taking of the Victory statue. I offered him money for information, but he wouldn't take it."

"Because *he thought* a patrician could pay more," Aemelia said still looking down. "I don't know how he figured it out, but we think he may have been at the temple that night and recognized Achilles. After the statue was reported missing, the Rat tracked Achilles down and began to threaten him. So I sent Achilles away, but that didn't stop him. Perhaps he had seen Achilles bring a large crate here and guessed what was in it. That's when he began to harass *me*. He came right to my front door and threatened me."

"I remember that," Alexander exclaimed. "I bumped into him as I was leaving your house. But I thought that he had been following *me*."

"No, he wanted me," Aemelia said softly. "He demanded a *lot* of money, or he would go to the Praetorians. It was more money than I could raise. So I lied. I told him the statue wasn't here and that he could go to the Praetorians for all I cared. I hoped that would get rid of him."

"But it didn't," Alexander continued for her. "I think he came back and he found the statue. That's how he got the chalk and paint I saw on his tunic and hands. ... and that's why you killed him, isn't it?"

Aemelia's head jerked up in surprise. "No, he didn't come back. He couldn't have or he would have demanded the money. I didn't kill him. "

"She didn't do it," said a soft voice next to Aemelia. *"I did."*

"No!" Aemelia cried.

Alexander stared at Rutila dumbfounded. She looked back at him, but she still had that same oddly vacant expression.

"I *had* to do it. Mother didn't know, but I overheard that dreadful man threatening her. I heard her tell him the statue wasn't there. But then I went and looked at our Victory statue myself and I knew it must be true. -- Just as I knew why Mother had done it, for me ... for us.

"I prayed with all my heart that evil little man would leave us alone, but he came back. It was late at night and I couldn't sleep because I was thinking about Alexander and me ... about how Mother was going to get the dowry money so that we could be married. I went for a walk when I saw that dirty man sneaking into the garden. He had a rope and he came over the wall. Then he went straight to that statue."

No one interrupted Rutila as she went on with her startling tale.

"I knew what I had to do. It was up to me. I had to save us all from that, that gutter filth. I slipped back inside and grabbed a marble statue from its niche. It was small, not too heavy for me. Then, I sneaked up behind him while he was looking at the Victory. He didn't hear me until it was too late. Just as he was turning, I swung that statue at his head as hard as I could.

"He fell down, but his *eyes* were still open. It was *horrible*. He kept *staring* at me. I couldn't stand it, so I took that little statue and hit them. I hit them again and again until his eyes were gone and he couldn't stare at me anymore. He made a mess all over of the little statue ... but it was an ugly statue, anyway."

Tiberius was the first to speak. "And then what happened, Rutila?"

She shrugged. "I wasn't sure what to do. There was blood all over the place and that horrible little man taking up space in *our* garden. So I went and woke one of the slaves. He said that he would take care of it. He helped me wash the blood off and told me to go to bed. I don't know what happened after that."

Rutila stood and held out her hand to Alexander. "So you see, Alexander, *I did it for us*. I couldn't let that filthy man stand in our way. Mother had to get the money for my dowry so we could be married. Because I love you, Alexander, and I know that you love me."

With her hand still outstretched, Rutila took a step toward Alexander. But Alexander could only step back in revulsion. She was the killer? He had seen the Rat's body; his death had been brutal. How could this gentle creature he loved commit such a violent act? She was the *killer*. *Killer.* The word filled his head shutting out all other thoughts.

Rutila took another step forward. "Alexander, you do understand, don't you?"

Speech failed him. Alexander took another step back. His mind cast about for something, anything that made sense. Then words filled his head, familiar words that he had said everyday during prayer for most of his life. Without thinking he began to utter them over and over.

"*Lo tirtsach. Lo tirtsach. Lo tirtsach! Thou shall not kill!*"

Rutila seemed unfazed. "It will be alright, Alexander. It's not like that man *mattered* anyway."

Lucius Servilius stepped angrily between Rutila and Alexander.

"Be silent foolish girl. Do you not realize what you and your mother have done? You have committed *sacrilege* against the State of Rome, stolen and defaced a treasure by perhaps *the greatest sculptor ever to have lived*, and ..."

A loud spluttering sound interrupted the *augur*. Lucius Servilius whirled to face Vatinius.

"What is it, man? Why do you interrupt me?"

The priest Vatinius had flushed red with his mouth working, as if he was trying to blurt something out, but the sound just wouldn't come. He kept alternating a beseeching glance between the *augur* and Tiberius, as if asking one of them to give him permission to speak.

"Well, what is it?" Lucius Servilius demanded.

"You, y-you're an *augur*. It, it- it's just that I th-th- thought you *knew*."

Lucius Servilius glared back. "Knew what?"

"About the, the statue. I thought you knew."

With exaggerated patience, Lucius Servilius replied, "Knew *what* about the statue?"

"That Alcamenes and Agoracritus worked in marble."

Vatinius looked about him nodding as if that had explained everything, but saw only puzzled expressions staring back at him. He nervously ran his tongue across his upper lip and tried again.

"His *students*, Alcamenes and Agoracritus. They worked in marble. ... *Phidias only* worked in bronze and ivory."

Seven heads swiveled towards the statue, taking in the large white marble wings and anticipated Vatinius' next words. *"The Phidias is a fake."*

26
VICTORY AND THE VANQUISHED

"THE Phidias is a fake."

There was a strangled cry and all eyes turned from the statue to Aemelia. Up to this point, she had spoken mostly distractedly, almost as if she were in a dream. But now she had turned pale and staggered toward the statue, her face in shock.

"No, no ... It can't be. I risked everything, *everything* and for *nothing*."

Aemelia's eyes rolled up and she collapsed onto the ground.

"Mother," Rutila cried as she rushed to her, but their door slave, Hermias, had suddenly materialized out of nowhere and was already kneeling beside her.

Then, in a surprise move, the priest Vatinius was suddenly at her side as well. But he wasn't looking at Aemelia; he was staring at Hermias.

"That's him!" he pointed. "That's Lucius Servilius. I mean, the man that I thought was Lucius Servilius."

Half a dozen heads swiveled back and forth between the slave Hermias and the *augur* Lucius Servilius. Alexander found the likeness uncanny. Both men were in their fifties with a small build, both were wrinkled and bald.

"Well, that explains *that* part," Agrippa said speaking up for the first time.

"He doesn't look a bit like me," Lucius Servilius protested.

"Oh, *forget him*," Rutila cried. "What about my Mother? Quickly, we must carry her to her bed; call a doctor."

"*No.*"

The word came firmly, and now all eyes turned to Tiberius.

"You," he pointed to Hermias. "Call for some wine, but no one, and I mean *no one*, leaves this garden."

Tiberius strode toward the defaced statue of Victory and stood staring up at it thoughtfully. The group behind him began to mutter amongst themselves.

"*Silence*," Tiberius commanded with his back still toward them.

The group fell silent each looking back and forth amongst themselves with their gazes continually returning first to Aemelia's prostrate form and then to Tiberius' back. A slave scurried out with a cup of wine and Hermias lifted Aemelia gently, while Rutila held the cup to her lips. After a moment, Aemelia gasped took a drink and some color returned. But she refused to get up and remained sitting on the ground where she had fallen.

Alexander forced himself to look at his friend Rutilus. Rutilus, who was always quick with a quip and a laugh. Rutilus, who found humor in everything, and could turn the most banal event into an adventure.

Now the smile was gone, as Rutilus stared at his mother and sister almost as if he had never seen them before. Above, the sun broke the clouds and fell upon a face that suddenly seemed much, much older than Alexander had ever seen it.

Rutilus seemed to be struggling inside. For a moment his countenance assumed a look of outrage, then changed to horror, then to disbelief. Then, finally, it softened. He sighed, then slowly walked to his mother's side, sat down on the ground next to her and put his arm around her.

"Mother, I didn't know," he spoke softly. "I *should* have seen what this was doing to you. ... I *should* have been the man you needed me to be, the man my father would have been."

With a sob, Aemelia buried her face into her son's shoulder. He held her tightly, and, with his other arm, reached out for his sister who scooted up next to him and placed her head on his other shoulder.

Tiberius returned. One by one, he turned to each member of the company and held their eyes with a piercing look.

"I have made up my mind," he said. "And *this* is how it is going to be."

Tiberius stood straight with his shoulders back, his look decisive. In the space of a few minutes, the man had transformed from the retiring heir to the stern general who had once commanded tens of thousands of troops on the battlefield.

"The truth of this event will *never* leave this garden."

There were mild exclamations and the *augur* made to protest, but Tiberius waved them aside.

"Think about it. This was not only a sacrilege against Victory; it was a crime against *all* of the gods and people of Rome. Rome has been defiled by this theft and her very foundations cry out for justice. By all rights, the perpetrators should meet a public and harsh retribution."

Alexander looked down at Aemelia whose face had turned from shock to terror. But Rutila's countenance still seemed oddly vacant, as if she couldn't quite grasp the situation and was just waiting for the angry people to go away.

"But, think further," Tiberius continued, "about who has perpetrated this most unforgivable crime. It was one of Rome's

316 Kass Evans | Toga of a Different Color

most respected matrons, a patrician woman, and the wife of a Senator. And what was the reason for her crime against the gods, the Senate and the people of Rome? *Greed.* Simple, common greed."

Tiberius looked from face to face as he let his words sink in. His gaze hardened as it lingered on first Aemelia and then Rutila.

"If word gets out that a patrician matron and wife of a senator committed this sacrilege, could Rome survive the scandal? Of course it could, but *not* without its consequences. For *forty years*, Augustus has striven to instill faith and morality into the Roman people. And now *patricians,* the very class that historically has been charged with the care and protection of Rome, have committed sacrilege. It is like a slap in the face of everything Augustus has stood for his whole life."

Tiberius shook his head and said sadly. "No, this is trouble that neither Augustus nor Rome needs right now."

The stern general's voice returned.

"The First Citizen has empowered me to resolve this matter and here are *my decisions.* Lucius Servilius, *you* will let it be known that you had forgotten that you had ordered the statue to be removed for cleaning and restoration."

"I will not," Lucius Servilius protested. "I would look like an utter fool, if I said such a thing."

Tiberius' face clouded and his voice turned menacing. "*You will* and I believe you know exactly why you will, and what will happen to you if you refuse."

The *augur* paled, but made no further protest.

Tiberius turned to the priest. "Vatinius, *you* must leave Rome. No protests. I can't have you around to accidentally let the truth slip out about the statue. We will find a suitable post for you out in the country, perhaps a nice roadside shrine in need of a gentle hand."

Vatinius swallowed and nodded.

"The statue must be restored. Lucius Servilius, I shall put you in charge of that. Have her restored and then arrange for a special public festival in her honor … at your expense, of course."

Lucius Servilius looked bilious, but nodded.

"A private sacrifice will also be required to purify the goddess of this defilement. I will speak to our *Pontifex Maximus* about arranging that. Yes, I think Augustus would prefer to see to that personally."

Tiberius turned then to Aemelia who was now cowering against her son's shoulder. For a moment he looked pityingly at her, then his face turned dispassionate.

"Aemelia, while I sympathize with the reason for your actions, you must realize that Rome cannot *tolerate* such an insult to her gods. Your husband, Sextus Fadius, will be recalled from Gaul immediately, and he will be advised to enact a quiet divorce. … But do not worry; he will not get off that easily. If he had been a good husband to you, this tragedy may have been avoided. Sextus Fadius will find his *future* career in political life to be, shall we say, *difficult*."

Rutila was looking blankly at Tiberius. He looked down at her and spoke harshly.

"Rutila, I charge you also with sacrilege. No doubt, you were justified to kill a man who had invaded your garden. But, *not* to hide the truth of the statue.

"There is *no place* for you in Rome. I *exile* you and your mother from the civilized world. Neither of you may step foot on Roman soil for as long as you both shall live. If you do, I will charge you with your respective crimes and you will meet your end by public execution. Do you understand?"

Rutila nodded vacantly. Aemelia had already fainted.

A throat cleared and Tiberius looked at Rutilus, who was still on the ground with his arms around his mother and sister.

"And what of *me*, Tiberius?" he croaked, then cleared his throat again and continued more firmly. "With my step-father gone, I was the only man in the house. I, I should have known. I should have prevented this."

Tiberius' look softened. "Better men than you have been duped by women before, Rutilus. This *I* know only too well. You are *not* banished, but I want you out of the City. Do you own land in the countryside?"

Rutilus nodded, "A small farm."

"Then you have a choice. You may go to live on your farm, or you may accompany your mother and sister into exile. But you must *petition me* personally, before you ever enter the walls of Rome again."

Rutilus looked sad, but determined. "I will sell the farm and accompany my mother and sister into exile. My place now is with them."

"Very, well. I suggest that you remove your women to the farm until your mother's divorce from Sextus Fadius is finalized. Their banishment will begin as of that date. Against my better judgment, I will permit you to take the two slaves who helped in the theft. Some ox carts will be sent here at sundown. I want you *out of Rome* by first light."

"But, what about Alexander?" a small voice asked. Everyone looked down at Rutila.

"Alexander *must* come with us. I did it for you, Alexander. Now we can be married. You will come won't you?"

Rutilus tried to hush his sister, as he clutched her head and laid it on his shoulder. But she would not be quieted.

"Alexander, why do you not speak? You love me. I know you do. Don't you want us to be married?"

Rutilus squeezed his sister's shoulders and whispered urgently, "No, Rutila. Alexander can't come. Remember? He must return to Egypt."

Rutilus gave Alexander a look of pure agony with tears welling up in his eyes. "Go," he mouthed silently. But Alexander stood transfixed and speechless, tears now forming in his own eyes.

"Alexander, if ever you loved me, please *go now*," Rutilus begged.

Tiberius took Alexander's arm and led him away, gesturing for the other men to follow. Alexander stopped at the edge of the garden and looked back at his childhood friend Rutilus sitting on the ground with his head bowed and his arms around his mother and sister. He knew that he would never see them again.

Tiberius led them into the atrium. One by one, he made each man swear an oath not to reveal the mystery of the statue. Lucius Servilius swore first and left quickly to arrange for the statue to be retrieved immediately for restoration. Vatinius swore next and Tiberius instructed him to return to the temple until he sent for him.

After Agrippa swore, Tiberius motioned for him to leave and held Alexander back. He paid no notice of Amarantus who had stationed himself at the edge of the room.

"I'll be waiting outside," Agrippa whispered and exited after the other men.

Tiberius looked at Alexander, who made no attempt to hide the tears streaming down his cheeks.

"You loved her?" he asked.

"*Them*," Alexander replied. "I loved each of them. I've known them all since I was a boy. ... At least, I thought I knew them."

Tiberius gave a mirthless laugh. "If there's one thing I've

learned about people, Alexander, it is that you *never really know* another person. You may know them a long time, think you know them. But when it comes right down to it, no one *really* knows what another person is capable of … for the better or the worse."

Alexander said nothing. His heart ached and he felt numb. *He did this.* He didn't mean to, but he did. Tiberius turned businesslike.

"Now, Alexander, do you swear never to discuss the theft of the statue to anyone other than Augustus or myself?"

"Yes," replied Alexander dully. "I swear."

"You have done a great service to Rome today, and Rome shall not forget it. No doubt, the First Citizen will wish to thank you personally."

Alexander just nodded. He had no desire to be thanked for ruining the lives of the people he loved.

"I will give the order that your client, Theon, should be released from the Carcer immediately. Will you accompany the messenger?"

Alexander started to say no, but then thought of Theon sitting in that prison cell, beaten and filthy.

"Yes, I will," he replied. "I suppose I should get him cleaned up before his family sees him again."

"Indeed," Tiberius responded briefly, then went to the door and called over a member of the Praetorian Guard who had been stationed outside. Tiberius whispered some instructions to him, then pointed at Alexander.

The Praetorian approached Alexander. "Are you ready now, sir?"

"Yes."

"Do you require a litter, sir? I can call one for you."

"No, I shall walk."

"What's with all the 'sirs'?" Agrippa murmured in his ear, as he fell into step next to Alexander. "Weren't these Praetorians trying to kill you just last night?"

"Huuh."

Alexander glanced sharply up at the Praetorian and saw that he had overheard Agrippa's words. The Praetorian seemed to glance about, as if to ensure that no one else was listening, before commenting, "Not all Praetorians think like Sejanus, you know; in fact, most of us don't."

He looked like he wanted to say something more, but instead adopted a stony look and kept his eyes on the road.

"Well," Agrippa said dryly. "At least we know we won't get attacked on the way ... speaking of which, where are we going?"

"To the Carcer; we're going to free Theon."

"Excellent," Agrippa replied.

They walked on is silence. Agrippa frequently cast worried looks at Alexander, but chose not to speak. Amarantus followed quietly behind.

***

Agrippa stayed with Alexander for the rest of the day. They freed Theon and took him to the nearest baths. Alexander was happy to learn that the beatings had stopped after his visit and that Theon had suffered no severe damage. Despite Sejanus' claim that he had been tortured, Theon assured Alexander that this had not been the case.

But, there was little question that Theon had left the prison a different man. They cleaned him up and dressed him in a new tunic and sandals, but he was not the old Theon. A little bit of light had gone out of his eyes. Alexander wondered if it would ever return.

He hired litters and he and Agrippa took Theon to his home across the Tiber. They were greeted with many tears of happiness from Theon's wife and children. Theon's friends, including Saul and Apollonius, soon arrived. Everyone wanted to thank Alexander and congratulate him for his efforts. Alexander could find no pleasure in it. He had done his duty and freed his client, but at such a cost. It had all begun with those stupid, stupid words, and now how many lives had been ruined because of them?

Sensing Alexander's mood, Agrippa stepped in and drew most of the attention to himself. He began by describing their many valiant efforts on Theon's behalf. Then he went on to regale them with the story of how the *augur* had forgotten that he had ordered the statue to be restored, and that it had never been stolen in the first place. Agrippa embroidered the tale freely and soon it involved several priests, too much wine, and a couple of dancing girls.

"I think the *augur* will like the story," Agrippa had whispered to Alexander with a nudge. "Not a single hairy, young man in it. – Kind of throws the hounds off the scent, if you know what I mean."

Then some new friends of Theon's joined the party and Agrippa was entreated to tell the story again. This time the dancing girls seemed to have acquired a trained monkey.

Alexander felt sure that by the end of the week all of Rome would be telling this story – or some version of it. The tale was good enough that Rome would soon forget that it had ever blamed the Jews.

Alexander was grateful when Agrippa had finally rescued him from the growing crowd at Theon's and had escorted him home. To his chagrin, Agrippa had insisted on joining him as he climbed up to his second floor apartment. Sure, he had been thankful for Agrippa's company that day, but now he really needed to be left alone.

To his surprise, Agrippa had stopped at the door and beckoned Amarantus to him. He spoke softly and Amarantus listened intently and nodded. Then Agrippa walked over to Alexander and held out his forearm. Without hesitation, Alexander clasped it just below the elbow and Agrippa clasped his firmly in return.

Nothing was said. Agrippa simply gave Alexander a long searching look, nodded once, and then was out the door into the afternoon sun.

***

Alexander remained at home for the rest of the day. The furniture was still smashed so he sat on the floor while Amarantus moved through the apartment sorting and packing what little had survived the Praetorians' rampage the night before.

That evening Amarantus brought him dinner and wine, then sat down near him, a pensive look on his face.

"What, Ranti? What is it?"

Amarantus hesitated then said, "Master, last night I thought you were sad because you thought that Rutilus took the statue."

Alexander jerked back in surprise. "Rutilus? No. I thought it was his step-father Sextus Fadius -- or at least his step-father's agents operating here in Rome. Why would you think it was Rutilus?"

Again his servant hesitated. "It was little things, Master. He didn't tell you that his family's client was a sculptor. When you went to the *Subura* to find the sculptor the neighbor recognized Rutilus immediately even though Rutilus said he had not been there since he was a boy. ... And in the sewer, he grabbed your tunic and kept you from questioning the Rat."

Alexander rubbed his chin thoughtfully and gave a wry smile.

"You weren't with me back when we were boys, but I can tell you that Rutilus the man looks very much as Rutilus the boy did. I was not surprised that he was so easily recognized. As for the sculptor as his family's client ... Aemelia remarried to Sextus Fadius when Rutilus was still perhaps nine or ten years old. He would have been a child when he had to give up his father's client to his step-father. No. It is not so surprising that Rutilus would forget about his father's client. He was never old enough to actually act as Achilles's patron.

"And as for the sewer, I'm sure he really *did slip* just as he said. After all, who would willingly risk falling into several feet of raw sewage? ... I know that I told Rutilus that he could wait outside, but it didn't surprise when he joined me in the sewer. Rutilus has always seen *everything* as great adventure – even a trip into a sewer with me."

Amarantus thought for a moment. "Master, wherever he goes now, I hope Rutilus finds it to be a great adventure."

Alexander considered for a moment then smiled a bit less sadly. "You know, Ranti, I think he will. ... I hope they *all* will."

27
THE TIES THAT BIND

THE following day, Amarantus moved what remained of their belongings into Agrippa's house. The Praetorians had left the apartment uninhabitable, and there was no point in replacing everything when Alexander had less than two weeks left in Rome.

Alexander went about his business as he felt his duty required, but he felt little enthusiasm for it. Once again, he was thankful for Amarantus who assumed the burden of making all of the arrangements for their upcoming journey.

Agrippa's mother, Berenice, returned home from her visit with her oldest son Herod. Berenice had been like a surrogate mother to Alexander when he was first brought to Rome as a boy. Of course, he didn't *need* a mother figure anymore. He was a grown man of twenty-two. *Still* ... he found her presence comforting.

Claudius never mentioned the affair of the statue directly, but somehow he seemed to know all about it anyway. Alexander assumed that Claudius had learned of it from his brother Germanicus. Or perhaps, Claudius had simply guessed the truth for himself. It was through Germanicus that the friends learned that any suspicions clinging to Sejanus regarding the attacks on Jews and the synagogue had been dropped. Apparently, what little evidence there was pointed only to the dead Praetorian Spurius, so Tiberius considered the matter to be closed.

On July 31st, the eve of Claudius' birthday, the remaining

friends met at the home of Agrippa for an early celebration. They had done that every year since they were boys. This year, the celebrants only counted as three, just Claudius, Agrippa, and Alexander. Rutilus wasn't there – and would never be there again. Alexander was leaving soon for Egypt – and he would never be there again. Even Germanicus no longer came – the duties of a Consul. A pall seemed to lie over the gathering. Berenice had tried to make for a cheery dinner, but in the end had sent the entertainers home early. The men retired to Agrippa's study.

As the wine flowed, Claudius appeared to be becoming increasingly distraught.

"Rutilus is gone," he said softly. "And now my dearest Alexander is leaving us, too. Who will be left for me now? ... You must not leave Rome, Agrippa, or I will be bereft."

Agrippa and Alexander stared into their wine cups and nodded their agreement.

Alexander thought half-heartedly of pointing out to Claudius that he still had his scholarly interests. There was a history that Claudius was planning to write. But, somehow a history seemed an inadequate consolation. Suddenly, he had a thought and sat up excitedly.

"Claudius, perhaps you could come with me. You too, Agrippa."

Claudius looked up blearily, not catching on immediately.

"*Cu*-Come where?"

"To *Alexandria*. You could stay with me. By day, you could use the great library to write your book and give readings for all the best scholars. And by night we will dine and play dice."

Claudius brightened visibly.

"What? Leave Rome? Never have to hear my mother and Livia call me a fool again? Never again have to suffer the disdain of my 'devoted' wife Urgulanilla? ... Alexander, this is a *splendid* idea.

And Agrippa, you *must* come, too. I know you love Rome, but you must come at least for a visit. And perhaps, after some time has passed, we can even have Rutilus, too."

Claudius looked from Alexander and Agrippa with an expression of delight that Alexander rarely saw. Immediately, he began talking animatedly about his plans for the trip, what books he would bring, what he wanted to see in Egypt, which scholars with whom he really must consult.

Alexander gazed at his friend's happy face, and, for just a moment, he caught a glimpse of the man Claudius might have been had it not been for the cruel names, the humiliations, and the bullies. Claudius was smart, smarter than most of those who made fun of him. And when given a chance, he could really shine in the most intelligent company. Perhaps Alexandria would be good for him, a fresh start.

Claudius was still planning out loud; he must have copies made of the Etruscan texts because those may not be in the Alexandrian library. Suddenly, he stopped in mid-sentence and his face fell.

"What is it?" Alexander asked.

"*They* would never let me go," Claudius replied crestfallen. He didn't have to define "*they*." Everyone knew he meant the imperial family.

"But surely they can spare you, Claudius. You have so few official duties, and there are so many others to do them."

"It's not that," Claudius shook his head sadly. "They would not want a 'fool' representing the imperial family in such an important province. No, they like to keep me where they can watch me and make sure I don't do anything to embarrass them."

"But, perhaps not, Claudius. Augustus knows you're no fool. … You could ask. Maybe Germanicus could speak in your behalf."

Agrippa had been silent so far in the conversation, but now looked at Alexander and shook his head.

"Claudius is correct in this, Alexander. Augustus is very cautious when it comes to the family. Maybe if it were any place other than Egypt, there might be a chance. Egypt is too critical for the welfare of Rome. You know that a Senator must get *permission* from Augustus before setting foot anywhere in Egypt.

"I know that Claudius is not a Senator – not even particularly political. But, even if Augustus believed that Claudius would never stir up trouble, he would fear that a more ruthless man might try to use him as a figurehead.

"We cannot forget that Claudius *is the grandson* of Marcus Antonius. There are many in Egypt who wish that it had been Antonius who had defeated Augustus at Actium, instead of the other way around. Having Antonius's grandson in Alexandria *could* be used be as a rallying point to incite rebellion."

Agrippa turned to Claudius. "You could still try. It couldn't hurt to ask. Maybe Augustus would let you go for a short visit. ... But I wouldn't mention Germanicus."

Both heads shot up in protest.

"What? Why not?" Alexander protested. "Everyone knows that Claudius is devoted to his brother."

"*That* is why," said Agrippa. "Germanicus is still young, but I can see the beginnings of it already."

"What do you mean?"

Agrippa looked from Alexander to Claudius and pursed his lips.

"Think about it. Germanicus is young, handsome, brave, just. Already the people love him and the soldiers admire him. ... And already the jealousy of him grows. Add to that, Germanicus *is also* the grandson of Marcus Antonius. People will assume that Germanicus is using Claudius to get a foothold in Egypt."

"*B-b-but,*" Claudius sputtered. "Germanicus would never... he's not like that."

"I know," replied Agrippa. "But do you think *Tiberius* would believe that?"

The three men fell silent. Long moments slipped by interrupted only by the refilling of the wine cups. Alexander glanced over at Claudius who looked miserable. So much pain, he thought, and so unfairly bestowed. And now Claudius was losing the comfort of two of his closest friends. Was there *anything* that could be done?

As if in response to his thoughts, Agrippa suddenly leaned forward and smacked his palm on the table.

"Listen," he said. "We've been close since we were boys, *right?* ... We've been raised together, educated together. We've been drinking and gambling together and had adventures together. We're more than friends. We are like *brothers,* are we not?"

Alexander and Claudius both nodded, wondering where this was going.

"Then I propose," Agrippa continued, "that we seal this bond of brotherhood. Seal it in a way that it cannot be broken by distance or time, no matter where we each may go."

Alexander turned to Claudius and raised his eyebrows. Claudius nodded back. They didn't know what Agrippa had in mind, but it seemed right so far.

Agrippa studied each man in turn. "I propose an oath; an oath that will bind us together as brothers. ... I will begin.

"Tiberius Nero Claudius, I swear to you that I shall always remain your friend, and that I will do everything in my power to raise you up to the position that you deserve by right of birth and ability. I am not without influence, you know. It may take awhile, but someday, you will achieve your rightful place and I will be there to cheer it."

Claudius said nothing, but his eyes had filled with tears.

"Gaius Julius Alexander," Agrippa continued. "I swear to you that my first born daughter shall be betrothed to your first born son. Your family shall rank among the Judean royalty and your grandchildren shall be heirs to the throne of David. ... I think that I shall name this daughter Berenice after the mother who raised us both."

Alexander was stunned. A sworn marriage alliance with the Judean prince and heir was worth as much as all of his family's wealth. Solemnly he replied.

"And I swear to you, Marcus Julius Agrippa, that my first born son, who will be named Marcus after you, shall be betrothed to your first born daughter, Berenice. And on the day of their wedding, I shall make a substantial gift to the Temple in both our names to mark the joining of our two families. "

Agrippa nodded and raised his wine cup. "To the marriage of Marcus Julius Alexander to Julia Berenice. May they live long and give us many grandchildren."

"To the marriage," Alexander and Claudius repeated, then each took a deep swallow of wine.

Alexander turned to Claudius.

"Tiberius Claudius Nero, I swear to you that I will always be your friend, and my second born son shall be named Tiberius after you. And when he is of age, I will send him to Rome to be with you, even if I cannot. My son will become a great Roman as a lasting tribute to a friendship that will endure the tests of place and time."

Again, Agrippa raised his cup. "To Tiberius Julius Alexander."

"To Tiberius Julius Alexander," the other two repeated and drank deeply.

Claudius' eyes were shining. He hesitated, but when he

spoke, he did not stutter.

"And to you, Marcus Julius Agrippa, I swear that I will always be your friend, and when the day comes that I gain the influence of my imperial rank, I will do everything in my power to restore to you the kingdom that is yours by right of birth. It may not come until after Livia dies, or until after my mother Antonia dies. But that day *will* come. ... It has been foretold."

Agrippa inclined his head to Claudius, an almost calculating look on his face.

"And *to you* Gaius Julius Alexander," Claudius continued. "I swear that I will always be your friend and that I shall guide and protect your son, and do whatever is in my power to ensure that Tiberius will become the greatest Roman of all the Julius Alexanders."

The three men fell silent for a few moments lost in the power of their oaths ... oaths that *could* change the course of both Roman and Jewish history. Alexander sensed that something truly momentous had just transpired. Only time would reveal exactly what.

Finally, Agrippa lifted his cup and raised it slightly to each man in turn, then said, "To the brotherhood of Tiberius Claudius Nero, Gaius Julius Alexander, and Marcus Julius Agrippa. May it long endure."

"To the brotherhood," returned the chorus.

***

Alexander stood in the stern of the ship watching as the port of Ostia grew smaller on the horizon. The past few days now seemed a blur. If it had not been for Amarantus, he did not know how he would have made it to the harbor and on board the ship taking him back to Alexandria.

Absently, he fingered the unfamiliar cloth of a new tunic bearing two narrow purple stripes, and remembered the day he had won the right to wear it. It was several days after the recovery of the statue, and Augustus had summoned him to the palace. Alexander had dreaded going, dreaded having to recount the events that had brought him so much pain.

Thankfully, Augustus had never mentioned the details and only congratulated Alexander for his skill and persistence in recovering the statue. Then, in a move uncharacteristic of the First Citizen, he had told Alexander to name his reward. Initially, Alexander had considered declining the offer. He needed no money. His family was wealthy; and, he could not forget that it was the desire for money that had set that luckless sequence of events into motion.

A sudden thought came to him. Looking straight at Augustus he said, "I wish a legacy for my sons; I wish for us to be made equestrians."

Augustus had raised his eyebrows at this. "You are not even married yet. You do not have any sons."

"But I will," Alexander assured him. "I plan to have many."

"*And so did I,*" Augustus had answered softly.

Alexander noted the look of sadness that had come over Augustus's face and immediately regretted his words. Despite having two wives and a long life, Augustus had only produced a single daughter and not the son and heir that all men desire. Even the beloved grandsons whom Augustus had adopted, had met with premature deaths. Alexander started to mumble an apology, but Augustus held up a hand to stop him.

"Very well, Gaius Julius Alexander, I will enter your name today into the census of the equestrian class, Rome's knights. ... Yes, I do believe purple stripes will suit you. Now, your time is short and I may not see you before you leave, so I will wish you now a safe voyage home."

Home. Alexander had thought that Rome was his home, but

now he found that he was not sorry to be leaving the City behind him.

In the distance, Ostia slipped behind the horizon.

"*Vale Roma,*" Alexander whispered, then strode to the prow of the ship where, somewhere out there, Alexandria and a new life lay before him.

EPILOGUE
FIVE YEARS LATER

ALEXANDER stood on the roof of his house in Alexandria staring out over the city. Dusk was falling and the usual hubbub of the city was quieting as residents scurried home to their families and dinner.

With a sigh, he lifted the letter in his hand and re-read its contents.

Aulus Rutilus to his dearest Gaius Julius Alexander. I say dearest for that is how you will always be to me. I have received a letter from Claudius who wrote that he believes that you still have many regrets regarding our last day in Rome together. I write to you now to assure you that neither I, nor any of my family, hold you to blame in any way for the events that transpired that day or since. In fact, in many ways the gods have smiled upon us in our new lives.

You may have heard that after we left Italy, my family settled in Britannia. My mother freed our old slave Hermias. Not long after that, they were married. Hermias is ten years my mother's senior, and has loved her since she was a child. Of course, inside the boundaries of Rome, a patrician woman could never marry a freed slave. But out here in the wilds of Britannia, no one knows or cares about the doings of patricians. With Hermias, my mother has found a contentment that she would have never known with Sextus Fadius.

Ephigenia, my mother's seamstress, was freed, as well, and together Ephigenia, Hermias, and I have started our own textile business. Yes, Alexander, you read correctly. I now work for a living. You would be proud to see how our business has finally begun to prosper.

My poor sister, Rutila, never recovered her wits after her unfortunate act in Rome, and for some time now her mind has been like that of a child. Fortunately, she kept her beauty and we were able to marry her to a local magistrate. He is older and a gentle man who treats her kindly. I believe that Rutila has also found happiness in her own way. She mentions you sometimes, but her memory has dimmed and I think she remembers little except for the name.

As for me, my sweetest Alexander, I finally settled down and married a local girl over a year ago. I did not marry for money, connections, or bloodlines, but only for love. We are expecting our first child this winter and I look forward to the rewards of fatherhood.

So you see, Alexander, you must have no regrets about whatever small part you may have played in my family's relocation to Britannia, for we have none. Each of us has made a life for ourselves here and we are happy – happier than we ever could have been had we remained in Rome. I will always think of and remember you fondly. Farewell.

Alexander lowered the letter, tears filling his eyes. *Regrets?* He wasn't sure what he felt now. Images of old acquaintances swam before his eyes. Aemelia. Old Hermias, the door steward. Rutilus with the freckles and impish grin. ... And beautiful Rutila, who he once believed would be the perfect wife.

"Alexander," a voice broke the silence.

Alexander turned to see his freedman, Amarantus.

"I was sent to retrieve you," Amarantus smiled. "The other

guests have arrived for dinner."

"In a moment," Alexander replied. "I will join you in just a moment."

Amarantus glanced at the letter in Alexander's hand and gave him a searching look, but simply nodded and returned to the party below.

Alexander turned back to watch first darkness encompass the city. Regrets? No, he decided. No regrets … for any of us. Then Alexander turned his face towards the heavens, and said a silent prayer for the unborn child of Aulus Rutilus – a child that he hoped that he would someday meet.

HISTORICAL NOTE

Dear reader, If you are like me, one of the pleasures of reading historical fiction is finding an historical note at the end of the novel.

Some years ago, when I was a graduate student at University of Pennsylvania, I published an article *"Alexander the Alabarch: Roman and Jew."* A scan of this article can be found at: http://kassevans.com/Alexander/ .

Since then, I sporadically have continued to research about the life and times of the Alabarch. Below is some of what I have learned and used for this book.

--ALEXANDER THE ALABARCH--

Alexander of Alexandria, also known as Alexander the Alabarch, was an historical person who lived during the first century A.D. He is known to us through several ancient sources including the first century historian Flavius Josephus (*The Jewish War* and *Jewish Antiquities*), one book by Alexander's famous philosopher brother Philo of Alexandria (*On Animals*), and several papyrus scrolls found in Egypt. One papyrus was written by Alexander's real-life freedman named Amarantus.

The historical sources indicate that Alexander was a very wealthy and important man in the first century. His influence spanned the Alexandrian, Roman, and Judean worlds. Much about his life, however, remains a mystery.

--His Name--

Alexander's Roman name of Gaius Julius Alexander has been reconstructed based on two pieces of evidence. The first is the Roman names of his sons: Marcus Julius Alexander and Tiberius Julius Alexander.

In the early first century A.D., Roman naming practices were very regimented. The father of Marcus and Tiberius would have probably been named *[first name] Julius Alexander*. His probable first name can be narrowed even further since there were only a handful of possible first names (*praenomens*) in common use by Romans at this time including: Aulus (A.), Gaius (C.), Gnaeus (Cn.), Decimus (D.), Lucius (L.), Marcus (M.), Manus (M'.), Numerius (N.), Publius (P.), Servius (Ser.), Sextus (Sex.), Spurius (S. or Sp), Tiberius (Ti.), and Titus (T.)

There are extant papyri from this time period that mention a wealthy land owner named *Gaius* Julius Alexander. All indications are that this Gaius Julius Alexander and Alexander the Alabarch are the same person.

--The Reliability of Josephus--

The most substantive information about the life of Alexander the Alabarch comes from the first century Jewish historian Flavius Josephus. This raises the questions, *"Can we trust him? Is he a reliable source?"* I say, yes, because he *had* to be.

There is no evidence to say one way or the other if Josephus was personally acquainted with Alexander the Alabarch. He was, however, undoubtedly acquainted with Alexander's *son* Tiberius Julius Alexander. Josephus was with Vespasian in Egypt shortly after the Prefect of Egypt declared Vespasian to be the new Emperor of Rome. That Prefect was the Alabarch's son Tiberius Julius Alexander.

Later, Alexander's son Tiberius was the Praetorian Prefect in Rome around the same time that Josephus was writing his books. It is unlikely that Josephus would have been publishing incorrect information about the family of the Praetorian Prefect who was very close to Josephus's patron Vespasian and to the the future emperor Titus.

--THE ALABARCH --

Josephus refers to Alexander as "The Alabarch," but never defined what an Alabarch was. The *Alabarch* or the *alabarchy* are mentioned in eleven ancient sources, but many of these have never been translated into English. Only one of the ancient sources, Emperor Justinian's *Edict* XI, described the historical function of the alabarchy.

Definition of Alabarch per Emperor Justinian, *Edict* XI:
The alabarch was the head of the alabarchy, which was a Roman magistracy in Egypt responsible for the assaying of gold (Latin: *obrussa*) probably including the ores extracted from the gold mines of Egypt and Nubia. The Alabarch reported to the Prefect in Alexandria who had overall responsibility for management of gold production in Egypt.

See http://kassevans.com/Alexander/Alabarch.html for a collection and analysis of all Greek and Latin sources on the alabarchy.

When Octavian (Augustus) took Egypt from Cleopatra and

Antony, he acquired its gold.   Egypt became Rome's largest supplier of gold (until it was surpassed later by the gold mines of Spain and elsewhere).   At the time, it was something new for Rome to suddenly have access to its own gold mines. For the first time in Roman history, gold became integrated into the economy as a means of exchange.   Gold coins were minted, gold bars were stamped and shipped for paying the legions, and gold flakes and nuggets were used for purchases. (*See* Timothy Green, <u>*Ages of Gold*</u>, London; GFMS, 2007, p. 187ff, images of assayer marks on pages after 200.)

Given this new importance of gold and Egypt's mines in the early first century B.C., it became critical that some Roman magistrate take responsibility for weighing and testing the purity of gold from Rome's new mines. Gold could only be a new medium of exchange if people could trust that it was accurately tested and stamped for purity.   This appears to be the function of the magistracy of the alabarch that is described in Emperor Justinian's *Edict* XI.

Note that readers may find other proposed definitions of *Alabarch* in some secondary or Web sources. These other definitions are usually derived from one or two historical resources and fall apart when one looks at the totality of the original Greek and Latin sources.

For example, some authors have suggested that an Alabarch must have been a leader in the Alexandrian Jewish community. Josephus does name two alabarchs who were known to be Jews. However, if one also considers the evidence of the Greek inscriptions and papyri, then we learn that other alabarchs were pagan or Christian. The Alabarch who prayed to the god Poseidon was almost certainly not a Jew.

Some scholars have suggested that an Alabarch was a tax collector, even though there is not a shred of evidence to support this in the *papyri*. The only evidence for this is a section in the

Theodosian, *Code*, IV.13.9 where some people (who may or may not be connected with the alabarchy) are *impudently claiming an exemption* from paying tax on the transportation of animals. People claiming an exemption from a type of tax, are not tax collectors. There is also a reference to the "impost of the alabarchy," but this appears to be some sort of tax on goods or services and not a type of tax collector.

--RELATIONSHIP TO CLAUDIUS --

Alexander and the Roman Emperor Claudius were described as *"old friends"* by the historian Josephus. Since Claudius never visited Egypt, how did he and Alexander become old friends?

We do know that Agrippa, the grandson of Herod the Great, future king of Judea, grew up in the circle of Claudius. Agrippa's mother Berenice and Claudius's mother Antonia Minor are also known to have been good friends.

It is suggested here that Alexander grew up in Rome in Claudius' circle along with Agrippa, the future king of Judea. It was a common practice for Roman provincials of consequence to send their sons to be educated in Rome at around age ten. Therefore, placing Alexander's adolescent years in Rome is completely plausible, although it cannot be proved.

It is also historical that Alexander was the *epitropos* for Antonia Minor, but it is unknown exactly what that entailed. Antonia Minor was Marc Antony's daughter, Augustus's niece, sister-in-law to Tiberius, Claudius' mother, and Gaius Caligula's grandmother. She was a Roman woman of great importance, so her *epitropos* must have been an important appointment.

The Greek word *epitropos* can be translated as trustee, guardian, or governor.   Another Greek word, *kurios*, was usually used for a woman's guardian who handled her legal and personal affairs.   Most scholars have assumed, therefore, that Alexander must have been some sort of trustee for Antonia's extensive estates in Egypt.   This will be explored further in a future volume in this series.

--VICTORY--

There was a temple to the goddess Victory (or Victoria) that stood off of Victory's Incline on Rome's Palatine Hill.   The original site has been located and the ruins partially excavated.   Historical references to the temple of Victory date back to the time of the Roman Republic so the temple was probably there in the early first century.

Although the temple would have contained a statue of Victory, there is no evidence that it had ever been attributed to the great 5th century B.C. Greek sculptor Phidias (who was never known to work in marble).

--TOGA TRABEA--

The author was very surprised to learn how little historical evidence there actually is for anything beyond a plain white toga. There are many statues and friezes that depict men wearing togas, but these are all solid white.

There is exactly *one* surviving wall painting from the Roman world that depicts a man wearing the toga *praetexta* – the white toga with the purple or scarlet border that is the style associated with Roman senators.   That painting is in the Vettii House that has been excavated in Pompeii.

Toga praetexta: The only extant visual evidence of the purple bordered toga worn by Senators is from this fresco in the Vettii House in Pompeii.

The evidence for the toga *trabea* is even more obscure. Of the material evidence, there is exactly *one* surviving statue where lines have been etched into the toga to indicate where there may have been stripes. That bronze statue is famously known as The *Orator* or *Arringatore* and wears a style of toga that is typical of the Roman Republican period being shorter that the togas of imperial Rome.

The bronze statue is weathered and covered with a green patina. There are, however, indications that the lines were intended to convey stripes on the toga at the neck, lower hem, waist, and just above the knees. There is a seam along the bottom that shows where a wide band was sewed to the toga. The apparent stripes on the toga of the bronze statue have led to the speculation that this must have been a toga *trabea*.

Toga trabea?: Reconstruction of how the scarlet and purple striped *toga trabea* may have looked based on the statue of the *Orator or Arringatore*. This is an example of the shorter version of a toga that was worn during the Republic.

The main literary evidence that applies here comes from the late fourth century writer Servius (*In Vergilii Aeneidem commentarii,* VII, 612).   He cites a lost work of Suetonius (late first to early second century A.D.) who wrote that there were three different types of toga *trabea*. The third type of *trabea* was the purple and scarlet 'mixed' toga worn by *augurs*.

There is no definitive historical evidence for the exact appearance of a toga *trabea* or even for who wore one. For this book, I've elected to use Suetonius that the toga *trabea* was a purple and scarlet striped toga that was only worn by an *augur*.

--Moral Reforms of Augustus--

Was it historically accurate to suggest that the *augur* may have been subject to blackmail because of his sexual preferences? Apparently, the answer is *"maybe,"* – partially because of his preferences, but also because of how they could have impacted his marriage choices and social position.

Augustus's idea of restoring morality to Rome was to require all men and women to get married and have children. He felt so strongly about this that he enacted laws defining and promoting marriage, enhancing the rights of those who produced children, and banning adultery.

The law that may have been applicable to the fictional *augur* was the *Lex Papia Poppaea* that was enacted by the Roman Senate in 9 A.D. It specified legal penalties against those who committed **celibacy**. The *celibate* was someone who did not get married and have children; not necessarily someone who abstained from sexual relations. There were also penalties imposed on a man and woman who married, but had no children.

If the *augur's* preferences meant that he did not marry and have children, then he would have been liable for the legal penalties under the law. Regardless of the letter of the law, however, it seems plausible that an *augur*, one of the top religious functionaries of Rome, would have encountered considerable social and political pressure to conform to the moral views of Augustus.

There is also another possibility for blackmail in that the *augur* is this story took the passive role in his encounter allowing a slave to take the dominant role. For a Roman, a man of rank choosing to take the passive role would have been taboo. If known, he may have been subject to considerable social derision.

--SEJANUS AND THE JEWS--

Lucius Aelius Sejanus (20 B.C.-31 A.D.) was appointed the Praetorian Prefect when Tiberius became emperor in 14 A.D. His continuing rise in influence makes for a dark tale of intrigue and power. Both Antonia Minor and her daughter Livilla will become critical players in his end.

The inspiration for developing Sejanus as Alexander's nemesis came from the writings of Alexander's brother Philo of Alexandria. Without any explanation, Philo makes it clear that Sejanus was perceived as an enemy of Jews in the two passages quoted below.

(159) And in the reign of Tiberius ...at that time things in Italy were thrown into a great deal of confusion when Sejanus was preparing to make his attempt against our nation [Jews]; (160) for he [Tiberius] knew immediately after his [Sejanus's] death that the accusations which had been brought against the Jews who were dwelling in Rome were false calumnies, inventions of Sejanus, who was desirous to destroy our nation...

--Philo, Embassy to Gaius, 159-160

Flaccus Avillius succeeded Sejanus in his hatred of and hostile designs against the Jewish nation. He [Flaccus] was not, indeed, able to injure the whole people by open and direct means as he [Sejanus] had been, inasmuch as he [Flaccus] had less power for such a purpose...

-- Philo, On Flaccus I.1.

Since Philo did not specify the bad acts of Sejanus against *"the whole Jewish nation,"* he may have assumed his audience was already familiar with those details. Interestingly, no other contemporary author except Philo mentions any particular animosity that Sejanus held towards Jews. The Jewish historian, Josephus, also does not mention any problems with Sejanus in his *Jewish Antiquities*.

--THE JEWS IN ROME--

That leads to the next issue of whether this novel reflects the actual situation of Jews living in Rome in the early first century A.D. To the extent that this can be reconstructed from sources, the depiction of Jews in Rome is as accurate as possible. Fortunately, there are both Roman and Jewish sources for this. This includes the extant writings of Alexander's brother, Philo of Alexandria, who described the environment of Jews in Rome when he went on embassy there.

Jews were one of many foreign groups living in Rome, and, like many of the others, they had adopted Greek names, dress, and language. The majority of Jews lived in the Trans-Tiber district along with many of the other foreigners. Romans, who were in little doubt of their own inherent superiority, generally looked down on *all* non-Romans. After all, the foreigners came from nations that Rome had conquered or otherwise subjugated.

Rome was notably tolerant of foreign religions and permitted the active practice of them within the City, as long as the foreigners paid adequate tribute to the Roman gods. This is where Jews diverged significantly from the other foreign populations. As monotheists, the Jews could only pay tribute to the invisible god who's one Temple was located in Jerusalem. Their religion forbade them to worship or pay money in tribute to the Roman gods, temples, or the deity of the emperor.

Fortunately for Jews, they won an early political alliance with Rome through Julius Caesar, because of their support for him during the Alexandrian War. The Jewish historian, Josephus, transcribed a number of decrees made by Caesar on behalf of protecting the religious rights of Jews (Flavius Josephus, *Jewish Antiquities*, 14.10.2-25). That these rights were confirmed and extended by Augustus, was recorded by Alexander's brother Philo (Philo, *Embassy to Gaius*, 315).

The distinctive rights and practices of Jews must have caused some friction at times. It is perhaps because of that fact, that there were several incidents recorded of trouble for Jews in Rome in the first century. For example, many Jews were expelled from Rome in 19 A.D. for proselytizing their religion to wealthy Romans. (cf. Josephus, *Jewish Antiquities*, 18.65-84)

Jewish religious practice in the first half of the first century in Rome included daily prayer for males using *phylacteries* (the small boxes containing scripture bound to the hand using leather straps). It also included prayer meetings held in synagogues. The Synagogue of the Agrippesians mentioned in Chapter 21 was a real place and is thought to be one of the earlier synagogues in Rome, perhaps dating back to the first century. While there is evidence for a number of synagogues in Rome, neither the exact date nor geographical location have been determined for any of them. Jews also collected tithes for their Temple and sent them to Jerusalem.

The title and function of *Mother of the Synagogue* was real and discussed at length in Bernadette Brooten, *Women Leaders in the Ancient Synagogue* (Providence, RI: Brown University, 1982). The character of Sara the Mother of the Synagogue is fictional.

Turning to the perspective of Roman authors, we occasionally find Jews ridiculed for their practices of circumcision and not eating the flesh of pigs. Of course, Romans ridiculed the "strange customs" of virtually every foreign element in their population. After the failed Jewish revolt against Rome in 66-70 A.D., the role of Jews in Roman life and literature changed considerably.

--ON THE TIES THAT BIND--

A final note should be made regarding the oaths that were made in the last chapter *"The Ties That Bind."* Although there is no reason to believe that these oaths were ever made as written, the facts in them are true.

Agrippa, who became King Agrippa of the Jews in 41 A.D., did marry his eldest daughter, Berenice, to Alexander's son, Marcus, forming a royal alliance between the families.

Alexander's other son, Tiberius, did become a great Roman achieving the two pinnacles of Roman knighthood as Prefect of Egypt and Praetorian Prefect.

In fact, all of the oaths that the three young men made to each other in the final chapter did eventually come to pass in real life – but the details will wait for a future novel.

For readers interested in learning more about Alexander, or in viewing images of many of the persons and places mentioned in this book, I invite you to visit my Web site at http://kassevans.com and click on the link for Alexander.

From the Author

Thank you for reading my first novel.

Your time is precious and I appreciate you spending it with Alexander *[the future]* Alabarch.

If you enjoyed it and would like to read more about Alexander, please leave a review on Amazon, or wherever you acquired the book.

Kass Evans
mail@KassEvans.com

****

Other books In the Series
Alexander the Alabarch

1. A Toga of a Different Color (2018)
2. A Toga in the Forum: Two Short Stories (2018)
3. *A Toga in the Wind – planned for 2019*